TA

D1066973

TAXI DANCER

Joseph Heywood

Guilford, Connecticut

An imprint of Rowman & Littlefield

Distributed by NATIONAL BOOK NETWORK

Copyright © 1985 by Joseph Heywood
First Lyons Paperback Edition, 2015

British Library Cataloguing in Publication Information Available

Library of Congress Cataloging-in-Publication Data Available

ISBN 978-1-4930-0903-9 (pbk.)
ISBN 978-1-4930-2399-8 (e-book)

♾™ The paper used in this publication meets the minimum requirements of American National Standard for Information Sciences—Permanence of Paper for Printed Library Materials, ANSI/NISO Z39.48-1992.

STRATEGY MEETING

'We're in this turkey trot together, Colonel Wainright. You, me, those bloodsucking reporters and LBJ-for-Jerk Johnson. You recommended me for the medal. You did the whole routine so that the country could have itself a public handjob over its first ace. You created me and now you're going to live by my terms. You copy this transmission, you hog-jowled son-of-a-bitch?'

Part I: Prologue

Thanksgiving Day, 1966

In combat there aren't any good guys or bad guys. Just dead and alive. And some cripples; they're in between. You do what you've got to do—play the cards you're dealt. God's got better things to do with his time than pull for one side or the other, or one guy over another.

Capt. Byron South, USAF
First Ace of the Vietnam Conflict

Three-Banger

The two MiG 19s came out of the morning sun from north of Haiphong. Obviously they were hoping for cover in the sun's rays, but the Navy's radar couldn't see the sun. Just metal. The air intercept technician on the cruiser in the Gulf of Tonkin 150 miles from the action had begun calling out the MiGs' positions, altitudes and headings as soon as the two blips popped up on his scope. The man cleared his throat and spoke slowly into the transmitter microphone.

Bandits. Bandits. Bandits. Blue. Lobster. Zero-three-seven Three-seven at two-seven miles heading zero-niner-zero Angelsten. Climbing.

Captain Byron South knew without checking the chart clipped to his legboard that the enemy aircraft were in their sector. He radioed his flight to assure that they had heard the warning call over Guard channel.

'Heads up, Beggars.' He didn't have to say any more.

'Beggar Two.'

'Three.'

'Four.'

They knew. Simple alert. Simple response. Nothing fancy. The four pilots continued toward their target while South calculated a likely intercept. Their target was a multiple 37-mm site dug into the red clay near what Intelligence believed was a small warehouse. Reconnaissance photos showed that the guns were sand-bagged to the gills and well concealed. Probably their attack would do nothing more than give the gunners a bad headache and some shooting practice. All around the target they could expect the workers from the warehouse to lie on their backs and blaze away at the incoming F-150s with small-arms fire. It

9

was always the same. Simple threat. Simple response. The gunners in the antiaircraft batteries would try to knock the Thuds down by using wooden silhouettes of the F-150s. The Soviets provided their Asian comrades with the wooden cheaters. The silhouettes were attached to a cross made of dowels that equated to the lead distance needed to hit a particular model of American aircraft. It was an ingenious device. Along the dowels silhouettes depicted the aircraft in a dive, a pullout or a flat pass. All the gunner had to do was identify the aircraft, snap his cheater onto his gun, match the silhouette to what he saw, line up the wooden marker with the real aircraft and pull the trigger.

If they were true to form, South knew, the MiGs would wait to make their run until after his flight was committed to its attack on the target. It was an effective tactic; properly employed − and the key was timing − it would pull most strikes away from the target or at least disturb the pilots' concentration. If the Americans broke off to engage the MiGs, the enemy pilots would immediately highball it to-ward safer airspace north of the city, up toward the Chinese border.

This time, South told himself, the MiG 19s might get themselves a big surprise.

'Beggars, clean 'em up, green 'em up and start your music,' South announced over the strike frequency.

Four gloved hands in four cockpits reached simultaneously for their weapons consoles. South ticked off the checklist items in his mind − the procedures long since memorized and assimilated into his being.

'Bomb Bay Selector Switch. Guard Release.' South snapped open the red metal cover. 'Master Arm Switch. Weapons.' He made the selection. 'Weapons Selector Knob. Conversion Bombs.' South had two dull-green two-thousand-pounders to deliver and now they were integrated into his attack system. 'Depressed Reticle Knob.' He cranked the pre-calculated wind factor into the small win-dow. All computations and calculations were made before they left the ground in Thailand. For missions in Laos, where there were forward air controllers (FAC) aloft to observe hits, they used a zero factor and made their adjustments based on the FAC's verbal directions. Setting a wind factor into the window put a fudge factor into the bomb drop — *if* the wind was correct. It wasn't often.

Based on the target's characteristics, South had decided to take his flight straight in and straight down from fifteen thousand. Shortest distance between two points, he reasoned. They'd try to drop their bombs right down the barrels of the guns. There were other options, of course, but he had ruled them out. A long, flat run at relatively low altitude. This would make it hard for the ground fire to be effective because they'd be past the shooters before they could react. A short run with a sharp vertical pull-out to toss the bomb at the target was another possibility — a lob — but the latter tactic was preferred for a target dug into the side of a valley and best for delivering something like napalm where 'close' was as good as 'on'. Given the configuration of this target, none of these made sense. It would be a straight-in, hairy-ass, steep, jinking dive from fifteen thousand feet; the added velocity from the descent would help them pull out of gun range faster when the weight from the bombs was gone. The North Vietnamese Army (NVA) gunners were good enough; there was no sense helping them. Dive. Drop. Haul ass. That was their plan.

South scanned the ground, checking for landmarks, now familiar from previous sorties into the area.

'Heads up, Beggars. Approaching target.'

'Two.'

'Three.'

'Four.'

Operating close to Haiphong was risky. The defences — both triple A and surface-to-air missiles, or SAMs, the latter courtesy of the Russians — were dense. And, to keep the Americans off guard, the guns and missiles were moved often to new locations. This target was like many other targets he'd drawn. Bad. The guns were in a triangular pattern about a hundred metres apart at the base. This was

11

a fairly tight package that improved both the attackers' and the defenders' chances for a good hit. For South and his men the guns were so close to each other that a good hit between them might do damage to all. For the gunners who waited below the triangulation of the arrangement gave them a tidy cone of concentrated fire above the area. The Americans, they knew from experience, wouldn't come in from directly overhead: that would be suicide. So they waited for them, fully expecting an attack to come from a flatter angle. South guessed their thoughts and chose the tactic based on what he believed the gunners would least expect. It was the kind of decision he was used to making, and the kind which the other pilots expected of him. When South led, those with him didn't worry. Usually his choices panned out.

At the pre-strike briefing Intelligence had warned them that MiGs might be operating in the area. Somebody had quipped that the NVA must've graduated a new pilot-training class and this had brought some laughter, but it had been a feeble attempt at a joke, too nervous and thin to produce a real response among the nervous pilots. MiGs were no joke. They were ferret-fast and could turn like roller-derby queens. Mostly they were flown by NVA jocks, but there were Russian advisors in the country and from time to time you didn't have to have a passport photo in your lap to know the face behind the stick on the other side had round eyes and a craving for vodka. The best way to survive was to assume that every MiG was piloted by a Russian. Assume the worst.

South strained against the Plexiglas trying to spot a formation of rock along the small green stream below. The target was nearby and he wanted to be sure to come down from the proper angle. He had his flight of four in a fingertip formation at twenty thousand feet, just above a scattered line of puffy white cumulus clouds.

By afternoon the area would be swollen with thunder-bumpers stretching to fifty and sixty thousand feet. The drafts and hail inside the huge cloud formations would tear an aircraft to shreds. South scanned his instruments. They were down to fifteen. He computed his pullout at four and pushed forward on the stick to begin a shallow descent. All four aircraft followed as if guided by a single hand – their wing tips less than six feet apart. They were one: a single instrument of war. Beggar flight broke through a haze of clouds and South watched intensely as they approached a small ridge ahead. Just beyond there would be crossroads and some huts. The guns and warehouse were a half-klick beyond the dilapidated village.

The flight leader rolled to his left wing and pressured the stick back slightly as he pitched out to a sixty-degree turn. The others flew straight on past him and at fifteen-second intervals made the identical tight turn taken by their leader.

The ridge was underneath. Altitude fifteen. This was it. South nudged the radio button on the stick. 'Lead's in.'

He rolled inverted, and immediately checked to see if there were white contrails from the guns that would tell him he was under fire. Clear. He nosed the throttle forward, pulled the stick back and grunted as the G-force pressed him against the parachute and the ejection seat. The targets were directly below and as he passed through ten thousand feet, orange flashes began to appear. Wispy white golf-ball-size contrails drifted close to his canopy, but he ignored the flak. His attention was locked on the southwest corner of the gun triangle. He set the crosshairs on his windscreen directly on his aiming point and held his breath as the altimeter unwound. Seven. Six. Five. Now the site was large and he could clearly see people running around, throwing themselves on their backs to shoot up at him with rifles and small automatic weapons. The muzzles of the weapons flickered and chattered, barking white-hot slugs of lead into the sky. At him.

At four thousand feet, South toggled his bombs with the simple movement of his thumb, and pulled back steadily but forcefully on the stick. His G-suit popped into life under the strain and he grunted to help keep blood pumping

13

to his brain.

'Lead's off,' he radioed to his flight as he pulled out and climbed back to fifteen thousand feet. He banked left to circle the area so that the other three could join on him as they finished their runs.

'Beggar Three's off.'

'Roger Three. You got lead in sight?'

'Negative — er, yeah, okay, wait a minute, now I got-chu lead. You on a southbound heading?'

'Affirmative. Fitting, ain't it?'

Click-click was the response. Because of the G-forces and because of the many things that required their attention during the actual attack the pilots usually kept radio transmissions to a minimum. For simplicity the pilots triggered the mike button twice for 'yes' or 'roger'.

'Beggar Two is rolling in.'

'Beggar Three, this is Four. Man, you started *mahk-mahk* fires down there. Gonna give the local bucket brigade a big workout today.'

Click-click.

South rolled into a shallow ten-degree turn to the east. An explosion near the target startled South and engulfed Beggar 2 as he pulled off his bombing run. The flight leader relaxed when he saw the F-105 pop though the side of a bright orange fireball and bank sharply to join.

'Beggar Two. Everything copacetic?'

'Roger. Toasted, but she's still flying. Must've torched some ammo.'

The conversation was interrupted by a transmission over Guard.

Attention all aircraft. Attention all aricraft. Blue Bandits. Blue Bandits. Bullseye one-eight-zero at sixty-five miles. Angels two-zero. Heading southwest. Descending.

Jesus! The two MiGs were almost directly overhead. Why hadn't Naval radar called them out sooner? There hadn't been a single intermediate-range call.

'Beggar Four's in.'

South knew what had to be done. 'Beggar Three, Lead.

Visitors topside. Drop your tanks, we're going up. Beggar Two, you hang with Four; clean it up down there, take a quick look and Return-to-Base. Copy RTB?'

'Two.'

'Three's on your wing, Beggar One.'

'Four copies,' the pilot of the attacking aircraft radioed just before he toggled his bomb load.

South glanced quickly at his starboard wing. Beggar 3 was in position just off his wing and aft.

'Okay Three, go burner *now*.' South shoved the throttle to the left and all the way forward, pulled the nose up and felt the added thrust slam him against his ejection seat.

The two F-105s rose quickly through the scattered clouds, broke into the bright sunlight and continued their climb, flame pouring from their tailpipes. South was blinded by the sun momentarily, but quickly he slid his sun shield down over his eyes and locked it into place. Instinctively he checked his wingman's position before rolling to put the sun at their backs. Beggar 3 stayed tucked in as their altimeters continued to mount. Twenty-four, twenty-five, twenty-six, twenty-seven thousand. By now they were above the MiGs' last reported altitude and position. South hoped that their sudden breakout had been undetected either by the enemy pilots or their Russian controllers who operated the radar defence net for the North Vietnamese. If they could locate the MiGs quickly and catch them in a bad position − waiting for the others to come up from above − they just might take them out. Luck, he chanted. Luck.

'Beggar One, this is Three. I've got problems. My controls are mushy.'

The flight leader took the news calmly. 'Rog, take her out over the water. I'll join you en route.' The other three pilots knew he was hunting. Normally single ships didn't engage apart from their flight, but there seemed little choice this time. Besides, he already had two kills to his credit and he was anxious for another chance. They didn't come very often. By taking a run at the MiGs he might buy some time for Beggar 3, who would need the help if his aircraft were

15

coming apart.

Click-click, Beggar 3 responded.

South turned his head often − as if it was on a swivel − as he searched the sky for the enemy. 'Beggar Two. Any sign of our bogeys down there?' They had disappeared. Not unusual. Often they made a pass and headed out. Chickenshit. He felt disappointed.

'Negative, Lead. We've got us a swell grass fire going down here. They stopped shooting after Three made his run. Nothing but small arms left and those cats are having a hard time because of all the smoke. We're headed for the pond. Beggar two.'

Attention all aircraft. Blue Bandits. Bullseye one-eight-five at six-seven miles. Angels one-seven. Descending.

South inverted and pulled back on the stick. In front and below, just above the cloud bank, he caught a glint of metal, then another. As he levelled his wings in the descent he could see the MiG-19s clearly. It looked like they were swinging toward the target hoping to pick off one of his mates.

'Beggars, Lead. Go burners. Bogeys at your back door.'

'Two.'

'Three.'

'Four.'

It was a bold move. For an instant he wondered if they were Russians. The NVA seldom did anything like this. South wriggled his shoulders to get the sweat-soaked flightsuit free of his back. He levelled sharply at eighteen thousand. The camouflaged MiGs had stopped their gradual descent and were silhouetted below and ahead. They had no place to go.

The first MiG exploded after a short burst of 20-mm cannon fire caught it amidship, just behind the canopy. Before the second aircraft could react, South swung his nose over, lined up the sights and fired another short burst. The MiG tried to bend a turn inside him as the fusillade of hot slugs began to strike, but it was a futile attempt. Too little, too late, South thought as the second

16

MiG-19 turned into a fireball directly in his path. Should've turned sooner, he chided himself as he flew through the momentarily-suspended debris. Clear of the situation he checked his controls and instruments. Free full movement; everything was in the green except for fuel. He was low; time to head for the tanker in the Purple Anchor refueling area over the gulf.

'Beggars, this is Lead. Say your angels.'

'Rog, we're level at twenty-two, heading one-one-seven, outbound for the Texaco.'

Click-click, South responded with his mike button.

South was just beginning to feel the exhilaration of the moment as he reached the coast. Below – along a strip of grey beach – he spotted something moving. Another aircraft, but not a MiG. Too low, way too slow. Defin-oot-ly not a MiG, he told himself as he nosed the Thud over to get a better view. Too big. He calculated its altitude to be under ten. *Very* slow. Couldn't be a friendly because it was too damn far north. What the hell was it? Spook ship? The CIA had all kinds of weird stuff in the zone and they always seemed to show up at the strangest times. South switched his radio to Guard frequency.

Slow mover south of Haiphong, please identify. This is Beggar One on Guard.

If they were CIA they'd better get on the horn, he told himself.

The aircraft was not camouflaged. There was no response from its pilots. It continued to drone northwest, inland. South tried to reach back into his memory, to pilot training and aircraft identification classes, but it was no use. He banked northwest and jerked off his gray calfskin gloves, letting them drop to the floor of the cockpit. Decision time. If he continued pursuit he might not get out. The tanker would have to come to him as it was and it wouldn't make the Great White Father of the Stragetic Air Command too happy to have his boys in the business part of a shooting war. SAC didn't like risking its expensive equipment for some fighter slob's behind. The Tactical Air Command

17

might be at war; SAC wasn't — at least by their definition. South's fuel gauges told him that his situation was getting critical. Suddenly he remembered something. There was a biweekly shuttle running between Phnom Penh, Vientiane and Hanoi — a remnant of the old International Control Commission operation. It had been making the run ever since the 1954 Geneva Conference had ended the French involvement in Indochina. No! Not right. The ICC's bird was an old patched-up Super Connie that ran only at night. Damn! The seconds were taking fuel he needed to get out.

Aircraft on guard, this is Navy two-seven-niner. If that slow-movin' sonovabitch is shaped like a swisher sweet ceegar and if'n it's got two props and an ugly square-like vertical stabilizer, that mother is an NVA courier. Take it out if you can get a shot.

South had no idea who was transmitting, but as soon as the term NVA registered in his brain, he nudged the Thud into position, trimmed it, lined up the sights, then walked a long burst of cannon tracers through the enemy craft. With the hits, the aircraft lurched, fell off to one wing and slid sideways. Black smoke belched from its engines as two small specks hurled themselves clear of the plane just before it went into a full flat spin and pancaked into the ground with a single puff of smoke and dirt but no fire. The two parachutes opened. Satisfied with the kill, South pushed up his power, made a quick victory roll over the parachutes and turned southeast toward the gulf, and his fuel.

'Purple Anchor Seven-One, this is Beggar Lead. I'm outbound, climbing to fifteen thou. Say your altitude. My beacon is on.'

'Howdy there, Beggar One. This is your friendly tanker nav. I have your beacon dead ahead, thirty-six miles. We are at twenty, descending to sixteen for the join-up; we're comin' at you, babes.'

'Thanks much, Purple Nav. Appreciate the service.'
Click-click.
'Hey, Lead, what's the haps? Beggar Two.'
'Knocked down a slow mover on the way out.'

'No shit?'

'Damn straight, babes.'

Aircraft on guard, this is Navy two-seven-niner. You score?

South switched frequencies again.

Affirmative, two-seven-niner.

The voice was excited, almost screaming.

Good shootin' Air Force. I seen that mother a half-dozen times but never had a chance to get after him. Been losing my beauty sleep thinking about them rice munchers chuggin' up and down the coast under our noses. I bet they make it into a night run after this.

South smiled. He felt good, intoxicated.

The Air Force thanks the Navy for its help.

Any time, Air Force. Keep up the good shooting and maybe we all can go home. Navy two-seven-niner out.

As South rolled up under the tanker's fat grey belly he felt jubilant.

The other three F-105s from his flight were tucked in along the sides of the tanker like baby geese with their mother.

'Lead, Three. How many you get?'

'Three,' South said.

'Hope your gun cameras got us some good pictures,' one of the pilots said.

They had.

19

January, 1967

TDY to The World

With the exception of having to make the trip with his wing commander, who brooded alone when he wasn't bootlicking, the whole temporary duty and associated events turned into a hell of a ball for Byron South. He even admitted to himself that he liked being in the limelight. What it all boiled down to was a three-week-long party, a big fat freebie. From the time Wainright informed him that he was going to be awarded the Congressional Medal of Honor, South set his mind to making the most out of their short trip back to The World.

The most amazing part of the medal was the interest it produced. South thought of himself as apolitical. Now he found himself immersed in the centre of the American political maelstrom. Senators crowed about him. Senior military officials strutted around in his presence like he was a grand champion show dog. Reporters elbowed each other in the face to hear every word he spoke. He was The Man, the first ace of the war. Despite the attention South knew it was a transient thing, a diversion for the folks back home. Personally the medal had no real meaning for him. He felt no linkage to those who had won the award before him. Its main advantage had nothing to do with career, or pride or any of the higher human states. The most amazing part of the medal was the effect it had on women. If the Medal of Honor was worth nothing else it was a carte blanche for getting broads into his bed. As it turned out, getting them into bed was a lot easier than getting them out.

South and Wainright were billeted at the posh Madison

20

Hotel in Washington, D.C. From their hotel suites they sallied forth by limousine to an endless series of receptions and cocktail parties. The Public Information Officer from the Department of Defense provided them with a full-time escort, a woman of thirty with a relish for her charge. She made sure that the two officers were where they were supposed to be, when they were supposed to be there. The first night she called about ten to see if South 'had a few minutes' to go over the next day's itinerary. Five minutes after she got to his room they were in bed, her above-and-beyond enthusiasm for the only ace of the Vietnam war quite plain. Why not? he reasoned. The whole affair was nothing more than an overblown bowling banquet. He was the trophy.

The ceremony at the White House took place January 3. President Johnson was just back from his Texas ranch and Lady Bird was nearby at all times, hovering. The audience for the actual medal ceremony was mostly media and White House staff. But there was an ample supply of military brass and wives with blue hair and hairdos resembling the business end of five-hundred-pound bombs. The newsmen scuttled about like crabs firing at will with their flash attachments. From the front of the room where South stood, it looked like the North Vietnamese defence of a SAM site. The President was apparently so moved by the Medal citation that he read it himself a second time after it had been initially read by his Air Force Adjutant, a young major with a West Point ring, an aura of arrogance and a thick Brahmin accent. That the President was overjoyed with South's accomplishment was obvious to all; he needed good news from the war and this was the best kind. *Our boys are still the best!* Despite his enthusiasm, the President stumbled over the text like an illiterate.

It was ironic, South thought during the early part of the ceremony, this whole boondoggle was over killing a handful of gooks. Hell, there were grunts in-country who killed as many every damned day with their shovels and no Medals of Honor were being draped around their necks. South

21

knew his was a public relations medal, kind of a living unknown soldier award. He was the war's first ace and as long as the North Vietnamese kept up their duck-and-run tactics, there probably wouldn't be many more. He'd gotten lucky. It was that simple. Virtually every pilot in his outfit could knock down the enemy as easily as he had. But it had been him who had the luck and got the opportunities. His weren't even all MiGs.

After the medal ceremony South, with the powder-blue ribbon draped around his neck, stepped to the rostrum to answer questions for the White House press corps. They fought each other to throw their questions at him. South didn't disappoint them with his fielding.

What is it like to shoot down another human being?
'Don't know. I shoot down airplanes.'
How good are the North Vietnamese pilots?
'The five I met, or the others?'
Is morale high among our combat forces?
'Depends on how much beer's available.'
What are your living conditions like?
'Imagine Miami in August. It's not as good.'
Do you have enough aircraft?
'Sure. They only let me use one at a time.'
Do you think we should be involved in this war?
'I don't pick 'em, sir. I just fight 'em.'

The crowd at the ceremony liked his spunk. Even some of the reporters applauded as he made his way out of the room.

As South was leaving, the President grabbed him by the arm and whispered into his ear. 'Keep kickin' their asses, boy.' His Commander-in-Chief's brute strength surprised him. A bruise had formed on his forearm by the next day; it lasted for almost a month.

The news media loved Byron South. He was cocky and witty. Despite a glib tongue, there was a coldness and aloofness to him that told each and every civilian he encountered, here was a man you wouldn't want to tangle with. At first the brass were shocked at his handling of the questions. But when they saw the favourable coverage that resulted, and as importantly, *how much coverage*, they knew they had themselves a winner and from that point on, anything he said, anything he wanted was okay with the powers that be. Byron South was on a roll and the U.S. Military Establishment was riding him for the duration. It was a powerful feeling.

His lady from the Defense Department was so moved by the medal ceremony that she pawed lustily at him in a small reception room just after the event as they prepared to leave for their next appointment of the day.

The week after the White House ceremony South and Wainright began a ten-day tour of major cities in the U.S. At each place they met with local civilian dignitaries and brass hurriedly rounded up from nearby military installations and recruiting offices. By trip's end they had their suitcases filled with keys to cities, city council proclamations and various awards and medals from state governments. He was an official hero and the subject of hundreds of media stories. He was interviewed on the *Today* show, appeared with Ed Sullivan, traded one-liners with Johnny Carson and he was even on the cover of *Time* with the simple red banner headline 'VIETNAM'S FIRST ACE'.

Wherever the entourage went, South faced a long line of aggressive women. In Philly a social worker let herself into his hotel room with a skeleton key early one morning and promptly accommodated him with a striptease and other personal services, courtesy of Philly's Social Services Administration. During the Detroit stop a Congresswoman twenty years his senior trapped him in a bathroom at a Bloomfield Hills cocktail party and maimed him with her drunken gropings. In Houston, a pair of female television talk-show hosts, twins called Annie and Emmy, cornered him in his dressing room before their programme. By air time he had barely enough energy to sit up straight, much less talk intelligently. By comparison, the twins seemed full of energy and even more exuberant than normal, a fact which didn't escape the attention of their producer, who knew their ways. In Denver, South met a twenty-year-old rodeo queen from Laramie and the University of Colorado who threw him on her bed and showed him how cowgirls got their jollies. In San Francisco a twenty-seven-year-old former high-fashion model and current wife of a Navy chaplain got to him, telling him that while she didn't normally engage in extramarital affairs, this seemed more like a matter of patriotic duty than a sin against God's laws. In Seattle three teenage girls climbed a fire escape, got onto his floor and ran up and down the corridor outside his room in the buff screaming for him to come out and show them his cannon. Security removed them before the dogfight could begin.

South's final press conference was in Honolulu as he and Wainright prepared for their return to Thailand. As usual the pilot wore his medal and he was glib and funny. But this time he was something more.

Would you characterize the Air Force flight forces as professional?

'It really bugs me the way you scoops throw around the word professional.' He had taken to calling newspeople 'scoops' in Detroit and continued the practice throughout the remainder of the media tour. 'First of all, the way you say it, it makes us out to be a bunch of cold-blooded, unemotional technicians — like a bunch of mechanical geeks. Come on a mission with me some time. It'll invert your yingyang and wrap a pink ring around your neck. In my business we have to be emotional. We live on adrenaline. But we're cool when the shit hits the fan. That doesn't mean we don't have feelings. In combat if you lose your cool, your ass is soon to follow. PDQ. Get it?

'Scoops never talk about the professionalism of our grunts — they're the ones who're in Charlie's back yard kicking his ass up one mountain and down the next. You want professional? Take a hike with those guys. Not in a base camp. Get out in the bush. They're as professional as anything you'll ever see. They have to be. The bottom line for all of us is to kill the enemy. To kill him, first you've got to find him. Then you've got to use the right tools at the

24

best possible moment. This is what professionalism means. It doesn't mean we get our jollies zapping some poor bastard who happened to be born in North Vietnam. When you're in, you're in. It doesn't matter whether you volunteered or were drafted.'

A reporter tried to ask another question, but South cut him off. 'Combat is pressure. Professionalism is your ability to rebound from pressure. To handle it and keep doing your job. You've got to understand, I'm talking *real* pressure. Take doctors. They have pressure. But it's not the same. Consider this. Some sawbones throws your Aunt Tilly up on his operating table and whacks open her belly. If he fucks up, she buys the farm, but he goes home to a Beefeater martini up with an olive and a boff in the sack with his old lady. Where's the risk? Malpractice? He's got insurance. Even if he loses his license, he's still got his life. Right? Where we work if you fuck up, it's over − C.H.I.-Dooey − end of the story. There's no insurance policy to bring you back from the dead. Blip-blap. They're using a dustpan to shovel what's left of your cells into a rubber bag.'

What's it like to knock down an enemy aircraft?

'Think of the best piece of ass you ever had. I mean *the* best − the one that drained your lizard for a week. It's better.'

How about the morality of the war?

South laughed hard and deep. 'When did wars start having morality? When countries start shooting at each other for any reason, where's the morality? Morality is an issue for schoolteachers, skypilots and philosophers, not for fighter pilots. Morality is something the winners of wars write into their history books − and winners *do* write the books − that much I know. Let me tell you something: the President and I have a great working arrangement. I don't tell him which wars to pick; he doesn't tell me how to fly my Thud.'

That evening South spent in the officers club at Hickam AFB drinking quart-size Mai-Tais filled with fresh pineapple chunks and watching Navy ships steam in and out the long deep channel that connected Pearl Harbor to the Pacific. He had his last fling in The World with a skinny but busty cocktail waitress who called herself Golden Fleece and claimed to have balled more pilots than any other woman on earth. She told him that she would give him the best lay of his life, then proved herself to be a woman of her word on a small lawn less than five feet from the rear exit of the Hickam Club.

The next day South and Wainright boarded a MAC C-135 bound for Bangkok. They were going back to war, South with a Medal of Honor, Wainright with new hope for promotion to general. *After all, Wainright had the only ace in the war.*

May 3, 1944

Fighting men speak of the 'fortunes of war'. In combat, luck cannot smile on all participants. Some are bound to lose.

The U.S. Fighting Man's Code

Flaw in the Fortress

Second Lieutenant Jergen Wainright watched the B-17 formations ahead of them and relaxed. There had been no antiaircraft bursts, no swarms of enemy fighters, nothing at all. Just a bluebird sky and clumps of rime ice on the windscreen. He'd expected something terrible this first time out. But now he was feeling more secure. For nearly a week he'd slept and eaten poorly. And he'd been thirsty all the time with an endless case of cottonmouth. Whenever some senior officer had found reason to talk to him, his voice had failed, the information spewing forth in the gasping, high-pitched tones of a castrato. He'd heard dozens of stories from the other flyers who'd already been over Germany. In orientation sessions they had shown the rookies films of crippled aircraft that, through some miracle, defied aerodynamic principles, and made it back. They'd also seen reams of still photos stuffed into green scrapbooks in no particular order, graphic photos of badly wounded and disfigured crew members. One picture showed a severed leg sitting crossways by itself on a stretcher on the ground near some B-17 wreckage. The nightmares began that night. He'd never seen a severed body part before.

But this wasn't too bad, Wainright congratulated himself. He pulled a soft apple from his box lunch, polished it vigorously on his sleeve and bit into it loudly. He turned his head to say something to his pilot but, instead, found himself gagging, immersed in a sudden stench of burning flesh.

The flak had hit them under the nose, directly under the cockpit. No warning. Just a violent thump against his behind and legs followed by a silent flash and heavy plumes of acrid, particle-filled black smoke that billowed from below

28

deck and temporarily cut his vision.

Several minutes passed before Wainright understood that the burning flesh was his own. The backs of his calves were numb, the cloth of the flight coveralls burned away. Narrow wisps of sweet smoke and body steam rolled up from underneath. What frightened him was the absence of pain. How many times had he heard there would be no pain with a fatal injury? Was he dying?

Cracking his window slightly, the young pilot was able to create a vent for the smoke and the cockpit cleared quickly. The only sensation that lingered was one of weariness. He felt the sudden need for sleep, but he fought it. He considered injecting morphine with a small Styrette from the first-aid kit, but there was no pain, and in any event, the narcotic would make him sleep. He'd save the drug for when it was needed. And hope it wasn't.

The B-17 was in a shallow descent of about fifty feet per minute. For a moment Wainright wasn't sure how long it had been since the explosion, or what their altitude had been. He tried the control column, but it seemed to be jammed. As he had been trained to do, he went through his options. Briefly he considered bailing out, but at the rate they had been bombing Germany, the Nazis and their civilians were not likely to be in any mood to take prisoners. They needed to keep going, home, to England.

The aircraft commander, Captain Lormis, was slumped forward in the left seat, unmarked and apparently dead, though the young pilot had never seen a dead man before and had no basis for comparison. Waingright pulled back tentatively on the control column several times, but it refused to move.

'Willie,' he shouted over interphone for his bombardier.

'Gone,' a voice said weakly.

'Who's this?'

'Corporal Mosher. Lootentant Williams is gone, sir. Looks like he got blowed out. Flak hit right on his bubble, I think. Ain't much left down here.'

'Okay, Mosher. Get up here PDQ. I need help.'

29

Seconds later the burly enlisted man stumbled into the cockpit and whistled in amazement when he saw the twists of steel. 'Geez, lootenant, we're lucky this friggin' thing's still in the air.'

Wainright's legs were beginning to ache. 'If we don't get the stick unjammed, we're not gonna be up here much longer. Skipper's dead.' Wainright hadn't checked. But he thought it was true. It was cold inside and there were no mouth clouds coming from the body. 'See if you can pull him out of there. I think he's jamming the controls.'

The sergeant pulled on the dead officer's shoulders until the upper torso was freed from the stick, but the body wouldn't come out of the seat and the stick was still locked slightly forward. 'Won't budge, sir.'

'Goddammit, get him out!' Wainright snapped. Mosher was a farm boy from Little Rock who did everything in slow motion; the man's lethargy had perturbed Wainright from their first meeting.

Mosher rested his elbows on the pilot's seat and wiped his forehead with his sleeve. 'His legs is pinned and all squashed up in some metal on the floor. He's jammed in there real good.'

'Use the fire axe,' Wainright said coolly.

'What's that?' the Southerner stammered.

'You deaf, Mosher? Use the axe. Cut him out of there.'

'That means ahm gonna have to hack oaf his legs,' the young corporal said in his thick Arkansas accent.

'Then do it. That's an order.'

Mosher folded his arms across his chest. 'I cain't do it, sir, I mean ... you know ... it's his *laigs*.'

'Get the axe.'

The gunner reappeared with the tool. Wainright could see that the man's jaw was set. He was frozen. He checked the altimeter again. They were still descending slowly and the rate was constant. There was time, if they could just get the stick loose. The young lieutenant released his safety harness and balanced himself between the seats on his left knee. His movement stirred the air and gave him another

30

whiff of seared flesh.

'You okay?' the gunner asked.

'Get back,' Wainright ordered. The feet of the corpse were enmeshed in the deck plating. The legs were hanging below deck. There were holes below and some of them were the size of the top of a large can of coffee. Through them he could see the German landscape passing underneath, some four miles below. Wainright sucked in a deep breath, gripped the axe handle firmly, took aim and struck hard just above the dead pilot's knees. The blade bit briefly into tissue and bone, then bounced out and skidded against something metal creating a brief but spectacular roostertail of sparks. The gunner fell backward against the bulkhead vomiting through his hands. Wainright inhaled again, held it and struck again and again, but the legs refused to come loose. He felt himself getting lightheaded as he sweated under the task. He had no idea how many blows it had taken, but finally the body separated from its legs, which somehow dropped through the holes below, deflected off part of the superstructure and fluttered into the sky. The lieutenant threw the axe to the floor and started pulling on the dead captain's shoulders.

'Dammit, Mosher! Help me.' The gunner grabbed hold, but Wainright did most of the work. 'Take it aft,' the copilot ordered as he slid into the left seat. Cold air came up from below and felt good on his legs. He tested the stick. It seemed to be all right. He levelled the plane and set the Altitude Hold on his autopilot. Satisfied that his immediate problem was solved, Wainright sat back in his seat and exhaled a long, controlled wheeze.

It was happening again. No matter how hard Wainright tried to do things right, something always seemed to go haywire. He'd saved for four years for a used convertible, then wrecked it less than six hours after it was his. In pilot training he'd ranked last in landing. It was not fear. It was just that when he got into the final flare he couldn't judge his altitude and invariably he bounced clumsily, and often hard onto the runway. In B-17 training his performance

31

during training had been flawless. Until the first check ride. Because he thought he'd seen a dip in oil pressure on one of the engines, he'd forgotten to retract the flaps after takeoff and almost caused the plane to auger in. His performance was rated unsatisfactory. Only an excellent mark on his second try kept him in the programme. It was always the same. Fate seemed determined to make it more difficult for him than others. Despite the stumbles, however, he still retained his dream and his lust for greatness, for 'making it big'. The military was a place where a man could get ahead, no matter how humble his beginnings. In his heart, he knew it was just a matter of time before his superiors and the world began to recognize him for what he was: a man of destiny. Now he was in command of a bunged-up B-17 and beginning to wonder if this was to be yet another test. Was there some built-in malfunction in him? Some supernatural spirit who had it in for him? It just wasn't fair.

After stowing the legless corpse, Mosher returned to the cockpit like a frightened dog. 'Get in the seat,' Wainright snapped.

The gunner eyed the bewildering rows of instruments: 'I don't know nothin' about flyin', lootenant.'

'That might change,' Wainright said grimly. While the corporal fumbled with his lap belt and harness, Wainright assessed their situation. Most of the instruments seemed to be working, though he couldn't understand how it was possible given their damage. He had no idea where they were. The rest of their bomber cell was long gone – inbound for the target. It was a long backtrack before they could pick up fighter cover out of England. On the good side, most of Germany's fighters were on the eastern front in Russia. But there were still a few Luftwaffe fighter units in France and Holland and all it took was one enemy bird to create a problem for them. On nothing more than instinct he put the compass on a southwest heading and decided to fly it until he passed over the French coast. He felt uneasy about such a simplistic decision, but it was all he could think to do and he was certain that doing something was better than doing nothing. But he needed information.

'Navigator, copilot.'

Mosher shook his head. Wainright stared at him, then understood.

'Crew, this is Wainright,' he said over interphone. There was no answer. He looked at his gunner.

'Navigator, bombardier, Sparky and the engineer all got blowed up in the nose. Tiny took a shrapnel through the head. Mose is unconscious . . . maybe he's dead. I couldn't tell. Never been in a mess like this afore. Couldn't see Andy nor Whit. They're aft. Maybe the interphone's on the fritz?'

'Go see,' Wainright told him. While he waited for a report, he adjusted the throttles and checked his fuel. The oil pressure on number one was low, too low, probably leaking. Eventually he'd have to feather it, he advised himself, but so long as it was still producing some power, he'd baby it as long as he could. It didn't occur to him that feathering it might conserve fuel. He'd be reminded of that later.

The interphone crackled in his headset.

'Heck of a mess back here too, lootenant. Had some small fires, but they're out. Took us some dandy hits. The port turret's gone. Andy and Whit are alive, but they're just hangin' on by a thread. I put a tourniquet on Andy's arm.'

'Tell him to loosen it once in a while.'

'Don't think he'll be able to. He's kinda in and out.'

'Morphine.'

'Already done. They're real groggy.'

Wainright tried to keep control of himself. He needed time to think. This was happening too fast. 'Okay, okay. Check for fires again, leave the drugs with Andy and come forward. Put Andy on the interphone and tell him he's gonna have to stay awake to keep track of what's going on. They got their chutes on?'

'Check. I'm on my way.'

Wainright twisted the frequency dial on his radio. 'Powder Room, this is Dusty Six.' No answer. He kept trying, but

33

got only static and silence.

Nearly an hour passed. Wainright kept trying to work out a plan, but everything he thought of presented problems. Or he had incomplete information to work with. That was the worst part. He wanted to get back to England. Deep in his mind were replays of the films showing badly crippled B-17s crawling back to their English bases. It had been done before. It could be done again. And this time he'd be the hero. The thought warmed him.

The coastline appeared in a mist ahead of them at the same time they finally made radio contact. 'Dusty Six, this is Powder Room.' Mosher grinned, revealing buck teeth that protruded almost like fangs.

'Powder Room, Powder Room. Dusty Six is a lame duck, proceeding home direct. Request fighter escort.' He checked his charts quickly, looked out the window for some kind of landmark. Seeing none, he took a guess. 'Dusty Six request rendezvous at Fox-Mike-One-Four, repeat rendezvous at Fox-Mike-One-Four, copy?'

The reply was stronger now. 'Roger, Dusty Six, Copy Fox-Mike-One-Four. You are requesting fighter cover. What is your condition?'

'Bad shape,' Wainright said.

'Casualties?' Powder Room came back.

'Affirmative. Dead and wounded.'

'Okay, Dusty Six. Confirm rendezvous at Fox-Mike-One-Four in three-zero minutes. Sorry about the delay but it's been a busy one. We're turning around some support right now. You guys are kinda early, ya-know?'

'Shit,' Wainright hissed.

'Come back, Dusty Six? I missed your last transmission.'

'Confirm rendezvous in three-zero minutes, Dusty Six.'

'Good luck, Dusty. Roll a seven.'

'We gonna make it, lootenant?'

Wainright grimaced. They needed fighter cover immediately. They were already near the French coast and if the Germans were going to be a problem, this was the time and the place. Thirty minutes could be too late. Miraculously they were still alone eight minutes before the rendezvous and the copilot was beginning to feel optimistic about their chances.

Mosher spotted them first. 'Bogeys, two o'clock high. Think it's our escort, lootenant?'

The young pilot knew immediately they were in trouble. As the two black specks rolled across their path he could tell by their silhouettes that they were ME-109s. Damn. His sphincter tightened and his stomach rumbled.

'Krauts,' Wainright gasped. 'We're gonna catch it.'

The pilot's mind raced. He had one engine with low pressure already and there was no telling how maneuverable the B-17 would be with all the damage it had taken. The two fighters were already sliding off in a wide arc and descending. He figured they'd come up from below and gut-shoot them. They were like wolves circling an injured sheep. That they were a lone bomber would tell the Krauts they were a cripple. When the fighters got close enough to make a visual inspection they'd throw away caution and pour it to them. 'Are any of our guns operational?' he asked the shaking corporal.

'Don't look like it,' Mosher said, his face against the glass, straining to see.

'Andy?' Wainright said on interphone.

'Sir?' a sleepy voice replied.

'Pair of Jerry fighters swinging in on us. You better cover up as best you can. I'm going to try to keep out of their way. Strap in.' There was no answer. Wainright switched to the radio. 'Powder Room, this is Dusty Six. We are under attack by two Germa aircraft. Repeat. *Under attack!*'

'Copy, Dusty Six. Your cover is up. You should have a visual any minute now. They got off a little faster than we thought. Hang on.'

Hang on? That asshole ought to be sitting here, Wainright thought. The aircraft shuddered as the Germans made a close pass. Wainright could feel the bullets whack against the wafer-thin sheet metal that was supposed to serve as armour plating. He knew they'd go for the engines on the next pass. There was only one option. Wainright switched off the autopilot and pushed the nose down into a tight spiraling turn.

The young pilot felt the problem before his mind could calculate it. There was too much drag. What the hell? Then it hit him: bombs. They still had their full load and no way to release them from where they were. They were screwed.

'It isn't fair!' his mind screamed as they shuddered and twisted earthward. The Germans rolled in tight and sprayed both wings. Fires broke out immediately and he began to lose pressure in three of the engines. There was no time left. 'Mosher. You got your chute on?' The corporal nodded. 'Andy,' the pilot called over the interphone. But there was no answer. No time, no time, his mind screamed. German tracers struck them again. 'Okay, corporal, get out. Now!' he screamed at the enlisted man. He levelled the aircraft, trimmed it as best he could and moved to the escape hatch.

Mosher had already jumped from his seat, but was frozen over the escape hole. Wainright pushed by him, grabbed the bailout bar and hung in the hole for a moment. Looking back and up he could see Mosher's harness wasn't snapped. He tried to say something, but Mosher, suddenly realizing what was happening, jumped on top of him, knocking both of them out of the aircraft. Wainright felt the blast of air in his face and Mosher's arms wrapped tightly around him. He got one hand free and punched wildly. The gunner let go and drifted away. Wainright reached for the D-ring and braced for the shock from the chute's opening. Below him Mosher's chute opened momentarily, then seemed to snap. He knew what had happened. Under the opening impact Mosher had been driven out of the harness. Wainright saw the enlisted man tumble toward the ocean below. The man's chute followed lazily like a white bird riding a gentle breeze. 'Dumb fucking hill-billy,' the pilot shouted as the German fighters climbed away toward the French coast.

Wainright spent several hours in the water before a

36

Coastal Defence Command boat pulled him out. He had a bad gash on his face and his legs were burned. The salt water had irritated all of his wounds and by the time he was rescued he was delirious.

For his effort, Wainright got a Distinguished Flying Cross. At the investigation, his squadron commander had vented his anger. The lieutenant should have been able to bring the plane home. But he had 'screwed the dog by the numbers.' He had failed to conserve fuel and he had forgotten about their bombs. If they'd just gotten rid of the bombs they would have had more maneuverability. The squadon CO wanted his scalp – as an example to other 'fuck-ups'. The deputy wing commander had intervened and saved him. In his judgement the young lieutenant had been through a bad experience. The plane was gone. They couldn't get it back. The men were dead. Not recall-able, he reasoned quietly for the board. On balance, he thought young Wainright had done the best he could con-sidering the circumstances, said the deputy commander. So they gave him the medal, told him to 'get hold of himself' and get back to work.

Wainright clearly felt the depth of his flaw for the first time in his life. He'd had his chance for glory and blown it. He didn't know how, but if another chance came along, he wouldn't lose it. He'd be prepared. He dedicated his life to preparing for greatness. By summer his injuries had healed and he was reassigned to a crew and flying missions again. As a copilot. But the opportunity for heroics never again presented itself and he came home with only his tarnished DFC and a half-dozen Air Medals to show for his war, the latter being automatic, given for numbers of missions, not for any particular accomplishments. And he was still a copilot. He knew it was not a great start on a career.

May 3, 1947

After all, a moron can press a button with his thumb and send an atom bomb out of the bomb bay. Smart college students can be taught which button to press and when to press the right button. But it takes an officer, a gentleman, and a *man* in the whole sense of the word to command the button-pressing, to direct and to get the best out of his airmen in a tense operation, and most of all to learn self-control and to command his own career to the advantage of himself and his service.

The Air Force Officer's Guide

Trouble in Berlin

Having been unable to sleep in the cramped space in the back of the C-54 transport plane during the long, bumpy ride across the Atlantic, Captain Jergen Wainright felt dirty and tired, in bad need of a bath and a drink.

As the plane let down to the base near London, Wainright found himself irritated. Now what? The telegram and orders had been cut by Lt. Colonel Hoyt Evans, his old deputy wing commander from World War II. Evans had been somewhat friendly during those times but hardly a mentor. He'd spoken up during the investigation and probably saved him from losing his wings and for that act alone, he owed the man. Wainright had heard nothing from Evans since, although he knew through the grapevine that Evans had been dispatched to Europe to serve on Curtis LeMay's staff at USAFE. What the hell did he want?

He got his answer at the bottom of the crew ladder. Evans was waiting in the mist with a broad smile and a snifter of brandy. 'Tired?' Evans asked.

'Beat to hell. What's up?'

'A problem. An opportunity. Depends on your perspective,' Evans said cryptically. 'Don't get too comfortable. You're going to take another plane ride.'

Wainright stared incredulously. 'Tonight?'

'Now,' Evans said. 'Soon as we can get the engines cranked up. We're headed for Wiesbaden. Germany.'

Wainright knew where Wiesbaden was. And what it was: LeMay's headquarters. 'It's going to be different to see it from the ground level,' Wainright said.

'Give you a good opportunity to see just how effective a job we did,' Evans said. 'It's not a pretty sight.'

It was raining hard when their C-54 finally bounced on

German soil and yawed to a skidding stop on the parking apron.

The two officers were met by a staff car and taken directly to a ramshackle quonset hut. LeMay was waiting for them. The general's desk was cluttered with stacks of paper. Blueprints and flow charts were tacked to a battered corkboard on the wall. His sleeves were rolled above his thick elbows and he was chewing on a long, fat, unlit cigar. He looked like it had been awhile since he'd slept. The general skipped small talk and got right to the point. It was his way.

'Damned Russians are tightening the screws in Berlin. Since March they've been doing white-glove inspection on all military vehicles going in and out of Berlin. They're checking passengers, baggage and materiel. Giving it a real Russky red-tape job, delaying shipments, the whole works. Everything has to be checked again at the East German border. That bastard Stalin is trying to throw a monkey wrench into the West German government. He doesn't want the West Germans getting into bed with other European countries during the reconstruction.'

LeMay paused for a moment, bit hard on his cigar, drew a breath and went on. 'But we're going to teach that sonofabitch a lesson in Yankee willpower, gentlemen. G-2 says Comrade Stalin will shut down all rail traffic to Berlin in a matter of weeks. He'll try to choke off the city. Without us, that bloodthirsty little bastard would be goose-stepping for Uncle Adolf right now. *This* is the thanks we get! When he shuts down the railroads we're going to supply that city with everything it needs and we're going to do it by air. We'll fly in everything: food, clothing, medical supplies, coal, coat hangers, rubbers, you name it, the whole damned ball of wax. You two have big jobs to do. Evans, you're going to be my adjutant. For the time being all your other USAFE responsibilities go on the shelf. You live, breathe and think this thing twenty-four hours a day. I've got some experts coming in from the states. They were the brains behind the resupply of Chiang over the Hump. Captain,

41

you're going to be my eyes and ears in Berlin – my inside man. We've got a few weeks – six at the outside – to get ourselves organized and ready.'

Wainright stared at the general, then Evans who was smiling again. 'Am I going to command a flying outfit?'

'Hell no!' the general thundered, 'I need *brains* in Berlin. Throttle jockeys are a dime a dozen. I want somebody up there with his feet on the ground and his eyes open. Evans says you're a man with some moxie. Now get some sleep. I'll cut orders for you tomorrow and arrange for a hop to Berlin.'

When they were outside Wainright nervously lit a cigarette, his hands shaking in the damp cold as he tried to shield the flame of his stainless steel Zippo. A staff car was waiting, its exhaust rising in small bursts like smoke signals.

'Why me?' Wainright asked. 'This is like some kind of weird dream. I don't even have the right clothes and uniforms with me.'

'We'll get you what you need,' Evans said to reassure him. 'This is reality. East against West. This is the real beginning. A new war. Undeclared, but a war any way you slice it. The Russians are going to be *the* fact of life for the remainder of our careers. Might as well get to know them now.'

'But why me?' the junior officer asked again.

'I remember the day you lost the B-17 and your crew. You had yourself a hell of a mess with that one.'

Wainright didn't reply. He didn't let himself dwell on that day. In his mind it no longer existed. Never happened.

'You survived,' Evans came back. 'That's the most important lesson. You can't teach instinct for survival. A few have it. Most don't.'

'But I don't speak German,' Wainright said defensively. 'I don't know anything about the Russians, or Berlin. I don't even know how we're organized over here, or who the key players are. I'm going in blind.'

Evans laughed. 'Welcome to the Real World,' he said as he jerked open the door to the waiting pea-green sedan.

May 3, 1950

In the military establishment an ability to adjust from job to job and to achieve greater all-around qualification by making a successful record in a diversified experience becomes a major asset in a career.

The Armed Forces Officer

One Short

Wainright clung to the polished bamboo rail of the bar trying to steady himself. His head was spinning from the sheer weight of the day's events, and from the too-many Manhattans that followed. He was filled with strong emotions that ranged from giddy elation to a sense of doom — the latter bringing whispers from his subconscious about a flaw, the flaw, his flaw. God knows, there should have been reason to celebrate. He'd shot down two MiG 15s during a midday raid, his third and fourth kills. Upon landing, his squadron commander had met him on the parking apron with a bottle of champagne and the news that he was on the major's list. And, barked his proud CO, because of the day's events he was recommending Wainright for a Silver Star. It was rotten luck again.

As it always did, the curse had asserted itself. A telegram lay crumpled on the bar in front of him. Hoyt Evans was being recalled from Japan to the Pentagon to assume a new Air Force planning job. He had selected Wainright to accompany him. The telegram congratulated him on his majority and reminded him of the good times they had had during the Berlin Airlift. 'Time for you to put the cockpit behind you,' Evans wired. 'Time to learn how to manage.' The reference was to the modernization and management programme the Air Force was about to undertake in a big way.

Wainright's stomach growled. There would be no fifth kill. He would not be an ace. He was going to 'fly a desk' — the victim of his own successes for Evans and LeMay. Somehow he had known even then that his competence as an administrator would come back to haunt him. In Berlin there had been no errors, no mistakes. No flaw and he thought he'd beaten it. But now it was clear that he hadn't. His competence at noncombat tasks was the latest manifestation of the flaw — there on his record for all to see. Certainly it was an effective credential but only up to certain ranks. Combat records still spoke loudest with peers and promotion boards and now he was being removed before he could get what he knew both intellectually and instinctively was the essential career 'merit badge.'

To be sure he was moving out of the line into staff with combat experience in two wars. He had four kills, the DFC and Air Medals from the big war and now there would be a Silver Star as well. A good record; not a great one. It was inadequate for what he wanted. Commendable, but not distinguished. The flaw lived.

Spring 1964

Maryland Shore

Elise Mantel was a regular on the weekend gin fizz and barbeque circuit in Georgetown and with the summer crowd at the Maryland Shore. In November of 1963 President Kennedy had been killed by a sniper in Dallas. Washington was in turmoil over the change in power. What would the new man do? Who would have jobs? Who would be out the door? The new man was not like Kennedy. He was a gangling Texan with a flair for backroom politics. His idea of society was cooking half a cow over an open spit at his ranch in the Texas scrub country or taking a wild ride over dusty Perdenales two-tracks in a Cadillac convertible. Insiders said that on balance the new longhorn power structure had more capital behind it than its eastern predecessor, but these were crude people without taste. The pall over Washington society was not so much for the passing of Kennedy as for what he represented. They all waited anxiously to see what the new man would bring to their lives. Or not bring. It cut both ways, said the wags.

In the spring the new President decided to visit Langley Field. A formal reception and ball were scheduled in the Chief Executive's honor. It was a cool and clear evening. The military was at its finest, decked out in their white mess dress uniforms. Rows of colorful ribbons and medals caught the glow of the lights and mixed musically with the harmonic sounds of Waterford crystal as they moved. They were specimens of straight backs and flat tops, spit-shined shoes, thin waists and deep tans from hours on the flight line and base golf courses. They talked their own language and thought their own thoughts. In their peculiar cosmos the color and cut of your cloth said all there was to say about you. By orientation and tradition the world was divided into two spheres: good guys and bad guys. Those who didn't share your values or who disagreed with you were bad. In their world they were paid to act and to do, not to intellectualize. Those who couldn't or wouldn't make the distinction were shown the gate.

Elise Mantel attended as the date of Major General Hoyt Evans, who while some years her senior, still cut a fine figure and looked like what she imagined a Greek warrior ought to look like. Her affair with Evans was one of pure lust, but even so, an on-again, off-again kind of thing. Because he had been shifted to Langley the opportunities to exercise what she calld her little 'lust-devils' were few. Evans went about his duty at his base, while she was left to her nightly parties in The District — as she called it. His invitation to the ball had not created much interest for her; but the general had considerable persuasive talents, not to mention dogged stubbornness and so the afternoon of the affair a blue Air Force staff car arrived to fetch her down-state to her general's side.

Evans enthusiastically supported the Johnson presidency. A Texan who started dirt-poor and fought his way up through American politics using raw power and the connections brought by a good marriage couldn't be all bad, he reasoned. The fact was, Evans liked Texans. They were scrappers, the kind of squinty-eyed, tight-jawed, hard-ass types who, once they bit into something, hung on like a Gila monster with purchase on a fat lady's ass. The Alamo said something important about such people. On the other hand, Kennedy was another matter. The missile deal with the Cubans had been his high point. After that Evans and most other senior military men lost faith in Kennedy. Too wishy-washy: the cardinal sin in a commander-in-chief. After the President and his rat-faced liberal brother left Cuban patriots stranded with their asses exposed at the Bay of Pigs, Kennedy's blue-suit and green-suit support evaporated. The failure to deal with Castro, they whispered in the halls of the Pentagon, would come back to haunt the country. Easier to kill a little mad dog than a big one, they reasoned.

At the ball Evans escorted Elise through the reception line and presented her to the President who smothered her long fingers in his massive paws and drawled great admiration for her 'git-up.' The First Lady stood close to her husband and watched like a bird of prey on its favorite perch.

Later Evans confimed her suspicions. Yessir, old Lady Bird calls some of the shots. When she yells 'shee-it,' the President squats. It was not like the general to be so crude; clearly he admired the First Lady's willingness to exercise power.

The Presidential party lingered until ten o'clock. The President danced with all the 'purty fillies' while dozens of Secret Service agents scratched at the collars of their rented tuxedos and watched him cruise the dance floor like a battleship with a crooked screw. What he lacked in grace, he made up in energy, Elise observed.

Around midnight a lieutenant colonel pulled Evans aside. Emergency of sorts. Couldn't wait until morning. Might take all weekend to straighten out the mess. Evans introduced her to Lieutenant Colonel Jergen Wainright. 'Take care of the lady, Jergen.' Yes sir, glad to.

Wainright immediately tried to apologize for being a stand-in. 'The general has a lot on his mind.'

'I know,' she said. 'He's getting ready for the war.'

The officer nodded. Obviously the Old Man kept her tuned in and that might be useful. There had been rumors that he was keeping a real 'looker' but few had actually seen her. Now that she was at arm's length, it was like calling Marilyn Monroe 'handsome.'

His car was an old white Buick Electra, a convertible with a black top and a fire-engine-red interior. It had delta fins that stuck out nearly a foot at forty-five-degree angles. Driving north out of Newport News with the top down, the woman suddenly told Wainright to turn onto Highway 17.

'This isn't the way home,' he protested.

'Scenic route,' she said. 'Please?' There was something about her that was hard to resist. It bothered him. A lot. As they drove along a series of narrow highways, then country lanes, a bottle of champange materialized from her purse. 'I liberated this on the way out,' she said, waving the bottle at him. Wainright was at a loss. She worked over the bottle with some kind of corkscrew, no doubt another trophy from Langley. It passed through his mind that she might be a kleptomaniac. When the cork finally gave way, it popped crisply into the night sky and fluttered behind them, spraying both of them with the sweet liquid.

Near the mouth of the York River she told him to 'pull over,' and there they sat for the better part of an hour, drinking from the bottle like adolescents and watching the running lights of small boats gliding on the black water.

'I love boats,' she told him. He admitted to a similar fascination.

'Ever been to Windmill Point?' she wanted to know. No, he'd never heard of it. She explained that it was the northern tip of land at the mouth of the Rappahannock. There was a cottage. It belonged to a friend. Nothing fancy. Your basic shelter. 'Dry roof and a warm bed with plenty of room to move around.' It wasn't clear to him whether she was referring to the cottage or the bed. He didn't pursue it.

Not sure of her intentions and fearing Evans he obediently followed her directions not quite sure what to make out of the whole thing. She was an odd creature. She looked soft and pliant but when she spoke there was a hardness that said she didn't ask for things; she demanded them, or took them. It was unnerving to be with her. But exciting. And more than a little tempting.

The cottage was a single-story affair with stone walls and a shingled roof. Very rustic. Newspapers were strewn around the interior. Dirty dishes in the sink. A large yellowing chart of the Rappahannock hung over a natural stone fireplace. The furniture was old. It was a place accustomed to being used. He sat stiffly on the couch while she disappeared down a dark hallway, returning minutes later with an arm-load of beach towels and two men's bathing suits.

'One of these ought to fit. If not we can always do it naturally,' she said, tossing the suits at him. 'You can change in the bedroom,' she said, pointing him toward the hallway. 'First door on the right. Light switch is to the right of the door jamb. Check out the workshop.' He had no idea what she meant.

As he squeezed into one of the suits he felt a surge of anxiety. So far there had been no funny business, but something inside him said this was a woman to be wary of. Most women operated inside certain constraints, letting men tempt them past established lines. It was a way to preserve certain conventions. But this one seemed more comfortable leading than following. It occurred to him, quite vividly, that if there was anything deep between Evans and her, his own ass might be on the line. She was a lot younger than the general. Younger women tended to have certain needs, some of them rather intense. He wasn't comfortable with the prospects and tried to steel himself against his own baser instincts. A dark voice inside him nagged mischievously: 'Don't get your meat where you get your bread.' The vulgarity of his own thoughts embarrassed him. Before leaving the room he opened two doors to look for a workship, but found only closets in bad disarray.

When the returned she was standing barefoot in the kitchen with a red towel wrapped around her shoulders.

'See the workshop?' she asked eagerly. She could tell from his expression that he didn't know what she was talking about. 'The bed,' she said as explanation. He blushed.

'Ready?' he asked, hoping to find a more comfortable subject of conversation.

'You tell me,' she said. She drew back the lower part of the towel, revealing the bottom part of a bikini. 'The bottoms are terrific,' she said. Then she let the towel fall free to the

50

floor. Her breasts tumbled free, the light dancing off them as she hunched her shoulders and made them swing in a kind of arc. 'My girlfriend's halter doesn't fit. Different architecture. I guess.'

He coughed in a nervous reflex, stunned far less by her naked flesh than by her apparent ease with it.

'I can get by if you can handle it,' she said. She grabbed his arm with both hands and pushed him toward the door. 'Besides, colonel,' she cooed, 'I always say if it feels good, do it.'

Thirty yards from the rocky shore, a large sailboat was lashed to a buoy, bobbing gently under a slight swell. She splashed into the surf ahead of him and swam toward the boat with powerful strokes. He tried to catch her, but she was too strong and easily widened her lead. She was already up the ladder and on deck by the time he got to the boat. He found her squeezing clumps of her dark hair to wring out the salt water.

'Water's nice,' he said as he climbed up beside her.

'Funny thing about this place,' she replied. 'Right here it's as warm as a bathtub, but just over the rocks — just a few yards away — it's like ice cubes. Don't you think it's fascinating how two things so different can be so close? You move just a little distance and everything changes.'

Once again he changed the subject. 'Anything on board to drink?'

'I'll look,' she cackled. 'My girlfriend is an absolute lush so there ought to be something.' She slid back a deck hatch and disappeared below. When she emerged she had a bottle of white wine which she had already opened. 'Can't vouch of the vintage, but it's wet.'

It took them nearly an hour to finish the bottle. Her head was afloat. He felt strangely anxious, but was not particularly talkative. She laid back and allowed her breasts to fall outward toward her arms. He stared at her, wondering what the hell was happening to him.

She was getting tired of the chase. She decided to help him out of his dilemma. 'Hoyt and I are friends. Sometimes we sleep together, but there's no commitment. Does that shock you?' She didn't wait for an answer. 'Despite what you may think, colonel, I'm a free agent and I would like for you to know that I am of an ever-increasing school of thought that subscribes to the notion that fornicating is extremely good for what ails you. It beats hell out of chicken soup. What do you think?'

'Evans,' he said weakly.

'Hoyt? He's a Teddy Bear. He won't care. Besides, who's going to tell him?'

'He'll find out. General officers can cause big trouble.'

'Nonsense. You're a colonel, not some fuzzy lieutenant.'

'A *light* colonel with hopes of being more.'

She touched her forehead with the back of her hand. 'God spare me. Another careerist. Aren't you of that generation of pilots whose motto was find 'em, feel 'em, fuck 'em and forget 'em? Whatever happened to those guys? I mean, where are they when you *really need them?*'

Wainright laughed. He couldn't help himself.

The woman leaned close to him, taking great care to push her breasts against him. 'Bet I can change your mind, colonel,' she cooed.

He pulled away. 'I can't,' he said. 'Don't you understand? Not with Sundown's woman.'

She sat up. 'Sundown?'

'General Evans,' he explained.

'What the hell does that mean?'

'His nickname. Sundown. He's had it as long as I can remember and he and I go back a long time. Every time he gets a new assignment he personally reviews the record of every key man in the operation. Those who don't meet his standards get until sundown the next day to get off base. Your Hoyt is one tough hombre.'

'He can do that?'

'Legally? Probably not. But he's always had the power and nobody can challenge that. He does as he pleases and it sticks. You see my problem?'

She slid her arms around his neck. 'I'm not waiting till

sundown tomorrow. Your commander told you to take care of me, now do your duty, light colonel Wainright.'

He gave in.

Around nine the next morning he awoke to the powerful scent and sound of cracking bacon strips. He stumbled out of bed, pulled on his pants and went into the kitchen. She was nude, with a full-front apron tied into place. He put his arms around her as she fiddled with a wide black skillet and a long fork, jerking her hand back every now and then to avoid angry splatters of grease.

'How long before they start shipping everybody off to the war?' she asked without warning.

'Don't you ever work your way up to anything gradually?'

'Never,' she said with a giggle.

'Soon,' he said. 'We have about fifteen thousand advisors and irregulars in there now. Until there's some kind of incident we'll have to officially stay out. We have to let them make the first move on us.'

'You mean you're waiting for Son of Pearl Harbor?'

'Roughly.'

'You say it like it's a foregone conclusion.'

'It will happen,' he said as he reached for a strip of bacon she had set on a paper napkin to drain. 'The Russians will see to it. Or the Red Chinese. Same difference.'

'Well,' she said, after they had eaten and after she had washed and stowed the dry dishes, 'I've made a decision. I think we should shack up – play a little house with each other.'

He backed away from the table. 'I don't think so. We can't just jump into something.'

'You and Hoyt can jump right into a war. This is worse? Poor, poor boy. We have to do something about your sense of values. We'll have some laughs and we can walk away anytime we want. As long as it feels good, what's the harm?'

'You're three hours away,' he argued.

'Not anymore,' she laughed. 'I can live right here. I

can arrange it this afternoon. How's that for solving a problem?'

He stared at her as she began to untie her apron.

'It's my sister's place.' she confessed.

That's how it began. Three months later North Vietnamese gunboats attacked U.S. Navy destroyers in the Gulf of Tonkin. The war was on.

Part II: Taxi Dancer

Two bits a ticket buys you a dance, mister. And that's all. You don't get my soul, just the dance. I may not be expensive, but I'm not cheap, get my drift? When I was a kid I thought it would be an elegant way to live. You know, expensive dresses, high heels, makeup, the trappings. Really something. So I got into the profession. That's what it is, you know? We have our own ethics. There's ways to do things and ways not to do them. It makes a big difference. In our heyday there were lots of us. Not now. Just a few old diehards. Not much elegance. Or sustenance. Business is down. Can hardly make expenses. Guess we don't know nothing else. We're the last of our kind. When we're gone, there won't be any more. Too bad? I suppose. Never really thought much about it. About all I think about is dancing. That's my first love. I'd do whatever I had to for that − to keep dancing. I don't know what the other ladies told you, mister, but I'm pretty good, you know? I think whatever people do, they ought to try to be good at it. It's in my blood; too late to change that.

From an interview in *Abstracts of American Sociology*, 1966.

May 1, 1967

Door Guard

The bulletin board inside the front entrance caught South's attention. Without knowing why, the pilot had taken to collecting various memoranda issued by the wing commander. After quickly reading the newest issue, he tore it off the board and stuffed it into a leg pocket of his flight suit. They already were having trouble meeting their mission requirements. Now Wainright was going to institute some kind of slow-learner's class for pilots who weren't making the grade on missions. It was the kind of thing you might do stateside, but not here. Didn't anyone have any idea what kind of an idiot was commanding the 39th?

South walked farther into the building. The floors were carpeted in a rich cerulean blue fabric with a long pile. The air conditioning in the headquarters building always seemed stronger and sweeter than elsewhere on the base. Which it was. By the wing commander's order.

The wing commander's reception area was fairly large. His receptionist sat behind a large gun-metal grey desk. Some soft chairs were lined up near her desk and across from her there was a huge emblem, in relief. Its main symbol was a skull with lightning bolts clenched tightly in its incisors. Ornate gold lettering on the curling banner below proclaimed: 'Taxi Dancers.' There were some Latin words as well, but South had no idea what they meant and no interest in finding out.

The receptionist was like everything else in the 39th Tactical Fighter Wing headquarters area: threatening.

South stood in front of the desk, but the woman made

no attempt to recognize his presence. Instead she continued to pound her electric typewriter at a speed South estimated to be approaching the limit of human capacity. She typed so fast that the hum of the IBM machine and the sound of the keys striking the paper all blended to mimic the high-pitched buzz of a Gatling gun. After several minutes, the secretary swiveled slowly in her chair and looked up at him.

'Have a seat, captain. The colonel is on a call.'

Her voice surprised him. He'd never spent much time around her. Usually she just pointed at Wainright's door and went back to what she was doing. Now he realized that her voice was much softer than he had remembered, or realized, and it had a quality that immediately captured his attention. He'd seen her hundreds of times, but it now seemed to him that he'd never really taken a close look. Early thirties, he estimated. Brunette. Hair cropped close, but the bangs in front were long and curled under invitingly. Not much make-up. She wore a summer shift that clung to her figure. Big tits, he noted. Her nipples protruded through the fabriclike thimbles.

'Can I have more than a seat?' he asked as he tumbled into the chair closest to her desk.

Her back was to him, but he could hear her shuffling papers. When she turned, she did so almost ceremoniously. Her eyes stared straight at him with incredible intensity. Her nostrils were flared. 'Do you think you can *handle* more?'

Her come-back caught him off guard. 'Say again,' he said weakly. But she did not respond. She had picked up a sheaf of papers which she was arranging in some kind of order. Her skirt was pulled high above her knees and the sight of so much white but tanned female flesh made him nervous. Round-eyes in Thailand were about as common as rednecks in Harlem. In Thailand where women took to sex like whitetails to a salt lick there was ample diversion for men. But even with the willingness of the little hairless Thais — what the airmen called Little Brown Fucking Machines, LBFMS for short — it was a shock to come face to face with the reality and sensuality of an American woman. He couldn't stop staring at the insides of her thighs, and while she surely realized the focus of his attention, she made no effort to tug her skirt down to a more businesslike altitude.

Her thighs were firm, like an athlete's. Just above one knee on the inside of her left thigh, there was a small scar, a long thin wisp of pink that curled almost like a swimming snake. Actually the colour was more like magenta, he decided, like the gills of a cuthroat trout flushed by spawning. Magenta was an unusual colour, even a rare one, for human scar tissue. South knew about scars; they spoke eloquently about their owners. Athletes had them. So, too, did firemen and cops and racing drivers. But no profession had scars like fighter pilots.

Taxi Dancer Jelly Roll Jessup bought the farm at McConnell, South remembered. Melted down to the ultimate: liquid scar. The trick in scar acquisition was to get just enough for effect; too much and you ended up like Jessup, too formless to identify. With Jessup, the body-bagging detail had to take a long smoke break to wait until the fleshy droplets cooled sufficiently to be picked up. The medics had used spatulas from the mess hall to put the pieces in the rubber bag.

Merchant did better than Jessup. His left ear had melted down to the skull, leaving only the stump of an earlobe, and his eyebrows had refused to grow back after the accident. It had been a bad cockpit fire, but Merchant had gotten out with minimal real damage and some great scar tissue. Now Merchant loved to greet FNGs — Fucking New Guys — by pointing to his face and hissing: 'You're in the clubhouse, asshole, but you ain't joined the club yet.' They understood.

Jasper Loo — called Chan by his comrades in the wing — was another case, somewhere in between Merchant and Jessup in the scar hierarchy. It had taken four hundred stitches and experimental plastic staples to put a face back on Chan's skull and, to be sure, the sawbones who'd done the work was no artist. Loo's new face was a patchwork quilt of discoloured flesh squares sewn to the muscles to approximate a human countenance. Even so, Loo didn't seem to mind. He was used to it now and besides, he said, split tails — especially young nurses — seemed fascinated by his deformity. The pilots were not so accepting. In the stag bar Chan was not allowed to stand in direct light. They insisted he stay in the shadows, lest he give them all nightmares. It was a joke. Sort of.

Jack Pasko's situation was about right. He'd lost his nose in a high-speed, high-altitude punch-out and he still swore that the nose had stayed right beside him, at arm's legnth, but too slippery to catch, as he free-fell from the bailout altitude to eighteen thousand feet when the aneroid in his chute inflated and automatically put him under the silk. The surgeons built a new nose for Pasko, using a chunk of flesh from his left buttock. The surgery had gone well, but there was a postoperative infection and problems with healing so that one corner of his left nostril contained a humped flap of skin and made him look like there were three entrances to his nose. The Flight Medicine Section wanted to fix the oddity, but Pasko — ever pragmatic — refused. His breathing was normal, his oxygen mask fit fine and undoubtedly there'd be more damage before the tour was over. The docs could just wait and fix the whole mess at once.

South especially admired Millette. His bottom lip resembled the battlements of a Norman castle. The surgeon who had done the job had worked in poor light and the mouth had been such a mess that his nurse kept leaving the room to puke into a steel basin. Given the circumstances, Millette felt lucky to have a bottom lip and besides, the jagged V's in it provided him with handy cigarette holders. Can't bitch, he said. It's there. It works. Everything else is gravy.

South and the Taxi Dancers knew about scars. But in their vast storehouse of such information, South could recall no previous specimen of a magenta hue. The discovery increased his interest in the secretary's thigh.

'Taking a snapshot for your wishbook, captain?' Her voice was oddly formal, but there was something else there. He couldn't quite put his finger on it. He smiled awkwardly. 'The colonel will see you now.' A small yellow light on her telephone was blinking.

Before entering the commander's office the pilot paused and looked back at Wainright's secretary. He was surprised to find her staring at him. 'I can handle more,' he said clumsily.

'We'll see, won't we?' she said with a smile. She tilted her head back and rotated her chair to the typewriter.

The Willie Mays Principle

Wainright was entrenched behind his desk, a hand-carved teak and rosewood monument imported from Hong Kong. Two ground-pounding lieutenants had spent a thirty-day TDY on the Chinese islands waiting for the artisans to finish Wainright's special order. The desk and its origins were designed by the wing commander to become part of the legend of the Taxi Dancers.

The office was richly appointed and elegant, in a peculiar way. It was said that a visiting Lieutenant General from the states had moaned in envy after his first view of the wing commander's office. In typical fashion the office was designed to let Wainright's visitors know he was in command. He might not be a West Point graduate, but he was a wing commander. He had power and the will to use it.

The carpets were thick and heavily padded to provide an almost weightless feeling. Silk flags with gold fringes were in individual Thai brass stands behind his desk. The furniture was covered with leather in a creamy chocolate tone. One corner of the expansive office was dominated by a teak bar nearly ten feet in length. The top was inlaid with a long

61

strip of unblemished onyx and the front of the edifice was surrounded by a polished brass rail, which looked more like gold than the amalgam it was. Behind the bar hung a large stainless steel eagle with huge blue star sapphires inlaid for eyes. The bird had been a gift from a Thai politician. The stones were at least fifteen carats each, so large and bright that they seemed to track you wherever you walked.

In Wainright's world every item had its purpose. Each was designed to make a particular point to visitors. Here was a system and order, *his* order. Neither the wing commander nor his system had time for those who could not or would not comply. Wainright had played by the system's rules and taken the hard times like a man. When it came to men who couldn't follow the rules, he had a short fuse.

Wainright liked to talk of Willie Mays. The Giant great had once told reporters the simple formula to his success. 'They throw the ball, I hit it; they hit the ball, I catch it.' Wainright loved Willie Mays because Willie had talent and followed orders. Because of it, Willie was rewarded handsomely for making his living at what remained nothing more than a boy's game. The essential remained the job. Getting it done. Those who deserved it, got rewarded. Reward was an important part of the system, all systems. Willie, Wainright often recounted, did not go so long without at least a few problems. Most notably the ballplayer had tried to move into a white neighborhood in San Francisco when the Giants moved from the Polo Grounds. This attempt to displace the system brought trouble to Willie and his performance suffered. But eventually Willie got himself straightened around and back into harmony with the natural order, and now he could look forward to immortality in the Hall of Fame at Cooperstown.

The wing commander appreciated that among truly talented people — thoroughbreds, he called them — there could be temporary 'disorientations'. Such people had a tendency to kick up their heels and let their natural individualism take command. To a point, a carefully and predetermined point, the supervisor of such people owed it to them and to himself to put up with such slippages and to gently nudge the thoroughbreds back onto course, *if* they could get back, and *if* they were producing. Some couldn't. They had to go. That was life.

Willie Mays was what military life was all about. That was the essence of Wainright's greeting to all new arrivals to the 39th Tactical Fighter Wing.

But right now Wainright had no time to contemplate Willie. His problem was Captain Byron South and his potential impact – both good and bad – on Wainright earning his first star. He had worked hard to get where he was, and where he hoped to be. Along the way he'd taken a few more chances than most, certainly more than the ringknockers from the academy who had their own old boy network to help boost them along to the higher ranks. It was not enough to know that you were the best in the Air Force at *managing* a wing. When you were a ninety-day wonder, you had to do more.

Most troublesome was the knowledge that in peace-time he would be a shoo-in for brigadier general; but this was quasi war and the market had turned bear on managers. The commodity in demand now was leadership in combat. Understanding the changing dynamics of the situation, Wainright had pulled some strings to get himself back into the line as a combat commander. But it was not easy. The Berlin deal had been easy. Look-listen-ask questions-learn-report-follow up. That was the way to manage. But this was different. Vietnam required that the old model be pulled out of mothballs, wound up and sent out to do battle. But it wasn't working. He didn't have the stomach for it anymore. He'd outgrown the old model and now there wasn't a damn thing he could do about the reversal.

Korea had been much easier. There you knew who the bad guys were – even if they all looked the same. At least they dressed differently. There the emphasis was on winning, on pushing the North Koreans and Chicoms back across identifiable geographic lines. It was a lot easier to keep score then. Now they were screaming for body counts and assessments of damage from their attacks – the enemy KIAs and BDA numbers they could flash over the evening news to the folks at home to show them that Johnny could still kick Oriental asses. It was turning into a bean counter's war.

Initially he saw the assignment as an opportunity to fill a long-standing gap in his record. He needed one more enemy kill to become an ace, and while it wasn't like doing it all in one war, being an ace over time was better than not being one at all. But now he harboured no illusions about this accomplishment; it wasn't going to happen unless somebody parked a MiG 19 on the ramp for him to shoot at. He'd made his try and not liked what he discovered. Worst of all someone else knew, too, and Wainright despised and feared him for it. South.

At first the man had been manageable. But since their return from Washington, things had been deteriorating fast. South knew the truth. In other circumstances he could simply run him out. But not now. South was The Ace. America knew him, even – God forbid! – admired the man. His last press conference in Honolulu had been a disaster. But since their return South had shot down three more enemy aircraft, giving him eight and putting him head and shoulders above anybody else in the war. He was one of a kind. That was the *real* problem.

Declaration of War

South sauntered slowly into the wing commander's office. He wore a faded orange T-shirt, his plastic batting helmet, flesh-colour shorts and faded orange knee socks rolled down over the tops of his jungle boots. Some pilots kept their boots polished, but South told his Thai housegirl, Twooey, that if she touched his boots with one speck of polish she'd be meeting Buddha a lot sooner than she or he expected. They were working boots, not ass-licking boots.

Wainright looked at him and sighed. 'Are you reporting to your commanding officer, or going to a masquerade party?'

'You mean there's a difference?'

Wainright drummed the desktop with well-manicured fingernails. 'South, I'm not going to put up with your crap.'

'Thank you,' South said with a grin. The wing commander's mouth opened and closed slowly like a fat catfish sucking algae off a river bottom. There was no sound, just movement. At one point, he started to stand up, but caught himself and pushed his swivel chair back from the desk. He ran his hands through his silver-grey hair and sucked deep breaths as he strained to control his composure.

Finally, when his colour had gone from white to red and settled back to a kind of murky pink, he smiled at the pilot. 'We've done this scene too many times. This time we're going to talk ... man-to-man ... get it all out on the table. We've got differences. Let's get them settled. For *your* sake.'

Before, it had always been a kind of perverse game whose rules changed from day to day. But now South could feel a different kind of intensity in Wainright, like he had an exposed nerve and was trying to hide the pain. He'd known all along that there would be a confrontation, but he was not sure he was prepared for it just now. In this world Wainright held all the cards.

'I'm a man of peace,' South said.

'You are a disruptive element in *my* world,' Wainright said menacingly. 'I *believe* in order; you *disturb* the order. I *don't like* the order to be disturbed. Colonel Horowitz tells me you were popping off this morning ... something about not flying tonight. He seemed to be a bit unclear about what you meant.' Wainright wanted to give the pilot a chance to back off.

'I say a lot of things,' South said quietly.

'To hear Horowitz tell this, the things you were saying are the kinds of things that illustrate my point — about disturbing order.'

'Back where I come from they call it shit-stirring.'

Wainright clasped his hands on his desk and tilted his head slightly to the side. 'Generally people who do this kind of thing have a reason. Sometimes they have a good reason. Sometimes it's the manifestation of hard feelings — a product of a breakdown in communications. These kinds of things can be cleared up, set right.'

'Could be,' South said. 'Never thought about it like that before. The shit-stirrers I know stir it because they like to. They don't need a reason; it's just the way they are. The more you talk to them, the harder they stir.' South looked directly at Wainright.

The wing commander looked past the pilot to a small shadow on the wall. He could feel the pressure building. They were jockeying. He warned himself to maintain control. 'Colonel Horowitz was under the impression that you might be encountering some difficulties that might temporarily require you to be off flying status. As I said, he wasn't especially clear, so if I'm inaccurate, I'd like very much for you to tell me. I simply want to understand you. I believe a commander should understand his men, and, of course, all commanders hope this will be reciprocated.'

'This was something I was supposed to have said?'

'According to Colonel Horowitz. He could have been mistaken.'

'And you want clarification?'

'Yes.'

'To help you to understand me?'

'Precisely.' Wainright was feeling better. For the very first time since they had first met he could feel progress. Patience was a virtue, he reminded himself.

'I think I said I was considering retirement.'

'You have a lot of years before you have to start thinking about that. It's too soon.'

66

South pushed his hands against his side and did a kind of trunk-twisting exercise. 'The way I see it, it might be a little late.'

The pupils of Wainright's eyes grew smaller. 'I know you're under a lot of pressure. We all are. This is a war. I've been through all this before. I've seen hundreds of men go through this. It's never easy.'

'Seems pretty easy to me. All I have to do is quit.'

'You can't quit. There are too many people counting on you.'

'Fine,' South said, his voice rising a bit. 'Who do I count on?'

'The other men. Your chaplain. Your commander. We have a complete infrastructure designed to provide everything you need.'

South gritted his teeth. 'What I need is out. Now. Today.'

'Out of the question,' Wainright said.

'Your opinion.'

'You've been a lucky man, captain. Eight kills. Medal of Honor. How would it look if you were to chuck it all in?'

'I can live with it.'

'You can't do it,' Wainright said, his voice intensifying. 'I can't allow it.'

'There,' South said. 'There's the fucking problem. *You* can't allow it. Of course *you* can't. If I walk away *you* lose your ticket and worse than that you look like a real asshole. The only wing commander in the war who had an ace quit.'

'You are going to keep flying, captain. Here I make the rules.'

'I'm not flying *period*. You know, small dot after a bunch of words . . . that time of month for a lady. Period. As in ever, which is to say, never. No flying. Zero aviating. Not just tonight. Never. With all due disrespect, I quit this chickenshit outfit. You want it in writing?'

So this was how it would be. Wainright sighed loudly. 'You can't quit.' It was going to be a championship bout.

'I can, if it's signed off by the medics. DNIF – Duty

Not Involving Flying. Section Eight. Combat fatigue. Call it whatever the hell you want.'

Both men were still talking quietly, their voices carefully controlled, neither wanting to provide an emotional advantage to the other. It was a contest; both knew the stakes were high. And they knew the fencing was ended.

It wasn't going to be easy, Wainright told himself. The wing commander considered South's idea. A Section Eight wasn't out of the question. Certainly South's behaviour qualified him for a psycho ward.

Two weeks previously South had barged into Horowitz's office. He told the vice commander that he was putting together the 'deal of a lifetime'. If he could get enough backers, he'd take a train up to Chiengmai and buy twenty young girls he could take back to Bangkok to sell to Chinese businessmen. Virgins, especially those who had not yet begun to menstruate, were worth a thousand U.S. dollars each. In northern Thailand life was hard and daughters a burden. Annual income up-country was less than twenty-five dollars U.S. Peasants in such circumstances would jump at a chance to make a few baht. They could buy them for the equivalent of a full year's income for the locals. Supply was no problem. Neither was demand. It was a perfect business proposition. The farmer gets rid of a burden and makes some income. The kid goes to a much better life than she could expect in the bush. And the old Chinese businessmen got a little prime young stuff. 'The potential return on investment is fantastic,' South said in launching his sales close. 'We've got no inventory to pay for. And it's a hell of a lot safer than smuggling gems and jewellery back to the states.' South was a born salesman, Wainright told himself. He'd known that the vice commander, like many other airmen, was shipping gems back to the states daily. With a good eye for stones you could buy quality stuff cheap and resell in the States at incredible profits. By regulation you could send twenty-five dollars in duty-free goods back to the States every day. You declared your package as worth the maximum allowable, then shipped back a thousand dollars worth of gems and jewellery. And you didn't even insure it. So what if it got lost? There was plenty more available and it was an easy process with virtually no risk.

Wainright smiled as he remembered Horowitz stumbling around his office like a wounded water buffalo. The irony was that South's plan was not without merit. A man *could* build a very nice nest egg dealing in women. Of Thailand's three million Chinese, nearly half lived in Bangkok and nearby Somburi and among them was a sizable number of lusty old bastards with some downright medieval ideas.

It was the kind of action Wainright had come to expect from South. Instead of a direct frontal assault, he'd needle somebody close to Wainright and create a mess that only the wing commander could clean up. It was a kind of guerrilla warfare and while it was tough to keep score, Wainright was beginning to feel like a loser. South was a disease – a virus – and viruses had to be killed – by whatever would do the trick.

It would be relatively easy to remove him; it would take no more than a quick phone call to the flight surgeon. But that didn't really solve the problem. They could pin a loony label on him, but that wouldn't shut his mouth; wouldn't keep him from talking about things better left unspoken.

He had hoped the Medal of Honour would help settle the man and for a while it had. They had gone back to the states together but it had not affected their relationship in any positive ways. Since their return it had continued to deteriorate at a steady but gentle rate. And then there had come that one day, one mistake and in the aftermath Wainright knew he had lost control. He had hoped that he could nurse the situation through, until South's hundred missions were complete and he was on his way home. Now the options were drying up, a situation precipitated by South himself.

Force was out. He had to try something else. Buy some time. His plan was to dangle a few milk runs before South, to get him through the final mission and out of his hair with both their reputations intact. Combat had odd, but predictable effects on most men.

In this war you came to combat knowing precisely when you were leaving. In that regard it was more like prison than war. When you reached your date, you went home. Or if you reached one hundred missions over North Vietnam. Whichever came first, you were finished; your duty was done. Every man who came to Southeast Asia knew his tour, and therefore his risk, was limited in time, and each man acted accordingly. This produced a documented, almost predictable sequence of mental changes and adjustments that the military shrinks had identified, and about which they supplied information to combat commanders to help them manage their people.

When the new men arrived, they tended to be green — very nervous and anxious, prone to errors in the most simple tasks. To ease them into the routine, you gave them some easy missions to start with. You sent them over Laos where the defences were for the most part sporadic. You watched them closely, studied them until you were sure they could handle what waited for them over the North. Up there, lives would depend on how they reacted to the pressure. The first time they went to Hanoi you sent along a good wingman, a pro. After the first trip they fully understood what they were up against. Reality crushed them and put them into an almost Zombie-like mode. They did their jobs. They learned that the mission came first and if you buy the farm, well, tough shit, babes. Somebody's got to do the work. The lucky ones and talented ones survived this stage, which lasted about six months. Then, suddenly, at about fifty or sixty missions, the attitudes of the survivors changed again. They got daring. Their eyes were hard. Now they were at their best. They had seen others die. They'd been hit by flak and SAMs. Their machines had gone sour on them and by now most had ejected at least once — some as many as six times. Where no serious injury was involved, they'd go right back into the sortie rotation.

These were the old pros and on their shoulders sat the responsibility for the lion's share of the fighting. By ninety missions, another change took place. Short-timer's fever. The same pilot who had battled his way through the last thirty missions suddenly got skittish. He began to dread every sortie, fearing that he'd be killed, or even worse, captured when he was so close to escaping Hell and returning to The World.

In South Vietnam, many Army commanders pulled their short-timers out of the field, disengaged them completely in order to avert mistakes. But fighter-wing commanders didn't have that kind of luxury and flexibility. The best they could do was make sure that the final ten missions in each pilot's tour were in less critical areas. Even so, the pilots were overly cautious during this period, not particularly effective, and the mortality rate was high. Wainright had had three different pilots killed on their hundredth and final mission. Each time this had happened the wing went into a kind of mass shock, all of the pilots wondering if the same fate awaited them.

After all, the main thing was to get home in one piece, more or less. The ultimate outcome of the war was irrelevant. Who cared? Certainly not the people back home. The war was something you watched on the evening news. It wasn't real unless you had somebody in it, and even then it wasn't like World War II. There were no rallies, no sustained government efforts to pump up the people to support their troops. Back home it was business as usual and fuck those stupid bastards who let themselves get caught up in the war.

Wainright knew there was no commitment to the fighting because the fighting had no purpose. That men reacted predictably was predictable.

South was unlike others. He slipped into the old-pro mode in his early missions and had been there ever since. In the air there were no signs that he was becoming cautious. But his behaviour on the ground was deteriorating and maybe, just maybe this was the symptom of his own peculiar

71

form of Short-Timer Fever.

Wainright understood that South might rebel at the offer. It was a gamble. In the end, he'd have to take more direct action. Right now, he needed time to plan a more thorough solution. And he still needed South in the lineup to assure that the wing's results were maximized. He could offer easy missions. If South refused, he could assign him to the worst. It was a double-edged sword and he had it by the hilt.

'You've got eleven missions remaining,' Wainright said.

'Wrong,' South corrected. 'I've got none. I've quit.'

'You'll fly.'

'Like you?'

Finally. Here it was. It was coming to the surface. He'd made one mistake and now he would pay for it.

'Seventeen missions. Hasn't anybody upstairs asked why the commander of the 39th has only seventeen sorties in all this time, and only two in the past sixty days? Hell, you've quit; why not me?'

Wainright felt himself flush. It was coming out.

'I was there that night, pal. I know what happened. You hauled ass like a scared rabbit when the shit hit the fan. Your wingman bought it because you bugged out. You couldn't hack it, colonel. *You* ran. You think they pin stars on cowards? I've got you by the balls, Wainright. You said you took a hit. You couldn't control your bird. But I looked at that sonofabitch myself. I talked to Maintenance. They couldn't find a thing. That bird was as solid as a nun's cherry.'

Wainright recoiled. He felt himself losing it. No junior officer, ace or not, could talk to him this way.

'We're in this turkey trot together, colonel. You and me — blood-fucking brothers. You got yourself to thank for it. You, those blood-sucking reporters and LBJ-for-Jerk Johnson. You recommended me for the medal. You sang my song. You did the whole fucking routine so that the country could have itself a public hand job over its first ace. You didn't miss a trick in pushing me to promote yourself.

72

You think I'm stupid? You created me, now you've got to live with it. *I've* got the medal. *I* shot down the MiGs. *I'm* the ace. *My* picture was on *Time*. And goddammit, when I get a sortie, *I* do my fucking job, all the way. Now you're going to live by my terms, you copy this transmission, you hogjowled cocksucker?'

Wainright trrembled.

'You think you're in command? Give it your best shot, asshole. Let's stop bumping each other and lay them down. You've got my raise; your call.'

Control, Wainright told himself. Control. The wing commander clasped his hands in front of him again, sat back in his chair and smiled.

South tapped his helmet down on his head, pivoted and swaggered slowly out the room. Wainright pawed through his humidor for a fresh Dominican cigar. It took several wooden matches to get it lit and to get himself under enough control to think. He couldn't crush South outright. Not yet. There'd be too many questions. It had to be done in such a way that South couldn't shoot off his mouth, and he'd have to cover all the bases. No loose ends. The short-range problem was to get South airborne. Then there was the more important problem. There were angles to play, ways to make it work. His career depended on his ability to pull it off. He picked up the telephone.

'Get Security,' he ordered. He dropped a live ember on the desk and brushed it away to the floor. 'This is Wainright. I've got a job for you people tonight and it damn well better get done right.'

Apparently the North Vietnamese weren't enough for South. Fine, Wainright thought. Now he's got a *real* war on his hands.

73

Anishinabe

A spring storm had blown suddenly down from the mountain ranges northeast of the base and was quietly but fiercely releasing its contents on the airfield. South stood under the long blue canopy that covered the walk to the headquarters building and considered the best route to follow to Chief Katsu's place. In the end he decided it didn't matter what course he followed; such storms tended to hang over the field for hours, sometimes days. He was going to get wet. Already, natural depressions in the compact red clay were gathering water; small lagoons were beginning to form, reaching from puddle to puddle until they would join and create a vast shallow lake.

South walked along the slight crest of the blacktop road. Ahead of him a Russell's viper darted from side to side in a zigzag pattern, studying the land along the roadway for a possible refuge. Near a green metal building by the road there was a small hummock with eroded sides. Several large brown rats were on the rim, scurrying about, nervously anticipating the reptile's approach. Their fears were not unfounded because the snake, spying the high ground, suddenly slid down into the water and began swimming with its head held high toward the rats. South laughed at the scene. As the snake grew closer the rats literally sprinted around the small hilltop, crashing into each other, squealing out alarms. One of the rodents, a large specimen with only a stump of a tail, hovered on the edge of the eroded area and as the snake reached ground, launched itself, hitting the water below in a clumsy bellyflop, raising a small splash and then propelling itself forward toward deeper water with its tiny legs pumping as fast as it could move them, apparently preferring death by drowning to serving as the

74

reptile's entree. 'Smart rat,' South called at the animal as it pulled away.

It was not that he was comfortable with reptiles; he wasn't. But South, like the other men of the 39th TFW, learned to accept their presence. What it came down to was learning to deal with them or allowing them to put your life at a standstill — a result Wainright wouldn't tolerate. The wing commander had issued a memorandum about what he termed Reptile Infestation Periods — or RIPs. To facilitate wing efficiency he would issue periodic status reports to help his men deal with the reptiles and rodents driven from their burrows and dens by the rains.

Back in The World snakes tended to stimulate extreme human reactions. Here things were turned around a bit. A Texan who learned in kindergarten to mash the head of every diamondback he encountered on the back forty here would simply walk around a cobra and go on about his business. Part of it was the almost mystical power attached to reptiles in this part of the world. Virtually all snakes were referred to as 'two-steppers,' meaning that after you were bitten you could walk about two paces before keeling over dead. To avoid confrontations with such deadly things was an eminently practical decision. If you were going to kill every snake you saw, you wouldn't get very far because there were so damn many of them. Even those that weren't poisonous were often so big and ominous that the temptation was too strong to walk past them. Newcomers snuffed a few snakes, or fled in an uncontrolled panic. But in a short while, having seen how the old-timers handled the situation, they too cast off the old habits of killing or running and instead just kept on about their business, giving a little room for the snake to go about his. For any man who'd ever been to the snake house in a major zoo and seen the world's deadliest snakes, this was familiar territory; only now the observers and visitors were both part of the exhibit. You couldn't let it get to you. If one of the damn things decided to make a run at you, so be it. Proximity to Buddha had its rub-offs. So to speak.

At night most airmen carried small flashlights called 'Habu Lights.' The flashlights were of Japanese manufacture, about half the size of a pack of butts, and rechargeable. In the various barracks and living quarters on base there were dozens of small Habu Lights plugged into electric sockets regaining their life-saving power. In The World you checked your readiness for action with the checklist 'spectacles, testicles, watch and wallet.' In Thailand the Habu Light became the fifth critical item. Cobras had an odd habit of crawling onto the wooden sidewalks at night and lifting themselves into vertical position to scan the area for four-legged meals. At night you kept the beam of your light straight ahead, pushing it out as far as its candlepower and your vision could handle. The appearance of a vertical shadow where none had been in daylight was reason to stop where you were and wait. At night snakes were more active, and much more aggressive than in the day. Generally you could step over a banded krait in daylight, but at night it would strike wildly at anything within reach. You learned these things. When you encountered a snake at night you either hung a one-eighty and found another way to get where you were going, or you waited for help. Eventually enough people would arrive with enough lights to make the reptile uncomfortable in the combined illumination and it would crawl off the walk and make way for the crowd to pass.

South accepted the situation and learned to deal with the snakes. Vincent 'Chief' Katsu, D.D.S., on the other hand was different than the rest of them. The Chief didn't like snakes either, but he chose to live in the jungle on the edge of the base with the snakes and that in itself made him somewhat of an odd bird. Officially Katsu was one of four dentists and a dozen or so dental technicians assigned to the wing medical group in the dental section. Katsu was in his second year at Takhli, having extended for a second thirteen-month tour. Like all officers in the wing he had an air-conditioned room in a small wooden hootch and privileges at the officer's club. But the six-foot-five Katsu was by nature a loner and more comfortable in the jungle than around the wood, steel and concrete world of the fighter wing.

During his first tour he had opted for an R & R leave to Chiengmai in northern Thailand. For his recreation he'd gone on a tiger hunt and killed a five-hundred-pound specimen whose soft hide now hung from a wood frame in his hut. Katsu had double value for the wing; he was a first rate dentist and his lifestyle provided the wing survival experts with a living field test. It had been Katsu who had discovered during one of his forays that leeches could be kept off the flesh by filling a bandana with tobacco and trying it around the arms and legs. By wetting down the poultice it would send a thin layer of tobacco juice down the flesh. Leeches wouldn't penetrate it. Many a downed flyer had been spared some serious health problems because of the Chief's innovation. Neither Wainright nor the hospital commander cared how his dentist lived as long as he did his job, didn't cause trouble and kept finding new ways to help the pilots of the wing. Besides, Wainright once said, Indians always did things a little differently.

Katsu was a full-blooded Ojibwa (he referred to himself as an Anishinabe, meaning 'original man'). He'd grown up on the Bay Mills Indian Reservation near Sault Ste. Marie and for the early part of his life had known a lifestyle not materially different than his ancestors. In the spring he went with his family to drain the sap from sugar maples and boil the mixture down to small cakes which they dried on pieces of birch bark and mixed with dried fruits and berries. They gathered wild strawberries, blueberries and other wild fruits over the summer, drying them for use in the winter. In the fall they fished for whitefish in Taquamenon Bay and the rivers which drained into it, dipping the spawning fish from the clear waters with long-handled nets in the same way the Anishinabe had fished for whitefish and sturgeon for three hundred years. And they propelled their canoes through the shallow lakes and swamps, harvesting wild rice by knocking the grain into the boat with small flat slabs of ash. At fifteen, Katsu and his brother, Joshua, had killed a three-hundred-pound black bear with a deadfall trap and now in his lodge in Thailand, Chief still wore the necklace he had fashioned from the animal's claws and from the sinew of a white-tailed deer.

Among his peers Vincent was the most accomplished at living off the land. The elders praised him and talked of his taking a place on the village council one day. But the young Indian wanted more and having finished the eighth grade — the point where most Indians ended their educations — if they got that far — Katsu arranged to live with a cousin in Sault Ste. Marie some twenty miles east in order to attend the public high school there. His move, to the white school, was viewed both with scepticism and pride by the minions of the Bay Mills community. They commended his courage, but to a man and woman, they knew it would not work out. The whites had no place for the Anishinabe. So it had always been. So it would always be. Vincent had no such concerns; he was graduated with high honors and moved west to Houghton to attend Michigan Technological University.

The faculty found him to be a rather shy and uncommunicative young man, but the mental acuity was apparent. He was graduated summa cum laude in chemical engineering with a half-dozen original research papers to his credit. He had devised a new family of resins that promised application in various forms of orthopedic and oral surgery. Katsu was accepted into dental school at the University of Michigan and upon graduation was enthusiastically encouraged by his professors to pursue a research career. Instead, he applied for a direct commission into the Air Force and requested assignment to Vietnam. They sent him to Thailand.

Over a period of months South and the Ojibwa dentist had formed a close relationship. It was South, in fact, who gave him the not-so-original nickname 'Chief'. They had been at the stag bar one night. Katsu stood off to himself nursing a Scotch. South pushed his way through the crowd and extended one of his large hands.

'Say, Chief. Any truth to all that shit about Indians and fire water?'

Katsu had stared hard at the pilot and the bar had quieted in anticipation. Then he had said with a straight face, 'We find it quite addictive. I'm particularly fond of a warm brandy, and of course a port at my club.' The Indian's black eyes flashed.

Whenever he was troubled, South sought refuge in the Chief's wigwam, and his quiet counsel.

The rain was still falling in sheets when South reached the dentist's small camp. It was built just below the crest of a small hillock covered with high grass with razor-sharp edges, some small hardwoods and stunted thorn trees whose roots were exposed above ground in an eye-catching tangle. The shelter itself was similar to a teepee, but its walls were thatched with leaves instead of animal hides. There was a small hole at the apex to allow smoke to escape.

South paused at the entrance. The rain was nearly a solid mass forming a layer on the walls of the structure; but instead of penetrating, it slid harmlessly down the leaves which were overlapped and into a deep slit trench around the base of the shelter. There was nothing elegant about the arrangement, but it was practical. The only concession made to the jungle was the elevation of the lodge on six-foot-high stilts of thick green bamboo.

'I know about snakes,' Chief had once explained. 'I just don't like living with them.' For added privacy from the reptiles, the Indian had installed a family of mongooses beneath his shelter. They lived in metal boxes that had contained 20-mm ammo and been brought to Thailand by merchant ships. The animals seemed prolific. There were always pups about. Now South approached as one such pup, a black-eyed little thing with a twitching nose, stared out at him from the darkness of its nest in an ammo box. It squeaked quietly as South passed by it. With the mongooses in residence one didn't worry much about snakes in the Chief's camp.

'Chow?' South called out as he climbed a ladder lashed

together with some kind of wild vine. It always amazed the pilot that the structure was so stable. From the outside and at ground level the platform looked like it might disintegrate in a wind that wouldn't push the lightest sailboat. But underfoot it was solid and unmoving.

'Lizard,' Chief responded with a grunt as South pushed back the slatted curtain that covered the entrance. The Indian was seated on the floor next to a metal box that contained a large bed of coals. The flame was small, but South could feel the heat all the way to the entrance some six or eight feet away. Raindrops occasionally found their way through the hole at the top and splashed into the coals with a hiss. The Chief wore moccasins that fit like oversize booties and a breech-cloth made from a tanned skin. His flesh was a bronze colour with a reddish hue. The Indian was holding a long bamboo skewer over the fire, turning it slowly counter-clockwise with one hand while he used the other hand to keep his place in a book in his lap. There was a gob of white meat on the stick. It was beginning to brown and emitted a pleasant aroma.

Katsu's hair was coal-black but it looked reddish grey because it had been cropped to a uniform patch of quarter-inch fuzz by military barbers. His cheekbones were high and his face flat, but his nose was small and straight, almost European. South often kidded him that some French fur trader must have gotten into one of his female ancestor's pants. Katsu had thick wrists and mammoth forearms. His hands were calloused like a common labourer and he was tall — like many Ojibwas. This was no scrawny half-starved Navajo or ferretlike Apache. The white men who first encountered the Chippewas must have been impressed; nearby Indian tribes certainly were.

The Chippewas had migrated to the shores of Lake Superior from Canadian territory to the north some time before the fifteenth century. By the eighteenth century they inhabited an empire that ranged from Huronia — the western part of Ontario — to the Turtle Mountains in the Dakotas and far north into the current Canadian province of Manitoba.

Yet the Chippewas were not a true empire. Chiefs were chosen based on ability, not bloodline, and even with the title bestowed, a chief had to lead, not simply give orders. If the leader wanted to go to war he had to work to convince his people that it would be worth the cost. It was a highly democratic society and individualism and independent spirit were valued above all. Despite the apparent looseness of their political arrangements the Chippewas were a force to be reckoned with. They had pushed the Sauk, the Fox and the Menominees west into Minnesota and had driven the Sioux out of their western hunting grounds, an act which resulted in a one hundred-and-fifty-year war between the tribes, a war won eventually by the Chippewas. Even the dreaded and savage Iroquois, before whom the whites in the New World quaked, tried only once to move in on the Chippewas. They were met with such violence and savage blood-letting that they retreated back to Huronia and never ventured west again.

Had the Chief been born in a bygone century there was no doubt in South's mind that he would have been a great chief. As it was the Chief made no claim to an interest in politics. His interests were in the bush and in his books. He was a voracious reader. The inside of the leaf-sided wigwam was cluttered with stacks of hardbound books from the base library, most of which contained a leaf bookmark sticking out from between the pages. The Indian had eclectic tastes and under ordinary circumstances was reading a dozen or more different things at any given time. In his lap now was the translated edition of an important treatise on Theravada Buddhism, Thailand's most important religion.

'I'm gonna pass on the lizard,' South said as he stood up in the shelter.

'Plenty of vitamins. Low in calories. Tastes great,' the Indian said with the high-pitched twang of a snakeoil hawker.

'I'll stick with greaseburgers,' South returned.

'Actually it's a lot like rabbit.'

'Forget rabbit, too.'

'So,' the Chief said, looking up for the first time. 'You got trouble.'

'Great insight. I drop bombs on mommies and babies while their daddies and brothers are trying to kill my ass. I'd say that's plenty of trouble for one person. Do I have to have trouble to drop by?'

'Usually.'

South ignored the Indian. He stripped off his flight-suit and sat down, his wet behind leaving a double print on the mats that covered the floors. He pulled his boots off and set them on the edge of the coals. The slight odour of burning rubber combined with the aroma of the meat. After propping his flight coveralls on a wooden rack near the fire, he sat down again, crossing his legs Indian-style. 'This kills my knees,' he complained.

'Wrong genes,' the Indian observed.

The pilot sniffed loudly at the cooking meat. 'Doesn't smell too bad. Is it really lizard?'

'Got him in a snare just over the hill. Just before the rain came. Real fresh. Up in the Yam River country they eat them differently. They strip the skin off and gut them. Then they fill them with fish eggs and spices. They wrap them in a kind of broad leaf that smells like a scallion and throw in a dozen pigeon eggs. Then they put the whole package in the ground and let it ferment for a year or so.'

'You *ate* such shit?'

The Indian smiled. 'Once you get past the smell you've got it licked.'

South laughed. 'Indian humour?'

'I first heard it from a white man.'

'Okay, I'll bite. Gimme a spear and a slab of that stuff.'

The Anishinabe smiled and handed his stick to South while he threaded another small haunch onto a bamboo skewer. When they had settled into watching their meat cook, Katsu lit a small clay calumet and they took turns with it. The tobacco was straight; neither South nor the Chief was interested in freak weed or other mind-altering substance. As a rule, none of the pilots dabbled in drugs.

They were of an older generation than the crazy bunch back in The World and their escape was in the bottle or can.

'I think I'm at war with Wainright,' South said.

'In a feud with another man it's best to know exactly what the status is,' Katsu said. 'With us, we declare it to everyone so that the situation is clearly understood.'

The pilot recanted the morning for him. The Chief listened quietly, letting the man speak until his story was told. South held back the information about the wing commander falsifying his flight records, and the puzzling but direct hustle put on by Wainright's secretary.

'He may try to get me on a medical,' South said.

'Pretty difficult. You've got to document more than erratic behaviour. Technically they have to bring in a shrink and get a diagnosis. Then it's got to be confirmed. Psychiatrists are fucked up; getting two of them to agree on anything is nearly impossible. Wainright will have a hard time with a Section Eight. More likely he'll go for disciplinary action.'

'Doubtful. Best he could do would be an Article Fifteen. If he filed real charges there'd have to be a court martial and then I'd get a chance to speak my piece. He can't afford that.'

The Indian grunted quietly. 'Then he's got to use the pressure he has through normal channels. He has the power.'

'Yeah.'

They ate their meat when it was cooked. South nipped at his tentatively until he was satisfied that the flavour was not what he might have expected lizard to taste like. In fact, he found it succulent. He ended up gnawing small muscles off the animal's rib cage. When they were done eating, they smoked again.

'You know Wainright's secretary?'

'A real wench,' Katsu said. 'She could bring big trouble to a tribe.'

'She hustled me today. I mean like a predator. She came on strong.'

'Too much trouble,' Chief said quietly, shaking his

head. 'There's a village about three klicks from here filled with friendly little ladies. No VD. Clean. The GIs haven't invaded yet. Can get all you want down there. Glad to make an introduction or two.'

'She said she's coming over to my place tonight. Think she'll come?'

'Among my people in the old days a man and a woman became one without a lot of formal ceremony. If a man wanted a woman, he killed a deer and dropped it on her family's cookfire. If they accepted him, they invited him to eat with them. Divorces were just as simple. With everything so simple there was no need for adultery. If a man's wife went with another man, the husband would take it out on her. Sometimes he'd bite off her nose so that all the tribe would know what kind of a woman she was.'

'Just as long as Wainright leaves her tits alone, he can have all the nose he wants,' South said.

'Bad manitu,' the Indian pronounced. 'If it must be war, let it be war with no quarter until one is finished.'

'Easy for you to say,' South said. 'War is in your blood.'

'War is in every man's blood,' the Chief said with a grin.

Buying The Farm

Major Oren Rudamaki was both queasy and uneasy. The diarrhea — a first-class case of Takhli TNT — had struck again just before the briefing. He'd thought briefly about calling the flight surgeon, but what the hell, the job had to be done and he was a lot more experienced than most. Besides, it was a routine mission. No big thing. What could the flight surgeon really do? Give you a handful of BB pills to cement your bowels? The problem was Thailand.

Mosquitos meant malaria. Malaria meant that you had to choke down your pale orange antimalaria pill. The pill gave you the shits. The way to beat the thing was to get out of the country. No threat, no pill. No pill, no diarrhea. Every mission you got under your belt put you one day closer to home. He'd rather fly the mission than sit on the toilet blotting his raw behind. Thailand and diarrhea: they went together. The trick was to keep your belly empty. No chow, no waste, no shits. A little liquid out the back pipe from time to time, but no bulk to blow its way out. Much easier on the anatomy.

Rudamaki scanned the tanker off his right wing. Pintail 4 was topping off. He felt aloof from the scene. Tankerdrivers. How could they fly something so damn big and clumsy? Too many engines to worry about. And too many people. One man, one plane, one engine. Much better. The Taxi Dancer way. Even the skins of the big birds were in poor shape; this one was beginning to wrinkle like a washboard just below the vertical stabilizer. He wondered if the crew knew, and if so, how they felt about it. He hated the colour, too. It was grey and discoloured from long baths in the salty mists of southern Thailand.

'Pintail Lead. Where do you want your dropoff?' It was the tanker's navigator.

Rudamaki checked his charts and watch and glanced at the ground passing below them. They were near the river. Born at the 16,700-foot level in the Himalayas, the wide, meandering yellow ribbon snaked its way across the whole Southeast Asian subcontinent, finally dumping its silt in the wide delta of South Vietnam before merging with the South China Sea. For the millions who lived along the Mekong, the river was life itself, a god to be worshipped and feared. The world's tenth longest river. Near it, they planted rice. From it they took a bounty of fish. They floated on it, lived near it, swam in it, drank from it. The mighty Mekong River. The Americans called it 'The Fence.' East was Bad Guy Land. West was home, safety and a gin and tonic. The Fence. It was the only real front line in the war; the only clear divider between good and bad, life and death.

'Blue Anchor Six-One, we'll drop off right here. See you later.'

'Have a good one, Pintails.'

'Roger. We'll be on three-twenty-one-point-eight.' The fighters always left their strike frequency with their tankers. It was more a matter of common sense than regulation or couresty. If your tanker was listening to the strike freak and you had a problem that involved fuel, he could get underway to meet you.

'Six-one copies three-twenty-one-point-eight. Thanks.'

Click-click. Rudamaki inhaled deeply, checked his position and nosed the F-105 down to slide under the belly of the tanker and head into the midday sun. 'Pintails, let's go Button Three.' He switched frequencies without looking as the fat belly of the tanker flashed overhead.

'Pintail radio check.'

'Two.'

'Three.'

'Four's up.'

Rudamaki checked his Seiko against the cockpit clock. They were the same to the second. Twenty-two minutes until their rendezvous with the forward air controller. He checked the name again. Covey 41. It was time to concentrate on the mission, and only the mission, but the growing rumble in his stomach made him wonder how much it would take to breach the dam. Three G's would do it for sure and he'd easily pull that on the bombing run. Stain his britches like a five-year-old too busy to head for the biffy. The idea disturbed him. Think about soumething else.

What would it be like to be a tanker driver? Bad duty. Combat support. Fill up the fighters and wait. Flying an underpowered Mack truck with swept-back wings and the aerodynamics of a brick. Through thunderstorms. The image made him shudder. Out of the action. It was good that somebody was willing to do the job. He'd come out of Gookville plenty of times sucking wind. When you were low on fuel nothing looked so good as a big grey hog wallowing along above the clouds.

Rudamaki adjusted his heading five degrees right to adjust for the wind drift and his flight followed. What a pain in the ass it would be to be in SAC. Suck-Ass-Command. LeMay had been one hell of a P. R. man. Bombers. Nuclear deterrent. Hold back the Russian hordes and their missiles. Peace is Our Profession — otherwise you got Russians diddling your fourteen-year-old cousin in Dubuque. What Russian would be so stupid as to launch a pre-emptive strike against the U.S.? Rasputin the mad monk? Russians aren't as stupid as Japs, he told himself. Or as smart, he thought, checking his watch again.

Everything was going smoothly. No sweat, he told himself. He scanned his instruments, changed heading slightly, trimmed the nose and adjusted his throttle. He'd ridden a tanker once. That was enough. They strapped him in the jumpseat between the two pilots — the seat was no more than a board. They rolled two miles before the nose came up and the bird flew. He'd screamed for them to hit their burners, but they'd only laughed at him. It wasn't natural for something that weighed three hundred thousand pounds to fly. The tanker pilots never flinched. In fact, they never looked interested. It was routine for them. No big thing. By the time they'd levelled off at two thousand feet, got the flaps up, trimmed it, pulled the gear and reset climb power, Rudamaki's flightsuit had turned black with sweat.

'Pintail Lead. Four's totalizer is fluctuating. Going to have to keep an eye on my fuel.'

'Copy. Did you take a full load?'

'Roger. Boomer saw it vent.'

Click-click.

His leg was beginning to ache again. It was hurting a lot lately. Don't need this. Usually didn't act up until the rain came and it got damp. Diarrhea and sore muscles. Maybe it was some kind of flu? There was always something floating around. Should have checked in with the flight surgeon, he chided himself as he changed the stick to his left hand and rubbed his right calf. As soon as he switched control hands, the aircraft went into a shallow descent and the other three aircraft followed, adjusting immediately to the change.

'The elevator going down, Lead?'

'Negative,' Rudamaki snapped. He pulled the nose up and levelled again. They were four hundred feet below altitude, but what the hell. His wingman was too quick with his mouth. Petit. Shit-hot first looey with twenty-five missions under his belt. Thinks he has the world by the balls. Rudamaki started to say something to the other man, but held back. No time for an argument; this mission was going to be tough enough without getting somebody pissed off. Just nerves, he told himself. Let him jaw. You've done this before and you know the refueling is always the worst time; too damn much time to think about what's coming.

As targets went this one was about a seven or an eight on a ten-scale. No picnic. He'd been there before. Suspected fuel depot. *Everything was suspected.* This was Intelligence talk for there aren't any photos and we don't have any information but we've got to find targets and, hell, that spot looks as good as any for a fuel depot, don't you think? He didn't blame them. With the jungle so thick you'd be lucky to spot the Great Pyramid down there. But they were right about one thing, it was a hot target area. It was right on the limestone karst in eastern Laos near Mu Ghia Pass.

On his previous visit to the target they'd gotten no secondaries. The target was nestled into the elbow of a small twisting box canyon, thick with vegetation. There were at least two 37-mm sites dug into the sides of the canyon – designed to set a deadly crossfire. In addition to the go he'd had against it, there had been a dozen other strikes by Taxi Dancer flights with no apparent success. In some ways he liked knowing that nobody had scored on it. POL dumps were the only targets that gave you a real clear report card. If you got a hit, you got a secondary explosion and fires that threw up thick black smoke. So far this target had cost two aircraft and one pilot, whose body the Jolly

Greens from Naked Fanny managed to recover. He hoped this trip wouldn't amount to more scores for the bad guys, but down in his stomach there was a feeling beginning to grow and it wasn't the diarrhea. No sense dwelling on it, he told himself. Let the FAC call the shots; put your bombs where he says to put them. You're the actor; he's the director.

'Pintail Lead. I got seven minutes to rendezous.' Rudamaki checked his watch again.

Click-click. Time to find out if the FAC was on station. He switched frequencies. 'Covey Four-One, this is Pintail Leader, flight of four Thuds.'

'Mornin', Pintail. Right on time. You wanna go three-twenty-one-point-eight?'

'Roger, Covey. Pintail One.' He switched back to the strike frequency.

'Covey's up, Pintails. How read?'

'Five-square, Covey.'

'Good. We got us a bad *motor-cycle* this mornin', gents.'

This was an experienced FAC, Rudamaki noted. The new one didn't talk much. This guy probably knew his business.

'This your way of building up confidence?'

'Nope. More a matter of truth in advertising, if you know what I mean. I was just up in the target area and those fellers hosed me down. Been through this area lots of times; never had them get so riled up before. A little nervous down there I reckon. Maybe they got a new load of petrol in their storage tanks. That'd make me nervous.'

Good FACs had a sense about such things. They worked the same areas day in and day out, learning every bend in the plentiful streams and rivers, every turn in the trails and roads, every hill, valley, canyon and unusual landmark until it was like home. When they saw something they hadn't seen before, they investigated. Because they were up there all the time the locals got used to them. So when the locals acted out of sorts, they investigated that too. Officially FACs were supposed to keep their aircraft seventy-five hundred feet above ground level – AGL – but the good ones ignored the regs and skimmed along the treetops at near stall speed hoping to stir up trouble, to tempt the hiding enemy into firing at them. Without help from the enemy there were lousy odds in producing any effect.

'Pintail Lead, what's your lineup?'

'Eight-one-thou-high explosives.'

'Confirm half-ton high explosives.' Rudamaki could hear the pleasure in the FAC's voice.

'Well now, Pintails. We might just get us some fireworks this time.'

'Where you at Covey?'

'Ahm 'bout five klicks south of the target area. You been to this one before?'

'Rog. Give me a landmark.' Rudamaki had not only been there before, he'd studied the target and area photos the afternoon before. He liked to be prepared.

'Okay . . . let me see. All right, I'm hangin' a lazy three-sixty over Sittin' Bull's Ass. You know the spot?'

'Affirmative.' Rudamaki looked up to the north-east. The landmark was a bare outcropping of ochre limestone that looked like two fat buttocks. Long ago some creative FAC had dubbed it Sitting Bull's Ass. 'What's your altitude Covey?'

'Twelve-five, give or take. Got some thermals up here. Little bumpy over these hills. Terrain's between five and six. Where you fellers at?'

'Descending to thirteen thousand about four klicks south-west of you. I've got a heading of zero-four-four.'

'Roger Pintail. Covey Four-One's got visual contact. I'm at your twelve o'clock low. Looks like you guys are coming through fifteen or sixteen right now.'

Rudamaki checked his altimeter. 'That's affirm.' Ahead he could see the FAC circling in his Cessna O-2 Birddog. 'We have Covey visual.'

'Shall we dance?' the FAC said his words trailing into a high-pitched giggle that shut off suddenly with his radio.

'Only if I can lead,' Rudamaki shot back to him.

'No way, babes. Out here *I'm* the leader.'

As they got closer Rudamaki curled his flight into a tight turn and picked up the arc being flown by the smaller slower craft. 'Covey, Pintails are in trail. Lead on.'

Click-click.

They flew northeast and passed over a place where a series of silver mountain streams converged into an area of white water. They weren't far from the target.

'About two klicks from touchdown, Pintail Lead. You'll want to make your run from south to north. You can expect heavy ground fire from all over the canyon. You been briefed on how they got those 37s in there?'

'Roger. We know. Are they active?'

'Does King Kong like big fucking bananas?'

Click-click.

'Okay Pintails. This is NVA turf. Some Pathet Lao too, but the NVA hold the high ground. If you have to step out, point your bird west as far as you can go. Target elevation is five-zero-three-three feet. Pressure altitude is five thou even. Altimeter two-niner-niner-seven. No wind. You copy?'

'Roger. Bailout heading is west. Elevation five-zero-three-three. Pressure five thou even. Altimeter two-niner-niner-seven. No wind. Pintail One.'

'Two.'

'Three.'

'Four.'

'You can't miss this target, Pintails. It's right at the end of the canyon. Looks like a crease. I'll put some smoke on it.'

'Okay, Covey.'

'No sweat. Hope you guys knock this thing out. I got a feeling about it.'

Click-click.

'Okay, Pintails. Make your break. I'll mark your target.'

Rudamaki banked hard to the left and the others followed at thirty-second intervals, spreading them into a single file line with a half-mile between the four attacking aircraft. Over his shoulder Rudamaki could see the camouflaged O-2 begin his dive into the canyon. A flash from the small aircraft's wing pod told him that Covey had launched a white phosphorous − Willy Pete − rocket. When it hit, it would throw up a plume of smoke they could use to mark the location of the target.

'Pin − Pin − tail − Pin.'

'Covey, you are breaking up. Say again?'

'Pin − smoke in − fire hit the − tail − Pin.'

'Covey you are about two by five. Garbled. Say again.'

'Roger, Pintail, how's this?'

'Great.'

'Sorry about that. That is one angry bunch of people down there. Got a couple of small holes in my starboard wing.'

'Triple A?'

'Nope. Small stuff, but a lot of it. Maybe some ZPU. My smoke's dead on and no wind. It's all yours, Pintails.'

Rudamaki banked left again. The smoke in the canyon was nearly vertical, curling upward like a tightly wound snake. He adjusted his arming release switches to drop all eight bombs at once. There'd be only one pass against this target. With 37-mm's hemming them in there was no sense taking too many chances. One run would have to do it.

'Pintails, Lead. I'm rolling in. One pass each. Hit the smoke. All copy?'

'Two.'

'Three.'

'Four.'

The flight leader concentrated on the brush-covered head of the deep ravine. It was drawing close and he could see the smoke from the rocket clearly. He pushed the throttle ahead, nosed down on his run, quickly ticking off checklist items silently. Zero K factor. He centered the crosshair on the base of the smoke. At five hundred feet he released his bomb load, plugged in his afterburner and pulled into a steep accelerating climb. But instead of climbing there was a dull crunch and the Thud slid sideways, its nose rotating in a tight circle. Heavy smoke flowed through the air-conditioning system into the cockpit. What the? The fire warning light was blinking. Geez. He'd been hit. Where? Automatically he switched off his oxygen.

'Hey, Pintail!' the FAC whooped. 'They threw everything but the kitchen sink at you that time. Those boys want your scalp.'

'Pintail Three is in.'

'I think they just got it,' Rudamaki said to nobody in particular.

'What's that, Pintail One?'

'Pintail Lead is hit. I've got a fire ... someplace. Got a light. I'm heading west.'

'Oh-my-God, Pintail Three! You hit the jackpot. Whole fucking canyon's coming apart. *Look at that!* Holy shit, look at the secondaries. Looks like a Christmas tree.'

'Pintail Three off. Where are you, Lead?'

'Heading two-seven-zero at seventeen thousand. You should see me easily. I'm belching smoke.'

'Gotcha. Three is joining.'

As Pintail Three joined on his flight leader, he examined the aircraft. There was some smoke. No telling how bad the fire was or where. But the control surfaces were another matter. They were hurting. The rudder was ragged and so was one aileron.

'You got a fire?'

'Light's out now.'

'How're the controls?'

'Seem okay.'

'Well the outside looks pretty nasty. You're full of holes. Better dump it after we get over the river. Might come apart if you try to land. Jolly Greens will get you, no sweat. I can cover you until the choppers arrive, I'll get the tanker in to cover me. It's gonna be okay, Rudy.'

By now Pintail Four had joined the other two, but there was no sign of Pintail Two. 'Covey Four-One, this is Pintail Four. You see Pintail Two down there?'

'Not since he turned east.'

93

'East?'

'Roger. Looked like he might have been smoking but I couldn't really tell. You guys set the whole area on fire. Visibility stinks down here.'

'Pintail Three, this is Lead.'

'Yeah, Rudy.'

'I-ah-got-uh-complications. Both my legs are numb. I think I'm hit.'

'Shocky.'

'Probably. Starting to have a little vertigo.'

'Okay, babes. Get on a hundred percent and breathe slow, *real* slow. Don't go hyper. You need a tourniquet? Can you tell how bad it is?'

'There's blood on the instrument panel. No pain. Just numb. Can't feel anything from the thighs down.'

'You got to take a look, One. If you're bleeding bad you've got to get it tied off. You got a scarf or some cord? Copy?'

'In my leg pocket. Flight suit's shredded. Nothing there ... it's ... God ...'

'Easy, Rudy. We're with you. It's gonna be okay, babes. Believe me. Pick up your speed. Keep flying that Thud. We got to get upstairs to our tanker. How's your fuel?'

'Can't tell. Gauge out. Smell fumes. Real bad. Real ...'

'No sweat, let's get upstairs and get a refill. I'll take the lead.' Pintail Three switched to the Guard channel.

Blue Anchor Six-one, this is Pintail Three on guard. Pintail Lead needs fuel badly. We're comin' out. How about meeting us? Descend to twenty-one thousand. We'll level at twenty. Copy?

'Pintail Three, this is Blue Anchor six-one on strike frequency. We've been monitoring. We're on the way, level at twenty-one and ready.'

'Good show, Blue. Pintail Lead, can you read our tanker?'

Click-click.

'Covey, this is Pintail Three. Any sign of Pintail Two?'

'Nope. Sailed over the east ridge. You want I should have a look?'

'Yeah, but let's get a Cap going first. Get on the horn to

94

NKP and get them off their butts. Good show, Covey. Damn fine job.'

'Thanks, Pintails. Nice work. I'll swing east and Cap your man till the cavalry arrives. Good luck. Pleasure working with you guys.'

Click-click.

'Pintails, this is your Blue Anchor boom operator. We're rolling over and in front of you now. Come on in. I'll do the talking. You get stable and I'll do the rest.'

The boom operator, a black technical sergeant with more than a hundred combat refueling missions under his belt, watched the F-105 wallow below him. 'Okay, Pintail. Get yourself stabilized. You're a little wild right now, sir. Settle it down and slide on up here.'

Rudamaki felt light-headed; his sight was beginning to blur. His hands felt like they were attached to lead weights. The tanker's belly lights were tough to see. Normally he ignored the lights, but this time he felt a desperate need for them and they were refusing to focus. Squinting helped, but it still wasn't enough. The two vertical strips of lights were extremely dim. They were designed to get him lined up on the tanker's midline. If he got too far to one side or the other they'd turn blue. If he was in the right position – in the so-called envelope – they'd all be white. All he had to do was keep flying his Thud and adjusting his heading until he had all white lights, then he could slip up under the backside of the KC-135 and start taking on fuel.

'Talk me in, boomer. I'm having some problems.'

'Glad to, sir. Six feet forward. Two left. Four up. Two left. Two up. Five left. Steady now, hold it steady for me, sir,' The Thud was off to the side a bit, but the boomer could see that it was losing fuel quickly so he lined up the boom and drove the nozzle into the in-flight refueling receptacle located on the top of the nose a few feet in front of the pilot. 'Contact Pintail, you're taking fuel.'

'Awful weak, boomer. Can't ...'

'No sweat, sir,' the boomer said calmly. 'You're hanging in there. Can always count on a Thud driver,' he lied.

This guy was all over the ever-loving sky.

'Rudy. How they hanging?'

'Weak. Wish — flight surgeon today. I just? Oh God! In my pants. God, God Almighty. Like a little baby I—'

'No sweat, Rudy. Hang tough, babes. You've got to fly that bastard, so don't think about anything else right now. Just keep flying.'

'I . . . shit . . . my . . . pants,' a strange voice screamed. The F-105 slipped off the boom, nearly tearing the control stick out of the boomer's hand. This guy was in bad shape.

'Okay, Pintail One, my fault. Slide back over here. Five right. Five right. Up three. Okay, that's good. I'm all set.' The boomer reminded himself to watch for another sudden disconnect. He switched his radio to intercom. 'AC, boomer. Better be ready for a break-away, sir. This cat's damn near out of control.'

'Rog, boom, thanks.'

The boomer thrust the nozzle back into the Thud, verified a solid connection and called contact. Up front the copilot started the refueling pumps again.

'Pintail One, this is Three. Rudy, you're venting from your belly tank. I think you're going to have to stay hooked up all the way.'

Click-click.

'Pintail Three, this is Blue Anchor. Understand a wet tow for your leader. How're you other guys doing for fuel? You want me to get another tanker over here?'

'Negative, Blue. I'm fine. I'll duck into Udorn with Pintail One. Can you let them know we're coming?'

Click-click.

'All right, Rudy. Just hang in there. We're coming up on The Fence and we'll be on the ground in Udorn in less than thirty minutes. You can do it, Rudy. You can do it.'

The boom operator stopped looking at the cockpit below and studied his own instruments. The fighter's cockpit was torn up inside. There were smoke stains inside the canopy and it looked like blood was spattered everywhere. It would be a miracle if this guy didn't buy the farm.

Doggie Detail

Wainright's secretary fought a yawn as she sat on the soft couch in his office. As usual she looked uncomfortable, a bit too stiff. Her posture was always a little bit too exaggerated — her back ramrod straight, head erect, chin jutted forward as if to challenge. It kept the lesser beings away. Wainright often told her she looked like an aristocrat. She said it was the effect of her 'boobs'. Such talk embarrassed him. Pillow talk was difficult: he liked to get his business done and get to sleep. Minimum of chatter, he said. Because he made so few concessions to her needs, she relished the few there were.

The wing commander marched up and down in front of the couch, his hands in his pants pockets. He dictated quickly, ticking off items nonstop like some kind of a computer. Over the years she'd learned that all pilots shared this quality. No matter how confusing a situation might get, they always seemed to be able to sort things out quickly and to organize their thoughts in a simple, logical sequence. In an organization that measured performance by the weight of its paper outfall, it was a blessing to have people in charge who weren't disorganized. And if Wainright was anything, it was organized. His abilities stretched far beyond anything she'd ever seen, and his constant development of new systems and procedures made her job a lot easier, even if the price was a state of continual change.

As he dictated, Elise Mantel filled her steno pad with crisp little squiggles and scribbles. Shorthand had long ago become a part of her; she could encode as quickly as he could speak.

Wainright dealt quickly with routine matters. Rotations. Letters of congratulation. Some minor disciplinary problems.

97

Recommendations for awards and decorations. Review of efficiency ratings written by his squadron commanders. Local matters.

'Letter to Camon Phrahamessett. Check the protocol directory for the amenities,' Wainright reminded her. The directory was published yearly by the American embassy in Bangkok and updated bimonthly as Thai officials changed jobs. Phrahamessett was the local *kamnan*, a sort of collective mayor for several local villages.

'My Dear Camon. The dog problem still plagues us. As you know, Colonel Thatchakorn agreed to implement a programme to eliminate the stray animals; he has been working diligently toward resolution of the problem. Nevertheless, the dog population remains a serious menace to both U.S. and Thai personnel on this installation. I have been informed that you have faced similar problems and because of your experience, I would sincerely appreciate the opportunity to meet with you at your convenience in order to learn how you resolved your situation. Colonel Thatchakorn believes that your assistance is essential if we are to solve this serious problem. If you can attend a meeting at my office next Tuesday it would be my distinct pleasure to welcome you.' Wainright rubbed his chin and pointed toward the secretary's steno pad.

'Miss Mantel, be sure to order two quarts of Johnny Walker Red. The little lizard is addicted to it.' He struck several matches to relight his cigar and finally it caught. 'Please excuse the directness of this letter and accept my deepest personal apology for any inconvenience that my request may cause you, but as you know we are at war with our mutual enemies and this necessitates our holding the meeting here.'

'Will he come?' she asked.

'Yes, The old bastard won't miss a chance to pick up a couple of free bottles of hootch.'

The dog problem. Phrahamessett could help all right. He was the key. Sergeant Major Robbins had learned that it was the *kamnan* himself who was importing dogs from

98

Bangkok and releasing them onto the base through a hole in the chain-link fence on the northern perimeter of the base. A few months before, a young enlisted man had been bitten by a rabid animal and had been forced to undergo the fourteen painful shots in the stomach. After the incident, Wainright had suggested to his Thai counterpart, Col. Thatchakorn, that they establish a bounty on the dogs – 20 baht per carcass. The United States would be happy to pay the bounty to Thai soldiers who could hunt the animals in their off-duty time. Good way to make some extra money, polish the old sharpshooting skills and it could be sporting. Thatchakorn had agreed quickly and promised to establish a very well-organized, number-one plan of elimination.

Wainright had been true to his word. In the programme's first month, he had paid out $1,350. From then on it had averaged around $600. Robbins had discovered that the Thai colonel was raking off 50 percent of each bounty. That didn't bother Wainright. So long as the Thai officer had a vested interest in the programme, it would be far more effective, he had explained to his sergeant major.

Unfortunately, the bounty plan had worked *too* well. Now a meeting was necessary. Thatchakorn was building a nice nest egg and so were his troops. Initially they'd done the job on the indigenous dog population but when it appeared that the demise of the Golden Goose was at hand, Thatchakorn had made a deal with the local *kamnan* who, in turn, arranged through his brother in Bangkok to have more dogs transported north by truck from Bangkok and Dhonburi – where they were abundant – to Takhli where they were in critically short supply. It was a satisfactory arrangement. Thatchakorn, because of a new payout to the *kamnan*, was forced to reduce his troops' share of the bounty to eight baht. The soldiers, of course, did not argue. The dogs were being killed too efficiently. Better eight baht than nothing; besides, now the animals were being delivered and it was far easier to kill them. No more stomping around in the snake-infested *bpah* where you might step on a cobra or krait. In fact, the soldiers' admiration of their commander increased. How lucky they were to have a leader who would think about the common *poochy* and find a way for them to keep taking the American dollars. Buddha be praised for their good fortune!

Sergeant Major Robbins had uncovered the intrigue after noticing that, despite seeing no dogs for more than two weeks, the monthly dog death report (MDDR) was still at a high level. A little snooping around − boosted by a few well-placed baht, boxes of laundry powder and American cigarettes − quickly brought the facts to light. Wainright had laughed hysterically as Robbins laid out the scheme for him.

'Free enterprise still flourishes in the Orient, Robbins.'

'Yessir.'

'I suppose we'd better do something about it.'

'You going to cut that Thai colonel down to size, sir?'

'Why do that? I just want those smug little bastards to know I've got the goods on them. Maybe get us some concessions later − understand?' Robbins smiled.

Phrahamessett was only a *kamnan*, but his district was on the periphery of Thailand's richest rice-producing country. He had very good connections in Bangkok and on rare occasions when Wainright could get away he might be able to depend on the contact for certain 'considerations'. Phrahamessett was a distant cousin of the foreign minister. Here was a contact that demanded nurturing. A dog bounty was small enough price to pay for so much promise.

While Elise knew about the problem − it was her job to make payment requisitions based on the MDDRs − she had no idea about the true nature of the Thai's arrangement.

Wainright puffed smugly on his cigar. She could read him easily. He was enjoying a private joke − something about the dogs. She hadn't seen one in months, but if he felt it was still a problem, it probably was. While she flipped through her notes to make sure that she could read the shorthand, she wondered about Wainright's meeting with South. Even with the heavy doors closed, she had heard them screaming. Louder than ever before. She had buried herself in her typing, purposely trying to shut them out. It was his business, their business. Not hers. She'd learned a long time ago to mind her own business.

But South had caught her off-guard as he slammed out of Wainright's office and up to her desk.

'Okay, my hootch or yours?'

'Yours,' she answered.

'Ten all right?'

'A little later,' her voice said.

'What'll you be drinking?'

'Scotch?'

'No problem. Got *mahk-mahk*. You want me to pick up some rubbers?'

She shook her head slowly, not believing.

He smiled. 'Good, I hate them bastards. See ya at ten, sweet cakes.' And he was gone.

Afterward, she was still unsure that it happened. There'd been no warning. And she found herself agreeing before she could think. Discretion was a practical consideration. She could still back out, she told herself. Stand him up. Would serve him right. But now, with Wainright's holier-than-thou attitude, she decided that maybe it wasn't such a bad idea. And it might be fun. It had been a long time since there'd been anybody else. She decided that she was glad it had happened. She checked her watch while Wainright scribbled notes on a legal pad. She'd learned long ago how to take care of her own needs.

Familiarity's Seed

'*Miss* Mantel!' a voice roared. She stirred, momentarily disoriented by the booming voice. Wainright stared angrily at her. 'Miss Mantel, I've been dictating for nearly three minutes and you haven't written down a single word. Are

101

you memorizing?'

She smiled weakly. 'Daydreaming, I guess. Sorry.'

'Snap out of it. Let's get on with this,' he ordered. 'I don't want to waste my whole day on dictation. We've got too much to do. Now . . . take a memorandum to Commander in Chief, Seventh Air Force. Subject. Weekly Operations Report. One. A full schedule of one hundred and eight (one-zero-eight) sorties was flown during the past frag period.' That would look good, he told himself. Flown as ordered with no discrepancies. While there had been late takeoffs, he always covered them with bad-weather-en-route reports after the fact. The Deputy Commander for Maintenance had standing orders to launch everything, even the marginals. Airborne aborts didn't count against the record as seriously as ground aborts. If you couldn't launch your birds it meant your maintenance was bad. If something went wrong after they were off the ground, that was an act of God. Wainright saw to it that the maintenance record of the Taxi Dancers always looked good. Always, no matter how much trouble it involved.

'Two,' he continued in a monotone. 'Bomb Damage Assessment, parens Bee-Dee-Eh, end parens, has been confirmed by actual body count via allied personnel, through visual sightings by forward air controllers and by airborne recce.' Verification phrases, he reminded himself. Evans had tipped him off when he first began rotating down from Okinawa. Write in your confirmations. Make sure they get everything in one report, single page if possible; that way you're sure they're getting the whole story and you're making it tougher for them to lose anything. Early in his tour Wainright was the only unit commander who included confirmations in his reports. Now the others were catching on and he had lost this small edge. That was the lever for success. Details.

'Results for the week,' he dictated, trying to decide his precise language. Intelligence reports were fine, but they always needed some embellishment, a little originality. 'All right. Let's see. Fourteen bunker-storage sites destroyed or damaged.' This was a good hedge. Don't tell them exactly how many were destroyed or damaged. All wings drew assignments to strike bunkers which the FACs referred to as 'suspected' sites. This meant that when the FAC chased a bunch of people into a clump of trees, they didn't come out again. Ergo, there was something in there they could hide in: a suspected bunker. If the pilot put his bombs into the general target area his wing got credit for a kill. If he missed, but not too badly − close enough to spray the area with shrapnel − he got credit for damaging the site. 'Make that item A,' he added. 'Item B. Twenty-two enemy vehicles destroyed, including six tanks. Item C. Sixteen probables.' This was his newest innovation. His competitors routinely reported probable air kills, but nobody but Wainright had thought to write in probable ground vehicle kills. It was ingenious. No one could dispute a claim on a probable, especially in North Vietnam where there were no slow-moving FACs to verify, and little recce against vehicle targets attacked in the rugged mountains.

Actually, probables weren't supposed to count, but he included them to enhance the total effect of the report. Probables, he believed, would begin to play an important role in arguments by higher headquarters for more men and materiel. Including them in his report, he reasoned, gave Seventh more flexibility in the reports it had to generate, numbers Seventh could play with depending on the political climate back home. If you could manipulate the data to do a better job in fighting the war, what was wrong with that? The North Vietnamese did it all the time. Alexander had done it; so had Bonaparte. Fudging the facts was as old as war itself.

Hell, it had gone on in World War II. Nobody really checked out the kill reports. B-17 forces would report shooting down 40 or 50 enemy fighters and damage to 20 or 30 more on a series of missions. The news would be blared across the Free World and everybody would feel better because of it. We were kicking hell out of the Nazis. But the data were inaccurate.

A German fighter would flit through a bomber formation. The guys up front would hit him and his engine would begin to trail smoke. Then the gunners in the middle of the formation would rake him as he slid by. Result: two visually-confirmed probables. If the rear element was lucky enough to see the bird go into a spin, they'd take a kill on it. After the war, German records showed that no more than six aircraft were lost on the same mission where 25 or 30 had been reported by the Allied High Command, verified in debriefings. The same thing happened again in Korea.

Stratoforts would motor up the peninsula toward a target. Russian Yaks would shadow the bomber formation — staying carefully out of .50 caliber range. Nevertheless the gunners would blaze away at them, filling the sky with tracers. When they'd finally get to the target area, flak would begin to burst all over and the Yaks would dive for safety. Invariably the crews would interpret the maneuver as a kill when, in fact, none were even damaged.

Commanders understood that these things happened, but such statistics, while not true, didn't hurt the war effort. Americans liked numbers. Willie Mays was bound for Cooperstown because of numbers.

'Item D. Six antiaircraft sites destroyed, one heavily damaged and out of commission temporarily. One mobile SAM launcher destroyed. One suspected 100-mm site destroyed.' That would raise eyebrows. Most of the NVA guns were 37-mm with limited range. But occasionally they stumbled over a sophisticated 100-mm gun, its computerized radar sights operated by Soviet technicians; such weapons could be devastating. Most of the big guns were in the Hanoi-Haiphong zone.

'Item E. One-forty-one MPA destroyed.'

The secretary giggled. Military acronyms amused her, especially this one. MPA stood for Military Pack Animals.

'Elephants or mules?' she asked coyly.

'The abbreviation will suffice,' he snapped. His voice was icy. She dropped her steno pad into her lap and stared back at him.

'Now ... Jergen,' she said, letting his name trail out slowly and thickly. He slammed his fist on the bar.

'How many times have I told you that when we're in the office you're to address me as *Colonel* Wainright?'

Her back stiffened. 'You're awfully touchy today.'

'Doesn't anybody in this organization do anything they're told?' he grumbled to himself. He waved a finger at her. 'I'm not going to repeat this again,' he shouted. Her features hardened immediately and he realized he'd made a mistake, gone too far. She'd make him pay. Damn South! This was his fault. South and the whole asinine operation. Military Pack Animals! For Christ's sake ... what asshole had thought that up? Some goddamn West Point asslicker with stars in his eyes. Not her fault. Of course it was funny. She was right. The whole system was funny. But it was his system now and he had to live with it and he couldn't let her or South or anybody else get in the way.

The woman stared at him. He had no reason to talk to her that way. The fact was he was becoming a bore. He was a bully. *Colonel* Wainright. Whatever it was that was between South and him, it was something powerful. And dangerous. She tingled with curiosity. What could it be? If Jergen wanted trouble, she'd give it to him. South was the answer. South. This was a game she'd enjoy – no matter the outcome.

Bad Packages

Wainright's face was contorted in disgust. His coffee was rancid, gritty *and* cold. 'Robbins!' he bellowed into the intercom.

Before the sergeant major could respond, Elise buzzed. Colonel Horowitz was outside, wanting to see him right away. The coolness in her voice was obvious. Even she was becoming a problem to deal with. His whole life was nothing but problems, endless, stupid and petty. Maybe it had been a mistake to bring her along, but what the heck, she served her purpose and besides, he wasn't the only senior officer in the war with a round-eye secretary. There were plenty of others. He felt no guilt about that. No one could argue with her efficiency; whatever else she might be she was a cracker-jack secretary. In fact there wasn't anything she did that she didn't do well, and virtually nothing she tried that she didn't do easily. The problem was, she'd try damn near anything, and while he'd thought at the beginning of their relationship he could come to grips with her impulsive ways, he hadn't. When they could get away from Takhli it wasn't so bad. But such diversions were becoming rare. She was getting troublesome. She wanted this; she wanted that. He didn't have time, but she couldn't − no, it was more like wouldn't − understand. She was a selfish one. His days were filled: telephone calls, meetings, strategy sessions, equipment to be checked, record reviews, reports to write. At night he wanted to be alone − in peace and quiet, not fending off her hot little hands and sweaty body.

She seemed to be in a constant state of heat − like some kind of an animal. Sex didn't seem as important as when they first met. He wished he'd left her in Virginia, or even on Okinawa. It had reached the point where it would be nice if she decided to chuck the whole thing in and go home. Pull out. It would make his life simpler and give him more time for the job. Besides, if he needed one, there were other women available. Brown ones, to be sure, but as the men said, they were still split north to south. You did what you had to do.

Colonel Alvin Horowitz rushed across the office and slammed a fat package of papers on his desk. Horowitz was a burly Jew, an intellectual who would be more at home in Intelligence than as vice commander of the 39th. An unwarranted intrusion into his well-ordered sphere, is how he characterized the orders which forced him back to the cockpit. Despite the man's bitterness, Wainright was glad to have him. He did as he was told and was an expert both with paperwork and with handling the men. It was a good thing, because Wainright himself was uncomfortable with the pilots.

'Problem, Al?'

'Goddamn Seventh has shoved it up our keesters again,' he muttered, fumbling through the pile of papers, searching for a particular report.

'Shoved *what* up our asses?'

'Targets. The split in target assignments!' Horowitz snapped. 'Look what they've given us,' he yelled, waving a paper at Wainright. 'Packages, nothing but packages for the next two weeks. You know what that means. Bastards! Brown's behind this − I can smell him. Spends half his time in Saigon licking Evans' ass so his people get the fat stuff and we get . . . interdiction packages!'

Brown. Colonel L. Gorman Brown III, commander of the F-4 wing at Da Nang. The long grey line of generals. Brown II had been commander of 15th Air Force during WW II. *The* Brown was a pre-Big War crony of General Hap Arnold, the father of the Army Air Corps. Wainright had known Brown III since Korea. They'd been in the same F-84 squadron, flying night interdiction. Wainright had been a new captain; Brown III a second lieutenant fresh out of West Point, class of '49. They'd made the colonels' list together in 1965. Wainright's number had been higher. Technically that made him senior, but for all practical purposes they were now direct competitors. Over the years they had met from time to time. Usually Brown III was between new assignments − in the line. He was always moving up. To new aircraft. Bigger units. More responsibility. Wainright was moving too; but in staff, on the periphery. 'Doing damn well for yourself,' Brown III would remark officiously, 'for an *outsider*.' Brown III wasn't a ring-knocker in the stereotyped sense, but he flashed the fat, gold U.S.M.A. ring as clearly as if he were banging it on a mahogany table. Wainright interrupted himself. Unproductive to think about Brown III. Concentrate on the real problem.

Packages were dirty. Until now he'd been able to duck them, manipulate Seventh in order to keep the more promising sorties for his own wing. Walther's Thud wing at Khorat AB in central Thailand caught the garbage instead, and Walther called twice a week to complain, never realizing that it was because of Wainright that his own wing was spending its time dropping bombs on banana groves and monkey colonies. They weren't dangerous missions; neither were they pieces of cake.

They simply didn't count because they were in Laos. That was the problem as far as the pilots were concerned. Every pilot wanted to get his one hundred in and head for home. But only missions over the north counted towards the one hundred. These were logged as 0-2 zone missions on the in-flight log. Most Laotian packages went down as O-1B sorties, and they got the pilots who flew them no closer to home.

Technically a package was a simple thing to insert. It meant dropping any number of weapons armed with various timing and detonation devices. They were dropped onto road intersections and near river crossings selected by FACSs partly on their own observations, partly on intelligence reports and in great part on instinct. The idea was to slow down traffic from the north and to instill fear in the hearts of the enemy. They were dramatically ineffective.

To counter such technology, the NVA had stored piles of gravel and crushed rock every few yards along the thousand-mile Ho Chi Minh trail. Whenever a trail was bombed, NVA conscripts, many of them hill tribesmen, quickly shovelled gravel into the holes and the convoys started moving again. More often than not they didn't even have to fill the craters; there was plenty of room to drive around them. Because of repeated bombing, many of the areas along the trail looked like lunar landscapes; it was an easy task to weave in and out of the craters with the four-wheel-drive trucks provided by the Soviets.

When the NVA suspected time bombs, they would rope

off large areas for forty-eight hours, then resume traffic. No bomb had ever exploded after forty hours. If the devices were suspected to be magnetic types, the NVA would strap sheet metal to the sides of a mule or water buffalo and send the beast stumbling down the trail to detonate the bombs and be blown to bits. Plenty of animals were available; the clearing process required only a few minutes before the flow could resume in earnest. It was a lesson of history that as war became more complex, more mechanized, simple solutions often neutralized sophisticated advantage.

The key was manpower. In North Vietnam it made the difference. When a train bridge was knocked out, the NVA would quickly lash together dozens of small sampans, cover them over with bamboo mats and suddenly hundreds of comrades would appear from nowhere, pushing their bicycles. They'd cross the river and unload the train. Each person would stack six hundred pounds or more on the bike, push it back across the makeshift bridge, and load another train waiting on the other side. While the cargo was being shifted, repair work would already be under way on the trestle. It was simple as hell — and right out to Mao's Little Red Book. Uncle Ho had done the same thing against the French.

Horowitz was right in being upset. The less valuable targets could upset their effort and demoralize their pilots. The plan had to be changed. 'Easy, Al. Calm down and get a drink.' Horowitz poured eight ounces of Canada Dry tonic water and chugged it down quickly.

'What did Brown draw?'

'Fives and Sixes. Some Mig Cap, too.' Wainright winced. North Vietnam was divided into six areas, starting just north of the demilitarized zone or DMZ with Route Package — Route Pack — One. Hanoi was on the southern border of Route Pack Six — the northernmost and most heavily defended. Even so, it was the juiciest area for success, even with all the political restrictions levied by Washington.

The President was leaning too heavily on his civilian advisors. He was trying to apply pressure to the North

Vietnamese, in order to get them to the bargaining table, but he was applying the pressure too damn slowly and often in the wrong places. What they needed, Wainright told himself, was a green light on the dikes and population centres in the north. And mines in Haiphong harbour to keep Russian supply transports out to sea. Without such moves he was certain the war was not winnable, which for the U.S. would be the same as losing. America was used to winning its wars. Now was the time to hit them with everything in the arsenal short of nukes; otherwise they just keep moving their materiel to the south and it would continue to be a hit-and-run contest with a phantom enemy. They might be fighting in South Vietnam, but if the war was to be won it would have to be done in the north. Without a propaganda effort back home there'd be no media support and without media support there'd be no popular support for the effort. They were in trouble and the more alert commanders like Wainright knew it.

Johnson had tied their hands, then bellyached to the press that his boys didn't seem to have what it took. There was a thirty-mile-wide strip of no-touch land along the Chinese border; a ten-mile circle around the deep water port at Haiphong; and even more red hash marks on the charts of Hanoi. Like a goddamn game of Monopoly. Pass Go. Don't Pass Go. Who's on First? Some zones were absolutely untouchable; others could be attacked, but only with prior top-level approval, and *only* if they contained Verified Military Targets – VMTs. It was an insane strategy that dictated unimaginative and costly tactics. Evans himself had complained to Wainright about it many times. The Joint Chiefs were trying to argue sense into the Chief Executive's thick Perdenales skull. Not a permanent green light, Evans had cautioned. Just a month to show what they could do. No holds barred. If Evans believed there was a good chance for opening it up, then it was probably true. Meanwhile it was better to be drawing the tough targets with restrictions than no-counters. Careers were being cemented in the far north and he had no intention of being

110

farmed out to sow stillborn Laotian seeds.

While Horowitz filled another glass with tonic, Wainright studied the Stat Board — what the pilots referred to as their 'report card'. It covered an entire wall, and contained, in neat grease pencil etchings, every conceivable statistic that Wainright thought he needed to determine how his wing was stacking up against others: MiGs destroyed or damaged in aerial combat; MiGs sighted, but escaped to Chinese sanctuaries; MiGs and other aircraft sighted, plotted for density and frequency on a map of North Vietnam; numbers of 37-, 57-, 85- and 100-mm guns sighted, attacked, damaged, destroyed, by month and week, by squadron and pilot; total enemy ground personnel killed, where and how (by bomb, rocket or cannon) enemy vehicles — trucks, pushcarts, tanks, APCs and autos, also bicycles, motorcycles and wagons; sampans, junks, barges, Mekong walk-alongs, and sea-going transports sighted, damaged and destroyed; fixed installations damaged or destroyed with estimates by percent of structure destroyed and converted from square footage to dollar value of replacement; number of secondary explosions touched off by bombs, with four subcategories listed.

Another part of the giant boards contained the names of the one hundred fourteen pilots who manned the wing's three squadrons. By regulation and manning ratios they were authorized one hundred twenty men, but because of casualties, late-arriving replacements, rotations, R&Rs, and other factors they were short six people. Each pilot's name was colour-coded according to the number of missions he'd flown against the north. Black for seventy-five or more; blue for fifty to seventy-five; green for twenty-five to fifty; red for fewer than twenty-five. No-count missions, such as package details, were noted in parentheses. Separate columns adjacent to each man's name told Wainright at a glance how many MiGs he had downed, what medals had been awarded (including oak leaf clusters), medals he'd been nominated for, total flying hours, flying hours in current month and previous month, total combat hours,

111

ratio of successful missions to aborts, number of times struck by enemy fire, number of bailouts, number of crashes, current health status (a critical category updated every eight hours by an enlisted man from the dispensary who used a red marker to write in names of men not able to fly; time remaining in tour; DEROS – the date when each man would leave the combat zone; rank and date of rank; current scores from gunnery and bombing practices; and forty other minute details which Wainright depended on to tell him how his machine was operating. He read the charts the way his pilots read the dozens of dials and meters in their cockpits. A slight shift in statistics, a hint of a change, sang out like a clinker to Wainright. Evans had taught him to anticipate. Treat symptoms early and problems won't develop.

Another wall held a gigantic relief map of North Vietnam. Pins and coded glyphs dotted the small mountains and valleys like confetti. Triple-A sites, truck parks, fuel dumps, cement factories, primary and auxiliary MiG fields, troop billets, key river crossings. The map was updated hourly, around the clock, every day, even on the rare days when the wing was standing down because of bad weather in the Route Packages – the various target zones in North Vietnam. A duplicate was also maintained in the wing briefing room.

One of Wainright's first orders had been to centralize everything. Before his arrival the three squadrons operated more or less independently, like three Greek city states in a loose alliance. Now everything operated jointly. There were still three squadrons, but only on paper. Wainright ran the show; that's the way he wanted it. Tight, instant centralized control was essential. Running the lives of three thousand men was a chore; something was invariably going wrong; getting fouled up. The two thousand Thai soldiers and their dependents in the area made it that much more difficult, especially because the Thai colonel was legally in command. The squadrons had fought the reorganization silently, but stubbornly. One young lieutenant in a drunken rage at the club one night had told him that familiarity between the staffs would breed contempt. It was a risk. But instinctively he felt that as they got to know each other better and better they would work more efficiently as a team. Quickly they'd learn each other's weaknesses and cover each other. That's the way it worked in units that were mission-oriented. It was a sound management technique and he knew it. Evans himself had complimented him on the reorganization — especially for keeping down costs in remodeling headquarters by using Thai labour.

Wainright scanned the board. A new month. Two more weeks until the new operations order would take effect. Meanwhile they could double their efforts. That would bring more results. It was time to do a little banking — just in case the pressure on Evans didn't work. Presumably he'd approach Evans on the pretense of wanting to know about action from the JCS, but during the conversation he'd find some way to express his displeasure.

In Horowitz's stack of papers he found the personnel list. South's name stood out as if a spotlight were on it. His involvement would be critical during the next two weeks. He would be the catalyst for the rest of them — set the example. It was incredible that one man could be so much better than those around him, but the statistics spoke for themselves. South was a natural. Not many of them came along. Wainright knew.

The telephone interrupted his thoughts. Direct line from the command post in operations.

'Wainright here.'

'Major Rawlings, sir. We've got a report from Lion. Our Pintail strike has run into some trouble.' Terrific, Wainright thought. Just what we need. When he had arrived, there had been a full complement of sixty aircraft; now they were down to fifty-two. Every loss had a greater and greater impact on their effectiveness, and replacements were getting harder to find. Republic hadn't made Thunderchiefs in several years.

'What's going on?'

'Pintail was Line 37,' Rawlings said. Wainright leafed through the daily operations schedule. Rudamaki, Urqhart,

113

Petit and Chones. Fuel storage area near Mu Ghia Pass. Wainright strained to remember the recce photos ... a box canyon, heavily defended, very tough to get an angle on. They'd been there before and it had cost them two aircraft that weren't balanced by two Purple Hearts. It was one of the few times he resented the Heart-for-Blood Rule — the simple fact that a man was wounded by enemy action shouldn't bring an automatic Purple Heart; they'd screwed up the mission pure and simple and deserved nothing. But medals were medals and you had to recoup everything you could from such situations.

'Brief me,' the wing commander said coldly.

'Pintail One is out of the target area reporting heavy battle damage. He had a fire, but apparently it's out now. The pilot's hurt, Pintail Three is escorting and Pintail Two is missing over the target area. Pintail Four is en route to Takhli.'

'What do you mean, Pintail Two is missing?'

'Just that, colonel. One minute he was rolling in on the target, the next minute he was gone. Nobody saw him go down, and nobody's seen him since. We have to assume he's down.'

'Where'd you get your information?'

'GCI relay from Pintail Three and Covey Four-One — oh, I almost forgot, the number-four bird is damaged too, but the pilot thinks it'll hold together.'

'Alert Maintenance,' Wainright said. 'I want a turn-around estimate thirty minutes after we recover the bird.'

'Wilco, sir. I've already called Crash Control.'

'Keep me posted,' Wainright said as he hung up abruptly. Rawlings stared at the buzzing telephone receiver. Why did he always draw the bad news assignments and why were wing commanders always slamming down phones? He drew a deep breath and picked it up again.

The wing commander answered. 'What?'

'Rawlings again, colonel. I didn't get a chance to finish ... Our Pintails got the depot and apparently it's still burning.'

Wainright grunted and hung up. That was better — at

114

least they got the target. More equitable. This would help balance the loss of an aircraft. It wasn't the kind of asset trade he preferred, but it was something to record on the other side of the balance sheet. Horowitz offered a cigarette, but the wing commander pushed the pack away. One aircraft lost, two in jeopardy. If they lost all three, they'd be down to forty-nine birds and even with fifty-two they were already scrounging and K-balling everything they could get their hands on. So far, he'd been lucky in meeting the schedule, but with three more birds out of commission it might be impossible. Transfers from Khorat were out of the question; the wing there wasn't much better off. Kadena was a possibility – depending on how many birds they had TDY in Korea for nuke alert, but they'd drawn hard on that resource for a long time and even if planes were available, it would take several days to get them ferried down and checked out; replacements from the States would take forever and even if they could get them, they'd be in shitshape.

Brown had a leg up when it came to replacement aircraft; the Phantoms were still being cranked out by McDonnell-Douglas, with an E-model nearing the production stage. Once Brown had the F4-Es he'd be in business as a MiG hunter. The 20-mm cannon mounted in the nose would do away with the gun pod and make the Phantoms more maneuverable. With F4-Es, Da Nang would be in fat city – it would be the end of MiG hunting for the Thuds.

The problem was to get the Thuds to last until he got his promotion. After that, they could go the way of the Mustang for all he cared. He remembered his first look at the F-80. He'd sat in the hangar half the night, staring at it. No propellers. It just didn't look like an airplane, but even so, he wanted to get his hands on it. Compared to the Thud, the F-80 had been a kiddie cart – a toy that tended to spin without warning and lacked range, making fuel consumption a constant problem.

They'd moved him to F-84s in Korea, and later to the

115

advanced F-86, and each time his new bird had been the most beautiful he'd ever seen – and more complex.

One night in Germany, in the Bitburg Officers Club, a drunk major had told him about a midair he'd had during a NATO exercise – with the goddamned Froggies and Eyeties – and how he'd been forced to punch out and make his own way back to the base where he found everyone running around in circles pissing down their legs, the French showing their scorn for everyone, the Italians claiming that it hadn't been their fault, the Americans trying to keep their allies apart and figure out just what had happened. The drunk had said that it was like a big log going down the Colorado River. Covered with ants – swarming with them. And every one of them thinking he was in control, showing contempt for the others who were not. Whenever things got tense, Wainright tried to remember that night in Germany. On this log, he *was* in control and he meant to keep it that way.

Several minutes passed before the phone rang again. Horowitz connected the call to the intercom.

'Rawlings here, colonel. We've confirmed a shack on the fuel depot. It's still burning. The Covey FAC had to abandon the area because of bad visibility but he said he counted at least fifteen secondaries.' Wainright smoothed his hair nervously. 'Rudamaki didn't make it, sir.'

'Who?'

'Rudamaki, sir. Pintail Lead. The tanker tried towing him, but it was no good. They vectored him to Udorn for a deadstick, but didn't think he could make it so he decided to punch out, but his cockpit was all blown apart and nothing worked, so he went ahead with the Udorn approach.'

'What about the bird?'

'Torn up, but salvageable. He ran off the end of the runway and folded his nosewheel. Cockpit's burned out – going to need extensive electrical work. Maintenance says that they can pull the gear and get it in good enough shape to fly back to Takhli in seventy-two hours. Instrumentation will take twenty-four to thirty-six hours more. The tail section and belly sustained moderate damage; sheet metal work will take another day. We could have it back in the schedule by the end of the week — twelve days at the outside.'

'Good — that's good news.'

'Rudamaki lost too much blood — legs were torn up. Petit is still missing.'

'What about the other two?'

'Urqhart's at Udorn and okay. Chones is almost home, reports that his bird is copacetic.'

Wainright thanked the controller and instructed Horowitz to take care of 'details' on the men. He'd sign them in the morning. It was ironic, he thought, that it took more paper to handle an MIA or KIA than to keep all the others flying. Dying really fattened a man's file. Someday he'd have to look into it; maybe there was some way to streamline the process.

After Horowitz left to call Udorn and dispatch a maintenance team, Wainright cleared his desk top and had freshly sharpened pencils and legal pad brought in. What had Pintail flight earned? What edge could he gain on Brown III?

A Purple Heart, an Air Force Cross and at least two Silver Stars, he calculated. He went to the board, erased the existing numbers, and wrote in the new figures lightly, adding them into individual totals and the wing aggregates. But it looked wrong. Wainright stepped back from the board, scanning it, absorbing all the information for the hundredth time, taking it all in like a pilot checking his instruments.

Why didn't it compute . . . where was the clinker? Ah! There it was. He'd been too hasty. The flight commander, Pintail One. The man was entitled to a Purple Heart, too.

Wainright heaved a sigh of relief as he added the number to the board. He had been so consumed by the prose of the citation that he'd nearly missed the other medal. The man had died from injuries sustained by enemy action. That would clinch the Cross, but he was also entitled to a Heart. Should have caught that before. Not a good sign to overlook

117

the obvious, he told himelf as the went back to his desk to begin roughing out the award recommendations.

Orders for the Cop Shop

'That's what the Old Man said. Bring him at gunpoint if necessary.'

Captain George Maxwell still couldn't believe the telephone call he'd gotten from Wainright. A 'special assignment' was how the wing commander had phrased it. And he'd left little doubt that the shit would hit the fan if he didn't bring South in for the mission briefing. Arrest 'Barney' South? Take him to a pre-strike at gun-point? At first he'd thought it was some kind of practical joke, but the CO's voice was serious and he wasn't the kind to engage in play games with his men. Who was crazy: South or the wing commander? Barney was a good guy.

Maxwell's stomach churned all day long. He'd never had an order so bizarre; in fact there'd been nothing that came even close to it. What the hell was going on between South and the commander? Of all the crazy outfits to be dumped into ... Taxi Dancers. What the fuck did that mean? Three more years and out. Retirement. Fifty percent of base pay. Settle in near a base. Do the shopping at the Px and commissary. Not bad. If he could hold on that long.

He'd been an enlisted man for eight years. And while it had been all right, it wasn't the same as being an officer. He'd worked at night to pick up a few credits through college extension courses − most of them during a two-year hitch in Korea. After that it had been relatively easy to be accepted into the Airmen's Educational Commissioning Program. Two years at Michigan State finished off his B.S. in criminology and it was back on active duty with brown bars on his shoulder and salutes from men who'd once been his equals. But with all his experience, nothing had prepared him for anything like this. If they'd had to take him to the briefing at gunpoint, who was going to get him to fly? Would somebody be strapped on the wing to hold a gun to his head? Insanity.

Staff Sergeant Nestor Scholz picked at his fingernails with the end of a small dagger and watched his commanding officer. Maxwell had laid out the situation for him. No fucking sweat, he told the captain. Wing Commander says arrest him; we arrest him. What's to think about? That's how he'd handle it. But not Maxwell. Maxwell had been the some way when he was a tech sergeant. A college degree and silver tracks on his fatigues hadn't changed anything. Same old Shaky Max; worry about everything. He deserved to be a goddamn officer; served him right. Now let him squirm with it, Scholz thought as he watched the sweat bead on Maxwell's forehead.

'Nestor. You pick your men yet?'

'Yessir. Four good ones. Strong.'

'No rough stuff unless you have to. And no rounds in the guns − sidearms only.'

'I told 'em, Cap'n. I explained it to ev' one of 'em.'

'Tell them again, sergeant. I don't want South hurt. Remember, we're taking him to fly − not to the lock-up.'

Bullshit! That's the problem. Goddamn pilots carry on like a bunch of spoiled college kids. Shit, who needed college to fly an airplane? Truck drivers didn't need no educations. So, why did pilots? Hell of a lot less traffic upstairs and a lot safer. Beat up a few of them; that'd show them they weren't so tough.

'I know what you're thinking, Nestor. Just follow my instructions and we won't have any trouble.'

'Where we going to find him? Everybody around here knows he'd a crazy fucker.'

'I'll have to think about it.' Maxwell shrugged. 'I've notified the gates. He won't get out that way. We'll start at the officer's club, then his hootch. From there I don't know. Just have to play it by ear. The briefing's at two so we'd better get started right after dinner. Once we spot him, we'll stay on his tail. We'll take him at the last possible minute. That'll keep him from thinking about it. Snap him up and haul him *reh-oh reh-oh*! That's how we'll do it.'

Scholz stood, saluted, executed a crisp aboutface and left Maxwell's office smiling. This assignment would be a pleasure.

Dinner Hour

South squinted in an attempt to accustom his eyes to the soft yellow lighting in the stag bar. There was still an aftertaste of lizard and while it had been pleasant he still half-expected to be sick from it. Damned Indian. Where were Buggs and Romero?

'Tommie, my man, lay a beer on me.'

The young Thai bartender flashed his toothiest customer smile and signalled thumbs up. 'One San Miguel quick-fast for Cap South.'

The pilot fondled the cool aluminium, noting a lighter gauge than usual. More cash for the corporate coffers. Nothing wrong with them making a few more bucks, he told himself, long as they don't screw with the beer.

The stag bar was relatively empty, making it seem larger than normal even though it wasn't much more than a large cedar closet built as an afterthought off the main dining room. From his seat he could see Thai waitresses taking orders in the dining room, hustling glasses of icewater for new arivals, delivering trays of hamburgers, clearing tables, all done with smiles and high-pitched chirping in their native tongue. He enjoyed watching them. English was nearly impossible for them, but they all tried hard to learn and to please, and it was their spirit as much as anything that he admired. Most of them learned to recite some

English by rote, but pronunciation was terrible, and often comic. When the base had first opened, the girls spoke virtually no English so a number system had been instituted in order for the officers to order their meals. Number One was ham and eggs. Two was a hamburger and french fries. The waitresses would stand beside their tables impatiently demanding to serve. 'What you want?'

With soft number-3 pencils they'd scribble the Arabic number down with a great flourish, smile at the customer and scurry happily away to the kitchen to squeal at the cook and anybody else in earshot, demanding their order first, to take care of their customer so that he would be pleased and leave a handsome tip.

South delighted in teasing them. They were like Wells' gentle and beautiful Eloi – quite attractive, childlike, with alabaster complexions. He would order in German and Italian, usually mixing the two and they would point at him and chide him. '*My! Dee poochy!*' The bad man. He was also a generous tipper so there was a certain amount of jockeying that occurred whenever he walked into the dining room. 'My table,' they would shout from all four corners and he would pause and study them very seriously before choosing a particular table. It was apparent to them that he moved around the room each week, giving everybody a fair chance, but that fact didn't reduce the competition for his attention. Thais loved to play and he obliged them.

When he'd first met Wainright he hadn't seemed such a bad sort. But he had turned out to be a leech. The medals. They were a big part of the rub. Them and the big board with the statistics. Like a big Keno board with Wainright as the only player. He was removed from the risk.

It was bad, South told himslf, for a commander to remove himself too far from his troops. You could understand a commander not liking his losses, finding them too difficult to accept. But Wainright was even delegating the writing of letters to next of kin and that was wrong. Nobody liked to write the letters. He'd written a few himself. To wives and parents of friends. But it had to be done and what better

121

reminder for the one who had the responsibility for sending them to fight? It was a good way to remember what this thing was all about. Without personal contact, it was too easy to get accustomed to losses, to begin seeing pilots as pieces on a chess board.

Instead of people, Wainright had numbers. Codes and coloured legends on the big board in his office. The colonel was withdrawing and that was dangerous for every man in the wing. This was a tough fight and everybody had to keep their cool, especially with rules set for everything. Caveats. Drop your bombs on this block, but leave the next one alone. Hit these Triple-A sites, but leave the others alone – even though they might blow you or your wingman out of your socks.

'Tommie-babes. Gimme some beer nuts.' South scooped a large helping and popped the red, sugar-coated nuts into his mouth. Their sweetness contrasted nicely with the bitterness of the Filipino beer.

Wainright was trying to run the wing like General Motors. His power was as great as a chairman of the board. He was more powerful than the captain of the Navy's biggest aircraft carrier. A ship's captain had to take most of the risks of his men. But Wainright had no such constraint. His power enabled him to push the wing and manipulate it instead of leading it. That was the big part of the problem. He didn't seem to know how to lead. Maybe, South thought, that's our Achilles' heel; men are promoted and given command authority by men who don't have to serve under them. The Chief said that leaders in his tribe were elected, but once in office had no real power, no way to compel tribal members to do anything. They elected him on his abilities. But once there he still had to convince them and sell them on his ideas and he couldn't act without the tribe's approval. The Ojibwa didn't go to war often; but when they went, it was a hundred percent effort and the men leading the way were there because they had the confidence of those who had chosen them. It was a strong system.

His can was empty. South crushed it and tossed it across

the bar into a large plastic barrel. Tommie immediately slid another full one down the bar top. It skidded to a halt inches from his hand.

The confrontations with Wainright had to stop. It felt good to get him going, but it wasn't smart, not in the long run. More and more it was beginning to cut into his own efficiency and it was an intrusion he didn't like. Couldn't allow it to happen. Too many new guys to train and babysit. And maybe, just maybe, the harassment was making Wain-- right fuck up, too. Stateside would be no problem, but here Wainright's bad judgement could cost lives.

What was it to him that Wainright was backing in his missions? From a practical view it was better that he not fly, even if it was his job and even if there was a moral responsibility. The cheating wasn't the main issue; it was more of a symptom. Wainright would do anything to get what he wanted and unfortunately he had the power to pull it off. What did it matter?

It might be tough to swallow some pride, but maybe it was time to finish the job and get the hell out. He had considered requesting an extension. Take a thirty day R&R in Honolulu, or Sydney and start all over again. But now that seemed out of the question. They'd probably leave him at Takhli and there was no way he could handle it anymore. Eleven more missions and he could go home. Back to The World. If they gave him a good assignment, he'd stick with it. Germany or England. But if they tried to dump on him, well, his five had been up for a long time and the commitment was ended. There were airline jobs, lots of them. Big pay, soft hours, lots of women. Pick up a lucrative sideline. The flying was the worst, but what the hell, you couldn't have everything. He had lots of options.

Best of all, keeping a low profile might get to Wainright more than a confrontation. The wing commander's woman seemed to be in heat. She might be a nice diversion till the end. Wainright would come unglued when he found out.

What kind of a woman was she? After all, she was Wainright's personal toy and that right there said something

123

about her. Maybe the bastard had redeeming qualities – like a Louisville Slugger for ... Or something. Power was part of the allure. The medal had taught him that. People liked to be around other people who seemed to have it made. Strange attraction. Did Wainright keep score on the wall of his hootch? Did his compulsion reach that far into his personal life? Number of orgasms. His. Hers. Theirs. Her first. Him first. Simultaneous. Doubles. Triples. More than three. Petting efficiency. Subcategories for endpoints. In her ass. Mouth. Ears. Armpits? Anything was possible. He seemed the armpit type. The image of a wall filled with sexual statistics amused him. How many categories were there?

'Cap South hab heaby mind?'

'Right, Tommie-babes, heavy.'

'You fry tonight?' The Thai asked carefully, working hard to make the correct pronunciation of the 'l' but it still came out as an 'r.'

'Why you wanna know? You workin' for the NVA. A snoop-snoop, like CIA?'

The bartender giggled. 'Sure, I numbah-one snoop-snoop. Go tell Uncle Ho where you go.'

'Then you're doin' a number-ten job, kiddo. They haven't got me yet.'

Tommie patted South's shoulder, a gesture he had learned from the pilots. Americans, unlike Thais, touched each other all the time. It was part of how they communicated.

'Keep ass down, Cap South, *chy?*'

'You bet.' There was something annoying about the way the Thais tossed around English obscenities. At first it had seemed cute, but now that it was routine, he found it demeaning. Did the Thais think all Americans were loud-mouth *farang* – barbarians? Probably so, he decided. The whole world thinks we're a pack of assholes. Sometimes with good reason.

'What time you fry?'

South stared at the boy. 'You trying to pump me?'

'No,' Tommie said, laughing. 'Soo-lee pump you! She

124

pump you numbah one if you got *mahk-mahk baht.*'

South grinned and crumpled another empty. He was getting tired. Tommie was right. Soo-lee would provide any service for a price. As a cocktail waitress she was a rank above the dining room waitresses who scribbled numbers and hustled trays. She was an interesting woman and he was fond of her. When she chose to, she could speak English flawlessly, but most of the time she played the native, chattering pidgin and flirting with the flyers who left her big tips and fantasized about her. Her rules were ironclad. No quickies. No freebies. No one-night stands. Sex for cash. Preferably a year-long arrangement. She'd be as true as any wife and a lot more attentive. Guaranteed.

As Tommie squealed her name, the waitress floated into the stag bar. She snapped off a long drink order in a mixture of Thai and English and then turned to South.

'Cap drink *mahk-mahk* tonight, go fly silver bird with thunder?' she whispered to him, blinking her heavily made-up eyelids. Her eyes were coal-black, accented against her golden flesh by a subtle blue-green eye shadow. Her lips were painted red and glistened in the light as if they were wet.

'Your English is improving,' South said sarcastically. She poked him hard in the ribs with a long fingernail.

'Smart ass,' she said, hefting a tray of drinks expertly as she sailed out of sight.

South ordered another beer but took only one sip from the can. It was beginning to taste sour. His mood was changing. The wall clock said six-fifteen. Probably be a good idea to head for the hootch and catch some z's. Briefing at two. He fumbled through his pockets for some change, but ended up leaving a dollar bill. With beer only a dime a can, the tip was enormous. But he enjoyed Tommie's company and the tip would assure good service the next time he visited. Wainright had established slave wages for the locals and even part of that probably was raked off by the Thai colonel who officially commanded the installation.

Tommie picked up the dollar bill and bowed low in a

proper *wai*.

Rawlings was coming into the foyer as South made his way out. The command post controller looked haggard, his face sagging with wrinkles, his flesh yellow. The controller had his back to the dining room as he talked. South could see Wainright and the woman at their corner table. He hoped she would look up.

'Hey babes,' South greeted him.

'Hi, Barn.'

'You look number ten.' Wainright's woman was sipping a drink from a long-stem glass but still she seemed unaware of his presence.

'Feel worse. Rudamaki bought it this afternoon.' South took the news stoically. The redhead had not been a close friend, but he had been a good pilot. 'Sitting Bull's ass. Routine mission, but apparently the gook gunners had a good day.'

'They get him out?'

'Didn't have to,' Rawlings said, shaking his head. 'He flew it into Udorn, but he'd lost too much blood, I guess. Petit's missing.'

'Same mission?'

'Yep. Weird. Might have been a MiG. Reports are still all jumbled up. Been on the phone with NKP and Udorn trying to find out what happened. The FAC says Petit left the target area trailing smoke, but he flew east. FAC says he thought he heard him say something about going after a MiG Red Bandit. Doesn't make any sense for a single ship to be out that far over the border. Maybe they've built some auxiliary fields in Laos. I don't know. Anything's possible in this mess. Anyhow, I got to get some chow before I head back. The Old Man wants confirmation if there was a MiG involved. You know how that plays.'

'Later.' Rawlings pushed by him and South stepped into the humid evening air. Two pilots. Bad day. Tough to lose the Rudamakis, but you had to expect to lose the Petits because of inexperience. Too short-handed to break them in properly. Wainright should be screaming at Seventh for more manpower or for a drop in the sortie load. Instead, he was asking for more missions. It was time to get the hell out before the roof caved in. How long could you push your luck?

Time to go, he told himself. He took one last look at Wainright's table. The woman's eyes made contact with him, but there was no signal, no clue as to her intent. She was something else.

South walked slowly back to his hootch. How could such a shack be home? It looked like an Okie chicken coop. Slanted tin roof. Clay-red slatted walls. At least there was an air conditioner, he thought as he kicked off his boots. He showered, towelled quickly, turned down the temperature and turned up the fan speed and crawled between cool, clean sheets. He was too tired to dream and too tired to spend any energy wondering if the brunette would show. Probably not, he told himself just before he dropped off to sleep.

Night Visitor

Somewhere on the distant flight line a jet engine screamed against its tie-down straps as maintenance men ran it up to check some pilot's complaint. Elise Mantel tried to calm herself; it had been a long time since she'd been with anyone other than Jergen. She felt like a schoolgirl sneaking out for a midnight handjob. She was nervous. What if South had gone off to the club and gotten drunk with the other pilots, or God forbid, that weird Indian dentist?

She built a scenario in her mind. She liked to be prepared. She'd knock on his door and if he was there, she'd show him what action was all about. There was a point during her walk where she stopped. A point of no return. She could have returned to her quarters and gone to bed. Or keep going toward the unknown. She had plunged ahead. He was a glib one, this pilot. But like most of his kind he'd probably be more talk than action. By going to his hootch she'd call his bluff and she'd get a big laugh out of it. He probably wouldn't even be able to get it up, a voice in her mind said. He'd better, another voice said. It's been nearly a month since Jergen paid any attention to me. That's what they called it: paying atention to each other. It was a silly, convoluted term, but the language of lovers was always bizarre.

She smiled as she considered the scene if Jergen found out. She wasn't afraid of him. Even so her heart was pounding as the thin soles of her high-heel shoes crunched on the gravel near the parking lot behind the officer's club. She moved quickly, staying in the shadows. She hoped that her new stockings wouldn't catch on anything. At the far end of the lot she climbed back onto a wooden sidewalk and made her way down a lane between a long line of identical hootches. If she wasn't afraid of Wainright, why was she sneaking around? A woman needed certain things, she told herself. It wasn't as if she made inordinate demands. She enjoyed sex, but even more than the actual act she needed the closeness of a relationship, the emotional attachment that went with it. Of course some sex was necessary. There was no sense taking a lover, then living a celibate life. If Jergen couldn't provide, she'd take care of herself. That was life's lesson.

South's hootch was dark. No light showed through the small windows or under the door. There were no numbers on the buildings so she had been forced to look in the files for the housing assignments. She located South's place by a number of landmarks. She hoped she hadn't made a mistake. As she paused before the door she had an impulse to leave, but she hesitated. She'd come this far; at least she could finish what she started. After all, wasn't that her trademark?

Not wanting to alert anybody in the nearby structures, she rapped lightly on the wooden door using the ends of her fingernails instead of her knuckles. Half asleep, South finally realized it was the door and he stumbled across the room to open it.

When the door was open only a slit, she bulled her way inside.

South stared at her silhouette in the doorway.

'What's the matter?' she asked. 'Cat got your tongue?'

'Well, kiss my ass,' he whispered in amazement.

'All in good time,' she said. 'Weren't you expecting me?'

He stammered. 'Yes and no.'

'I thought you might be all talk; now I know.'

She turned to leave, but he moved quickly to block her path. 'I was trying to catch a little nap. Got to fly in the morning, you know . . . lead the Forces of Righteousness?'

'I assumed that you knew that this morning when you made the offer.'

'You must be early,' he said.

'Right on time,' she came back. 'I'm always prompt.'

'I'll remember that for the future.'

'If there's one.'

He laughed nervously. 'Okay, I confess. When I left you this morning I figured there was no way anything would come out of it. I figured we were being cute . . . you know, making boy-girl talk.'

She liked that. He was honest. Most men would have kept trying to cover themselves.

'But now that you're here, I'm really glad,' he said. 'But you got me.'

'Not yet,' she said. 'But soon, *very* soon.' She pulled him away from the door, closed it, latched it and led him by the hand to his rumpled bed. She pushed him down and reached for the lamp switch. The room illuminated with a faint light from the bed stand. Her deeply tanned legs glowed and the shadows produced by the dim lighting made her ample curves seem more so. Normally she wore straight dresses that hid her body, but now she was wearing a light blue thing with a tight waist and a low cut. Her top was held up by two tiny straps and she bulged to overflowing.

129

'Whew,' he whistled. 'You do a hell of a job hiding your assets in your work clothes.'

'I've been told not to ... *excite* ... the men. I always follow orders.'

'Orders that would cover you up are downright immoral.'

'Our colonel is afraid that a white woman in anything more than a burlap bag might boost more than the men's morale.'

'I don't agree with him very often, but I think this time he's right.'

'You two don't get on very well, do you?'

'Not very.'

'What's between you?' she asked, her curiosity getting the best of her.

'How about a drink?' he asked, changing the subject.

'What's available?'

'Bourbon. Scotch. A beer?'

'Too late for beer. Scotch. Neat.'

'On my way,' he said as he hurried toward the small bathroom where he kept his liquor stash.

She watched him go, wondering if he was excited. She admitted to herself that she was attracted to him. She'd caught him off balance, but he had recovered quickly and efficiently. The nervousness she had felt outside in the night air was gone, replaced now by a kind of gnawing anticipation that made her feel giddy. It had been crazy to get involved in this, but now that she was in his room she couldn't wait to see what happened next.

He emerged carrying a single glass with golden liquid.

'Nothing for you?'

'Gotta fly.'

She accepted the drink and sipped it, letting the Scotch pause on the back of her tongue before swallowing it. She nodded her head toward him. 'Is the way you're dressed supposed to be suggestive?'

He looked down at himself. 'Shoot.' He was clad only in green jockey shorts.

'Don't worry,' she said as she took another drink from

the glass. 'I've seen it all before.'

'All?'

She laughed. 'In case you didn't know, captain, there's just two standard models. Helmets and anteaters. Which are you?'

'I'd prefer if you'd peek for yourself.'

She smiled, stood up and raised her glass to him. 'Wilco.' Now she felt herself in full control. There was no longer any question of backing out. She welcomed the finality of it, the commitment to it. She finished her drink and stood up.

'You shouldn't be here,' he said.

'Cold feet? Look at it this way. I've got to walk all the way back to my place. Be a wasted trip if I got spotted on the way back. Jergen's going to think I'm servicing one of his men. If he's going to think it, I think I ought to do it. The sin is in the mind. Understand?'

'You're here to stay.'

'Now you've got it,' she said.

South sat on the bed and reached for her leg, touching her just inside the knee. She held her ground as his hand slid upward to the top of her stockings.

'Nobody owns me,' she said firmly, but quietly. 'Not him. Not you. I choose.'

South's hand found the wide spot between her legs and she began to sway gently.

'I'm not for sale. I make my own choices. I do what I want, when I want. I'm different than any other woman you've ever known. You'd better get used to that right now. You're about to have the experience of your life. I choose to live in a man's world, so I operate like a man.'

'You don't feel like a man,' South said softly. 'Lie down.'

'Not yet.' she gasped. 'I want to get something straight between us.'

'Me too,' he said, 'but you won't shut up.'

She pulled away from him and slipped out of her dress. She unclasped her bra and let it fall to the floor. 'Your bed tonight, maybe somebody else's tomorrow night. Can you

131

handle that?' She peeled down her panties and stood before him.

'Whatever you say.' he said. 'Is the speech over?'

She threw herself on him.

Round Up

Staff Sergeant Nestor Scholz caressed the forestock of his M-16 Armalite, inserted a full clip, and rammed a round into the chamber. The black surface of the automatic rifle felt cool in his hands, and comforting. It also had felt good at Tuy Hoa the night three dinks slid under the concertina wire in front of this guard post. They had been dark shadows duck-walking awkwardly through the high grass trying to keep low profiles. But Nestor had the good night eyes; he spotted their silhouettes when they were still fifty metres out. As they approached he guessed where they would come through the wire and moved to intercept them.

The perimeter was made of five winding rolls of wire spread over a thirty-foot swath which had been bulldozed by combat engineers from the elephant grass and ferns. Scholz waited until the last man was on his back and under a coil before opening fire. He finished them with his knife.

Basking in the memory, Scholz moved to the front of the truck where the others and Captain Maxwell were waiting.

'Nestor. Pull the round.'

'Sir?'

'You heard me,' Maxwell said sharply. 'I said pull the fucking round.'

Maxwell the Worm. The officer. Shit, if the old man wanted this guy South, then they ought to fetch his mouthy ass any way they had to. Not Maxwell. He believed in all that officer and gentlemen horseshit. Scholz popped the round and slung his rifle loosely over his shoulder.

'Listen up,' Maxwell told the group quietly. 'I'll fetch him. You people wait here. Wainright said to bring him to the briefing – alive and able to fly. He hasn't done anything wrong that I know of. Let me handle it. If I need muscle, I'll call for it.'

The security police officer checked his watch. Three minutes. He'd called the motor pool dispatcher and told him South wouldn't need a pick-up. Crazy war. Blue school buses carrying men in baseball hats to drop time bombs on stone-age gooks and monkeys. What was between South and Wainright? Tough enough to manage men without making them do their jobs at gunpoint. If South was a psycho they should move him out on a Section Eight. Not much else you could do when a man's dipstick stopped touching oil. It was difficult to imagine anything wrong with South. He had the Medal of Honor. That in itself made him special. Had his picture on the cover of *Time*. No way they could court-martial him. What was going on?

Maxwell moved up the wooden sidewalk carefully. How would South react? He hoped there would be no trouble. Nestor, on the other hand, would love it. He was a beaut. He'd jump at the chance to use his weapon. Maybe he had the same problem as Wainright. Scholz was good. Maybe too good. That's why they had shipped him out of Tuy Hoa. They called it inadvertent. Dark night. Mortars and rockets coming in all the time. The men were jumpy. Sapper teams made regular tries at a penetration to get at the F-100s on the flight line. Nestor couldn't have known it was a South Vietnamese Army scout team. Hell, they didn't come through the regular ARVN check point. It was their mistake – their own fault. Of course, Nestor had shot them at point-blank range, then cut their throats. If he could see them coming through the jungle, he sure as hell could see by their uniforms that they were good guys. Officially an accident. Off the record, they called him an executioner. A probable psychopath. The Air Force couldn't condone an NCO who killed in cold blood – even if there was some reasonable doubt about his motivations.

133

Maxwell rapped lightly on the door to South's hootch. 'Barney?'

'Yeah,' a voice came from inside.

'It's me. Max. George Maxwell.' The door opened a crack.

'Hey, Max, what the hell you doin' out there?'

'Wainright sent me,' Maxwell said nervously.

South peeked out the door and looked down the walkway. 'Got your boys with you?'

'Over by the trucks.'

'Hope they got their bullets in their shirt pockets.'

'Barney, the old man wants me to drive you down to ops,' Maxwell said apologetically. 'No trouble, okay?'

'You got that crazy NCO with you? The one who cuts gooks?'

'Yes.'

'No problem then. I'm a pacifist. Just keep that jerk away from me.'

Maxwell walked to the corner of the building and yelled. 'All set, sergeant. Take the other truck and vamoose. I'll see you later.'

'I'm stickin' with you, Cap'n,' a voice called back.

'Go with the men.'

'But sir ...'

'*Sergeant*, take the other truck and get the hell out of here. *Now.*'

South heard the muffled curses, then Scholz was barking orders at the other men like a Parris Island DI. The doors to a double-cabbed pickup slammed loudly, the motor roared into life and the vehicle peeled out, its tyres screaming on the hot pavement, sending a small cloud of loose gravel into the air. Maxwell heaved a sigh of relief. At least that complication was taken care of. Keep situation simple; reduce the chance of error. That's what they taught in OCS and it worked. He'd learned the hard way as an enlisted man.

'All right, Barney. They're gone. We'd better get moving. Little past one now.'

'No sweat, Max. Gimme a minute.' The door closed and a light snapped on, but Maxwell couldn't see through the blinds on the windows. After ten minutes he began to get edgy. No back door, he told himself. No way out but here. What the hell was South up to? He began to feel panicky.

'Come on, Barney. The old man's gonna have my ass if we don't hustle,' he yelled. Finally the door opened and South stepped onto the porch. Although his view was partially blocked, Maxwell could see that someone else was inside. Clothes were strewn on the floor and there was a long white leg on the bed. A female. Not a Thai. Oh God! Maxwell thought. It's Wainright's honey. As South pulled the door to, the security officer moved to the side and saw the woman clearly, all of her.

'Geez, Barn. That's Mantel in there. You're gonna start a war. No wonder the old man's after your ass.'

'Settle down, Max. Rest your bowels, boy. He doesn't know. Besides it's strictly platonic.'

'My ass. She had her clothes off.'

'Air conditioning is lousy. Besides, *you* gonna tell him?'

'No, but all the same...'

'Forget it, Max, I've got to get to the briefing. You coming?' South hopped off the porch and jogged across the road to the truck.

God Almighty, Maxwell thought as he started the engine. This man's out of his gourd.

'Hey, Max, can we stop along the way? I need a can of V-8 juice.'

A Matter of Time

Pre-strike briefings had become ritualized by hundreds of repetitions. The pilots went through them more or less blindly, each reacting in his own special way according to

135

his own needs. None of them questioned the format or the organization of such meetings; they simply showed up when they were supposed to be there and went through the prescribed motions – like good Catholics, reciting Latin without meaning, standing, sitting and genuflecting on cue.

Each man handled this time in his own way. Some swaggered down the aisles of the briefing room, while others snuck to their places as if they were afraid to be seen. All of them made it a point to visit a small stand near the front stage. A yellow telephone was enclosed in a plastic sound hood and a hand-lettered sign proclaimed: 'Time Hack.' The dedicated phone line linked them to a master hookup through the wing communications centre with WWV radio which produced a tone burst every minute and ticked off its seconds electronically. Every five minutes a voice dripping a wet British accent announced a precise Greenwich Mean Time. They called it Zulu time.

All time was relative to the Greenwich Meridian – the zero longitude line on the earth. Travel westward and you gained time at the rate of one hour for every fifteen degrees of longitude. Beyond Hawaii and Wake Island you flew into the back end of the coming day and time began to increase at one hour for each fifteen degrees of longitude. It was all very confusing, especially during early flight training. The decision of mathematicians, South swore. Arbitrary and capricious! His revolutionary fervour was torched every time he heard the WWV hack and the lisping limey accent – which he called the 'Fag of Falworth'.

Time was both important and bewildering. Time was the pilot's pilot – especially in wartime. It was the ultimate idol, a deity more important than God Almighty. Time controlled all.

How long till bus time? How many wake-ups until your DEROS? Start-engine time. Taxi time. Takeoff time. Rendezvous time. Boom time. Air refueling control time. Drop-off time. Time over the initial point. Time on target. Time over target. Post-refueling time. Pucker time. RTB time. Touchdown time. Weather time. Night time and day time – both weather and simulated weather. First pilot time. Penetration time and approach time. Chock time. Mission time for the Form 781. Debrief time. Breakfast time. Dinner time. Lunch time. Booze time. Sad time. Good time. Fuck-off time. Jack-off time. Solo time. Single-engine time and multi-engine time. Time-time-time-time. And always, without exception, related to the imaginary line splitting the seam of Mother Britannia. Strangest of all, Greenwich Mean Time was called 'Zulu'. The limeys were masters at complicating the uncomplicated.

Romero and Buggs slid into aisle seats in the second and third rows. Mulkey, a surly ex-wrestler from Toledo, was already in place in the fourth row – as leader of the fourth flight of the strike force. He was half-asleep so the two late arrivals were careful not to disturb him as they took their seats. Neither wanted to rile Mulkey, who Buggs said was big enough to hunt grizzlies with a switch.

Most of the pilots were subdued; those who felt the need to talk kept their conversations low in respect for those who needed quiet. Some used the time to daydream; others brushed up on procedures. Each man had his own way of psyching up for battle and in this they were much the same as millions who'd gone before them. Part of their quiet approach involved their concept of professionalism. You were paid to do the job. People depended on your competence. There was little need for pep talks and Rockneish tricks. As a professional it was your own responsibility to prepare yourself for the job. Very similar to businessmen. But instead of briefcases and seersucker suits, they lugged heavy parachutes, green plastic helmets and wore loose-fitting, grey-green flightsuits covered with zippers and pockets. Their orientation to their jobs was the same. Concentrate on what you must do. Stay cool. Think things out. Prepare for the unexpected and, above all, trust in the instinct acquired from experience.

It was a job. And like all jobs, there were routines and procedures to adhere to. The bus came two hours before takeoff. Briefing at one-plus-thirty. Get the weather; study target photos when available; trot on down to Personal Equipment to pick up chaps and chutes and baby bottles filled with water. Stop at the Green Weenie for a moldy hot dog smothered in onions, relish and mustard. Start engines thirty minutes before takeoff. Taxi five minutes later. Stop on the hammerhead for a leak check and weapons arming. Take the active runway one minute before takeoff. Set the parking brakes and watch the clock unwind. Release brakes, plug in the throttle, watch the gauges, plug in the afterburner, pull the nose off, pop the gear handle, retract the flaps, set your climb power and you were on the way. Just like being in an office. A radio for the boss to call you. Colleagues in nearby offices doing their jobs. Absolutely no difference. Except terror.

But it all began and ended with time. First task at briefing: set your watch. Ten minutes later, the briefing officer comes in and what does he do? Picks up the phone to WWV and orders that all watches be synchronized. At the end of the briefing, you look up on the wall and check your watch against the master clock — just in case. There is always doubt.

Hey, babes, you got the time? This here Accutron don't work for shit. Stop a crew chief on the flightline: Got the time, sarge? Radio the Command Post: Need a time hack, sir. To the tanker: Hey nav, what time you got up there? To the forward air controller: Okay, Covey. I got you visual over the hump of red trees. Understand you're taking heavy ground fire. You got a time hack for Rainbow flight? To the bartender: Hey, Tommie. What time is it, man? Clock on the wall says six. I got three to. Hey, Buggs, what's Seiko say? Two after? No way. Somebody call ops when you're up for a piss. Fucking Thais can't keep these clocks straight. At a poker game: Bought this goddamn Seiko up at Oki just last month. Now look at the sumbitch! Losing twenty-three seconds a month. Guaranteed, that Jap outlaw told me. Just send it back, he says. Send it *where?* Where the fuck *is* Seiko? In the hootch: You think that's bad? You ought to have one of these electric bummers. Hear that sucker buzz? Yeah, Accutron. Gave a hunert an' five on sale — regular $165. I got it a month, see, an' I'm wadin' through the BX and pow! I rap this fucker on a glass counter; ten minutes later I got a Class Six on my hands; damn thing is totalled. So I ship it back to Bulova and six months later I get it back, so I buy a new battery, only now they're up from a buck and two bits to a buck-seventy-five and I screw the little bastard into the back ... and nothing! So I send it back to Bulova again and another six months go by and finally it shows up and there's a bill for $78 for parts and cleaning. My goddamn warranty ran out! Can you believe it? I own the bastard a year; it's been on my wrist two days. Where the fuck are the Swiss when we really need them?

Every man has a watch. Timex. Omega. Rolex. Accutron. Seikos are most popular — and least expensive. It's a big decision. A watch has to fit your personality and it's got to be easy to hack. One of a pilot's four essentials: spectacles, testicles, watch and wallet. Never take it off — even in the shower. Waterproof, shock-resistant, easy-to-read dials with luminous hands that sweep through 360 degrees like Father Murphy marching the stations of the cross.

No longer an instrument on your arm; it's a growth. Thais laugh. Whores howl over them. How you know he American pilot? Easy. Got big watch and *nit noy* dick! You real pilot, *chy?* You bet, sweet cakes. Here's my watch and you checky-check the other ... but before we get started, you got the time, sugar?

May 2, 1967

The Phuc Yen Briefing

One minute before the briefing South walked slowly down the centre aisle to a seat in front of Buggs, Romero and Muley Dragotte, a six-three mesomorph who'd been a third-string offensive guard at Stanford and whose claim to fame involved eating bar glasses.

'Where you been, babes?' Buggs attacked. 'Lopin' your mule?'

South ignored them. He carefully lifted the tab on a can of Snappy Tom tomato juice and pulled it upward, bending it out of his way. He broke open small paper packets of salt and pepper, poured them into the opening, then sealed off the opening with his thumb and shook the can to mix in the seasoning. The relief of the other pilots over his arrival was evident. Having him on strike calmed things considerably. Luck rode with South, and in this mess you needed every bit of luck you could lay your hands on. He couldn't fly your plane, but he helped settle frayed nerves when all hell was breaking loose. In a crisis he was Bing Crosby hustling bucks for St. Mary's.

Sipping his juice, South thought about the look he'd seen on Maxwell's face when he'd spotted Elise. There was little doubt that South's life was about to get more complicated than it had been. It had been some session with her. His legs were still weak. He wanted to see her again, but there was no way they could tiptoe back and forth every night. What was she up to? A game? Maybe she just wanted a little strange stuff on the side. By the time this mission was over she might look at him like she'd never seen him

141

before. Women did that every now and then. On the other hand, she could be for real. It seemed more her style now that he knew her a little better. She was direct and to the point. A lot different than the image she put forth in Wainright's office or when she was out with the wing commander. He wondered how she came to be at Takhli. It took balls to come to the war this way − to be the only round-eye in camp. If Wainright found out about them, there'd be hell to pay. Wainright had the hammer. You never knew when or how he'd use it. He'd pushed him to the limit; hard to say if there was any elasticity left. So far South tried to keep the wing commander off balance, but it was getting tougher and the man was far from hamstrung. The damn medal had been a curse. Before it hadn't been too bad; but after the way Wainright carried on in Washington, you'd have thought he was the Red Baron puffing over the success of a protégé. Too much hoopla over luck and that couldn't hold forever. What about Richter? He'd pushed his luck too far − the fool. Actually destroyed records so he could fly more missions and it had cost him. Got beat to death on the rocks in a bailout. In a way, Richter had been lucky. What if the NVA had gotten him? That was the real fear − becoming a long-term resident of the Hanoi Hilton. Hard to say what they were up to there, but it had to be rough. It's the one thing Byron South refused to think about. Capture. It was his personal view of hell.

' 'Tench-hut!' Sixteen pilots struggled to their feet and faced straight ahead as Wainright and Horowitz strode to seats. South took the opportunity to salute them with the juice can.

Wainright waved his cigar at the briefing officer. 'Let's get on with it.'

The briefing officer, a young nervous first lieutenant named Garside with a pencil moustache, pulled a cord and a curtain parted to reveal the twin of the huge relief map that hung in Wainright's office. From a distance the twenty-by-thirty-foot monster looked like a porcupine with red quills. Small red surface-to-air missiles were pasted to the chart

142

along with circles in red, blue, yellow and orange to mark 37-, 57-, 85- and 100-mm gun sites. Restricted targets were outlined in red and crosshatched in black. The Taxi Dancers didn't put much stock in the information depicted on the board. Intelligence kept it as updated as they could, but most of their information was at least a week old — the time it took for most routine information to be processed in Saigon and relayed to operational combat units. Most of the NVA's defensive firepower was mobile and by the time the reports got to the unit, the enemy equipment was usually someplace else. Even so, the board was impressive and served Wainright well as a public relations tool for visiting dignitaries.

'Gentlemen, this morning's target is in Route Pack Six.' Garside's metal telescopic pointer hammered against the map, its tip resting on Phuc Yen, the NVA's primary MiG farm in the Hanoi area. Until now it had been off limits.

'*Here* is the target,' Garside said, his pointer striking the map again like a gun shot. 'This morning we're going to hurt the NVA where they're going to feel it . . . Phuc Yen.'

South sat straighter in his seat. Everything was forgotten except the target. This could be the war's big turkey shoot.

Garside picked up the phone and plugged it into the intercom for a time hack: 'This is WWV Radio. In fifteen seconds, the time will be ten-thirty-five Greenwich Mean Time EEEEEEEEEEEEEEEEEE tick-tick-tick-tick . . . '

Watches were punched on the tone and the pilots settled back to concentrate on target information. 'Phuc Yen is a primary air operations and training centre,' the briefer explained. He spoke slowly and deliberately, like a teacher adhering to a prepared lesson plan and detailed notes, careful to cover every point lest the students miss a salient fact. His voice was a monotone, his face impassive. He had developed his style over twelve months. Now he was down to eighteen wake-ups and he was determined to do his job like a professional. Arrive at the office, pour a cup of tea, review the day's briefings, saving for himself the ones Wainright was likely to attend. Some days, because they were short of briefers, he would give as many as ten briefings; on other days he did none. For nearly a month he'd been carefully breaking in his replacement, but because of the importance of this target, he chose to do the job himself.

When it was over, he would return to his office, open the middle drawer in the gun-metal grey desk and extract his mimeographed short-timer's calendar. It was a simple line drawing of a well-endowed female divided into thirty parts — with the final part outlining a bulging pudendum between muscular thighs. Each day he coloured in another part of the puzzle; on his final morning, he'd blacken in the triangle, pick up his bags and head for Da Nang to catch the Pan Am flight that would return him to The World.

This briefing was like any other. A well-practiced and polished routine to accomplish within a predetermined time limit. It had been done just so before he arrived; it would be done just so after he was gone. He had neither improved nor impaired it. He preserved it.

With watches set, Garside flipped another switch on the intercom and a voice from the meteorology shop in base operations coughed. Television receivers in the corners showed a fat greying man standing in front of a map of North Vietnam, scratched up with the same symbols that weathermen used on the eleven o'clock news in Green Bay, Hartford, San Diego and dozens of other places.

Garside had considered his role carefully and he was convinced that he should be primarily an emcee rather than an entertainer.

The weather over the target would be clear. The weather briefing was over quickly and that was good. They could stay on schedule. Early in his tour, Garside had envied the pilots, but after finagling a free ride in a two-seat Wild Weasel, during which he spent most of the time vomiting breakfast into his hat, he had decided that maybe flying wasn't quite as glorious as it seemed from groundside. After the episode, his desire for combat ebbed and he settled into the routine in his own world. It hadn't been easy . . . and it bothered him that the pilots probably didn't

144

understand just how demanding staff duty could be, not because of danger, but because of boredom. Alcohol was the preferred anesthetic for most staff types, but he passed it up. Not good for a young staff officer to be tagged as a booze hound. The older men told him that this was war and nobody was watching, but he couldn't accept that. This was the best place to watch people and see how they performed. His method was better. He slept ... and waited for the time to draw up his own short-timer's calendar.

'Our objective today is to destroy as many enemy aircraft as possible. For this mission, the ground restriction is lifted.'

South grinned. Ground restriction lifted. These were sweet, sweet words. This time they could attack the MiGs in their parking areas. When the restriction was on, they had to wait for the enemy aircraft to be airborne before attacking. It was a stupid rule – a concession to politicians and, like most arbitrary rules, designed to cover somebody's ass in the event a Russian or Chinese facility or ship was hit. This time they'd catch the gooks squatting.

A buzzing sound filled the room as a movie screen lowered into place behind the briefer. A slide appeared. An aerial photo flashed on the screen and the pilots could see the layout of the Phuc Yen facility. Like Kep and the Paul Doumer Bridge, it was a target they seldom got a crack at, but each of them knew it well. Garside quickly detailed the location of MiG revetments, fuel storage tanks and an on-site ammo dump. A row of one-storey wood-frame buildings were thought to be troop barracks; they would be attacked by the Navy. Their birds were to concentrate on the field and its parked aircraft.

Garside hit the slide-change button and another photograph appeared, this one much closer and in more detail. A MiG was sitting on the end of the runway and heavily sand-bagged gun sites were visible all around the perimeter of the field. There were also several vehicle clusters that looked like small camps of silver Airstream travel trailers.

145

These, the pilots knew, were the mobile control units for the SAMs – Soviet-made SA-5s and SA-6s.

'As you can see, the triple-A is heavily concentrated,' Garside said. 'Mostly 37-mm – but there are two confirmed 100-mm sites ... here ... and here.' The lieutenant's pointer flashed in the light like a surgeon's scalpel. South closed his eyes and made a mental note.

'When were those sites confirmed?' Romero asked.

'Yesterday, sir. That's when these photos were taken.'

South leaned forward. 'Did we tip our hand?' He was concerned. Intelligence had a bad habit of trying to dope his big targets too close to a scheduled strike. The NVA had learned to react by moving their equipment into such areas. In effect, unusual recce flights told them where and when to beef up their firepower.

'Negative, sir. We've photographed this target eleven days running. They're used to us by now.' Garside understood South's concern. He'd been pinned against the wall several times after missions which resulted in losses. He'd tried several times to convince Seventh to be more subtle in their information-gathering activities, but generally they had ignored his advice and continued to schedule reconnaisance flights expediently. The pilots paid the price.

Garside's pointer tracked a wide arc around the perimeter of the airfield. 'Everything inside this area is free fire zone, gentlemen. There will be no restrictions of any kind this morning.'

The pilots reacted predictably. This was the kind of license they could understand, the kind there had been in Korea when everything south of the Yalu had been fair game. In this war, targets of opportunity were few and far between because of all the red tape that had to be waded through to get clearance to strike.

The lieutenant rapped his pointer on the side of his podium to regain their attention. There was only so much time to get this done and his time limits were no less binding than those that governed the pilots when they rocketed away from Takhli.

146

Wainright listened to the pilots and glowed. Usually these missions were accomplished in a morguelike silence, but today they were alive and buzzing, eager for the action. This was how the war should have been fought all along. There was no way the Russians were going to mash the button over the death of a few technical advisors. And the Chinese certainly weren't going to create a stink. You can't deliver nuclear weapons by ox cart.

The growing number of restrictions were obviously the result of an increasing national guilt and the wailing of a few malcontents and reporters who used the media to further their own causes and reputations.

He was also certain that Dulles and Eisenhower had been off-base in their domino theory, but even so the Soviets and Chinese were committed to creating pressure and tension wherever they could — as a way of keeping U.S. resources committed and wearing down the spirit. This was their strategy; not the annexation of North Vietnam. No way crusty old Uncle Ho would stand for that. He'd been independent too damn long and used to running his own show. Nevertheless the little bastard was taking help from all corners; for the present, assistance from Russians and Chinese suited his purposes.

It was a challenge. The American forces were fighting fiercely in each and every place Ho chose to stir up; but this wasn't the way to battle them, not like it was being done in Vietnam. You had to overreact; crush them ruthlessly. That would keep them at home a little longer before they came out of their holes to poke and prod again.

This war could be won, with or without the South Vietnamese. It was criminal that it hadn't been ended already. More operations like the Phuc Yen show were what was needed. This time Wainright's people could do the job they were trained to do in the way they were trained to do it. They were going to clobber the smug little dinks right where they least expected it.

'Pre-strike refueling in Orange anchor; tanker-receiver matchups are listed on your mission briefing forms. Route of entry will parallel the Red and Black rivers.'

The pilots groaned. 'Jesus Christ.'

'Quiet,' Wainright snapped. 'Intelligence believes that we should follow S.O.P.; by doing so we'll catch them by surprise. You people are constantly complaining that our routine works against us; this time it will work *for* us.'

Buggs shook with anger. 'I've lost three wingmen in six weeks,' he whispered to nobody in particular. 'Every damn one of them right along Thud Ridge.'

'Cool it, Buggs,' South said. 'I think they're right. Besides we've been following this route so long our airplanes won't take any other heading.'

'Gentlemen.' Garside pleaded. He wanted to restore order, but it was too late. South's voice was getting louder; he was taking over.

'What the hey, Buggs? You can't fly a steady enough heading or altitude for any of them seven-level gunners to get a bead on you.' Several pilots laughed.

South got to his feet. 'Standard procedures. Stay off the horn unless you've got trouble. Keep the elements tight. Standard bail-out procedures – and remember, there are no safe areas in downtown Hanoi. Any questions?'

No response. 'Okay "fell-hose," kick your tyres, light your fires and go. First man off is lead. Check in on Guard.'

South grabbed his gear and started to leave, but was blocked by the chaplain who coughed loudly in order to catch his attention.

'Padre?' South purposely used the term because the cleric didn't like it. South had no use for sky-pilots at pre-strike briefings. If a man needed religious gobbledy-gook, he should take care of it beforehand. 'Sorry to step on your foreskin, Padre.'

The chaplain, a red-haired major with a massive moustache, moved down the aisle to stand between the pilots. He lowered his head and clasped his hands together so gently that he appeared to be trying to hold onto a delicate butterfly.

'Let us pray. Heavenly Father.' Most of the pilots bowed

their heads. A few blessed themselves. South studied his mission briefing form. Wainright blew a perfect smoke ring, an exquisite 'O' that raced toward the ceiling, slowed and dissipated in tiny wisps, halfway to its target.

'Heavenly Father, these men are about to go into battle against our enemies and soon they're going to be very busy and they may not have time to pay much attention to You. But Lord, we ask humbly that You don't forget them. Amen.'

'And let no man be taken prisoner,' South added.

'Amen,' Buggs said.

South led them out of the briefing room. Garside watched the room clear, folded his briefing materials carefully and returned them to his leather portfolio. He closed the telescoping pointer, slid it into a breast pocket, and went back to his cubbyhole. He opened the middle drawer of his desk and spread the mimeographed calendar on the blotter. He coloured in a small puzzle section near the female's belly button, examined his handiwork and returned the calendar to its place in his desk.

'Eighteen more,' he noted smugly as he searched for the rest of the morning's briefing schedule.

Command Post Watch

Major Billy Ogden of Moscow, Idaho, watched Horowitz suffer and felt nothing. It was like watching a laboratory rat squirm in a vacuum jar after the air was sucked out, or a live frog writhing and jerking under a student's scalpel and not enough anesthetic. The vice-commander was perched on a high-backed captain's chair near the head of the battle staff conference table − a table not unlike those decorating the board rooms of the Fortune 500. For the moment Horowitz was still. Ogden was thankful for that. For an hour he had to contend with the chunky colonel shuffling around the room at double time like a ruffed grouse drumming for action, wringing his hands, popping his knuckles, flapping his elbows, sweating so heavily that what began as small underarm circles and a tiny dot on his lower back had grown and joined like mating jelly fish, leaving the entire shirt black and sticky.

Ogden tried to choke down another cup of lukewarm coffee, but it was no use. Three cups were enough to make him hyper; this morning he'd already had at least six and his kidneys were beginning to pulsate. As senior controller on the graveyard shift, he was required to remain inside his cubicle, protected by a thick clear wall of bulletproof plastic. Why this was so he didn't know and didn't care. What he knew were the regs, and for his own self-preservation he followed them — without exception. He was the main link in a communications system that could put the wing in instant contact with any of several higher headquarters spread from Thailand to Japan, or, with luck, he could even connect by radio to their airborne strike forces in North Vietnamese air space. For six months he'd taken his turn in the saddle, flying missions every day with the other Taxi Dancers, but when the position had opened in the CP, Wainright had asked him to step in, and he had been damn glad to. He was relieved to be out of the heat.

The war was a tactical nightmare — bad beyond belief — and his stomach had nearly disintegrated under the pressure of combat, four packs of Kools and three rolls of orange-flavoured Tums each and every day. Command post duty was no free ride; but its challenges were more subtle, and its risks not so drastic.

No way was it a picnic. The hours were tiring. Five days of twelve-hour shifts. Two days off. Seven days of eight-hour shifts. Three days off. Overall it meant a lot of time loitering in the dimly lit communications centre worrying about eight other controllers and their problems, not to mention last-minute mission changes, coordinating Cap operations when a pilot was down, making sure that the

150

field was ready for cripples coming back, and full loads going out.

Ogden was especially proud of the work schedule; he'd put it together himself. It was damn sound from every possible angle. It was designed to make the men think that their lot was getting better – improving – each day as they made their way through the seven-day cycle. It hadn't been completely his own invention. One of his sergeants started designing a schedule for a business course out of the University of Maryland extension. The deaccelerator had been his own idea – the key component. An accident. He'd seen it suddenly after several mistakes in arithmetic and it supported what he'd always suspected – that most novel ideas come from serendipity.

Something else had been confirmed, too. One of his officers, a captain, had done a staff study analysis of the schedule and potential application to other units. The report had earned the captain a promotion to major below the zone and a transfer to Saigon and Seventh where he'd have a hell of a lot more opportunity to pick up a senior sponsor to ride to higher ranks. The situation still bothered Ogden. He tried to tell himself that he'd learned something from it – never let a good idea slip by through inactivity. Promote your ideas. Championing your ideas was as important as creating them. He tried to convince himself that there'd be more opportunity, new chances to capitalize on. Nonetheless there was a large part of him that kept telling him that he'd missed out. The millionaire's proxy had come knocking on the door and he'd been out. It just didn't seem right – especially when Wainright had written up the captain for a bronze star for pushing papers, while the pilots were shedding blood to earn them.

Wainright, of course, had been right in sending a medal with him. That was S.O.P. Get a man started off on the right foot in a new assignment, but a Commendation Medal would have been adequate, and far more appropriate.

The captain's good fortune had produced negative results, too. Now Ogden's men spent a good deal of their time trying to find ways to repeat the feat, and nearly everything they were producing was harebrained. Not a serious problem, but there were symptoms.

'Major Ogden — hey, Billy!' The senior controller lost his train of thought and looked up to see Horowitz's face mashed against the plastic.

'Sir?'

'Any word yet? Let me know the instant you hear — the very instant, all right?' Horowitz thumped his finger against the plastic like a pointer. 'Just as soon as you hear, Billy.'

Ogden swiveled in his chair and studied the control console. It had been a while since the last report. Nearly thirty minutes. He picked up a small yellow telephone from a box underneath and dialled 333, the code number, direct line to Lion Control at Ubon AB near the Mekong in eastern Thailand.

'Lion, this is Ogden. Right, Sy. Checking again. Yep. Blazers, Banjos, Blivets and Baltics. Okay ... right ... I'm going to switch you to the horn so hang on for a sec.' The major depressed a blue button on his console, returned the phone to its hook and turned up the volume so that Horowitz could hear the conversation through a speaker near his table.

'Okay, Sy — I've got you plugged in over here so watch your language.'

'How m'I comin' through?'

'Five square. Shoot.'

Horowitz signalled that the speaker on the battle table was transmitting. Ogden could see that the colonel was nervously tinkering with the volume control. No wonder he didn't fly. He'd be a disaster up in the Packs. Horowitz was a comedy to watch. He finally got the volume adjusted and immediately switched his attention to the zipper on his khaki pants.

'Fucking 1505s,' Horowitz complained. 'Cheap shit. Like to know who lets the damn contracts for this crap.' Horowitz wondered how many people had been mortally wounded screwing around with the zippers. 'Have they

152

crossed the Initial Point yet?'

Ogden leaned close to his transmitter. 'Don't know, colonel. Lion's working on it right now. You'll hear the same time I do.'

Wainright walked stiffly into the room and took the chair his vice-commander had occupied earlier. Ogden began to sweat. Jesus, he thought. Sy baby, don't blow it now. C'mon, Sy, give us the word before the old man starts boiling.

'Bill?'

'Rog, Sy.'

'We've just talked with the lead tanker in Orange Anchor Extension. All your chicks are off and in the green. They all took full offloads and their radios are working fine. Looks smooth. I have a teletype from the Navy reporting the gulf strike force off tankers in Brown Anchor right on time and they are now pressing north. Looks pretty goddamn good, Billy. Damn good!'

'Thanks, Sy. Let's keep the hookup and if you get any airborne contact, patch them right into us. You copy?'

'That's a rog.'

Wainright rolled the cigar butt between his fingers and leaned back in his seat. 'I can feel it. We're really going to catch them. Burn them right where they sit. Wish I was along on this one, right this minute at pucker time, just before the shit hits the fan. That's what you remember afterward, Albert, how tight it was just before they opened up. You remember what it was like?'

'No, sir. I put it out of my mind a long time ago. I don't ever want to remember again. I don't need it.'

'We've got to remember, colonel. It's our job to remember.'

'Hey, Bill,' the telephone connection interrupted. 'We're starting to get some dope. Gulf force is in the target area and Navy pickets are reporting heavy flak and numerous SAM firings. Adams Radar says that MiGs are taxiing at Phuc Yen and Kep.'

Wainright thrust himself forward in his chair. His palms were flat on the table top; a long cigar wrapped in cellophane

153

sat precisely halfway between his hands.

Ogden tapped his ballpoint pen nervously on the control console. They were really going to catch it. He was damn glad that he was where he was. He'd already had his turn in the barrel.

Eavesdropping

Banjo Two, go head's up on your left! Rajah, babes — got him visual; I see him, Eddie — let's break left now . . . No! Left, dammit. Go left! Hey Lead, you got company at your six low, climbing and closing — break right.

Dancer Four on guard. I've been hit — smoking bad, unable to hold heading or altitude, repeat sick controls!

Uh, Rog Four. Just a minute. Head for water.

Click-click. Okay there, Three, I copy you . . . the . . . ah . . . green hooch-like building at the end of the hammerhead? *Click-click.* Okay there, Three, I gotcha; let's swing to the west right here and cut back to the northeast.

Beggar Two, follow me down, I'm getting out of this thing right now.

Buggsy, that muther is swinging back to the east and he's picked up a comrade. Yeah, I got them eyeballed; no sweat, let's go right and teach 'em some chicken. *Click-click.* Roger, followin' you round the bend.

All aircraft vicinity of bullseye, multiple SAM firings, multiple SAM firings. Repeat —

Hey voice on Guard, shut the fuck up . . . we can see the goddam things.

Dumbass bastards always clogging up Guard. Burnhams check in. Two. Three. Four. Let's head —

Banjos, this is Two, we got sticks coming up at three o'clock — break now!

Hey, strike leader . . . you see the guns dug in near the

154

tower? Roger, guns. I have them in sight. Let's get after them. Negative! Still two hangars on the northwest end of the field; we'll take those while we've still got something left. *Two!* God, man. You got to pull up better'n that or you're gonna spend the night with Uncle Ho. Uh ... ah ... I uh ... okay, Lead.

Nash Lead, this is Three. I'm hit and I'm —

Three, this is Lead. You're garbled. Say again? Please repeat. Banjo Three? Save it, Lead, he's gone. *Click-click.*

Jesus, Four, watch that yoyo behind you. Who's singing? *Ah don't care if it rains or freezes long as ah got mah plastic Jessus plastered on the Daaaaashboard of mah caaaar.* Can it, Buggs. Hey, babes! Call coming off target there, Burnham. It's gettin' crowded up here. C-H-I dooey man. Sorry about that! Had my head down, I guess. Okay, *nit noy,* just a *nit noy.* Blazers, Lead. Let's take one more pass and cook some meat down there. Two. Three. *No chute in north quad, beeper but no chute. Streamer! Poor guy's got a streamer!*

beepbeepbeepbeepbeepbeepbeepbeepbeepbeepbeepbeep beepbeepbeepbeepbeepbeepbeepbeep

Beeper — somebody get a fix on that beeper. Four suck in tight, you're too far out, man. *Click-click.*

All Thuds, this is Strike Leader on Guard. Let's are-tee-bee eh-sap. Repeat, this is Strike Leader. All Thuds are to are-tee-bee eh-sap.

Two, this is Baltic One, you got some ... ah ... fire I think ... it's aft. Baltic Two has ejected. Good chute. Repeat, I see a good chute. Roger there Baltic Lead, I have Two visual and I'm going to swing down an' Cap him.

Negative Baltic Three. Negative cap ... Strike Leader on Guard. Baltics and all aircraft are are-tee-bee posthaste. Egress the area. Do not cap!

Sandies, this is Blazer One, Strike Leader. How far out is your force? What? Okay, hurry, babes. Nope. Unable. Sucking wind for fuel right now. Not left; you'll have to work your own magic, okay babes? Strike Leader, this is Splake One —

Hold on there, Splake One, I'm trying to coordinate the

Sandies. Let's move out now. *Click-click.*
Dancer, Baltics are outbound.
Orange Anchor ... damn ... uh ...
Orange Anchor, this is Strike Leader on Guard. We're coming out estimating on time but need for you to turn east. Copy? Okay eastbound turn. Roger. On our way, Orange. Okay, Blazers. Make sure you're clean and green. Shake 'em loose, gas is on the way.

Mixed Messages

Ogden felt a chill sweep over him as the preliminary post-strike messages began to clatter in from Lion on the tele-type, and by direct phone hookup.

'Billy, the radio is a mess. I think some of your people are down, but I don't have any call signs yet. Everybody up there is screaming at everybody else on Guard. The Navy say that four MiGs have been shot down, but that's uncon-firmed and you know how fucked up the navy is.'

'Okay, Sy. Just keep us informed as best you can.'
Click-click.

Wainright smashed his cigar in a stainless steel ashtray. 'Damn radio relays. Can't track anything. Kaput when you need them ... why the hell aren't our people following radio procedures? You'd think a country that can produce a camera that will show you the colour of a Russian's eyes from outer space could make a goddamn radio that worked right.'

The intercom crackled again. 'Blue Strike Force is egressing the target area, Bill. That's confirmed.'

Wainright leaned back in his chair. 'Good.'

'Billy, Sy. I'm hearing now that MiGs are in pursuit. That's not normal. Your people must've really pissed 'em off.'

156

Wainright leaned toward the intercom, which was only a receiver. He had no transmission capability. 'All right. This is what I want,' he said into the device. 'You'll have to take them into Laos, South. Suck them out after you, then *turn on them*.' The wing commander was forward on the lip of his chair, his hands clasped so tightly that the knuckles showed white. Ogden stared in disbelief.

'Billy, Sy again. All quiet now. They must be clear and running for their tankers. Cap force is executed and inbound – bet they don't get too many out. They're too far north. Get maybe one sweep through the area. No more than that. No good in the Hanoi area. No good at all.'

Wainright lit another cigar and walked toward Ogden's Plexiglas cocoon. 'Major. Call SAC at Utapao. I want to patch through to their tankers.'

'Working on it already,' Ogden said quickly. He'd already talked with the SAC command post a hundred miles south of Bangkok. Just in case. He'd hoped that he could've made the suggestion – to show Wainright how efficient he could be under pressure. But the colonel had been too fast and robbed him of his chance. At least he'd see how fast he could work. That would be worth some points. The phone rang.

'Spider Control.'

'Spider, Colonel Wainright wants to talk to our people. Can you patch us through your tanks? Rog, Orange Anchor Extension. We'll stand by until you get it set.' Damn SAC assholes. Everybody at war except them. Peace is Our Profession. Horseshit motto for horseshit people. Why the hell don't they hurry?

Ogden was getting uneasy with Wainright pacing back and forth in front of him. Through the distortion of the plastic, the wing commander looked like a catfish vacuuming for algae.

'What? Colonel Wainright, this SAC weenie says they can't get through. He recommends we try a patch through Udorn.'

Wainright slapped the wall, his face bright red. 'For

157

Christ's sake — tell the bastards to work an HF contact — and signal them it's a priority.'

'Hey, my boss up here is venting his fuel load. We've just put sixteen birds through hell and he's wide-eyed,' Ogden whispered, even though the two colonels couldn't hear him. Surely the SAC people had been in tight situations. Couldn't they understand that his job was on the line? 'What? You can?' Thank God. 'Okay babes, put it through — and I owe you guys a brew or ten.' He nodded at Wainright to let him know, but the colonel banged his fists against the plastic again.

'What the hell's going on?'

Ogden hung up and reached for a yellow telephone. He pointed at the speaker on the battle staff table. Wainright looked puzzled for a moment, then turned and moved away from the console.

'Lion — hey, Sy, clear the line. Thanks for your help.' Ogden quickly dialled the unit's eight-digit priority code as he transferred the system back to the speakers. The code tied their communication system into a powerful radio-relaying complex in Bangkok which could raise any aircraft in the theatre at any time. The tankers, they hoped, would be about to get South on the frequency so that Wainright could talk directly to him.

'Orange Anchor Seven-one, this is Spider Control on Guard. Please come up 327.5.' C'mon, you bastards, get on the horn, he thought.

'Spider, this is Orange Anchor.' The words were faint.

'Orange, this is Spider Control. You are two by five. Jack it up.'

'Roger, Spider. We're—'

'Orange Anchor, your transmissions are badly broken. You are garbled. Copy?' Ogden adjusted the volume on his receiver.

'Roger, Spider. How do you read Orange Anchor now?' The voice was louder, but still raspy. 'Spider, our chicks are coming in now — about three miles out. If we break off for a few minutes it'll be because we're trying to join up.

We've got some weather up here and some of your birds aren't handling too well. You copy us there, Spider Control?'

'Roger. Go ahead and hook up and give us a callback. We'll stand by.'

Click-click. 'Thank ya, Spider.'

Five minutes passed with no further transmissions. Ogden, Wainright and Horowitz kept to themselves. Ogden thought about the people who were down. He'd been there himself. It had been dusk when he'd parachuted into the trees on a small hillock. He had released his harness and scrambled on all fours into the thickest foliage he could find. After dark, he'd made his way to higher ground and dug in. The next morning, at sunrise, he made voice contact with the Skyraider pilots who raked the area with machine-gun fire and led in the Jolly Green Giant choppers. The minnowlike CH-3C hovered over him, almost nervously, as he watched the rescue loop spin slowly down toward him. He let it touch the ground, to clear it of static electricity, slid the loop over his head and under his armpits and signalled thumbs-up to the pararescue man looking down at him from the open hatch near the winch.

The chopper bolted into forward flight before he had been winched halfway up. Below the ridge he could see North Vietnamese firing at them, but an AIE swung low and tore up the ground with machine-gun bullets and the shooting ceased.

Initially he had been certain that the bailout hadn't affected him but two weeks later he was jolted by a 37-mm burst northwest of Vinh and he had frozen. He was sure that he was going down again and it kept running through his mind that this time they wouldn't pick him up. Luckily his wingman had screamed at him, jarred him out of the spell, and he had nursed his bird home. When Wainright came through with the Command Post assignment, he'd pounced on it. You push your luck only so far. Now others were down and he wondered what kind of luck they'd have.

'Spider Control, this is Orange Anchor Seven-one. We've got receivers in tow and we're headed for home.'

'How many souls?'

'Eleven, but two or three are in rough shape. Can't say whether they'll make it.'

'What's your position?'

'Ah ... just a minute, Spider. My nav has us about seventy-five northeast of Luang Prabang.' Ogden computed the distance on a wall chart. They were still a good forty minutes away.

Wainright hunched closer to his speaker. 'Orange Anchor, can you get Blazer One up this frequency?'

'We'll give it a try, Spider ... sir.' Ogden smiled. The damn SAC bugaboo for courtesy. Six miles above the earth at six hundred miles per hour, but still it had to be 'sir'. Nuclear nice guys in starched green tuxedos, silk scarves and buttons on their baseball hats that proclaimed, 'Kill a Commie for Christ.'

'Spider, I just got off the line with Blazer One. Says he's kind of busy right now; he'll brief you when he gets home.'

Wainright grabbed the transmitter and shouted into it: 'Orange Anchor, this is Spider *One*. You tell Blazer to come up on this frequency *now*. You copy, Orange?'

'Give it a try, sir.'

A steady low burst of tone filled the speakers. Ogden played with his controls, but couldn't reestablish contact. 'Patch is out, colonel. Dead. You want me to put it through again?'

'South!' Wainright hissed.

'He is busy,' Horowitz said in the pilot's defence. 'He's trying to hold them together.'

'They've all been through this before. We've had losses before. They're supposed to be professionals. They don't need a goddamn mother hen. If the planes hold together, they fly. If not, they get out.'

'Yes, but ...'

'Shut up, Al.'

'Colonel Wainright.' Ogden waved another telephone at the wing commander. 'I've got some information, sir. Six of ours down, not five. Three cripples and two of them are

160

pretty bad.'

'What about BDA? Is there a mission report?'

Ogden shook his head. 'I reckon recce went in on their heels. Probably launch more sorties in an hour or so. We should have word from South before recce can process the photos.'

Wainright pushed his wheel hat down tight and started for the door. 'Call Udorn, major. I want their photos as soon as they're processed.' Ogden grabbed for the phone. 'We've got to know how many MiGs we've got, Albert. That's crucial right now. You stay on top of it. I'll be in my office so let me know immediately,' the wing commander said as he pushed open the heavy metal door that guarded the command post.

Odgen waited until the wing commander was gone before saying anything. 'Colonel, Udorn says they'll get right on it, but they said to remind you that gun cameras are primary confirmation on MiG kills.'

'Only when they're airborne, Billy. Call the tower and approach control. Brief them. Get everybody alerted. If South is crippled, I hope he can hold together long enough to get the rest in. I don't want one of them tearing up the runway. Get their fuel status — tell approach control to get that first. If we have to overfly and recover into Don Muang or Khorat, I want to know early. Get SAC on the horn and tell them we need a tanker holding near Khorat — just in case. They can pull one out of the lower anchors.

'Get Maintenance. I want all passes cancelled. Everybody on alert as of right now. We may need them to put our people up tomorrow.' Had he covered all the bases? It was up to him. Wainright was gone; it was up to him to get them home and ready to fight again.

Hanging On

South arched his back in his parachute harness and wiped at the sweat rivulets trickling from his temples and hair into the corners of his eyes. 'Damn.'

'What's the haps, Lead?' Buggs was still giddy – his normal post-strike euphoria. Going into strikes he was near catatonic; you could hardly get him to make necessary radio calls. Coming out, when the pressure was off, he was plagued by diarrhea of the mouth. A number of times South had been forced to come down hard on him so that others could concentrate, but this time he was too busy with his own problems to worry about Buggs' bad habits. Besides, when they got home the euphoria would fade into post-strike phase two – light depression. Every man had his ways and most of them, including Buggs, were predictable. South was attuned to all of them because a break in habit might signal a problem. He took pride in knowing the others and in listening carefully. Often what he didn't hear was as important as what he heard.

'Oil pressure's fluctuating,' South said in simple explanation.

'Dropping?'

'Not sure yet. Too soon. Fluctuating like a Polish steeplejack – down two steps, up one. Have to let it settle.'

'Might be the gauge,' Buggs offered.

'Um, don't think so,' South came back. As soon as he noticed the oil pressure dipping below thirty-five pounds per square inch, South had briefly extended his speed brakes as a check. The needle danced. He knew then that the gauge was functioning properly. Something else was wrong. Maybe a leak in the reservoir or in one of the many miles of tubing. Somewhere in his Thud, oil was draining out of the system and without lubrication the engine bearings would eventually disintegrate and freeze the engine. As soon as he knew that the gauge was operative, he realized there was a good chance he wasn't going to make it back to Takhli. He felt oddly calm.

One part of his mind held out on the side of luck, while the more dispassionate side told him to prepare for the inevitable. If it was a small leak, the engine might hold together long enough to make it home ... but that was a big *maybe*. Depending on luck, he reminded himself, was stupid and weak – not the smart choice. Ejecting was part of the job; he'd done it before, so why ignore the obvious? He began to get ready even before Buggs noticed that something might be wrong.

Buggs had been watching South's aircraft for several minutes. There were several small holes in the vertical stabilizer and a piece of aluminium the size of a *Bangkok Times* was flapping in the slipstream. Even so, there was no visible leakage, nothing venting into the sky leaving a telltale green skidmark on the metal or blue contrail in the sky. 'What now, Lead?'

South pulled back his throttle, checked to his right to make sure he was clear of the others and banked slowly to slip away from the rest of the element. 'Buggs, I'm gonna slow this muther down and fall back. Maybe I can hold it together long enough to get it home.'

'Rog, I'll take your wing.'

'Negative. Take them home. If I have to step out, at least it'll be over friendly territory.' South grinned beneath his oxygen mask. Friendly country! The triple canopy of jungle and thick underbrush glued to steep limestone ridges below him were anything but hospitable. 'After I slow this hog down, my fuel's going to be in pretty good shape, so inform Takhli Approach that I'll be the last one in.'

'Roger – but last man buys.'

'Gladly,' South said sullenly. Already the other elements were beginning to pull away from him and he felt relieved to be rid of the responsibility. Now he could concentrate

163

on his own problem. Dropping back wouldn't solve it, but it might just delay it. In any event, he was alone and that's the way it was meant to be in an airplane. Flying was safest and best when you were by yourself. Wars should be fought by single aircraft – drifting on thermals in the night like owls, waiting to plummet earthward and strike. Real flying was being alone in the bird, inside the machine, feeling the surge of the engine, aglow in the soft red lights with nothing but a blue-black sky above and a pegboard of white stars diffused by the curvature of the canopy.

A buzz in his earphones forced him to refocus his attention on the cockpit. He reduced the squelch on the UHF receiver and scanned the forward instrument panel, his eyes intent on the oil pressure and tach gauges. It was strange, he thought, how a human being could be so comfortable inside a machine.

He was the robot in *The Day the Earth Stood Still* – standing smugly before the army, knowing his own power, that they were at his mercy. It was the power of the metal, of the closeness and compactness of having your whole world within reach. It was seeing yourself reflected in the radar scope, the sun visor snug against the latex mask – the face of an insect, something sinister, almost grotesque – a perfect costume to add to the mystique of flying, the mystery whose secret was known only to those with the nerve to take hold of a machine and tempt it away from the earth.

As he watched the oil pressure needle wobble, South's hand found the radio and rotated the function switch full counterclockwise to BOTH and the mode selector to GUARD TRANSMIT. Now he could send and receive on the emergency frequency and every aircraft within range would hear him. There would be no need to change frequencies.

'Strike Force, this is Blazer One on GUARD. I am down-bound for angels two-zero, dropping back – save me some beer!'

He pulled back on the throttle with his left hand and

164

watched as his indicated air speed began to fall off. Satisfied that he was well clear of the others, he nosed the stick forward and set a moderate descent rate of three hundred feet per minute on the vertical velocity indicator. As he approached twenty thousand feet he eased back, flicked in a touch of trim, checked his heading and adjusted the throttle to new tach and exhaust gas temperature, or egt, settings. Now it was clear that he was losing oil; the pressure was down to 33 psi and, as the book said, the trouble would be nearly imperceptible in the beginning. But at some point it would take off like a downhill skier and race toward the inevitable conclusion. He reminded himself of the importance of keeping a firm grip on the stick because it would be the stick that ultimately would telegraph the end to him and tell him if the engine was really dying.

As more and more oil oozed from the lines, the bearing would encounter more and more friction and the aircraft would begin to vibrate. If the vibrations started, they would signal the end. He would feel them in the stick.

He was determined to get the aircraft home, not because Wainright needed it, not because the President might need it as a pawn in some cockamamie poker play to make the NVA negotiate, but because it was his job. You began by getting into the plane on a concrete sea and it wasn't over until you put it back in the same spot. When you took a bird, you did everything in your power to get it back and a lot of people had died trying to do just that. Even so, it wasn't as bad as the Navy. You didn't have to go down with your ship, but as a professional you were compelled to do everything in your power to not give it up until you were certain your life was in jeopardy.

Adrenalin flooded South's body. He was hyper-alert, sensitive to every sound. The nine-ship formation had moved ahead of him. They had lost six men and aircraft — too many. It was the worst beating they'd ever taken, but this wasn't the time to think about it, he warned himself. Don't make it seven.

Egt was creeping up, oil down to 31 psi. He concentrated

165

on the stick, but it was still smooth. How many minutes before the F-105 would begin to buck itself out of the sky?

How long before he'd become a politically embarrassing statistic? How long before the system would cringe at his name. South ... ech! Lost another aircraft. Jesus Christ! Don't those goddamn pilots care? The system was going to be upset and why not? It had a life of its own. Put together by people and now it called the shots. First job of any system is survival. Stay alive. Not much different from a person, he thought. Got to think of it as a person. That's the only way to cope with it. Frankenstein's monster. It had gone berserk.

Back in Washington, the President and his cronies gathered every Tuesday afternoon for late lunch in the private dining room on the second floor of the White House. Secretary of State, Secretary of Defense, head of the CIA, the whole damn gang huddled around some antique mahogany table grading 'sensitive' targets like schoolmasters.

Every week the Wainrights of the war forwarded their tidy lists of suggested targets. Seventh Air Force looked them over first, scratched off a few, added a few, and passed them along to PACAF Headquarters in Honolulu. From there the list was pared and sent on to the Joint Chiefs' intelligence staff. They sent the list on to civilian experts in the Pentagon who sent it back to the Secretary of Defense. Then State got into the act. Couldn't let the brass hats screw around with politically sensitive things. No, sir. Assistant Secretary of Defense shipped the list downstairs to the basement of the granite building where the computers could run it through the grid, determine mathematically just what the probable effect might have on foreign policy. After State sterilized the list, it went back to the Secretary of Defense who gave it to a Ph.D. from Princeton who put together a report card — Target Evaluation Sheet — for each item. There was even a system to make sure the TES forms got printed. Once a year. In January. Every January.

On Tuesdays, the Presidential coffee klatch trickled into the White House just after noon from various places in the city. Lots of hand pumping and smiles, South had been told. Flop down in the padded captains' chairs around the table and start grading report cards. They had to be careful. Suck on the sharp point of a No. 2 pencil and analyse each target thoroughly. What kind of military advantage? How many planes and pilots will be lost? How will the Chicoms and Soviets react? Kill any civilians? How many? Can we break down the number of women and children? The process took two hours. At the end they totaled the points on each target and applied a modified bell curve. High scores got hit first – *after* the President said, 'do it'.

The Secretary of State took the approved TES forms with him and from them his staff made out official authorizations on special forms. In hours the forms would travel down the chain of command, through the National Military Command Center to the Pentagon, across the Pacific to Honolulu. From there the Navy got its assignments directly; the Air Force in Saigon took its and distributed them to field commanders like Wainright.

McNamara himself set the guidelines for targets. 'They must improve South Vietnamese morale and bolster their resolve to fight for themselves. They must reduce the flow of material from the north and undercut the NVA will to fight.' About all the strikes did was make the dink truck drivers take a detour on subsequent trips.

Of course the system allowed for flexibility. That was an essential; it was imperative to preserve the on-site commander's initiative. If you were airborne and spotted a vehicle filled with troops you had a blanket authorization to attack. But fixed targets were something else again. They were the President's business, and his alone.

Now it was starting to tighten up. A few targets had been missed; a few fixed targets had ben obliterated without Presidential decree. Things were getting out of hand, so a couple of F4 jockeys from Khorat were court-martialed. Examples for other Yankee Air Pirates.

That's why the MiGs usually were left alone on the ground. The system had eaten six more people this trip and in a short time he was going to have an even shot at being the seventh.

The stick was rattling. Vibrating slightly in his hands. The sudden realization startled him. How long had it been going on? Jesus! He'd broken his concentration. He scanned the instruments. The mileage readings from the Distance Measuring Equipment were just beginning to lock onto the Takhli TACAN station and were chattering between 190 and 200, working desperately to find a radial.

If he could hold the J-75 together until time to descend he might have a chance. Shut it down and deadstick it in. Maybe they could foam the runway . . . if the engine would just hold together. Close. He had to get close so they could get to the wreckage and K-ball it. Need the parts. He looked at the fuel gauges. Running on fumes. Damn! Need a nice soft spot to put it down. Have to make it. His instinct told him there was no way. He took a deep breath and cinched the straps on his parachute harness tighter.

The Hard Part

Buggs leaned against the wall in the maintenance debriefing shed bar and rubbed his neck. It still ached. Tension, he told himself. You never really got used to Mr. G; you simply learned to ignore him and get on with the job. Mr. G is a curious bird. One minute everything is normal; then your arm weighs three hundred pounds and a simple task like moving a toggle switch six inches from your leg seemed harder than climbing Mount Everest. The mountain might be high, cold and starved of oxygen but at least a hundred-and-fifty-pounder still weighed a hundred and fifty even on the goddamn top. The worst part came later. Like the morning after a bad car wreck when you find muscles in places where you didn't know there were places.

168

Mr. G was a particularly nasty fellow.

'Me too,' Romero said as he loudly crunched the ice cubes from a glass of Dr. Pepper.

'Me too *what?*'

'Sore. And tired.'

A WAF who worked in the administrative offices of the maintenance squadron walked by with an armload of papers. The blue skirt to her uniform hung below her knees. She wore black leather shoes with square heels and toes — miniature combat boots on lifts.

'An hour like that might change my outlook on life,' Buggs said sullenly.

'Hers too,' Romero added.

'Right,' Buggs said. 'My old lady wouldn't appreciate me dipping into something like that.'

'Too ugly?'

'No, too young.'

'With terminal acne and hair you could use to refit a broom.'

'Michael me-lad. You're very insensitive to the lady. She's always spoken well of you.'

They laughed.

One of the intelligence officers came from a room where he had been meeting with other pilots on the mission. 'Hey G-2, they got a fix on Barney yet?'

'No beeper,' the man said with the emotion of a book-keeper. 'Chopper crapped out. We're taking some trucks up there. Launch some Jolly Greens from Udorn later.'

'Technology,' Romero grumbled lowly.

'Let's hit the bar,' Buggs suggested.

The Takhli stag bar was an exclusive establishment with a unique clientele. Technically any member of the officer's open mess could drink there, but unofficially (and no less binding) it was clearly understood that it was the haunt of the Taxi Dancers, those who flew the missions. The out-siders knew their places and kept them. Low profile. For the administrators, the weather men and intelligence briefers, the officers who directed mechanics and saw to the work of the photo lab and the myriad of other functions needed to support the three flying squadrons, the war was a vicarious experience and being close to the pilots was enough.

For many in the wing, maybe even for most, drinking was the main recreation, but being the competitive animals that they were, the Thud drivers took drinking to new heights, and lows. Dead Bug. Kick the Candle. Chorus Line. Power Bar. Child's play for grown men. Many of the pilots were scarred by the games but they played anyway. What was a few stitches in the arm from a broken bottle against a sixty-foot-long surface-to-air missile up your tailpipe?

Occasionally newsmen visited Takhli, especially since it was widely known as South's home base and because the Taxi Dancers were unanimously declared to have the worst mission in the war. The reporters came to hear what the Thud jockeys had to say about the war up north; invariably they ended up in the stag bar, drunk and disoriented, their notes destroyed. Most of them vowed to write about what went on in the club, but no story was ever published; the censors saw to that. Wouldn't do to have granny know that sonny-boy was letting down his hair between missions. It would distort reality and the perspective on the wing's real mission; or so went Wainright's argument.

How would it look if the local paper carried a story telling the folks back home that their eighteen-year-old volunteer was taking a military bus to a whorehouse every night and that U.S. doctors were checking the prostitutes every week for venereal disease? Not a pretty picture. Accurate, but not pretty. And never written even though the whore operation at the SAC base in southern Thailand had reached legendary proportions.

One night Buggs and South cornered a reporter in the bar. A little fat man from the *Boston Globe*. He slobbered when he talked and belched after every swallow of beer. The man had horn-rim glasses and a receding hairline. He wore a Hong Kong suit − still shiny − and penny loafers caked with red dust.

'You're supposed to write the truth, right?' Buggs was right in his face with the challenge.

'My editor wants me to write about the war.'

'*This* is the war,' Buggs insisted.

The reporter looked around the room trying to understand. 'I mean the real war,' the reporter croaked. 'You know, what you guys do up there in North Vietnam.'

'You asshole,' Buggs hissed. 'This is the real war. An ape can drop a bomb, but it takes a man to put up with this shit. It's what happens *between the missions*; that's the real story.'

'Feature stuff,' the reporter said. 'I write news.' In the end the reporter shrugged and went back to his drink.

Odd that he remembered the story. It had been a minor paragraph in a long chapter, time spent with a creature he instinctively loathed, an outsider looking in. Now Buggs wished the reporter was back so he could try to explain it one more time. Carefully. This was the real war, the hardest part. Waiting to hear if a friend was dead. Or worse.

Ejection

By the time the F-105 began to buck like a bronco on the world's toughest rodeo circuit, South was prepared for the ejection. He had nursed the machine and hope all the way from North Vietnam, but he had known from the beginning that his chances of keeping the bird together were small. When the engine bearings began to scrape and heat up, they would come apart and put the F-105 into violent convulsions that would lead ultimately to an explosion. He was ready; the loose gear from the cockpit was already stowed in various compartments and bags. What he wanted to take with him was either in a survival vest pocket or zippered securely into his flight suit.

While he had prepared he had carefully scanned the geography below, hoping to find a place he could aim for if he had to get out. When he had to get out. He had descended to fifteen thousand feet in anticipation of a direct penetration and approach into Takhli, just in case a miracle occurred. At fifteen thousand he could see what he was jumping to and maybe the airplane would land close by. In any event he could make the rescue effort easier with a little preplanning and he used the opportunity.

Reminding himself to control his breathing, the pilot ticked off the items on his Before Ejection Checklist. The gear was already stowed, but he scanned the cockpit again to be sure. A loose piece of equipment could shatter a bone during the ejection and make survival that much tougher on the ground, especially if he ended up in a tree, which was beginning to look pretty likely considering the terrain below. He reached up and retightened the sun visor on his helmet. With the plastic secure in front of his face there'd be less chance of losing an eye or getting cut.

As a precaution he checked his altitude again. Still fifteen thousand, but the plane's worsening condition was making it ride like the Jones Beach roller coaster and getting progressively more violent. It was time to get set.

He rammed his head hard against the headrest and tucked his chin in tighter than a plebe in a brace. His arms were on the armrests and his pelvis was snug against the back of the seat. Posture was critical; if it wasn't perfect his back would snap like a dry bone. He placed his feet evenly on the rudder pedals to keep his thighs down. If his feet slipped inward, which was the natural tendency, his legs would lift during the egress and catch on something as he rocketed out of the cockpit.

South was being swung from side to side as he raised the yellow-and-black-striped leg braces. Both popped into place easily. The good old next-of-kin sticks. It was time to get out. He focused on the instrument panel, gritted his teeth and squeezed the triggers inside the brace handles as deliberately as a professional sniper.

Nothing happened. For a moment he was confused. The triggers should have blown the canopy and less than half a second later he should have been shot clear of the aircraft. Fuck! Now there was real danger. The bird was wallowing and bucking all over the sky.

He reached for the auxiliary canopy jettison handle and jerked it violently. Moving quickly, he pulled open the canopy lock lever on the side rail. Canopy control switch . . . where was it? There. He held it open. Okay, cool it now, he told himself. Get the damn thing off. He triggered the canopy actuator release handle and pushed upward with a gloved hand until the canopy cracked open like a mussel, caught the slipstream and popped open. Fumbling, he disconnected the ejection seat firing cable. Goddamn, this was going to be a bitch! Manual bailout. Shit!

Hurrying, South pulled his survival kit emergency release handle, snapped open his safety belt and tugged the leg lanyards through his leg garters so that the chute wouldn't get hung up. No time to screw up, he told himself. No luxury this trip; everything has to be done right the first time. He unsnapped his oxygen hose and connections to his 'G' load until he got the plane onto its back. Now the ground was on top of him, directly overhead. He let go of the stick and shoved hard with both feet, with as much power as he could muster with aching muscles.

Cold air ripped at his face and the whine of the F-105 only a few feet away nearly deafened him, but he tried to concentrate and spread his arms and legs like a crawling baby to stabilize himself in a free-fall position.

He waited until the aircraft was well clear before jerking the orange 'T' handle with one powerful motion. Pffffft! The metal plate on the pilot chute popped free and the smaller chute opened and pulled the larger twenty-eight foot mushroom out of his backpack until it opened with a sharp crack into a fat circle above him and sent a sharp pain tearing into his groin.

Should've cinched the harness tighter, he told himself, as he released his oxygen mask and checked to be sure that the chute was fully deployed. Round, full and working as advertised. When he got back to the base, he'd have to stop by the Personal Equipment shop and deliver a bottle of Chivas to his favourite parachute packer. It was one old custom every flyer endorsed. When he landed, the first thing he'd do was fish the chute inspection report out of the pack and safe it away in his flight suit. But first he had to get safely to the ground.

The aircraft was behind him now, gyrating wildly and growling like a wounded animal as the engine disintegrated, screaming and whining in its death throes. He was glad to be free of it, of his outer skin, but he felt bad that it would end up in a smoldering heap of molten metal. It had been a damn good machine to take him so far.

Below him was a line of low ridges, green and thick, almost gray in the rising morning sun. He was going to end up in the trees again. Jesus! Just once it would be nice to land in a wheat field, a nice soft plowed pillow of earth. The land was coming up quickly, but below and to his right he spotted an open area — a swamp! At least it wasn't a forest. No damn trees. If he could slip his chute, make it drop faster, he could make it, he figured. He pushed his hands up the risers, grabbed them, and pulled them down to his chest, his arms quivering under the strain. Immediately the front lip of the silk canopy dipped and his descent steepened into a near dive.

By the time he had dropped below the ridges he knew that he had it made, so he released the risers and they snapped back into place. He held his heels together, refastened the bayonet clips on his oxygen mask, rechecked his visor to make sure it was locked, reached back up the risers and turned his head to the side, relaxing himself for the impact.

The last thing he remembered was a blur of green all around him.

Seconds later he was flat on his back. His head was buzzing and his flightsuit was soaked. The back left side of his head throbbed and was covered by a sticky substance.

174

At first his vision was blurred, but it cleared quickly. He was down. What was the damage? Wait, he cautioned himself. Lie still for a few moments. Take your time and assess the damage. Don't make things worse by crashing around like a bull.

South wiggled his toes. Okay. No pain. Full movement inside his boots, but there was water in them. He rolled his head to the side and stared. He had made the swamp. He was in a foot-deep pool of green slime topped with clusters of pads and yellow lilies. He tried to roll over, but his suit was caught on something. It was a stump — just below the water line. From the air it had been invisible, but now he could see that the entire swamp was dotted with them. The knowledge made him shiver. He could've broken something. If he had known, he told himself, he'd have put himself in the trees.

In any event, nothing was broken and he was thankful to be in relatively good shape. For the moment, that was enough. He unhooked the metal release covers on his chest straps, dug his thumbs into the tight cylinders and popped them open. He was free of his parachute. He rolled up to his knees and tried to stand, but his legs were wobbly so he perched on the stump and unsnapped his oxygen mask and chin strap. His helmet bounced off his shoulder and splashed into the swamp. He picked up the pieces and stared at them. He'd never seen a helmet with a crack much less one split in two like an egg. No wonder his head throbbed; the plastic brain bucket had saved his skull.

He fumbled through his left leg pocket for the cigar pouch, but was disappointed when he discovered that it was badly crushed. The cigars were dry, but he could only salvage a half-dozen small stumps from the shards. If he was alone for long he knew he'd have to ration them, but he had to have one to calm his nerves, so he picked the smallest remnant and lit it carefully. It had been near dawn when he tried to punch out, but now the light was beginning to flood the crests of the ridges. He was damn glad that it was daytime. Much better than bailing out at sundown, he

175

reminded himself. Spending a night in the jungle was bad news. He'd already been that route once and that was more than enough for anybody.

Inhaling the cigar smoke deep into his lungs, South studied his swampy basin. It was huge – much larger than he had estimated from above. Maybe five hundred metres across and oval-shaped. He was within fifty metres of a hummock of hard ground. Move to the high country, he told himself. Remember your training. Climb now while you've got adrenalin working for you. Don't wait; get moving. And don't panic. That's the Golden Rule of staying alive. Be cool like a poker player. Remember that poor bastard they told you about in Survival School. He'd punched out of an F-102, they said, in the Pacific Northwest. Landed in a tree upside down, hanging about four feet from the ground. Rugged, mountainous country. An elderly couple driving by in a truck had spotted the orange and white chute and had found the body. The man had drawn his revolver, stuck it in his mouth and pulled the trigger. Panic. Keep that poor bastard in your packet, he told himself.

It would be just like Wainright to charge him for any equipment he lost, South thought, so he rolled his parachute into a soggy ball, rammed it into the remains of his helmet and tied the whole package together with the chin strap and shroudline. Then he slogged his way to shore.

No way to fix the position, he decided. He'd have to mark it for the choppers. Using his survival knife – a specially modified bayonet – he tore away an orange and white, pie-shaped section which he spread out to dry in the sun while he cut some small bamboo stalks to anchor the marker.

Back in the water again, he anchored the sticks in the flat tops of the rotten stumps and tied the silk to them. The result was a crisp arrowhead pointing toward the ridge he had already decided to climb. He placed the marker well out into the swamp so that by climbing a tree he would be able to look back and see it. It was an easy way to keep his own bearing. Finding your way in the jungle, he knew, was a tough proposition. Any possible way to mark a trail or location was worth a little extra effort.

Satisfied that the marker would hold, even in the event of a hard rainstorm, South moved into the thick jungle. Nearly a half-mile up the ridge, he discovered a large clearing in the forest. It was covered by spongy red ground moss and waist-high golden ferns that crackled as he waded through them. Here a chopper would have an easy time picking him up and it would be far more comfortable for him than down by the swamp where insects congregated in swarms and the humidity was heavier. He'd fetch his equipment and establish his camp in the clearing.

On the edge of the swamp again, South surveyed his situaton. Takhli Approach knew he was down ... or did they? He wracked his memory. Had he followed the checklist? The Mayday call. That was last on the list ... damn, he couldn't remember making the call. He kicked the ground angrily. Jesus Christ! He hadn't radioed his situation: a goddamn stupid-ass rookie mistake. They'd know, of course, but they'd have no idea of where to look. Hero! he scolded himself. This would create a delay ... but no real danger, he tried to reassure himself, but something else was gnawing at him: if his instruments had been correct he should have cleared the hills and landed somewhere near the great swamps north of the base. Obviously, he was farther north than he had reckoned and if the F-105 crashed into a valley between the craggy ridges, they'd play hell locating the crash site. The situation would make a good film, he thought: 'Mr. Perfect Fucks Up in Spades.'

Eventually the choppers would find him; he was sure of that. But they could use some help. He could spread his chute out over the clearing.

South moved back to the clearing, spread out the chute, tying it down, so that it billowed gently in the slight breeze that seemed to be trying to build itself. Now there was nothing to do but wait; he stripped off his flightsuit and cringed at the sight of a dark grey leech stuck to his calf just above one sock. He knew he shouldn't pull it off; too much chance for infection. Burn them off, they had said at

177

Clark. Use your lighter; but he found that his leech was not impressed by the open flame and the Zippo was getting too hot to handle. The Chief swore that tobacco juice would work. Romero had been on the ground in Laos for five days and had used tobacco drippings to keep the leeches off him. Maybe it would work now. South gathered several shreds of cigar, mixed them with water from one of his baby bottles, and squeezed the rancid brown juice onto the leech, which immediately began to wiggle and squirm. Finally it backed out and he flicked it away with a violent thump of his forefinger. 'Asshole,' he shouted at it.

Guard against infection. He pawed through his survival vest in search of an antiseptic. He found a tube of antibiotic ointment which he squeezed onto the wound, rubbing it in with his little finger. He'd apply the ointment every six hours, he told himself. That would hold until he got back to the base where he could get proper medical treatment.

Satisfied that he'd done everything he could to aid his rescuers, South spread his flightsuit on the ferns to dry in the sun, and leaned back against a tree to rest. Already the pain in his head was becoming unbearable and the fetid stench of decaying vegetation, the putrid-sweet smell of the jungle, began to overwhelm him. He hoped he wouldn't be around long enough to get used to it.

No-Go-Cap

Charlie McAdams, alias 'Bucky the Beak,' felt like shooting his squat little HH-43 helicopter. Fucker wouldn't fly. Couldn't raise enough power to stir a cake mix, much less lift the squat little monster off the ramp. Ought to draw my Python and waste this hunk of iron, he told himself. Torch it off like won-a a them Buddhist monks in Saigon.

'Takhli Towah, this hyere's Peppahmill One an' ahm

178

abortin'.'

'Say again Pepermill?'

'Ah said Towah, that Peppahmill One is a No-Go-Cap. No powah.'

'Try it again Peppermill. Somebody stepped on you.'

'Ah said, uh suh, thet this hyere piece of tinfoil 'n' rubbah bans is awl screwed up lahk nubah tee-in. Yew copy thet, Towah?'

'Uh, think so. Peppermill. Understand you are a nogo?'

'Rajah, Towah. Yew called thet pocket. Let ev'body know now ... all-rat y'all?' McAdams shut off his radio, swung down to the ground beside his aircraft and glowered at his machine. Itt was the third time in two weeks that it had skunked on him. Maintenance had tried everything they knew, but even Loosiana Voodoo wouldn't help the bastard work right. 'Sheee-it!' he hissed as he walked away tapping at his holster. Wainright was gonna be some kind of pissed this time.

McAdams' crew chief approached cautiously.

'Again, sir?'

'Yaay-up,' the young lieutenant said disconsolately.

'How they gonna cap without our bird?' the crew chief asked anxiously.

'Not mah problem, boy,' the pilot said. Then he swiveled on his heel, lifted his left arm slowly and pointed his forefinger at the little helicopter. 'Pow! Yew piece a Yankee hoss-bleep.'

Trouble Under Glass

'That's correct. I need to talk to the colonel right away. Yes, ma'am, it is urgent.' Billy Ogden sat inside his Plexiglas cage and fumbled to light another cigarette as he cradled the telephone between his neck and shoulder. Damn HH-

179

43. Never worked when you needed it. Always crapping out. And why the hell did they have only one?'

'Sir? Major Odgen. Yessir. South's overdue. Right. Captain Buggs and the others reported that he was losing oil and that he dropped back to slow down and try to nurse the bird home. That's right. If he lost the bearing he probably didn't have much choice but to punch out. That's why I'm calling. We've assumed that he's down but our HH-43 is out of commission again. Can't get more than sixty percent rpm's. It's sitting on the ramp and that's where it's going to stay. With your permission I'd like to call Udorn and Naked Fanny and get a couple of Jolly Greens over here to help out? I know it'll take some time, but the only alternative to that is to send some trucks up there after we spot the wreck and that could be a tough go. Might take a lot of men.'

Wainright granted the permission. He was unusually calm, Ogden thought.

'Right, sir. Can't guess at a delay right now. Maybe they got something they can send over in a hurry — maybe not. I'll get on the horn soon as we're done. Sir? I also thought you might want to consider launching a couple of our own birds to recce the area. All we need is a fix on his beeper. That could save us time when the choppers get here.'

Wainright refused. 'Can we put one up without screwing up our schedule?'

'Don't think so, sir,' Ogden told him. 'We'd have to make some adjustments.'

'Then no-go and no dice. I don't want the frag jeopardized for a cap in friendly territory.' Wainright hung up on him.

Ogden studied the large chart on the wall. No spares would be available until early the next day and if their frag was upgraded during the next watch there'd be nothing available. Wainright's termination of the phone conversation made it quite clear to the controller that the effort to locate Byron South was in his hands. He didn't like the feeling.

Ground Pounder

By mid-morning South's flightsuit was dry, but his head was still aching and it seemed to be getting worse by the minute. If a search-and-rescue operation had been launched, he should have heard choppers by now. It had to be the Peppermill again: the little HH-43s just weren't cut out to do more than hose down a fire, which is what they were designed for in the first place. Only the Air Force would think of turning a fire truck into an ambulance. Every base needed at least a couple of Hueys but nearly all those were forward, concentrated at the bases along Laos and at Da Nang.

Just before ejecting, South had noticed several streams in the area; They ran downhill, in a generally southerly direction between the steep ridges around him. If he could get to a stream and follow it down he might locate a village and from there get to a road. This was prime timber country and the hills were supposed to be dotted with small logging camps. At least that's what the Chief claimed.

From his clearing South could see a cluster of tall trees on the nearest crest. They had been girdled by machetes — marked for harvest. There *had to be* loggers in the area. But he also knew that they only took the trees during the end part of the rainy season and that was still some weeks in the future. Even if he found a camp, it might be empty. Even so, he decided to try. It beat sitting in the heat.

The stench of the jungle and the continuing attacks by insects of various sizes and temperaments helped influence the decision. From experience he knew it would get worse and, if he had to spend the night, it would be downright unbearable. It was time to move out. He stowed his beacon in his vest, took a swig of water from one of his six baby bottles and started uphill, carefully taking a compass bearing on the high grove of trees protruding from the brushy crest.

An hour later his flightsuit was soaked again, and even though it stuck to his skin like wet paper, the moisture helped to repel the heat. The sun was climbing rapidly and would hang in the sky like an interrogator's spotlight. It felt good to be moving and even his head was beginning to feel better. He might be getting lost, but at least he was doing *something*. When things went sour you sometimes had to take things into your own hands. Do something, even if it's wrong. Besides, the You-Ass-Air-Farce didn't seem to be overly concerned that he was on the verge of a jungle camporee. There should have been choppers, but there had been nothing. It was unlikely that Wainright would release a Thud for the duty if the chopper was out of commission; they were just too damn short.

Oddly enough, in the jungle it felt almost like being home again. He'd spent a lot of time in the woods as a kid in New York, hunting frogs in ponds along the banks of the Hudson north of Poughkeepsie, spearing them expertly, carefully noting size and colour, marking kill sites so that he might come back again and find more of the brownish bulls. Sometimes a willowy whitetail would bound from its bed and he would point a stick at the waving flag and pretend to shoot.

His uncles brought fresh venison to the table each November and he devoured the tangy meat, looking forward to the day when he would be included with the men, to go out and bring home his own deer. The day came, of course, but it was neither as challenging nor satisfying as it had been in his imagination. It was a cold and dispassionate sport; one where patience took precedence over courage. At its simplest measure, it was nothing more than a very exacting method of harvest, not much different than going into the chicken coop with an axe. He found that he excelled at it and seemed to find bucks where others found none, but he saw it as a mere exercise in willpower. If you could sit and wait, you could be a successful hunter. If you used all your senses, not just your eyes, you could kill often. The trick was concentration. As simple as that.

Now, alone in the forest again, he felt the same serenity that had enveloped him during the hunts of his youth. Instinctively he sensed something moving slowly ahead of him, a dark, compact shadow in the undergrowth. He moved cautiously toward the form, stopping several metres away in order to catch a glimpse of it. He scanned the area slowly, finally spotting a patch of reddish-brown fur. An animal. Now he moved again, a step at a time, intent on flushing the animal from hiding. When the tiny deer could stand it no longer, and bolted from a bush, he shouted at it and laughed as it tore through the jungle, shifting gears and jinking like an F-105 on a Hanoi bomb run. It was tiny, much smaller than New York's whitetails, but if worse came to worst, he told himself, he could shoot one for food . . . assuming, of course, that he could hit anything other than a stationary human silhouette with his pistol. At the range, they blazed away at paper targets, life-size humans with black hearts printed on their chests. The time Romero had been shot down, two NVA troopers had walked within fifteen feet of his hiding place. South had later asked Romero why he hadn't fired at them. 'No heart painted on their chests,' he'd offered weakly to a chorus of guffaws. South wasn't sure he could kill in cold blood either − even an enemy. In an airplane it was different − much easier at six hundred knots. You gave it about as much thought as eating.

Below him there was a small stream, rolling quickly down a steep grade. Beyond, around a small bend covered with overhanging branches and a thick bamboo grove, he could hear the chatter of rapids and white-water. The discovery pleased him; it was the first water he'd encountered since starting out. He decided to follow it downhill. If there were camps or villages in the area, they'd be built in clusters in the elbows of tight valleys, not far from water. It was the same throughout Southeast Asia, they'd told him at Jungle Survival School at Clark. The school's instructors had been very thorough in explaining precisely how to locate people — mostly so that they could be avoided.

Two hours after noon, South finally found what he had been looking for. The stream had been widening ever since he started following it, growing from a rough trickle into a relatively wide, fast-moving swath of silvery-brown murk.

Because the banks were steeper, he decided to cut across a small ridge and when he crossed the crest he saw below him a very wide, nearly serene stretch of river. The sight of three elephants stopped him in his tracks. All three were wallowing in the shallows on the other side, blowing water on each other. Elephants, he knew, were used by loggers to drag logs to the rivers; he also knew that the jungles had a number of wild animals. If these belonged to a camp, they wouldn't be out here alone, he figured. Somebody would be nearby, keeping an eye on them.

He watched them play for a few moments and decided to cross the river. There were no tracks and no trails on his side. If there was a camp it would be on the other side of the river. He'd cross downriver and downwind; he didn't want to start a stampede with a strange scent. Beautiful headlines that would make: 'Medal of Honor Ace Trampled by Loggers' Elephants.'

After a quick hike downstream he found a narrow place to his liking, similar to a Venturi tube. It was too deep to wade, but he could swim it easily. Because everything was already wet he simply checked to make sure the snap on his holster was secure before moving upstream slightly to enter the river so that the current would sweep him across to roughly the spot he had in mind.

The strength of the river caught him by surprise. It carried him too quickly and he had to claw his way toward the other shore, a chore made worse by his broken helmet, which acted like a sea anchor and kept tugging at him. By the time he crawled onto the muddy bank on the other side he was exhausted. The bailout had taken its toll. The heat was taking him apart — that and Elise. What an hour they'd had.

After a brief rest, he moved back upriver, carefully skirting the elephants. Dogs he could handle. Cats and horses. But not elephants. Stupid bastards might step on him and not even know it.

Crossing the trail he'd seen from the other side he followed it uphill into a small valley and several hundred yards from the river he found a camp. It wasn't much, but it was worn and looked promising to him. At first it appeared to be empty, but after standing for a moment he heard a peculiar grating noise, a raspy whine from behind one of the flimsy hootches. Behind it he found two Thais, one apparently in his teens, the other an old man, wrapped in a brown-stained, plaid *phanung*. The two were bent over a large foot-powered grindstone, sharpening several dark-bladed machetes and small hand axes. Both of them jumped with fright when South rounded the corner.

He raised his hands, then joined them and bowed in the *wai*. The other two quickly recovered their wits and greeted him similarly.

Now all he needed was an interpreter. Damn! He thought of the pointee talkee and blood chit in his vest, but decided to hold back. After several minutes of trying with improvised sign language to explain who he was and why he was there, he gave up and decided that the pointee talkee would be better than nothing. He unfolded the silk and spread it on the ground, motioning for them to come closer and look at it. In several languages the cloth read: 'I am a stranger in your land. I mean you no harm. I am from far away and my government will give you gold if you help me.' The two Thais studied the silk banner for a moment, but South could tell by their expressions that it didn't mean much. What the kit needed was a literacy test!

Obviously they were more impressed by the embroidered American flag than the words on the chit; they clearly admired the bright colours. South gave it to them and indicated he was hungry by opening his mouth like a baby bird and rubbing his belly. The two bowed in deep appreciation for the gift, and led him into one of the huts.

It was sparsely furnished and reminded him very much of a deer camp. Several earthenware pots were stacked in a corner near a large urn filled with what he guessed was rainwater. In another corner there was a low table made from rough-hewn slats of dark wood lashed to bamboo legs. Kerosene lanterns were hung from ceiling hooks; rattan mats were scattered around the hard dirt floor. This hut, unlike the others in camp, was at ground level, its stilts only a foot high with the single room recessed. The other hootches were traditional and much higher — perhaps seven to ten feet, with rickety bamboo ladders hanging from narrow slatted porches.

The older Thai signalled him to sit. The boy disappeared and South stretched his legs — his first real break since morning. It was cool in the hut and immediately he felt drowsy, but he fought it and soon the boy returned carrying a wooden bowl filled with fruit and a small crock of sticky rice laced with greens and what appeared to be diced meat. He sniffed the offering carefully but it was relatively odourless. Certainly not fish, but what it might be he had no idea. Anything from dog to monkey, he figured. Or fermented lizard. The rice, although sticky and clumped, looked inviting and it was difficult to stop himself from eating it. The fruit would be safer. There was no telling how or if the meat had been cured or cooked or what the greens might do to his stomach. He'd had several tough bouts with Thai diarrhea already and he didn't relish another.

The fruits were familiar. He selected a thorny one which he peeled with his knife and ate quickly. The two Thais ignored him for the most part, preferring to study their new acquisition. South leaned back and sucked the fruit, enjoying its sweet juice and chewy flesh.

After devouring several pieces he felt his stomach tighten, so he took several pulls of water and wiped his mouth with the sleeve of his flightsuit.

Temporarily sated, he slid out of his mesh vest and emptied the contents on a brown mat in front of him. Three radios. The water bottles. His knife, pistol and twenty-five rounds of ammo. Compass. Signal mirror. Two packs of Cherry Blend tobacco. Wallet and check-book. Tree climbing device. Toilet paper. Two small first-aid kits. Windproof lighter. Water purification tablets. APCs. Needles and small skeins of thread. Assorted fish hooks and one hundred yards of black, braided fishing line. Several small wire snares for trapping small animals. Three Okinawan Habu lights. Some nylon cord. Several plastic survival maps designed to double as shelter halves, but no good for navigation here because they depicted areas of North Vietnam and Laos.

The array of gear was incredible because it wasn't much good without a rescue effort to back up the downed pilot. And it was absolutely useless in Thailand. Everything, including procedures were geared to being shot down or crashing over enemy territory, not friendly turf. Planners, he snorted to himself. Know-nothing ground pounders.

The Thais grew more interested when he began spreading out his equipment, but they really didn't react until he laid out his three radios and beacon. The old man nodded repeatedly, his dark eyes focusing on the green packages. He pushed the boy toward the door and moments later South saw him pedal by on a rusted bicycle, churning hard.

The boy's departure was cause for immediate concern; a warning signal buzzed in his head. This camp might not be all that it appears to be, he told himself. Lots of smugglers and insurgents operating in the belt across the northern part of the country, moving freely between Laos and Burma. He'd naturally assumed that the elephants belonged to the camp and that first impression had been borne out of bits and pieces of equipment strewn about, but now he was not so sure. What if the kid was fetching a bunch of gooks with AK-47s and Red Chinese relatives. He decided to clean his pistol. Shooting somebody from ambush was one thing, but if this turned into a hassle he'd protect himself.

187

At sunset the old man, who had gone back to sharpening his machetes after South began to work on his pistol, returned with another basket of fresh fruit and a bowl of boiled fish. The odour was overpowering, but so was his hunger; he attacked the thick white lumps of flesh, licking the grease from his fingers. He tried to chew to avoid bones, but there seemed to be none and the food, generously sprinkled with saffron, was delicious. He ate quickly, figuring that if trouble was on the way, this might be his last chance for a while.

As he finished, the old man came back again, this time with a thin wooden bowl that appeared to be filled with cucumbers. South nibbled tentatively. They were cucumbers! He wished he had salt for them, or vinegar, but since he couldn't talk to the old man, he resigned himself to having the food itself and he literally inhaled the fish which reminded him of black bass.

'Dee,' he said to the old man, who had settled down Indian-style across the room from him to shovel sticky rice into his toothless mouth with wooden chopsticks. The old man smiled and nodded repeatedly. Once he waved a bony finger at the pilot, then at the radios, and said something which South couldn't understand, but which he thought might relate to the boy's hasty departure.

After eating he followed the man outside and chewed on an unlit cigar while the man worked on his axes. South inspected his work; the blades were razor-sharp. The old man pointed to his survival knife and reached out. South gave it to him reluctantly. In less than two minutes he had it back, its blade sharper than it had ever been before.

After a while he grew bored with watching the old man and decided to explore the camp, but hesitated when he remembered the elephants. Did they stay by the river all night? He'd seen only the two Thais so they were probably left to roam free, in which case he decided that it would be smarter to restrict his explorations to the actual camp perimeter and its buildings.

He wanted very much to scale one of the ladders to look

into one of the elevated hootches, but the boy had been gone for quite some time now and he didn't want to be caught upstairs if he brought back friends. He contented himself with poking around underneath the platforms.

At one point he thought he heard the whirp-whirp of choppers, but after straining for several minutes to hear, he decided it was only the wind rustling the tops of the hardwoods that towered over the valley.

At dust the old man lit several lanterns that were mounted on poles around the camp and again returned to the grindstone. South had explored all that he could so he went back to the small hootch to rest. At first he stayed awake, afraid that intruders might come back or that a snake might crawl in to keep him company, but he was so tired that he fell asleep. Just before giving in, however, he tucked his pistol under his arm. If anybody tried to surprise him he'd get off at least one shot at the door and that might be enough.

He slept fitfully, dreaming over and over again about the bailout, remembering that he had forgotten to make the emergency radio call and had himself to blame, at least partially, for being in his present fix. In a kind of half-sleep he tried to think about Elise, but their meeting had been purely physical; nothing more complex than animal coupling. She had groaned and grunted louder and longer than any other woman he'd known and seemed to genuinely enjoy herself, but the memory of the session was blurred and half the time he was seeing a parade of women from his life — before Elise.

After nearly an hour of tossing and turning, of trying but failing to get into deep sleep, South realized that somebody else was in the room. He blinked several times trying to clear his eyes. The boy was back. With him was another Thai — or was he? He stared at the man, who wore Levis, heavy workboots and a widebrimmed Panama with a bright red felt band.

'Good evening, captain.'

He spoke English.

'Evening,' South replied, sitting up, rubbing his eyes

189

with the back of one hand while keeping a firm grip on his pistol with the other.

'You've lost your aircraft?' the stranger asked brightly.

'This morning. You find it?'

'No. The boy came and told me you were here. Why have you not been picked up by your helicopters?'

The man seemed friendly and not at all threatening, but South was edgy and determined to be careful.

The stranger sensed South's tenseness. 'Don't be alarmed, captain. I am Manuel Marques, directing supervisor for Incomnia Corporation. My company has a lease with the government of Thailand to cut the trees in this forest. I am from the Philippines.'

'You speak damn good English.'

The stranger beamed. 'Thank you. I was a member of my country's air force for nearly ... ten years. I was in the United States − at your Davis-Montham Air Force Base in Tucson. I studied radar electronics. And I was an officer. A captain ... like you.'

'Is this your camp?'

'One of several. We are preparing for *fohn* − the monsoons. There are few people in our camps now, but soon there will be many working very hard. My own camp is several kilometers from here.'

'Is there a telephone?'

Marques laughed very hard and translated into Thai for the others who also laughed.

'No telephone, captain. I have a truck, however. I will deliver you.'

'When can we leave?' South asked anxiously.

'Now, if you're ready − are you sure you are feeling well?'

'I'm ready,' South said, shoving his pistol back into its holster, but leaving the snap unfastened. They went outside and South thanked the old man and the boy for their help. The Filipino translated and the two bowed politely. He shook hands with each of them and followed his benefactor back down the trail he'd first followed into the camp. Near

190

the river the trail forked.

'My truck is parked farther down the trail,' his guide said happily, 'where there is a road — what you Americans call a two-track. Logging in Thailand is like logging everywhere. We live simply, work hard and our roads are bad ... but we have nobody to blame because we build them ourselves just like in your Pacific North-west.'

'How long you been in this business?' South asked as he followed along behind a bobbing flashlight.

'Two years. My brother and I are owners of Incomnia. I find it is better to look out for my own investments than to leave it to others. You agree?'

South laughed. 'That's how I ended up in your camp. I guess I was a bit off course when I punched out. When nobody showed up I figured I had to help myself.' He omitted his failure to make the Mayday call.

The stranger walked just ahead of him and South tramped along quietly, wondering how the other man could see, even with the flashlight to help. It was pitch black. It took them nearly half an hour to reach the truck, a four-wheel-drive Toyota that clearly had seen better times.

'You fly from Takhli?'

South leaned against the cab. Here it came. He clenched the pistol grip, stiffening his thumb against the scored hammer.

Suspicions increasing, he answered quietly. 'If you just get me to a town, I can call for help.'

Marques laughed and slapped his thighs. 'That would add five days to your journey. You know how the Thai authorities are. Especially our local *kamnan*. He will feel compelled to conduct his own investigation; after all, you will be the most important thing that has happened here in years. Then he will probably fine you for damaging Thai property with your aircraft.' The man stopped and slapped South on the back. 'No, captain, it will be faster if I drive you to Takhli. Besides, I had planned to go to Bangkok at the end of the week. A few days sooner will make little difference and I would enjoy your company.'

'I'm too tired to argue.'
'Your day has been demanding?'
'Ummmm. The night, too.'

Word Games

Romero and Buggs walked slowly toward the base exchange. Though neither man said so, the thoughts of both were on South. They had left him trailing behind them and he never arrived. Both were feeling guilt. It was a shock to the men who survived the mission and the news had travelled across the wing's grapevine at close to the speed of light. For now the two men were keeping their own counsel, not wanting to talk about what both were thinking and feeling.

'Ever tell you about my hometown?' Romero asked.

'Five thousand times.'

'Right,' Romero said brightly. 'Very famous place. Hereford, Texas. That's what it called.'

'Jesus Christ!' Buggs snapped. 'Can't you people learn the King's English? Not "*what it called*". You say "*what it is called*," or if you're in a hurry, "*what it's called*".'

'Right,' Romero said, ignoring the interruption. They played this game a lot. 'Cattle ranches. About eight thousand people and four million cows.'

Buggs stopped and grabbed his friend by the arm. 'Four *million*?'

'Sure, within a fifty-mile radius of Hereford. Beef is big business down there.'

Buggs shrugged and began walking again.

'Hey,' Romero said. 'They made a movie about it once. With Jimmy Stewart. Some English *puta* brought a bunch of Herefords down to Texas and she took a whole lot of shit from the longhorn people. That's the way it is down there. People don't light right up to new ideas. Like when

192

I showed up in my dress blues and wings: it didn't make them too happy. This is West Texas — about ten clicks from the earth's asshole. Down there a Mexican is supposed to sleep a lot and carry his tacos on his burro.'

'*That* I can relate to,' Buggs grunted.

'Anyways, old Jimmy Stewart hires on with this lady — foreman I think — and pretty soon Jimmy's stickin' his willy to her and their bull gets lost for the winter.'

'What bull?'

'The one she brought from England. Name was Vindicator or something like that. Come winter he trooped out onto the panhandle with the longhorn cows and they didn't see him again till spring. By then most of the longhorn cows were all knocked up. The Hereford had arrived in America. The end of the longhorn was near and old Jimmy and Vindicator, well, they were set up with a life's supply of poontang.'

'This really happened?'

'Sure,' Romero said. 'Saw the movies in the fifties — when I was a kid.'

'No, I mean the real thing.'

'I don't know,' Romero said. 'Been nothing but Herefords there since they let my family swim the border.'

They reached the entrance to the base exchange, a square building with thin metal walls and grey paint. 'Why you telling me all this shit?' Buggs held the door open for his friend. They moved down the first aisle to the section where stereo equipment was piled in boxes nearly ten feet high.

'You know those four million cows? Well, they're a real problem for the folks back home.' Romero explained.

'Man, it takes you forever to get to the point.'

'The problem is in the nature of the bovine propulsion system. Efficient as hell. They eat and dump on nearly a one-to-one ratio.'

Buggs tore open the corner of a box containing an Akai 1800 SD recorder and looked inside. 'Thing's busted. Score one for the quality of union labour. Get to the point, asshole.'

'Shit. Manure. Feces. Dung. Hoya. Guano. Steers eat about a hundred and fifty pounds of grass a day and just as regularly they put it back out through the rear exit. Heck of a problem. Say quarter of a million cows times a hundred pounds each, you get twenty-five million pounds of manure to be cleaned up every day.'

'That's why you can smell Texas before you can see it, right?'

Romero shook his head and toyed with a small transistor radio. 'There are some guys down there who got the idea they can make gas from that stuff and sell the gas to make heat.'

'Capitalism,' Buggs said with a sigh as he moved toward the magazine rack.

'Barney,' Romero said.

Buggs' head jerked as he looked around the area. 'Where?'

Romero patted his friend on the shoulder. 'No, not here. What I mean is that you got to look for the good side. Have the faith. If those crazy cowboys can see a fortune in manure, there's hope in any situation. I'm thinkin' that Barney's like that old bull Vindicator. Come spring, he'll still be hanging in there. No sense in worrying too much.'

'I hope you're right,' Buggs said as he reached for the latest issue of *Playboy*. 'Sooner he gets back, the better I'll like it. I don't want people thinkin' I *like* hangin' out with Mexicans.'

Bad Physics

Buggs watched light specks dance on the wall behind the bar. It was nearly dark. After their visit to the BX the two pilots had gone back to their respective hootches, but they had each found the isolation too much to bear and had drifted over to the stag bar in the O club. They'd arrived around dinner time, but neither had eaten and now they were engrossed in what they generally termed a power drunk – the kind of drinking bout that frequently ended with the phenomenon Romero described as the real-life, real-time intersection of the drunk curve with the barf curve.

For Buggs the light specks were a diversion. His real interest was the wing emblem behind the bar. He had been staring intently at the skull in the emblem for nearly an hour.

Romero amused himself with building a tower of flat toothpicks, the construction getting more and more difficult as the hours passed.

'Did it again,' Buggs grumbled.

'You're gettin' drunk,' Romero said. 'Stop lookin' at the bastard and it won't wink at you no more.'

'*Any* more. Don't they teach English at the academy?'

'That's what I said.'

'*Can't* stop,' Buggs mumbled. 'I'm serious,' he whispered. 'That thing *winks* at me . . . *See!* Did it again. Can't you see it? Fucker's right there on the wall. Got eye sockets the size of Carole Doda's titties.'

Romero turned slowly to avoid destroying the tooth-pick structure and examined the emblem on the wall. He was silent for a moment; there was no movement. 'Nope. It don't compute, Buggs. That bastard's made outta plywood and I never heard of plywood that could blink. It's bad physics.'

'Not a blink. A *wink* – like this.' Buggs turned and pushed his face close to the other man's. He winked slowly, several times, to demonstrate. 'See what I mean? A wink. Blinks are in—'

'Involuntary reflex actions.'

'Yeah. You can't help doin' blinks. But winks are deliberate. You got to want to wink and then do them *on purpose*. It's no accident when you wink, Mike. I don't need no Zoomie physics degree to know that. If your old lady winked at some gringo stud and you caught her you wouldn't swallow no shit about a blink, right? There's a big damn difference.'

'You're drunk.'

'What's that got to do with this subject? Sure I'm drunk. I ain't saying I ain't.'

'You want me to straighten out my English?'

'I'm tellin' ya that the skull up there is winking at me and if it don't stop I'm gonna rip that sumbitch off the wall.'

Romero stood up, grabbed his friend by the shoulders and marched him around the bar, arriving in front of the emblem. He pushed Buggs' face forward. 'Look. See the blood dripping out of the eyes? There's your answer.'

Buggs touched the sculpted figure with his hand and traced the contours of the skull's eye sockets with his forefinger.

'Now I know why it's blinking at you,' Romero explained. 'It's got something stuck in its eyes. Hell if it had arms it would probably just reach right up there and pick out the nit, then everything would be back to normal. It's not supernatural; it's a normal response.' Romero pulled Buggs away and led him back to his seat. 'Now, we solved that one. Let's talk about something else.'

Buggs cocked his head to the side and stared at the emblem. Then he turned and looked at his friend. A smile crawled over his face, almost a leer of disbelief. 'You are one fucked-up G.I., captain. Out of your ever-lovin' gourd. How in hell could a piece of plywood have something stuck in its eye? More important, why would a piece of plywood *give a shit?*'

'I rest my case,' Romero said.

'I'm confused,' Buggs said.

'In direct proportion to your blood-alcohol level.'

'I admit only to being maybe a little high. Tops. Not drunk. Not yet.'

'Good. We're starting to get someplace. You're beginning to get un-confused. If you clear your head and admit to being drunk I'll see what I can do about getting us a couple more snorts.'

'I'm drunk,' Buggs said with a wide grin. 'Smasheroo.'

Romero stood. He yelled for the bar to be silent and the other pilots turned to listen. With incredible dexterity he peeled the label off a bottle of San Miguel beer, wet the back with spit and stuck it to Buggs' forehead.

'Now hear this,' he said loudly so that all could hear.

'Cut the sailor talk,' somebody shouted.

'My apologies,' Romero said. 'Let it be known that Captain Daniel E. Buggs on this day in this year of our Lord on or about four a.m. local time with no fucking consideration whatsoever for Zulu time did log his sixty-seventh encounter on the conflict between North Vietnam, hereafter the Forces of Evil, and the U.S. of Eh, hereafter the Forces of Righteousness. Captain Buggs, like any old sweaty body in the cockpit, did in a calm and unaffected manner penetrate the hostile air space of the Forces of Evil and did destroy with malicious intent all within reach of his Thud. Captain Buggs' bravery reflects great credit upon himself and the Forces of Righteousness and those few remaining good guys in the world who agree with us – which, according to the latest polls, ain't too many. Ninny-event, for his courage I do hereby award to Captain Buggs whom you all know with some variance in opinion as to his worth the first ever Marvin J. Furphy Exemplary Conduct and All-Around Good Guy Medal.' Having completed his speech Romero snapped to attention and crisply executed a salute which he held. 'Speech,' he whispered to Buggs who struggled off his stool.

Buggs surveyed the pilots, coughed, began to speak, paused and grinned, picked up a can of beer and took a long pull on it. When it was empty he let it fall to the floor, wiped his mouth with his sleeve and faced the others. 'How's it goin', guys?' he shouted as he fell straight back-wards knocking over a line of bar stools.

When he came to several minutes later he found an im-provised ice pack tied to his head. The fall had left him with a small but messy cut on the back of the head.

'How's my speech?' Buggs asked feebly.
'Perfect,' Romero grinned.

Touchdown in a Toyota

South crawled out of the Toyota at daybreak and stared at the main gate to Takhli. A crudely fashioned sign was hung on a fence about fifteen metres from the entrance. It read: 'Through These Portals Pass the Toughest Mother Fuckers on Earth.' South felt the aches in his muscles beginning to intensify. 'With all due respect,' he said to the sign, 'I don't feel so tough.'

Marques stood on the other side of the small truck, his arms folded on top of the cab. 'Home again, Señor Captain.'

'Let's just keep it at this is where I hang my hat.'

The Filipino laughed deeply and walked around the front of the truck to face the pilot.

'Thanks much,' South said.

'*Nada*. I was glad to have your company on this journey. I'm happy you were not injured in your ... mishap.'

'As it turns out the only thing that's really bent up is my pride. I figured they'd have half the Air Force out searching for me. Just goes to show you.'

'Withdraw your hand from a container of water and there is no evidence of it ever having been there. So it is with a man. A very important thing to understand, you agree?'

'Asian philosophy?'

'Hollywood. Your Esteban McQueen.'

South grinned. Despite his early misgivings he'd come to like this strange man very much.

'Do you visit Bangkok often, captain?'

'Just now and then ... once a month maybe.'

'Have you met Mr. Jim Thompson?'

'Nope.'

'That is very surprising. You are his "kind" of man . . . Mr. Thompson is what you call an . . . adventurer,' the Filipino explained. 'Officially he is the leading importer-exporter in the city . . . but he has many different businesses, exciting kinds of businesses. It was he who suggested that I come to Thailand to look after my own business interests. The next time you are in Bangkok you must meet him. I will tell him about you, and you will find him very hospitable . . . with a special affection for flyers. I suspect he is in the employ of your CIA and its Air America, but he denies it. Big Jim denies everything. But I know that he has several light-grey flightsuits in his closet,' Manuel said with a wink. 'You must meet Big Jim.'

'Don't expect to get to Bangkok again: I've only got ten missions left until I head stateside.'

'A shame. You would like Big Jim. You two have much in common. Perhaps you could extend your tour. Others have done so.'

'Not me. The way this show's going I wouldn't make it through a second tour. In fact, I've got some doubts about this one.'

'You are bitter?'

'Nope. Just saturated. I've had enough.'

'Tired?'

'That's part of it.'

'It's a bad war, *si*?'

'The worst.'

'But for a good cause,' the Filipino said brightly. 'It is good to kill communists. In my country we still hunt them. Communists must be stopped.'

'We're not stopping anybody.'

'The United States is *losing* this war?' Manuel asked incredulously.

'Not exactly losing. We're just not winning.'

'I suspect that your superiors would not approve of your attitude.'

'You assume correctly.'

The little man sighed and extended his hand. 'I must be going. I pray for your safe return to your country and for victory against the communists.' South shook hands with him and stepped back as the Toyota roared away.

South paused in front of the gate; another bizarre experience. What had Hemingway written about war? That it intensifies experience. True. Politics might make for strange bedfellows, but it couldn't come close to the result produced by war. How else could you meet the Manuels of the world?

South flashed his ID card to the guard, hoisted his gear, and limped slowly through the gate. A hundred yards down the road he stopped to flip his cigarette into a huge stone fireplace. A sign next to the area read: 'Norman Morrison Memorial Bar-B-Que.' Norman Morrison was the Quaker who protested American involvement in Southeast Asia by setting himself on fire. In North Vietnam the Quaker was a hero. At Takhli his memorial firepit was filled with cigarette and cigar butts.

First Aid

'For God's sake, Barney. Stop wiggling!'

He pushed her away. 'I can't. Feels like you're using sandpaper.'

'Well,' she said indignantly, 'I can't hit a moving target. If you don't keep still I'm going to pick up the phone and call the flight surgeon — it should be him working on you anyhow.'

He sat up on the bed. 'You'd turn me in?'

'If you don't cooperate, I will.'

'Okay, okay, I'll be a big boy. I just can't stand you poking around inside me.'

Elise giggled. 'I don't have *that* aversion.' She pushed

him gently and he rolled onto his stomach. She went back to trying to clean the various scratches and abrasions, some of which already showed signs of infection.

'Amazing how fast things get infected here,' she said as she washed festering sores near his shoulder blades. 'That hurt?' she purred as he jerked under the touch of the washcloth.

'Hell yes,' he swore.

'This isn't going to be good enough,' she told him. 'I think a doctor ought to have a look at you – especially that cut on your head. You look like you took a pretty bad beating.'

'Not so bad. I can still sit up and take nourishment. Figure I hit a stump – or maybe my chute dragged me into one. It's not too clear right now.' He stretched his arms out and moaned. 'Feels like somebody used a sap on me.' She tried to get up but he pulled her back into the bed with him.

'I've got to get to work,' she said half-heartedly as she tried to pull away. But he was persistent and she gave up and fell back beside him. 'If you get your way I'm not going to be fit for work.'

'That's my plan,' he whispered, pulling her closer.

'This seems like a dream,' he whispered. 'I mean ... one minute I was upstairs trying to nurse home a cripple, then there I was in the jungle watching elephants play in a muddy river. It all runs together. A musty hootch and an old Thai who smelled like a bad belch – a crazy Filipino ...'

'Never mind.'

'It's weird how fast things can change. Snap your fingers and it's a whole new ballgame. There are all these people around here, all living *separately*. We all know about each other, but we pound forward all alone. We're down here making a war. Two hundred miles away there are people cutting down trees and floating them down the river to Bangkok as if this ... war ... doesn't exist. I don't think they even hear us fly over anymore. Manuel told me that if I had gotten into a town looking for help that the government probably would have charged me with damaging private property with my airplane. It's crazy as hell. Insane. Southeast Asia is an outdoor looney bin and we're all inmates. Christ, we're just like crazies! I mean we're fighting this stupid war very calmly and deliberately as if we were sane and rational.'

'You're in shock.'

He laughed. 'I'm beginning to realize that I've been in shock for months. This is mass hysteria. None of us know what we're doing. I get my ass shot down and I hitchhike home so I can get another bird, go up there and get it again. That's not sane.'

'War's not sane,' she said. 'It can't be. You spend your life learning what the limits are, the constraints, and suddenly they tell you to forget all that for a few months. Almost anything goes. Nobody expects you to be sane, Barney. They just want you to be efficient. The saner you are, the less likely you are to be efficient. These are the rules and even if they're not sane, at least for normal standards, they make sense for here. The only difference between this mess and the big war is that back then everybody apparently understood the distinction.'

'Maybe.'

'No maybe. Look at me. I'm on my way to breakfast and I see your boots on the porch so I let myself in and start taking care of you. You were *shot down*; you belong in the hospital. The Intelligence people need to talk with you. Those are the rules. I shouldn't be here.'

'Then, why are you here, for Christ's sake?' She shrugged and reached for a cigaratte. 'Maybe you were hot for my body?'

'Not hardly,' she hissed, fumbling with a book of matches.

Several minutes passed during which neither of them spoke. South admired the bruises on his arms and shoulders and the dozens of tiny cuts from his walk through the jungle. He studied her too. She was a strange broad, and as soon as he formed the words in his mind he felt guilty. She was unpredictable. Soft and pliant one minute; ruthless

202

and cold the next. After their first love-making she had summarized his life quickly: fly, drink with your buddies, and fuck when you can get it.

'What are you so smug about?' she asked.

'I was wondening about the aerodynamics of a brassiere.' She poked at him and he yelped in pain as she struck his ribs. 'Seriously, how do women with big tits learn how to hook a brassiere?'

'Practice,' she said, rising from the bed.

He tugged at her, but she fought free. 'Where you going? What's the hurry?'

'I'm going to work ... and you're going to the hospital. You need an X ray; I think a rib is cracked and I wouldn't be surprised if you've got a concussion.'

'Wait a minute' he protested. 'Why don't you check my helmet; be a crime if that little devil was busted.'

'Let the doctor do it.'

'It won't be the same.' he said. 'He won't give it the TLC that you do.' South tried to stand up, but slumped back to the bed. Jesus. His head was pounding. 'I don't understand this. The Souths have long been known for hard heads. Always thought mine was hard as a can-nonball.'

'Well ... it seems that your cannonball has been bruised, big shot. Your cannonball's really an egg and it's cracked.'

'Then the yolk's on you,' he chirped. She frowned and rolled her eyes.

'You're no comedian either.'

'Give it time to work. It'll grow on you.'

'So will a fungus in this climate. Get dressed.'

'Okay, but no hospital. Don't care for our sawbones. I'll get some coffee and wander down to Intelligence. I'd like to know what happened to my cap.'

She waited for him to dress, then held the door open for him. He gently cupped one of her buttocks and shoved her out into the humid morning.

May 3, 1967

Dead Bug: A Game

Many of the pilots who gathered in the bar after the strike stayed through the night. Wainright and Horowitz arrived late and for the most part were ignored by the others. Three Jolly Greens had been dispatched from Udorn nearly four hours after the crash and it had been one of the smelt-shaped HH-3Es that South had heard hovering over the ridges while he was in the logging camp.

Tommie the bartender was exhausted. It had been a bad night. Ordinarily good-natured, the pilots had been surly throughout the evening. Several fights had erupted and a dozen chairs and tables had been shattered in the various bouts. The baseboard along one wall was littered with broken glass. The mound of debris was nearly ankle deep in the area and still piling up as the pilots downed drinks and smashed their glasses against the walls. Tommie had seen them in foul moods before, but never anything so sustained as this.

Wainright stood at one end of the bar, hacking quietly as he inhaled too deeply from one of his cigars.

'Bartender,' he said loudly. 'You . . . bartender!' Tommie loped quickly to the end of the teak strip. Colonels didn't like to wait − especially this colonel.

'Sir?'

'Another one,' Wainright ordered, pushing a glass at him. 'Make it a double,' he added as the Thai bowed lightly and barked at one of the bar girls whose crime was nothing more than one of bad timing. Wainright tapped his cigar ash onto the bartop and brushed it off to the floor with the side of hand.

A lieutenant colonel from the operations section approached cautiously. 'Still no word on Captain South, sir,' the thin officer said nervously. 'They think they've located the wreckage, but no sign of the pilot and no beeper.'

'What about the MiGs? The film was sent over yesterday. Has the confirmation come in yet?'

Horowitz listened but tried to not be too interested. Wainright had been obsessed with the MiGs since the strike had returned. In debriefings they had figured a preliminary kill of eleven enemy aircraft, but that couldn't be verified without Seventh AF examining the gun-camera films and making further interviews with pilots from other bases who had been in the area during the attack. Wainright had been as nervous as a cat as they waited.

'Uh ... no, sir.'

'Where'd they find the wreckage?'

'North of the plains and the big swamp. Rough country.'

'Dirty bastard!' Wainright said suddenly.

'Sir?' Horowitz interrupted.

'South, Albert,' the wing commander hissed. 'That bastard South. This is no accident. No way. This is sabotage — you hear me? Sabotage. South put that plane down intentionally. He knows how bad we need it here and he sacrificed the aircraft to spite me. I know how his mind works. I understand him now. For a long time, he had me off balance, kept me guessing. But now I'm on to him, Albert. He won't get away with it.'

Horowitz flushed.

'Sir ... I don't think that South ...'

'Yes, I know. You're inclined to side with him and that's all right. He's fooled a lot of you people. Not anymore. That man has deliberately undermined this organization since he arrived. He has methodically reduced our efficiency and planted the seeds of a serious morale problem. This is my wing, Albert. Nobody is going to fuck with it.'

'South has done a lot for us, sir.'

Wainright smiled and patted Horowitz on the shoulder.

'True. On the surface, his value is irrefutable. But think about it. *Think* about South. What if you have an individual who undermines the morale of the other pilots so badly that they become inefficient? If that happens, then an average pilot, or the slightly better-than-average pilot, might look extremely good in comparison. What we have here is − is the *appearance* of excellence.'

Horowitz felt a chill and quickly gulped down his drink. The wing commander was talking crazy and the scariest part was that he was so serene. How could he conjure such an incredible situation? South had accounted for more BDA than anyone in the SEA − not just this wing. His entire record was one of excellence. He was a hell of a pilot − in combat and stateside. As for a morale problem, there was no question that South didn't help things, but it stemmed from a lot of causes, not the least of which was Wainright's own style.

Tommie scurried back with Wainright's drink. 'I come back *reh-oh reh-oh*, Colonel Wainright, sir. Bring your Salty Dog.' Wainright took the drink and waved off the Thai, turning again to Horowitz. 'Better get yourself another drink, Albert. You look like you need it.'

Horowitz nodded, and moved quickly to the other end of the bar, trying to catch the bartender's attention. Wainright walked to a nearby table and sat down. After several minutes his vice-commander joined him again and they drank in relative silence.

Buggs and Romero had been at the bar nearly 12 hours. Both of them had ignored the two senior officers.

The controller had lingered after Wainright moved to a table, stood beside the two pilots. 'You guys had a rough one yesterday.'

'Yeah,' Romero said. 'Pretty rough. You got word on Barney yet?'

'Nope. Choppers from Udorn knocked it off for the night. Going back in the morning. Think they've got the bird pinpointed. Maybe he moved off to get help. Probably left the area when nobody showed up,' he said reading their thoughts. 'We sent some trucks up there. We'll find him.'

'Yeah. That's got to be it,' Buggs said, not so sure of his own words. Anyone could get it any time he went up. Everybody understood that. It was in your guts every time you went to briefing. It made your hands shake when you started engines and it made it hard as hell to talk during pre-strike. It hit everybody differently but there wasn't a man who didn't think about dying every time he went to fly. Barney handled it better than most; it was impossible to imagine that he could be dead.

The phone behind the bar rang and Tommie yelled at Wainright, who nodded, got up and left the stag bar. He always took his calls in the privacy of the club office.

It was still early and the airman on duty jumped to attention when Wainright entered.

'Wainright. Right.'

The airman watched nervously as the colonel's expression lightened. 'Yes. Good. Get on the wire right away and put the confirmation on my desk.' He hung up and walked quickly back to the stag bar where he stopped in midroom.

'Gentlemen. I have just been informed that the thirty-ninth has been credited with destroying twelve enemy aircraft.' Horowitz hadn't seen him as excited since the day the paperwork had come through on South's Congressional Medal of Honor.

'I propose a toast,' he said loudly, raising his glass. The other pilots lifted their glasses and drank, but the bar was silent. Wainright emptied his glass and immediately called for a refill, tossing it toward a startled Tommie.

'Another for me, boy, and a round for everybody in here. We did a hell of a job yesterday,' he chirped as he walked to Buggs and Romeo.

'Damm fine job. Twelve MiGs ... you had a couple, didn't you, Romeo?'

Buggs stared at the thick-jawed wing commander and nodded toward his friend. 'Name's Romero, colonel. Read my lips: *R-O-M-E-R-O*. Ain't changed in the eight months he's been here.'

'Yes. Right,' he said clumsily, trying to cover his mistake. 'I know that. But the excitement ... a little joke. Just a joke. How many kids you got, Romero?'

'Five, sir.'

'Well then,' Wainright said brightly, slapping the Texan on the back, 'Romeo's not too far off, is it?' The captain tried to smile, but his effort produced more of a sneer. Horowitz sensed trouble and inserted himself between the commander and the pilots.

'Captain Romero was responsible for two of the MiGs,' Horowitz said quickly, trying to cut the tension.

'Two? Good God, man! Why didn't you say no? Bartender. Another round for the captain.' Suddenly Wainright snatched up a large plastic hammer and struck it so hard against the bar that the mallethead cracked. 'Dead Bug! Dead Bug!'

Instinctively Horowitz threw himself to the ground, hoping there was no broken glass underneath. Everyone in the bar except Romero and Buggs followed suit with less than their customary enthusiasm for the game. It was one of many they played with a rigid set of rules. The commander had the option to call the game at any time. Otherwise it was the last loser who retained the right by virtue of having bought a drink for every person in the club. When Dead Bug was called, everyone had to fall to the floor on their backs and extend their arms and legs upward, like an insect which meets its end from a deadly bug spray. Last man down bought.

Horowitz, lying flat on his back, had an unusual vantage point. Wainright was standing there holding the battered hammer like a spoiled child. The two pilots stared at him silently as he waited for them to fall. Seconds passed before he realized that they weren't going to cooperate. When he finally spoke his voice was soft, but quivering. The veins in his neck stuck out like thick blue tubing.

'I said, Dead Bug. Hit the floor. That's a *direct* order!'

Romero was the first to move. Buggs and South were

crazy. They weren't concerned about careers. Test pilot school at Nellis was sure to be coming and he couldn't take a chance on blowing it now – not over something so minor. If Barney was dead, he was dead. Their belligerence wouldn't change that. The living had to press on. That's what South always said. He slipped off his stool and lay on the floor beside Horowitz, carefully flipping broken glass away with his hand as he got down.

Buggs stared at Wainright and continued to sip his drink. Romero tapped him on the ankle. 'Forget it, man. It's not worth it.'

For a moment, Buggs stood his ground, but finally he relented and handed Romero's drink to him as he slipped down beside him.

Wainright's tight-lipped frown turned immediately into a wide smile. 'Hey – I'm still standing. Drinks are on me. Tommie, drinks are on the house!'

'*Reh-oh*,' Tommie chirped at the barmaids.

Buggs remained on his back staring up at the wing commander. 'Maybe I ought to piss on his pant leg,' he whispered to Romero.

'Naw. You'd probably hit me and I already feel as bad as I want to.'

'How about I kick his legs out from under him and cut his face up with a broken glass?'

'Shut up for Christ's sake. Too late to get back our honour. We had our chance and we blew it.'

Suddenly a commotion erupted in the dining area. Barney strode into the bar and up to Wainright. South yanked the hammer away from the colonel and slammed the head down. A few of the pilots, who had just gotten to their feet, crashed back to the floor again. 'Dead Bug, you yard-apes.'

South and Wainright were the only two left standing. 'You too good to play with these men, colonel?' South's sudden appearance and challenge caught Wainright off guard. Elise's sudden appearance behind the pilot startled him even more.

'I-uh ... '

'You're insulting these men, colonel!'

'What?'

'Just between you 'n' me and the walls, colonel, I'll lay you five to one that you can't hit the deck before me. You copy?'

'See here, South. Your crash . . . ' Wainright was beginning to recover his senses so South crouched as if he were going to dive to the floor. 'Dead Bug,' he whispered.

Instinctively, Wainright dove, caught off guard by the sudden command and tension. Lying on his side, he looked up at South and grinned weakly. 'You lose, South. You buy for the house.'

Elise joined South at the bar and stood beside him, looking directly at Wainright.

'Yessir, colonel. I concede. You can fall flat on your ass faster'n me. Got everybody here as an honest-to-God witness. All right, you pirates, drinks are on Byron South.'

As Wainright struggled to his feet, men pushed their way toward South, slapping him on the back and laughing. The wing commander backed away from the onrush, busying himself with brushing off his well-pressed khakis and smoothing his silver hair back. He had to have time to think.

Apparently, the choppers had finally located South. Now he was back and acting crazier than ever. It would have been better if he'd not come back. It had been a tough mission, but the results made it worthwhile. Clearly it was time to do something about the man. Not this instant. Wrong place. But soon. This should be a fine moment, but it had deteriorated, become an intolerable mess. Be calm, he warned himself. Leave it alone.

But South wouldn't allow it. He stepped toward Wainright and pushed him. When the colonel sputtered and stared wide-eyed at him, he grabbed him. Two buttons popped off his shirt and skittered across the floor like small flat rocks skipped on an evening pond.

'Butcher,' South said. 'For what? Everybody here has been bleeding. Everybody but you. You've been sitting on

211

your ass playing with your grease pencil.' His grip tightened on the wing commander's throat.

'For *what?*' Wainright struggled to get loose.

'Somebody stop him.' Buggs was first to regain his senses. He shoved his arm between the two men and broke South's grip.

'All right, Barney. Enough's enough. Don't push it, babes, or this weasel will ram one up your tailpipe. Wait till you get home, man. Get him through channels. This ain't the way to do it.'

South shoved Wainright, sent him stumbling into a wooden chair and table which collapsed under his weight. South rubbed his neck. It was beginning to stiffen badly. Elise had hold of his hand and was pulling him toward the door.

Buggs helped the woman push the pilot away from the room.

'Where the hell you been?'

'Fender bender on the highway.'

'Jolly Greens give you a lift?'

'Nope. A Filipino lumberjack.'

'What?'

'It's a long story.' They moved outside the club and South put on his sunglasses. His head was hurting worse now. Beginning to throb near the temples.

'Finally froze up?'

'Yep. I blew an emergency call. Guess that's why help never came.'

Horowitz joined the group. 'Glad you're back, South. You had us pretty worried.'

'You should've been with me, colonel. I could have scared the shit out of you.'

'You ought to get over to the hospital for a checkup. In fact, I'll drive and I don't want any lip. My truck's out back. I'll bring it around by the pool. Buggs, you keep him here. That's an order. I don't want him disappearing again.'

Buggs saluted sloppily and smiled. 'You can count on me.'

Elise clung to his arm. 'I'm glad you're going.'

'Hell, I'm not there yet ... but I guess maybe some X rays won't hurt.'

'You take a crack on the head?' Buggs asked.

'I must've. Don't remember it. I thought I got out without any trouble but now my whole body's a mass of bruises and sore spots.'

'Yes, well, anyway, you beat the old strikeout. Third punch out and you're still stumbling around with the rest of us sheep.'

'Odds weren't made for me,' South said with a laugh. 'I've been giving heart failure to actuaries all my life. I've got nine lives − maybe nine times nine. I might even live to be forty.'

Buggs elbowed Romero who had joined them. 'You hear that? Forty? Don't think I've ever known anybody that old before.'

Tumbling Gyro

With South and the slut off the premises Wainright had more drinks fetched to his table. After the violent confrontation, the pilots had pretty well deserted the area and it was just as well. Wainright wanted to be alone. He needed time to think, time to carefully analyse his problem, to be rational about it.

South could be humoured for the remainder of his tour, even ignored if that's what it took, but that would solve only a short-term problem. Now he was certain South would make trouble when he got stateside. Wainright prided himself in an instinct from such things, projecting what he might do in a similar situation as the basis of his analysis. Probably get hold of some Young Turk congressman hot to make a name for himself by slinging mud on the military establishment and its senior officers. If he had his star by that time, South's efforts probably wouldn't matter. It was his word against South's that the aircraft hadn't been operating that day. Despite what South thought, there was no proof of anything out of the ordinary. He'd seen to that. But if the star hadn't come, then there could be real trouble. They wouldn't promote him. The war was already too unpopular and undoubtedly would get more so. They'd back off the promotion; that was a certainty. It would be better, he thought, to think of South as a permanent problem, and that being so, a permanent solution was in order. It would be better for everyone if South simply didn't come back from a mission. A hero's death for a hero. That was something everyone could accept, something all could understand, and maybe even what most people expected for the pilot. The Brass would assume he had been consumed by his sense of duty, just as thousands of others had. The public would mourn his passing; another example of the high cost of a cruel and unjust war.

Evans had made it clear that his star was in the bag. A sure thing. A formality. His name would be near the top of the board's list.

Elise was a problem, too. It was clear that she and South had something going. What was hard to tell. Or how long. He'd been working long hours recently. Not paying much attention to her. She could have been screwing half of China and there'd be no way of telling. She had always been headstrong. It was time to change that too, or get rid of her. Either way, that part of the problem would be taken care of.

'Tommie, get me another,' Wainright cried loudly. He was alone in the bar now. The wing was already starting another busy day. Outside, he could hear the roar of jet engines as another strike taxied out to the runway. For a moment he considered heading for his office, but he rejected it. He needed time alone, away from the constant interruptions of the office.

The bartender brought the drink and Wainright chugged it down, wiped his mouth with the back of his hand and handed the glass back to Tommie for another refill.

'Another re-few-ring, cornel, *Reh-oh reh-oh.*'

'Think I'll sit at the bar,' he said, following the Thai. Seree and Soo-lee were seated near him, talking quietly. He smiled down the bar at them and they giggled nervously. It wasn't like the commander to be in the bar, especially in the morning.

Tommie brought another drink.

'To the Thirty-ninth!' he said to the women. 'Taxi Dancers!' They smiled at him and wished they could leave, but he was the commander and it would be an insult to leave him. He finished his drink and threw the glass. His head was beginning to spin, but he didn't care. He owed this to himself.

For another hour, the bartender made drinks for the wing commander who drank them quickly. He was sitting on his stool and visibly reeling from the alcohol.

Soo-lee shored up her courage and slid over to the colonel.

'Colonel, we must close up to clean stag bar. Tommie will not leave until you do. He has been here all night.' Seree joined her friend and slid her arm around the colonel.

'Colonel Wainright like to make love to Seree? You want short-time or all-day?'

'Huh?' Wainright didn't understand.

'She want to know how much you pay her,' Soo-lee interrupted.

'Pay?' Wainright looked dizzy. 'Why'n she say so? Minimum wage. Pay minimum wage. That's fair. Wha's mi'mum wage in Thailand? Is one?' Wainright raised up on the stool and fished through his pockets for change which he dumped on the bar and began to count with great difficulty.

Seree ducked under the bar and grabbed her purse. She signalled for Soo-lee to follow as Tommie closed out the register and gathered up the drawer. They moved back under the bar gate and pausing at the door, dimmed the lights.

Wainright was alone.

215

The money was spread out on the bar in front of him. 'Thir'y five dollars an' some bahts,' he muttered out loud. 'Got lots of bahts, S'ree baby.' He looked around anxiously, squinting into the darkness. 'S'ree.' Where the hell was she? 'S'ree!' He tried to stand, but one of his heels was caught on the bar stool and he fell heavily to the floor.

'S'ree? Goddammit, S'ree!' His voice wavered. 'I got lossa money. Good bahts money. All day at mi'mum wage. Okay, I know you got to sleep. Been workin' all night. Jus' short one. Quickie.' He giggled. 'Give you all the moneys for quickie. Right here good place,' he cackled. 'Nice dark place for quickie.'

Finally his voice trailed off. He strained to hear a response. 'S'ree!' he was getting angry. 'Lil'-Brown-Fucking-Machine. S'ree. Where's my LBFM? Colonel loves LBFMs, S'ree. Come here, let Jergen give you quickie in dark.'

Before he could say anything else, nausea overwhelmed him and he vomited until he was light-headed.

'Tommie? Ol' Tom? Hey! You hear me? LBFM. Funny joke ... Okay Tommie. You right. Jergen should go. Got work to do. Not good to get like this during day. Men might see me.' He laughed hard. 'Okay-okay. Don' nag. Like *her*. S'ree, you a nag? What? Uh-huh,' he giggled, 'jus' my LBFM.'

Wainright tried to sit up but toppled over into his own vomit. He rolled onto his side and closed his eyes. 'Time to sleep. Later S'ree. Don' bother colonel now ... hey South! You hear me South! Captain Byron South? I got news for you, South. Big news. I *am* channels!'

An hour later Horowitz found the wing commander snoring on the floor of the stag bar. He'd overlooked him at first, but heavy breathing had tipped his presence. Horowitz dripped sweat as he half-dragged him out the back door of the club into his truck.

What a fucked-up war, he thought as he started the engine.

216

In Check

South sat with his feet propped on his desk. He wore a faded green T-shirt and a Hawaiian bathing suit with a splash of colours that blended into a kind of murky purple. Elise half sat and half laid on the bed propped up by some pillows. A large, flat glass ashtray from a Bangkok hotel was piling up with cigarette butts. Her skirt rode high up on her legs and there was a long run in one of her nylons that looked like it had been gouged out by a chisel.

'What now?' she asked pensively. They had been back from the hospital for some time. The danger was clear to her, but he was in no mood to talk seriously. She'd spent the better part of an hour fending off his advances, torn between wanting him and wanting to talk.

'Ten missions. Then home to the You-Ass-of-Eh. I'm short.'

'Be serious,' she pleaded. 'That was a bad scene. He's not going to let it alone. He's capable of anything; I know.'

'What can he do? Send me north to get shot at? Make me wear funny clothes?'

'Barney.' She was begging. 'This isn't just another argument. You pushed him. You were insubordinate. And there were lots of witnesses.'

'There won't be a court-martial. Believe me. It's okay.'

She studied him for awhile. He had a smug little grin on his face. 'You've got something on him?'

South lifted his hands, held them out to her backs down and made a squeezing motion. 'By the proverbial and biological balls.'

'Tell me,' she urged. Now her curiosity was rising.

'It's between Wainright and me. I want to keep it that way.'

217

'Don't underestimate him,' she cautioned. 'I'm serious. Really. What's going to happen?'

'Predictable. I fly my missions. Then I go home. Strictly routine.'

'The future.'

He laughed deeply. 'There isn't a future here. It stretches out to six hours from now. I've got a DEROS on my calendar like the rest of the slobs in the wing but it doesn't mean a damn thing till the day you leave. My orders are supposed to say McConnell. I'm going to train new Thud drivers for awhile, but it can't last too long. Not enough rolling stock left. If this thing drags on, eventually they'll have to phase into something else. All the Thuds will be in building materials up north. What's the big interest? Aren't you the one with all the rules about no rules?'

'I'm going to leave when you do.'

'So sudden?'

'It's been coming for a long time. You've helped me to see it. I'm used to moving on.'

'Some place in particular?'

'I hear McConnell is a friendly place.'

He grinned and reached for one of her cigarettes. 'You are what the boys used to call "fast".'

'I prefer to think of it as decisive.'

'Not much future in tagging along with me. I'm a floater. No roots.'

'We'll be good for each other.'

'Maybe,' he said.

There obviously was something else he wanted to say. She could see it. 'A piece of ass isn't the basis for a relationship. Is that what you're thinking?'

'Not so bluntly. Maybe we ought to sit on this thing for now. Keep our options open.'

'You're turning me down?' She smiled weakly and fell back against the pillows. 'I've never handled rejection well.'

'Your problem is that you like to be the boss.'

'No different than you single-engine, single-seat types,' she shot back. 'Control is what it's all about. Take care of

218

number one first.'

'I guess,' he said. She had an air about her that was difficult to cope with. When she talked to you it was as if you were the only person on earth. Her presence flowed over you like some kind of invisible shroud. Even her perfume overwhelmed and put you into a kind of trance. There had been a lot of women in South's life, but none quite like this one. 'I'm tired of everything,' he added.

'Ah,' she said with a knowing exhalation. 'Male of the species wants to talk. Female antennae pick this up very quickly.'

He blushed slightly and reached for another smoke. 'When I got over here I thought it was the Great Adventure. Man's essential rite of passage. "Yeah, babes, I was in the war. No big thing." Like that. More of this I see the less I like it. When Wainright and I were back in the States I could see the paranoia. We're into a shooting war now, only nobody knows exactly how we got into it. Maybe there aren't any reasons. Twenty years ago Uncle Ho was a good guy; now he's a bad guy. Maybe forty years from now some bookworm will figure it all out. All I know is that I'm tired of the whole thing.'

'Not exactly your basic warrior speech,' she said quietly.

He shook his head slowly. 'Some warriors. Like punching the tar baby. Every time we hit them we hit ourselves and get tied into more knots. Hit them, trouble at home. No trouble at home, problems here. Like a snake trying to swallow its tail. There aren't any options here. It escalates, it recedes, but nothing changes. Sometimes I think the object of all this is to field-test new technology. Only machines can't beat resolve. They flat out don't care what the score is today. All they care about is the score when it's over, and they're prepared to keep playing until they win. The NVA are in South Vietnam. They say they aren't. We say they are. Everybody's missing the point. Turf isn't at issue even if you look at them as invaders. This is a war of philosophies. They learned from Ho who learned from Mao and created his own wrinkles. Hit and run. Drive the enemy crazy. We operate with one foot on the gas pedal, the other on the brake. Go-stop. Ho doesn't want to beat us; he can't. Never was an option. The game is a head game. String us out. Get us tired of it. Stir up the home front. Play the p.r. game.'

She pulled him to her. 'Worried about the last missions?'

'I worry about every mission beacuse it could be the last one for me. We bomb the same targets day in and day out. We take the same routes in and the same routes out. We hit at nearly the same time every day. We come from the same directions, the same altitudes and in the same formations. Thank God the NVA are for shit or we'd all be dead. There's so goddamn many rules about what you can hit and can't hit that you've got to have a photographic memory just to remember where the fuck you are and what you're supposed to be doing.'

He paused, radiating his anger. She put her head on his shoulder and waited.

South put his head back on a pillow and looked up at the ceiling. 'You know what kind of war this is? The Medal of Honor winner, your favourite lone-star ace bombed a hospital.'

She blinked. 'Where they keep sick people?'

'The same.'

'Intentionally?'

The pilot nodded. 'We were trying to get at a 100-mm site right next to it. We lost a couple of birds there. We were trying to get in at a narrow strip but this gun had it cold and they were clobbering us. First day I went in there and tried to do what they wanted. But after that I knew what I'd do if I went back. The gun was built on the corner of a parking lot right under a four-storey building. A hospital.'

'You knew it?'

'Sure. Briefers told us to be damn careful to stay away from it. They didn't want any acccidents − no atrocities. On my second trip I didn't even look at the target. I drove down the old pike and dropped my load right against the side of the building. Whole damn thing dropped right on the gun and that was that. It was an expedient. I'm at Mach I. The gun's pumping away. I just did it. Period.'

'And afterward?'

'Felt terrific. Fantastic. Damned hospital started blowing secondaries. They had ammo and fuel stored inside. There were patients, but they were just a front for the important stuff. The NVA made a real stink about it afterwards. Jap TV crews did a long documentary on it. The Russians raised hell in the U.N. The whole world was pissed off at the Yankee Air Pirates.'

'I remember,' she said.

'This isn't a confession,' he said. 'I don't think I feel any real guilt. I did my job and in the long run that saved more of our guys. At present our lives are more important than theirs. That's the bottom line of a war.' He stopped and looked at her. 'I sound like Wainright, don't I?'

'You're not like him,' she said firmly.

'Your opinion,' he said.

'He doesn't let people inside his head. It's off limits. I've been just a diversion for him. Something to do in bed and something to show off. A power symbol.'

'We're all pawns,' South said. 'And right now I've got that bastard in check. That's all I need to finish up and get out of here.'

She was not so confident.

Isolating the Part

Wainright fumbled with the intercom button under his desk. It was noon and his head was still spinning from the alcohol. Horowitz had appeared at just the right time. Only the Thais had seen him in his 'state', and they didn't count.

The memory was dim and confused, but he remembered the vice-commander dragging him to a truck and he remembered a dizzying ride on the floor in back. He'd passed out on the bed in his hootch, then spent most of the morning in a cold shower, drinking hot, bitter coffee, doled up one at a time by Horowitz. It helped but his head and neck ached now and his hands were still shaking badly. He waited for Robbins to respond.

'Yessir, Colonel?' the voice rasped.

'APCs. Four of them.'

'Two now, two later?'

'All of 'em now, and hurry it up.'

'Right away, sir.' Wainright flinched at the click of the intercom. Bad time to be hung over. The South thing was out of hand. Ordinarily Wainright suffered minimal effects from heavy drinking, but not this time. Stress, he told himself. His stomach was jumpy; he'd tried to eat a piece of toast, but it had come right back up. He'd just have to avoid food and drink until his body adjusted and the blood levels normalized. The past two days had frayed his nerves. Everything seemed to be dropping out from under him. South's sudden return had been the final blow. He had been so sure he was dead. It had been a feeling ... but it was wrong and that irritated him too.

It had gotten worse when Horowitz called to Intelligence. South, not Romero had been credited with two of the MiGs. That would make it even tougher to do something about him. His first impulse was to not forgive, but to forget — a path of least resistance. But South continued his belligerence and it had gotten to major proportions. Of the event, which is how he thought of the day he aborted a mission and was accused by South of cowardice, he was confident that the pilot had no case. He had said he'd been hit, but holes in the airframe weren't necessary to such a claim. Heavy buffeting would be adequate. The key was that the bird didn't seem to be functioning properly at that time. And only he could make that assessment. That maintenance could not reproduce the malfunctions was not unusual. And he'd covered all his bases with an ironclad paper trail. In reality, what could South do? Deep inside, he knew. A frightened voice screamed inside: eliminate him, cut out the cancer. In life you had to deal with two extremes; the truly evil and the truly good. The former were easier to contend with because they were practical. But the other kind, they were impossible because they would do what they believed to be right, no matter what the personal cost. These were the most dangerous of all, and South was one of them. Wainright didn't need evidence; his gut told him all he needed to know. When South got back to the States he would make trouble. He was the kind. That the other captain had made reference to it was proof that South had been talking it up with some of the other pilots.

And South wasn't the only one. There seemed to be more and more like him. Today's pilots were better trained than in World War II, better educated, and book-smart. But they were stupid when it came to understanding how the game was played. The problem was in the transient nature of the war. No dedication. With rare exceptions the new men reporting to the Taxi Dancers were not committed to anything but themselves. The war was one of self-preservation. Communism, the tyranny of large over small, none of that mattered. All the pilots cared about was getting home in one piece. He'd tried to understand their attitudes, but couldn't. He knew what it was to fear dying. But this was war and in war some people had to die in order for the mission to have success. It was the way and it hadn't changed since men started battering each other with their bare hands. South had no sympathy for him and his position. Command was a terrible burden. That should have been clear to all of them, especially South since he was just the type they liked to promote. You had to steel yourself against emotion: in war you made decisions with your brain, not your heart. During his time in Berlin, LeMay had told him many times how tough it had been for him to order straight-in bombing runs against German targets. Before his arrival the formations ducked and darted their way in and most of the time missed hitting what they were after. It had to be

223

changed. He knew full well the losses were going to be high — on both sides. But America had depth and what it lost it could replace. The Germans couldn't. It was the only decision that could be made. Of course LeMay had the benefit of an American public which solidly backed that war; now public sentiment ranged from the majority who simply didn't care and wouldn't be bothered to an outspoken few who were vehemently opposed and beginning to get the ear of the press. Hard times loomed on the home front. But it didn't really matter. His mission was to attack and to give the orders. South's job was to follow them and keep his mouth shut. That was the balance required; the Taxi Dancers had lost it. South's fault.

Robbins rapped sharply on the door jamb and marched rigidly to Wainright's desk. The aspirin were in a plastic vial beside a glass of ice water on a small plastic tray.

The wing commander picked up the tablets and swallowed them quickly, washing them down with a large swallow of the cold water. 'Thank you, sergeant.'

The first sergeant knew Wainright well, and therefore how to live with him. They'd been together since before Langley; the sergeant's armful of stripes was clear evidence of how well he'd learned to manage his colonel. Robbins held no affection for the senior officer and no misgivings about his ability to get the job done; he'd taken care of the wing commander's needs and, in turn, the wing commander had repaid him with rank. The job was to get both of them promoted as high as they could go. That's how the system worked. It was all a professional could hope for. It was a great source of pride that early on he had seen in Wainright a drive that was angled steeply upward; Robbins had nurtured the relationship by making himself the indispens- able man. He'd picked his horse and put all his money down. Back when he'd been a private, a drunken Army master sergeant had told him: 'Boy, find yourself a sponsor and ride him. Don't look for the heroes. They get their asses killed. Look for the ones that fuck up and walk away smelling like a rose. They're the ones that are going someplace.' It had been sound advice. Wainright fit the profile. And his subsequent investment became the dearest kind, one soaked with sweat equity. Robbins did his duty, thoroughly and promptly without omission and without flair. He didn't ask questions that took him beyond the bounds of the officer-non-commissioned-officer relationship. It was strictly business. He made himself into an indispensable man, and rode it. He could read Wainright and now because he could sense the colonel's mood swings before they happened, he knew the colonel was going to close down shop and take a nap on his couch. It had happened before.

'Looks like the colonel could use some shut-eye,' Robbins said in anticipation of his commander's thoughts. 'A lot of pressure these days, sir.'

Wainright shrugged and twisted in an attempt to loosen his stiff back muscles. His shoulders and arms felt like somebody had dropped barbells on them.

'The pressure's on every man here, sergeant. But I am a bit tired. Usual procedure,' he said as he sat down on his couch. 'Hold all calls except for my priorities.' That meant Evans and higher.

'Right, sir, I'll tell the girl.' Robbins never referred to Elise Mantel by her name or by her position. She was always 'the girl'.

Wainright lurched forward. He hadn't thought about her. 'She's *here?*'

'Bright and early. Just like always. Something wrong, sir?' The wing commander's emotional reaction and surprise clinched the scuttlebutt he'd heard at breakfast. The big-titted split-tail was screwing around behind the Old Man's back; word had it she'd left the club in the wee hours with one of the pilots. Robbins shuddered. Somebody was going to catch some heavy duty flak over it.

Not that the Old Man gave a shit personally about the girl; that was beside the point. It was more a question of property. You learned your first few days in an open barracks that there was your property and the other guy's property. You kept your hands on your stuff. *Only* your stuff. If you caught somebody with something that belonged to you, you educated him. In spades. A man had to take care of his own property. Otherwise all kinds of trash would be sniffing around waiting for you to look the other way so they could steal you blind. Property demanded respect and respect was the bulwark of military life. Until Wainright declared that the girl was no longer his territory, she remained his and that was that. What the girl thought didn't matter. Her job was to keep it wet and waiting. This was going to be an interesting process to watch, he told himself. This was when the Old Man was at his best.

'Nothing wrong, Robbins. Let me sleep.' When the sergeant was gone, Wainright collapsed on the couch. The air conditioning was going full bore. A blanket would help keep off the chill. Robbins would soon realize this and fetch one. It wasn't the kind of thing he had to say.

So she had come to work? Maybe the alcohol had blurred what he thought he'd seen. She was with South and they were holding hands and hanging all over each other. Or were they? If so, why was she in the office? Didn't the slut *understand*? He'd had too much to drink, he admitted it to himself. His memories were dim. Mostly what lingered was an intense hatred for the pilot. The image of her grunting and squatting over South made him suddenly feel sick to his stomach but he fought back the nausea by focusing his sight on a spot on the ceiling and by concentrating on nothing else. He called this the exclusion method. The bitch. She was trying to antagonize him, hoping to get at him and *this* for nothing more than a mild reprimand. And like all the other problems of the Taxi Dancers, South was right there in the middle of it. He defiled everyone he came in touch with.

After Robbins brought his blanket, Wainright pulled it up to his chin and propped his head against an angular armrest. He knew he could solve the problem. It was a matter of pride. And survival. It was the talent that stood out most in his efficiency ratings. He was the supreme

226

problem-solver. Problems were constructs, made of many parts. In order to get the solution you had to understand the interrelationships of the parts to the function and operation of the construct. You had to take it apart one piece at a time. In an orderly and patient manner. Once you had all the parts in your mind, it was a simple matter to pick out the one causing the problem. Then you eliminated it. It was a formula that never failed him.

Commander's Prerogative

'Colonel.' The voice was dim, far away and fading in and out. 'Colonel Wainright.' The wing commander blinked. Deep sleep. His eyelids felt like they were stuck together with wet sand. 'Dammit, Jergen! Wake up. We've got problems.' He awoke to find Horowitz shaking him violently.

'What?'

'Screw-up. Our MiGs have been credited to the Eleventh.'

Wainright swung his feet to the floor and stood up, the blanket cascading ahead of him. He crossed to his desk, pushing his hair back with both hands, trying to clear his mind. 'How?'

'Don't understand it, but our data came back on the teletype this morning and it's all fucked up. The Eleventh was fragged against the thermal plant and the power station. Navy Air was against the Red River Bridge and Phuc Yen. It's all jumbled up and we're being tagged with a minor pump on the power plants. Eleventh's getting the MiGs. Fucking paper apes in Saigon have gotten the whole thing botched up.'

'Recce follow-up?'

'Nothing. Low ceiling. Camera problems. Too much groundfire and smoke. You name it. Same old bullshit. Photos won't do us any good now. They're not going to credit us with the birds we got in the revetments. They were off limits. The only ones that count are those that we caught off the ground. We don't need pictures of burned-over MiGs and the bricks of power plants.'

'Gun cameras,' Wainright said. He was beginning to wake up. 'Where's that film?'

'Going over today.'

Wainright realized that if the reports were simply screwed up, then Saigon would figure it out. All they had to do was match the frag order to strike photos and gun films and it would be obvious. Until it was cleared up though, they'd be out twelve aircraft. It would be cleared up, he tried to assure himself. It was simply a stupid mistake. Mistakes always happened in wars. They were always made by non-combatants, he reminded himself, and his temper began to flare.

'Robbins,' he snapped into the intercom. 'Coffee and lots of it.' Robbins appeared immediately with a large pewter urn and two cups. He slid the tray onto the commander's desk and disappeared.

Horowitz filled two cups and began to pace. The wing commander weighed his options. He could do nothing and wait. Play it tight. The mistake would be detected in due course and corrected. But how would Seventh see that? Careers were built on kills. It was his duty to protect the accomplishments of his wing. Keeping quiet could look bad. If he knew there was an error, wasn't it his duty to let them know? How would that look? The board would know about it. They knew everything. His pilots shoot down twelve MiGs and the commander makes no move to correct a mistake that could affect all of their careers. That wouldn't look good to them.

He could call Lohr. But that would get out, too. And he'd look like a jerk at Seventh. Lohr was a rival. You don't call your rival and ask him to square it. He'd laugh in his face. And he'd tell everybody. No, that was no answer at all. Right now Lohr was sitting at Da Nang laughing at the screw-up.

228

What about calling headquarters? But the timing would have to be right. Not right away. That would look as if he were hanging on every report, every kill. Can't look too eager, he told himself. At Seventh, appearances were critical. To wear a star, you need a degree of coolness. The call would have to wait a couple of days.

But those options simply weren't workable. Wainright sipped his coffee and lit a cigar. Boldness was a key sometimes. So was lying low, but the latter didn't seem to fit. 'Al, what's our latest information on Than-Lohn?'

Horowitz blinked at the name. Than-Lohn was the most restricted potential target in Hanoi. It was marked for destruction only if an all-out green light came from the President. For years, they had received reports that pinpointed Than-Lohn as the nerve centre for the Hanoi-Haiphong Electronic Defence Sector. It was also reported to be the billet for five hundred Soviet technicians. Striking it would instantly take away the NVA's radar capability. Their area net would be destroyed. It would also create an international incident. With the Russians so damn active in the Middle East, the U.S. didn't want to risk an open armed confrontation.

'No change,' Horowitz said calmly. The target was a fortified villa on the old French university campus in southwest Hanoi. It was surrounded by Triple-A and SAM sites. Casualty-cost estimates on the target were high. At present, the theatrewide cost was running four men and four birds per one thousand sorties at a cost of $20 million. One strike against Than-Lohn could raise the theatre average. It was that kind of target. They had marked it long ago with a red pin in the map. The op planners had a standing joke that the red symbolized the blood that would flow if they ever went after it. It would make the February attacks on the Thainguyen Steel Works look like a picnic. It was also right in the middle of a dense population band. Any attack would kill a lot of civilians and that wouldn't stand too well with the Secretary of Defense who'd laid down strict targeting guidelines.

'Casualty estimate?'

'High as fifty percent on first strike. Could be even worse. We don't really know what the hell they've got there.' Why the hell was the Old Man worried about Than-Lohn? They had other problems to take care of. 'First strike could be a bitch — a *real* bitch!'

'Not if the attack was being made by a single aircraft,' Wainright said. 'One bird stuffed to the gills.'

Horowitz considered it. With a late and sustained pre-strike and a quick post-strike it could work. Single aircraft were hard to detect. Even the recce outfits who usually operated twin bills cut back to one when they needed pictures of a tough target. One bird could pick time and place. No routes to follow. It could work.

'What's the frag today?' Horowitz picked up a sheaf of reports and read through them. 'Steel Tiger. Laos. Got in our new shipments of Self-sterilizing Gravel and Button Bombs. We're going to spend the next few days seeding packages along the Anti-Infiltration Barrier. It stretched across the DMZ into Laos running north of Tchepone to the vicinity of Muong Sen. Twenty sorties,' he added after quickly counting the number of scheduled flights.

'A single ship could piggy-back with eight birds and drop off without detection after they get into the Steel Tiger area, right?'

'Sure,' Horowitz said. 'That's one way of doing it.'

'Even if they detected the solo they'd figure it was recce.'

'Maybe. Recce's been flying three birds. Two picture-takers and an armed escort. Been pretty hot. We've been keeping it stirred up for more than ninety days now. Even so, I don't think they'd suspect — until it was too late.'

Wainright scribbled 'Than-Lohn' on a note pad and circled it in red. 'Okay, Al. We've got work to do. Fuel up a single ship. HE all the way. Check with operations and verify sunset and end of evening twilight. I want the hit just before it gets too dark to see. The pilot will only get one pass. You understand what we need?'

Horowitz nodded.

'Where's South?'

'Hospital released him just before noon.'

'Get him over here at three.'

'He's pretty bruised up, sir. Besides, he's got three days coming. Anybody steps out, they get a three-day blow. That's the rule.'

'I make the rules, Al. Get South for me,' Wainright said.

'Who do you want on spare?'

'Nobody. Prep two birds. South will fly this one or it won't go at all.'

'Shall I schedule a tank?'

'No,' Wainright snapped. 'Opportunity. Just make sure that there's somebody in Red, White or Blue when he gets there. This has got to go smoothly.'

'Right, sir.'

'Albert?'

The lieutenant colonel stopped at the door.

'I haven't made up my mind yet. I have the right to hit it, you know. Commander's prerogative. They won't like it, but they'll buy it — especially if we take it out. I've never said it before. Albert, but you've got a good shot at your full bird this time. I'm seeing to it. You and I will brief South. Nobody else is to know anything until it's over.'

'I understand, sir.'

'I knew you would, Albert. Now get on with it and check on your courier to Saigon. Did our gun film go out?'

'This morning at eight-thirty. Stops at Khorat and Ubon, then straight in to Saigon.'

'Our mess will be straightened out today. Right?'

'I hope so, sir. I hope so.' Horowitz saluted sloppily and left.

Wainright leaned back in his chair. It was risky, but this wouldn't be the first time someone had made a unilateral decision. The trick was to pull it off. Now he had a trump card. Horowitz would keep his mouth shut. No backbone. If South got the target? Great. If not? All right, too. He wouldn't come back from this one. And it would look like it was his own decision. They could fix the paperwork. Enough people had seen South. He was overwrought. The medics said he was too beat up to fly. Why he even passed up a three-day rest to get even with the NVA for getting so many of his friends. Than-Lohn was a good trade for the MiGs. He was satisfied. It had factored out once again.

Hercules on The Fence

At 1324 hours local time a camouflaged C-130 Hercules lifted off the runway at Ubon and began a straight-ahead climb to its clearance altitude of twenty-eight thousand feet. In its wide belly, several metal canisters of gun-camera film were tightly lashed to the floor, checked and rechecked for security by the crew's load-master. The sky was overcast, a front moving west toward the base from the Mekong River. Normally the thunderstorms built during the day and didn't move in until nightfall, but the monsoons were beginning to test their muscles in the area and they were coming earlier every day.

At three thousand feet, the shuttle's pilot, Captain Elgin Masters, was only slightly startled by a sudden drop in oil pressure on number four. The 130s used to shuttle between Thai bases and South Vietnam were logging a lot of hours in all kinds of weather, operating frequently from makeshift airfields and dirt landing strips. The planes and their crews were getting tired. But Masters knew this and watched his instruments religiously for any hint of trouble. At thirty-three, Masters had two combat tours under his belt. He was soon to be a major and took great comfort in the thought of it. He had more than three thousand hours in the air and a lot of close shaves with eternity. His copilot, Captain Robbie Allen, was equally experienced in the air-craft, but only recently arrived in the zone, and therefore still suspect in his competence. You treated all newcomers

232

like lepers until you knew they were clean. That was the way to stay alive.

'Better watch the oil on number four, Allen,' Masters told the pilot in the right seat.

'Roger,' the copilot said lethargically, not really paying attention. Engines always fluctuated. Besides, this was a milk run. Big deal. If you had to be in the war this was the way to do it. Could be a lot worse. Maybe a fighter with a good chance of getting your ass shot down. This was no sweat. Okay Jose. Easy duty.

'AC, you better take about thirty right. We've got a small cell dead ahead.' The navigator sat behind the pilots and slightly above them. In weather his face was buried in the long black rubber cover to the radar scope. He was the eyes of the plane and it was his job to help them pick their way through mazes of thunderstorms until they could find smooth clear sky on the other side. When there was no weather, Captain Robbie Allen spent most of his time reading lurid paperback novels he referred to simply as 'one-handers.' Now he was engrossed in his work.

'Fifteen more to the right. This is a real mess in here.'

Masters clicked his mike button twice and rotated the autopilot control to the new heading. The sky was black and rain was pelting off the windscreen in front of him. The turbulence was getting worse and even over the roar of the turbos the could hear thunder around them. 'Goddamnit, Robbie. Get us the hell out of this shit,' the pilot snapped nervously. It was always a pain in the ass to be blind, to be depending on a navigator's directions.

'Twenty back to the left and you better crank the bastard over — we're right on the edge of a big fucker.' The engines screamed and whined in the rain as the pilot put the aircraft into a steep left turn away from the storm cell. As they rolled out on the new heading, the aircraft began to vibrate as if someone was pounding the fuselage with a single hammer then thousands of tiny taps that rose into a roaring crescendo and made their ears pop and eyes flinch.

'Hail,' the copilot said, matter-of-factly. All four engines

233

began to cough and sputter under the deluge of the hailstorm.

'Thirty more to the left,' the navigator screamed over the interphone. Masters started the turn but the aircraft was sluggish and seemed to yaw. Suddenly there was a fireball on the column between the pilots, a ball of flame about the size of a honeydew melon, white hot and crackling. All three men froze as the ball bounced lazily and seemed to suspend above them. From behind, the navigator could see that all the generator lights were illuminated. They had lost power, but when he tried to call out to the pilots, no sound came from his mouth. Instead of trying to yell across the cockpit, he lifted his feet and watched the fireball singe its way aft, burning a black strip in the rubber matting as it travelled toward the rear of the aircraft.

Masters grabbed the control column and checked his attitude indicator which showed them to be in a 30-degree bank to the right. When the lightning had hit they had been in a left bank. Hadn't they? What to believe? Three thousand hours. What have you learned? Trust your instruments. Trust your instruments. The aircraft was being buffeted heavily by updrafts in the storm. The altimeter read twelve hundred feet. Running out of sky. Nothing more useless than altitude above, the old saw ran. Masters leaned on twelve years of experience and jerked the aircraft left. For the first time in his career, the instruments were wrong.

'Air start,' he yelled at Allen who tried to reach for the switch but was held in his seat by extreme G force. 'Attitude indicator out!' he screamed at Masters just before the C-130 dropped wing-first into the jungle.

The Jolly Green crew from Ubon found the neatest pile of wreckage they'd ever seen — a single ball of fused and burning superstructure surrounded by a raging brushfire.

'Looks like somebody done whomped it on the ground like a frog on the sidewalk,' the pararescue man in the belly door said as they hovered to check for survivors. 'No fucking way anybody walks from that one.'

Crap Shoot

Wainright stared out the window. Three airmen, stripped to their waists, were hunkered down over the lawn, trying to manicure the stubborn patch of ochre grass. It had been like that as a cadet. Go to class. Fly your missions. Hope you didn't wash out. Shine your shoes. Go to class. Be enthusiastic. Follow orders. It was a simple life with simple rules and now as he watched the men he realized how insulated they were from the real pressures, from the decisions. All they had to worry about was who they were going to screw, or who they were going to get drunk with. They could paw at the grass during the day and do what their sergeant told them and never worry about whether the task made any sense or had any purpose. Their job was to do. Others did the thinking. Wainright found himself wishing his life were so uncomplicated, so orderly. He wished he could go out there on the lawn with them, enjoy his own sweat and the warmth, but he knew this was a condition he could never return to. He had passed it. When they pinned on his gold bars it had ended. The game was different now.

The phone call had clinched it. The shuttle had crashed and with it had gone any hope they had for getting full credit for the MiGs. They would interview the pilots and try to reconstruct the mission but it would take time and there would be losses. All the camera film had been on board and it was gone, consumed by the fire. Even Horowitz accepted that they had no other choice. The mission was on. He was going to send South against Than-Lohn. Brief at fifteen-thirty. It was time to take control of the dice and act with boldness. In a crap game, balls and confidence influenced luck. But it was even better when you could use your own dice, loaded to your specifications and touch.

Faint heart ne'er won fair lady, he reminded himself. Even with verification from debriefings they'd get no more than four of the kills — six at the outside. Not enough. He had the first ace of the war. The first double ace. And now his wing had shot down more MiGs in one mission than any outfit in the war. He couldn't let it slip by. He was ready.

He had some final details to attend to. South would arrive soon. For his final mission. If it worked out.

Dreaming

South stiffened his forefinger and thumb and drew back the rubber band with steady pressure, gently releasing it only when he was satisfied with the sight line. The folded paper wing rocketed away and hit squarely in the crease of the creamy buttocks of the red-haired Play mate of the Month pinned to the bathroom door. He had just gotten off the phone with Elise. She didn't know anything, but she cautioned him to be careful. Wainright had been locked in his office all day, first to sleep off the hangover, later because Horowitz said it was essential to burst his reverie. Something was up, but Wainright had not communicated with her and she was in the dark.

South smiled at the thought of the wing commander finding the secretary at work this morning. She had guts; South conceded that. Her voice on the phone had been warm and full, penetrating. Her ways made him uneasy, almost violated. He hadn't felt so bad in years. His body ached in places where he had forgotten there were places. They were from the ejection. But he was sore in other places too. She was a very demanding woman. His stomach was churning because of her, his head light. It was a feeling

236

he hadn't experienced in years and now he was not sure he was ready for it again. He'd tried marriage, thank you. Too confining. Women were fine at the start, open to everything. But once that permanence set in, they went to work. They worried, they wanted security, no risk. The marriage had lasted eight months. She said he didn't give it time to work. She was right. That was the point.

Arming his makeshift slingshot with another round he turned his mind to Wainright and what was ahead. Horowitz hadn't given him much to go on. Get some sleep. Fifteen-thirty briefing. For what? He argued with the vice-commander. He had three days of R&R coming. That was the rule. Horowitz was very calm on the phone, working just a tad too hard to be effectively reassuring. They had a special mission. When he got back he could have his three days, in fact a whole week. And he should consider taking the woman with him – just to relieve the pressure a little. It was the kind of fatherly advice he'd come to expect from the vice-commander. The whole thing did not set well with him: in Romero's words he suspected that there was a gringo of another colour in the carbon supplies.

He checked his watch. Ten before two. Not enough time for a real nap. But he'd take what he could get. He set his alarm and leaned back on the pillows, crossing a forearm over his eyes to help keep out the sunlight.

Wainright. Elise. A special mission. Nine more. The future. There were lots of things to think about.

The wing commander. He chickened out on a mission. So what? His word against Wainright's. No proof. Backing in missions. He had proof – on paper. But he was just as certain that the main records were already doctored so that his information would look out of line, not the commander's. Word against word. It was check all the way. He could make it uncomfortable for the colonel, maybe even make it so messy that he'd never get promoted. But what kind of penalty would that be? It would hurt Wainright personally, but he'd still be in command of a wing somewhere. Check. All the way.

He'd already taken Elise from him. That had to make him smart some. But what was it really? An irritant. No more. Sleep seemed no closer. His head hurt. There was no way out save one: shut up and get it done.

No, his mind cautioned. You've forgotten the ultimate mission. You and Buggs have planned it a hundred times. Even walked off distances from landmarks to pin down the best aiming points. It would be a beautiful run. No flak. No SAMs. No groundfire. Roll in on the brown building, hold the crosshairs on the peak of the roof, squeeze them off. Wainright would never even hear the scream of the big J-75. He'd do it on his hundredth mission. Make a couple of passes over the base, blow out a few windows, give the ground pounders a show they'd never forget, then for a finale — the headquarters building. When he was done he'd drive a fire truck to the scene, wash it down with foam and prop Wainright's corpse in the seat next to him, haul him over to the club for a drink. Tut-tut, no hard feelings, old boy. He'd smash the saltwater aquarium in the service club with a baseball bat, and eat the fish! Yeah. Even the piranha! That would give them something to remember. Nobody had eaten the fish before. Not just swallow it like a college kid during hell week, but eat it raw, scales, bones, guts and all. Straight out. He'd buy every man on the base a drink, or two, whatever they wanted. Going home!

And the poker players. He hated the bastards. Their own little clique. Never talked. Never ate. Just sat there, dealing their cards, the money and chips tumbling back and forth across the green felt, clinking softly like cheap chimes. Maybe he'd tip over their table during a big pot, or better yet, throw a snake on the table. Have to handle it, but it was worth the risk. Nobody would expect him to haul a krait into the club. Maybe Chief could get one for him, a big fat one.

He saw himself standing beside the poker table, swinging the snake around his head like a lariat, its body whistling through the air-conditioned environment, its black and yellow colours flashing in the light, blending together, its mouth open in anger, the tongue searching wildly for heat, reciting the Pledge of Allegiance in a helium-induced falsetto. What room? Where's the poker table? Ceiling covered with statistics. A door opened slowly and Elise wandered in, naked, her breasts swinging heavily like pendulums, like they were loaded with mercury that drew them earthward. The snake was still swinging. He felt detached from it and watched. It had changed. Wainright. The snake's head was Wainright's and it had teeth with gold fillings — like a carnivore — not fangs. Its eyes were wide, covered by a clear sheath, smiling, flashing in anticipation. It floated to the floor and made no sound when it landed. It made its way across the floor toward the woman. She stood, balanced on needle-heeled high heels, her legs wide apart like a cheerleader ready to leap, her skirt jacked high, her nipples rotating like two red marbles trapped in a cylinder and she smiled, laughed, drooled as the snake wound its way up her long leg, her eyelashes crashing down and opening in anticipation, her hips beginning to move, chanting a guttural *wetwetwetwetwet*, her voice rising higher and higher until the snake's head — South sat up suddenly in his bed, hurting his back in the process. Sweat poured from his forehead. Three o'clock. Thirty minutes until briefing. He felt terrible.

The Than-Lohn Gambit

The lights were dim in the empty briefing room. Just enough time. South slipped into the projection room and dropped a 35-mm slide into the tray. This one would really ring Wainright's bell.

With his side mission completed, South walked into the briefing room and took a seat in the front row. He popped a tab on a can of orange pop as Horowitz arrived and sat nearby.

'What's up, colonel?'

'Wing commander's on his way,' the older officer said.

South leaned forward in his seat. *'Wainright's* going to brief me for a mission?' He whistled quietly. Horowitz nodded and fished for a cigarette in a crumpled pack. 'Isn't this unusual?' South prodded. 'I make major below the zone?' The colonel laughed nervously, wishing the wing commander would arrive and take him off the spot. 'Lighten up,' South said good-naturedly. 'Is he going to use the slide projector?'

Horowitz shook his head, but before he could say anything, Wainright strutted stiffly into the room. He was carrying a clipboard and a large black leather map case from Intelligence. 'Pity,' South said as Wainright closed the door, and pushed a button. Outside a sign illuminated. 'Briefing in Session: Top Secret.' When the light came on the door was automatically locked from the inside. There would be no interruptions. The wing commander got right to the point.

'You're going to hit Than-Lohn.'

South nearly choked on his orange pop. Than-Lohn! It housed a shit-pot full of smug Russians running the NVN radar net. Than-Lohn was *the* target: the big one. Immediately he was suspicious.

'Take off at seventeen hundred. Pre-strike refueling in Red, White or Blue Anchors at seventeen-thirty.' Wainright turned to his vice-commander. 'Tankers are available in those anchors, correct, Albert?' The fat colonel nodded eagerly and gave a thumbs-up sign. Wainright nodded his understanding and continued. 'Fifty minutes from tanker to the target. You should get there a few minutes after sundown. The weather will help you on the way in and out. If you can shack it, you won't have to sweat the radar on egress. At least not a complete net.'

'Whoa,' South said. 'Not so fast. I've got a few questions. Why Than-Lohn so suddenly? Why me? And why me *alone?*'

'I'll take them as you put them. Than-Lohn because it's

240

the President's order. You because you were hand-picked and much as I find you personally repulsive, I fully support their choice. You alone because they believe that a single ship has a much better chance for success than a flight might have. If you follow your route they may think you're a solo recce ship until you're right on top of them. We can't afford to lose birds or pilots right now.'

South sat back. 'A neat little package, just like that.'

'Just like that,' Wainright said. The two men's eyes met momentarily. Wainright sat down on the edge of the low, front stage and peeled the cellophane off another cigar. He chewed the end to make it fit more comfortably between his teeth and licked the tobacco leaf to keep it from flaking.

'What's going on? What's the President's reason for this little . . . surprise?'

'I don't know. We may never know. I am certain that our President and the Secretary of Defense have their reasons . . . good ones.' The bait was out. Wainright prepared to set the hook.

'Your opinion, not mine.'

'They have given us an order. They have not chosen to share the reasons with us. So be it. I can't query the order. I have to follow it. If you can't or won't do the job, I'll get somebody else. What's it to be?'

South was startled by the words. 'What about my three days?'

'Take them when you get back.'

'Horowitz said I could take seven.'

'That was my instruction to him.'

South paused for effect. 'What if I take your secretary with me?'

Horowitz writhed in his seat but Wainright was perfectly calm, his voice unwavering. 'What you and the secretary do with your personal time is your affair. I'm concerned only with the efficiency of this wing and right now that efficiency boils down to this mission. Yes or no?'

South's suspicions were being overridden by other emotions. Than-Lohn. It was a target nobody could turn down.

241

That the President might choose to hit it was not unreasonable, although he'd feel much better knowing why. That they would choose him specifically also made sense. And the rationale of sending a single ship was sound. He'd thought about Than-Lohn before. Every Taxi Dancer had.

'Okay,' South said.

Wainright grunted and dropped a package into his lap. 'The target. Study the photos. You've got some time.' He stood up, but South intercepted him in the aisle.

'I want to see the execution order.'

Wainright smiled, unfastened a paper from his clip-board and handed it to the pilot who read it quickly and tossed it toward Horowitz. 'Seven days off when I get back. That's the deal.'

'Seven days,' Wainright repeated firmly. 'Get the job done and I'll forget everything that's happened. Clean slate. Bury the hatchet.' South did not reply.

At the door the wing commander stopped and turned. 'One more thing. It's in your flight plan. Egress along the Red River and post-strike in Orange. It's longer, but they'll expect a single ship to run for the water. You'll head west instead. It may give you an edge.'

'Rog,' South said. He sat down and carefully opened the package of target photos. The plan was all right, but inside there remained a healthy portion of doubt. The whole thing had a bit of an odour to it.

When he was alone, South exited the briefing room, found an empty office in the Intelligence section and dialled a number. Her voice warmed him. 'Listen,' he said. 'I don't have a lot of time. Find out if Line 24a' — he checked his paperwork again to be sure — 'I need to know if Line 24a has been executed.'

She repeated the number. 'Something wrong?' He could hear the apprehension in her voice.

'Probably not. I'll call you back in a little while. Gotta go. Keep it warm for me, sweetcakes.' He hung up before she could answer.

Line 24a

Elise waited until Robbins was out of the office and tied up with something else before picking up the direct line to the command post.

'CP, Sergeant James,' a deep male voice thundered.

'Sergeant. This is Colonel Wainright's secretary. He would like to know if Line 24a has received an execution yet.'

'Twenty-four A? Don't sound familiar, ma'am. Lemme check the frag. It's here someplace.' She tapped her fingers nervously. 'Miss Mantel?' She still found it unnerving when men she'd never met called her by name. 'It's not on the frag, but that don't mean much today. There's weather on The Fence and on the border and everything's bein' cancelled and rescheduled and scrubbed again. At this rate we'll have to buy a paper factory just to keep up with the changes. Fact is we've got all kinds of changes we haven't caught up with yet. Won't get all the TWIX changes into the paper mill till later tonight after the war goes to bed. Be twenty-one hundred or thereabouts. Controller told me to tell you he had a whole slew of executions a little while ago. Twenty-four A was probably in that batch. In fact, he says he's certain it was in there. Colonel want the paperwork sent over?'

'No, no. He doesn't want a copy. He just wanted to verify it. Thank you for your help, sergeant.'

'Glad to, ma'am.' She hung up and waited for Barney's call.

In the command post Technical Sergeant Marvin Jerami chuckled to himself. The controller was out taking a leak. They didn't need the wing commander butting in. It was a screwed-up day and he had no idea whether there'd been any executions in the last few minutes. He'd made it up. Sergeant Jerami considered himself an expert in dealing with Brass and their doorguards. She'd never know the truth and besides, what difference could one lousy mission make to a wing commander?

Gizmoville

The personal equipment section was housed in a single-story metal frame building just across a blacktop parking lot from the headquarters-operations complex. Not much larger than the concession stand at a Little League ballpark, PE was a storehouse for all the gear each pilot needed to operate in the cramped environment of the F-105. To South and other Taxi Dancers the section was Gizmoland.

At first glance the casual visitor was struck by the facility's resemblance to a locker room. Near the entrance, there was a cage that looked like there might be a junior high school coach waiting to pass out towels to pre-pubescent jocks. Here the pilots picked up their helmets and specially-fitted oxygen masks — checked by P.E. specialists after every mission — their handguns, ammo, survival vests, radios, parachutes and the myriad of other special equipment used by each man or carried in case it was needed.

The main part of the building was separated into three sections by long rows of lockerlike bins — similar to those used by professional sports teams.

P.E. men thought of themselves as trainers. Each day they scrubbed and cleaned, repaired and inspected the equipment needed by their pilots. Oxygen masks had to be cleaned after every flight; every thirty days they were disassembled and sterilized. Every man carried several UHF radios that had to be attended to, batteries replaced, switches checked, antennae studied for wear and tear. On the ground their radios, more than anything else, could spell the difference between being picked up and captured. The men in P.E. were keenly aware of their mission and what their failures might bring to their pilots. Colt Combat Master .38-calibre revolvers had to be inspected and oiled every few days to keep them from rusting and malfunctioning. Soft-steel survival knives – modified bayonets sold to the government at ten bucks a copy – were honed razor-sharp until they could cut paper with the effect of a razor blade. Parachutes had to be inspected before every flight by the pilot, carefully scrutinized monthly by the P.E. experts, then disassembled and repacked twice a year.

Like professional trainers, the P.E. men went about their tasks with great energy, burying themselves in the details of their work and toys with the glee of children turned loose in an Army surplus store. A pilot's oxygen mask rubbed against the bridge of his nose and needed to be exchanged for a wider and longer latex mask to fit his peculiar proboscis. Another's G-suit had gone hay-wire and inflated several times under normal G; it had to be inspected. One pilot had accidentally popped his chute after landing and torn the silk as he tried to prevent himself from being smothered by it in the cockpit. Camouflage designs had to be repainted on scratched helmets and cracked sun visors had to be replaced.

The bins were stuffed with a wide assortment of gear, reflecting in part the requirements of the job shared by all pilots, but also the personality of each man. Buggs' locker was plastered with pinups from a Swedish nudist magazine; Romero's area contained several abbreviated checklists in glycene covers to remind him of critical procedures; he had tacked a small plastic crucifix to the head of the bin. Browning stalks from Palm Sunday hung from a thin shred of flypaper. South's area was the cleanest of all, marred only by a collection of hard plastic ten-ounce baby bottles lining the top shelf.

For South his time in Gizmoville was a pleasant experience. He thought of it as a knight's tent. Its specialists were squires readying their master's equipment for the contest. Here technology and attention to detail ruled supreme; fine workmanship and ornate designs were openly admired. Barbarians fought in the mud with their hands, choking the life out of each other with brute strength. Here the war was different. Even in flight on those rare occasions when they encountered a MiG 21 over North Vietnam, the confrontation was handled with ease and confidence and only minor physical inconvenience. The Taxi Dancers embraced the fact that their foes were like them: men of skill and technology, able to manipulate their aircraft and fight with courage. They were knights, no less familiar with their field of battle above the earth than their historical counterparts had been with obscure grassy knolls.

South entered the building, went directly to his bin, picked up a handful of baby bottles and skipped them across the counter to the P.E. specialist. Behind the counter a gray wall was covered by a brightly coloured sign: *Survival Rule Number One: Check Your Own Gear.* This was the way his ritual preparation always began.

'Gin or bourbon, sir?'

'Double H with an O, sarge. I'm on the wagon this trip.'

The enlisted man grimaced. 'Rot your stomach, cap'n. Best you can hope for is rust.'

'Roger that,' South said over his shoulder as he returned to his bin. Each time he flew his actions were the same, never varying. Even the same words were spoken with no variations. Ritual was ritual and every man understood it.

South's parachute was hung on a triangular pattern of wooden pegs. Reaching for the heavy chute, he turned it around so that the back was facing out and unzipped it to make sure the cotter pins were straight and connected. Bent pins could leave the silk folded inside its canvas uterus like a stillborn fetus and leave him tumbling to the earth like a broken maple wing. Next he examined the straps to make sure that none were frayed. This was a new chute and it needed a careful going over; the old one had worked well enough the day before, but with parachutes you couldn't bank on family history. Every individual had to do the job. It was like checking the balance in your checking account against the institution's computer. The bank was always right, but it didn't cost anything to be certain. Just in case.

Satisfied that the chute was in good order, the pilot shifted his attention to his survival vest and G-suit. He went through each pocket in the vest slowly, methodically extracting the contents and examining them to be certain they would perform in the way they were supposed to. Of all the things in his possession, he spent the most time on his radios, checking for extra batteries, pressing the 'press-to-test' buttons, examining them for moisture, damage or leaking acid. All three radios were in the green. His freshly oiled .44 magnum was back in its holster and he remembered how reluctant he'd been to use it. Nevertheless he examined it in exactly the way that the armourer had done in oiling it for him. He plopped six fat rounds into the cylinder and put the revolver back in the shoulder holster sewn to the vest, taking special care to fasten the leather strap over the hammer of the weapon to keep the pistol in. It was funny about the gun. The bullets were stored in different pockets of the vest, but when you took them out and put them into the gun the vest always seemed to be heavier, a greater burden than when the items were separate.

After checking the rest of the contents of the vest. South carried his G-suit to a test station on a nearby wall and plugged the hose from the chaps into a metal receptacle. The meter reading showed that the suit was functioning properly.

Back at his bin, he wiggled into the G-suit, which fit over the legs and squeezed him tight around the abdomen like a green sash. He had to work hard to get into the vest with its bulging pockets. Once he had his arms in, he slipped it onto his shoulders and sucked in his sparse gut while he zipped up the front. The parachute was last. He slipped into the shoulder straps, attached the chest snap, but left the leg straps dangling down the backs of his legs. As an afterthought he slid his knife from its scabbard and tested the blade by sliding it across a thumbnail — a trick he'd learned as a boy. Everything was in order.

South pushed his oxygen mask into his helmet, pushed his plastic Tiger helmet down over his forehead and headed to the back of the building to catch a ride to the flight line with a maintenance crew. As he moved slowly through Gizmoville the P.E. technicians watched him. He looked like a man the North Vietnamese would not want to do business with.

In a small office near the back of the building he picked up a dust-covered telephone and dialled a four-digit number.

Last Call

'What's the deal?' he asked tersely, his mind already in the aircraft.

'I'm not sure. The command post says everything's a mess up there today and they're behind in the paperwork. They didn't have an actual execution on 24a but they said they're pretty sure it's been executed. A little while ago.'

South considered it. He wished the information were more solid, but it made sense. When the weather was bad the command post always turned into a mess. They probably couldn't find the execution order; it wouldn't be the first time. It was probably real. The decision was made. For the first time he began to feel peace. He began to shift his mind to the task ahead. Than-Lohn. This was going to be something special.

'Barney,' Elise interrupted his thoughts. 'There's been some kind of mistake in Saigon. Jergen's angry. The shuttle with the films crashed near Ubon and he's sure the wing isn't going to get credit for what you guys did.'

248

South's stomach knotted immediately. What were the odds of Wainright getting an execution on Than-Lohn at this precise moment, under these precise cricumstances? But the TWIX had been real. He'd read it carefully. It had to be a coincidence. What to do? He thought for a moment, then made up his mind. A pilot had to trust his instruments, not his instincts. It was time to go.

'What's going on?' she asked. He could hear the fear in her voice.

'Gotta go fly. Pack your bags, we're going to Bangkok when I get back.'

'I *can't* leave,' she whispered into the phone.

'Hell,' he said with a laugh, 'it was your boss's idea.'

He hung up before she could get any more out of him. She felt sick to her stomach.

Blazer 1

South handed his helmet and leg board to an assistant crew chief, pulled his checklist from a leg pocket and began his safety checks and the walkaround inspection. The crew chief, a three-striper with an emerging reddish-blond moustache followed close behind, anxious to please.

South examined the nose gear. The torque links were connected and the safety pin was in place. Moving aft and stooping, he looked over the main landing gear, pulling the safety pins and handing them back to the chief like a reverse pass in a relay race. South removed the pins from the fire bottles and arresting hook. He opened the 781 and checked to be sure no maintenance items were on red slashes or red X's; the record was clean and what minor items there had been, had been cleared by maintenance action.

'How's she running?' he asked as he started to climb the

ladder to the cockpit.

'Humming,' the crew chief said proudly. 'Couple of months ago we had to do some sheet metal work on the belly. Ground fire. But we got her back on the line in a week and no trouble since. She's a good bird,' the airman said proudly.

'Good,' South said from the top of the ladder. He leaned over the canopy rail to see that the ejection-seat pin was in place in the right leg brace. It was snug. He pulled the canopy jettison safety pin and dropped it to the crew chief. Its long red cloth streamer fluttered as it fell. Quickly, South arranged his parachute harness straps, like a woman lifting her gown to step over an obstacle, then with a long reach of the leg, swung over the rail into the seat. He felt like he had come home.

His checklist rested on his right leg. Electrical power off.

South adjusted the rudder pedals for the length of his legs and shoved his map case into the storage bin on his right console. Everything else was in his survival vest so there was no need to stow any other gear. He gripped the stick and felt for slight back pressure. Check. He ran the palm of his hand over the circuit-breaker panels to make sure they were all in, depending on touch rather than sight.

Intercom was set. Temperature controls, set. He turned on the electronic cooling switch. Rain removal off. Temperature control level; he wiggled it and it moved free and easy. Check. Side panel defroster off. Windshield defog and pilot hit switches off. Cockpit heat: he moved the rheostat to the 10 o'clock position. Camera mount to automatic.

Next he turned his attention to the fuel control panel. His mind worked quickly and efficiently as he set the various knobs and switches that would control the flow of JP-4 from tanks to the J-75 engine. Throughout the flight he'd have to balance the fuel load to control his centre of gravity. If he didn't the aircraft would become mushy and possibly unflyable. Main tank boost pumps on. Guard cover down on the tank jettison switch. Fuel shutoff to engine feed. Override checked in normal position. Air refueling rheostats turned off.

Flight controls. RAT level to TURB RETRACT. VAI set to cruise mode. Pitch on. Stick-grip override to normal. Stab lock to normal with guard down. Flap roll to cruise.

Radio off. Now his hands, mind and senses were racing together, touching, smelling, listening for telltale clicks in switches and knobs and in the innards of the aircraft.

Radar fire control system power off. Set map mode. Tilt full up, gain off.

He wiped the sweat from his forehead as he set the throttles and closed the speed brake switch. He was hurrying.

Finally the checklist was reduced to a single task. Check the landing gear warning test button. He pushed it and the red light in the gear handle illuminated, a warning buzzer sounded and the gear windows flagged three red unsafe signs. He stared at the little flags as he let off the button, then checked his watch against the clock on the instrument panel.

Below the crew chief was plugged into the intercom and awaiting his instruction. He held up five fingers and the airman flashed the signal back to him with a broad smile.

Five minutes. He fastened his chinstrap and rolled over the pictures of the target in his mind. He wanted to have a precise idea of where he was when he got there. No time to look around. In and out. Or else.

South began strapping in, first connecting survival kit straps on both sides of the ejection seat, then lacing the left leg lanyard under the left leg, inserting it through the right garter D-ring, finally into place with lanyard and lapbelt. He adjusted his shoulder harness and pulled the safety pin and dust cap from the parachute firing cable. The last task required him to connect his oxygen and communications leads. Now he was tethered to the Thud by several straps and tubes. Its heart and brain were in place.

'Okay up here, chief,' he said into the intercom. 'Let's get this thing started.' He meant more than the aircraft.

251

'Roger, sir. You're clear to start.' South looked down to get the visual signal and saw the crew chief windmilling his arms.

He switched on the battery power and put the fuel system back into operation. The instrument clock and his watch showed thirty minutes until takeoff. They were right on time.

'Starting,' he said into the interphone.

'Copy, starting engine,' the airman echoed.

South turned the fuel tank selector to the main tank, checked the fuel shutoff to engine feed and the throttle off, touching the black-knobbed lever with the heel of his hand to make sure it was locked in the off position. 'Battery's on, sarge − gimme some air.'

'You've got it, sir.' South watched the tach move up. Nine-10 − 12 percent RPM. He pressed the ground start button and notched the throttle up to the IDLE position. Immediately the engine surged and began to wind up. He kept his eye on the fuel flow and it was normal. The engine lit with a thump and the RPM kept increasing. The aircraft vibrated beneath him as the oil pressure approached 35 psi.

Now his attention was riveted on the tach . . . 20 percent, 25 . . . 28 . . . 30 percent.

'Cut the air, chief.'

The crew chief disconnected the air hose which provided the power to initially turn the big turbine; he threw the hose over the top of the yellow MA-1A cart. He snapped the access doors shut on the Thud's belly and stepped back so that South could see him, adjusting his Mickey Mouse ears to reduce the assault on his hearing.

'You're clean, cap'n.'

Click-click. 'Thanks,' South said, his headset buzzing with the background wail of his engine as the tach hit 70 percent. The exhaust gas temp was stable at 320 degrees. He switched the AC generator on and glanced again at all the instruments. Check. Everything was copacetic.

'Takhli Tower, Blazer One has engine start at zero-one-hundred Zulu, standing by for taxi instructions.'

'Roger, Blazer. Cleared to taxi runway one-eight. Altimeter is two-niner-niner zero, wind one-eight-zero at five knots, pressure altitude six hundred feet. Leak check on the north hammerhead.'

South repeated the information to confirm that he had understood. 'Uh ... thanks, tower. I'll be taxiing in about two minutes.' A high squeal filled his headphones but his hand shot out to the radio squelch to cut the mind-jarring noise before it hurt too much. He continued the checklist, first making sure that the left-side circuit breakers were all in. Rain removal off. He depressed the fuel-vent indicator and the light popped on. That was okay. Now for the boost pump. He turned it on. Radio on, mode set to Both. Fire control to standby. Check the fuel; flow okay, throttle back to idle. Emergency fuel switch to emergency fuel system. Light's on, ignition buzz present. System checks. Turn it off. Lights out. Antiskid off; caution light works. Inverter to standby – gear pressure within limits. Altimeter checked to field setting 29.90. VAI to automatic; CADC to low setting. Duct plugs to full aft: he checked both sides to make sure they were back. TBC check.

The mission was progressing without a hitch; he wasn't so sure that it was a good omen. He continued with the checks assuring in turn that the automatic pilot, weapons and navigation systems were ready and working. Finally it was complete. He removed his seat pin, waved it at the crew chief to let him know it was out, and stowed it in the storage bin with his charts. Now the aircraft was hot; he could eject even while taxiing and probably have a chance of surviving. At takeoff speed, it would be a cinch. As a final preparation for taxiing he checked to make sure the hydraulic pressure was in the green and it was. He leaned on the brakes and while the crew chief pulled the chocks from under the tyres, he turned on the anti-collision light.

He watched the airman struggle with the heavy wooden chocks, push them to the side and turn to salute sharply. South returned the salute and signalled thumbs up.

'Takhli Tower, Blazer One is taxiing.'

'Roger, Blazer, you're cleared to taxi.'

Than-Lohn. The target photos flashed through his mind as he released the brakes and evenly applied more thrust to get the F-105 moving. The engine screamed to overcome its own inertia but as soon as the nose moved, he stamped hard on the brakes, making the nose dip violently. The brakes were okay.

He checked left and right to make sure that his wings were clear of any maintenance vehicles and engaged the nose-wheel steering, which he tested by tapping the left brake pedal. The nose moved left, the system was okay. He depressed the nose-wheel steering button on the control stick, advanced the throttle and moved left between rows of aircraft revetments. He watched the hydraulic-pressure gauges for fluctuations as he turned on to the main taxiway that paralleled the north-south runway. Gauge readings were as steady as his hands.

Like most pilots, South had certain mechanical problems that concerned him more than others. Some pilots lived in constant fear of losing an engine on takeoff and monitored their instruments like archaeologists scraping dirt away from an artifact with a toothbrush. Others were afraid of setting their altimeters improperly and still others sweated gear failure or forgetting to put the wheels down before landing. South's concern was focused on hydraulics. Even though there were three separate systems on board, he watched the gauges like a hawk. In the Thud, a small leak could grow large in a hurry and even with three systems the fluid could drain out and when it was gone, so were the flight controls.

As he approached the hammerhead. South could see a blue panel truck waiting for him. He taxied to an area that was painted with yellow and black hash marks, stopped and set his parking brakes. Airmen poured out of the truck and scurried beneath the plane, pulling pins from the fuses of three 1,000-pound bombs that hung from wing pylons. Some of the airmen checked to make sure that no fluids of any kind were dripping from the aircraft.

While the munitions technicians examined his bird, South pulled out his light-grey kid gloves and shoved his hands into them, carefully tugging down the creases between his fingers to make sure they were snug. Once airborne, they'd not only keep his hands warm, they'd keep them from slipping on the stick. They made his hands feel streamlined and he never felt completely ready to fly until they were on and comfortable.

As he rolled down the tops of the gloves and tucked them under the sleeve of his flightsuit, two airmen emerged from under his left wing and held up the safety pins and streamers from the bombs. He counted them and nodded with great animation. Again, they saluted. When the truck cleared the area, he resumed his checklist.

Rain removal on. He wouldn't need it, but it had to be checked. Throttle up to 75 percent. Good airflow on the windshield; if he needed it, it would be there. Throttle back to idle. Rain removal turned off.

'Bluebird Six-three on final.' South looked up to see a clumsy EB-66 lumbering toward the runway, its nose rotating as the pilot fought the sluggish controls to line up with the strip.

Poor bastard, he thought. Flying that piece of junk. The old bombers had been converted for electronic warfare and the engineering had been so dismal that the inside of the EB-66 cockpit looked like the guts of a pinball machine. Before the modification there had been places for two pilots; now there was one, and the seat was located in mid-space, just out of effective reach of everything the pilot had to be able to get to in a hurry. Add lousy visibility from windows the size of the back screen of a Volkswagen and ejection seats that killed more than they saved and the sum total was rotten.

The idea of flying into NVA airspace to jam radar and SAM sites was not exactly the ideal mission. The EB-66s got shot down just a little less frequently than Thuds — but only, because there were fewer of them, South figured. Nosir, the old Thud might be a dog at high altitude, but you could fly it. And no belly-full of spooks and navigators in back of you to complain about bumpy rides and bad landings.

He watched the albatross-shaped aircraft waddle onto the concrete just to his right and went back to preparing for his own takeoff. He connected the chute cable and again checked the fuel tank selector switch to make sure that everything was properly positioned. Main tank, he noted. It never hurts to double-check yourself. Autopilot off. Stab-Aug engaged. Trim set. He spun the small wheel into position and then set the flaps. Speed brakes in. Seat pin out. Doppler to PPI — he squinted to see the coordinates in the small windows. The longitude and latitude display checked with the actual. Transponder to Mode III, code 44. System on.

'Roger, Blazer One. Taxi into position and hold for takeoff runway one-eight. Wind light and variable. Altimeter two-niner-niner-zero with pressure altitude six hundred feet. Squawk Three, forty-four. Contact Takhli Departure Control on Button Three after airborne.'

South read back his clearance verbatim and thanked the tower controller. He pushed the canopy control switch and the Plexiglas hummed as it slid into place over his head, immediately intensifying the heat in the cockpit. He pulled the lock lever tight on his left console and checked it. The lock hooks were over the rollers and the caution light was out; the canopy was down and locked.

Pitot heat on. Temperature control to RAM air. Defog off. Wouldn't need it. Windshield defrosters and side panels off. De-ice off. Rain removal off. All caution and warning lights out. The F-105 was ready.

'Tower, Blazer One's taking the active.'

'Roger there, Blazer One. Cleared for takeoff. Have a good one, sir.'

Click-click.

The runway was scarred and discoloured by long black patches of rubber burned into the concrete by thousands of landings and takeoffs. When it was wet it was worse than ice. He guided the F-105 into place, stopping with the nose wheel on the centreline strip that ran the length of the 8,700-foot runway. He switched his radio to channel three, stretched his neck and legs and drew a deep breath. Antiskid on. HSI and magnetic compass readings were the same.

'Blazer is rolling,' South radioed as he pushed up the throttle to MRT and watched his instruments jump like goosed matrons. Quickly he scanned every instrument like a speed reader flying down the middle of a page taking everything in at once. Oil. EGT. Tach. Fuel flow. Hydraulic pressure. Everything looked good. He wiggled the rudder and stick; the control surfaces were free. From habit he reached down and checked the speed brakes with the heel of his hand − just to be sure. This was no time to be shooting for a land speed record. If the spoilers came up he'd never get airborne.

When he released the brakes, the Thud lurched and moved very slowly, banging heavily against the seams of the runway. As he applied the throttle, the speed increased rapidly and the aircraft shook wildly as the concrete battered the solid rubber tyres. When the engine temperature hit 226 degrees, South rammed in the after-burner. It jolted him back against his seat. He turned the water injection switch on and the acceleration smoothed like a hydroplane finally on top of the water.

This was the part he loved best; the raw power under his hand, the thumping of tyres against the pitted pavement, metal rattling like giant chimes in a gale-force wind, the base and parked aircraft an orange and green blur on the right side of his peripheral vision, an eye catching the acceleration check, knowing he was committed, responding automatically to everything that had to be done, checking main airspeed indicator against the standby instrument, knowing he was committed to takeoff, a goer, watching the speed build to 190 to 210 to 225, approaching takeoff speed, the two-thousand-foot marker flashing by, speeding to 230, easing back on the stick, pegging the VVI on ten degrees and holding it rock-steady, feeling the F-105 come off the ground in his hand, flying.

Did the surgeon feel like this when he cut into his patient? ADI showing nose up, straining to come up, lifting, settling momentarily as ground effect disappeared and flight began. South slammed the gear handle up and waited for three up signals to pop into the green indicator windows ... appearing at their own time with their own minds ... nose ... and two main. Three up and in the well. Speed, 254. He set the flaps for cruise and maneuvre and checked the indicator for verification. Check. Water injection to dump. Burner off. Temperature to automatic. Oxygen to normal. Radio to button three.

'Takhli Departure Control. Blazer One is airborne. Three in the well.'

Topping Off

'Takhli Departure, Blazer One squawking Code three-four, heading zero-five-zero, climbing through angels six.'

'Roger, Blazer. You're cleared to twenty thousand. Climb on course. Squawk ident.'

South reached for the transponder and pushed the spring-loaded switch without looking. 'Ident, Blazer One.'

'Radar contact,' the controller reported. Now South knew that he was not alone. Everything he did until he entered North Vietnamese air space would be monitored and tracked by men at GCI sites, staring at their twenty-four-inch radar screens. Even so, they couldn't really help him. Once inside enemy territory nobody could help him. He was his own boss. His fate was in his own hands. And that's the way he wanted it. In the States the air traffic controllers were in charge; they dictated every move, but here the GCI people simply tracked the many aircraft that passed silently over them. In emergencies they could be

258

counted on to control the loose traffic to help alleviate the pandemonium above. But for the most part, they were onlookers, not participants.

Steadying on a new heading of zero-six-zero, South adjusted the throttle and relaxed a bit. The sky was still the blue of natural sapphires. To the northeast, thunderstorms were building toward seventy thousand feet, spreading their rain like a thin veil of muslin, the sun's rays defracted to create an extraordinary display of interlaced patterns. Most of the time South was too busy to pay much attention to such gaudy displays, but this time he felt a need to let his mind wander, if just for a moment, and to absorb the scene. The sun felt warm and comforting and he leaned back and soaked it in, his senses alive.

'Takhli, Blazer One is through eighteen thousand,' he radioed as he reset his altimeter to 29.92 and turned two fuel valves to drain fuel into the main tank in order to keep his centre of gravity near the cockpit.

'Thank you, Blazer. Call when level.'

Click-click. He eased back on the stick as his altimeter crept close to twenty thousand, but at nineteen-five his climb ended and even when he increased his power, the aircraft was sluggish in attaining the clearance altitude; it was the Thud at its worst — a heavy load and thin air. At thirty-thousand, it would have handled like a Greyhound bus.

'Takhli, Blazer is level at twenty.'

'Thank you, sir. Contact Lion on three-four-three-point-seven.'

'Rog.' South turned the radio selector to channel five and adjusted his power again. Better to burn the fuel now, he thought. Make it easier to handle during the refueling. After that he could take it downstairs where it handled best.

'Lion, Blazer One at twenty.'

'Blazer squawk Ident.'

Again South triggered the transponder.

'Radar contact, Blazer. Are you scheduled for a tanker? I

259

don't have you on my board.' Suddenly the knot in his stomach was tightening again.

'Lion, I'm a late add. Can you fix me up?'

'Roger, sir. Take your pick of Anchors.'

'Need to get something as far north as I can. I'm loaded down so I don't want a tag game with the weather.'

'Understand, sir. Climb and maintain twenty-four thousand and turn port to heading zero-four-three for vector to Red Anchor.'

Click-click. Damn. Not on his board. Goddamn Wainright! But the TWIX had been real — it *had* to be. He opened the storage compartment on his right and extracted the target photo package.

Powerhouse to the northwest. Three big smokestacks. No way to miss the landmark — even better than the island in Mono Lake in Nevada. It was a weird area — like a college campus, with lawns and groves of palm trees. But this campus was dotted with sandbagged gun sites and lines of one-man concrete bunkers along every sidewalk and narrow street. The NVA were smart — Hanoi was a spread-out affair. People were no longer clustered in the city and suburbs. The bombs had taken care of that. Children and schools had been moved far from the city and instead of group shelters, North Vietnam was busy putting together the most comprehensive system of one-man shelters in history. Now when the sirens began to wail people stopped, pulled over the concrete cover and dropped into the four-by-six-foot hole. Often in strike photos South had seen NVA soldiers in the little 'hidey' holes firing up at his aircraft, safely surrounded by cement. There was no way to get them short of a direct hit.

Than-Lohn itself looked like a large villa — an administration building on a California college campus. The roof and several gables were covered with a red tile. HE would disintegrate it, he figured. But only if he could hit the roof. From the side the walls would probably withstand a pretty good explosion. Whey wasn't the flight on the GCI schedule? Have to be very precise, he told himself. Hit the roof. What

260

was Wainright up to?

'Blazer — you've got fast-moving traffic at one o'clock northbound, well clear.'

South glanced to his right. A KC-135 was headed north with three F-4Cs in tow. Business as usual. A whole sky filled with planes and people going to and from a war while the Thais below tramped around their rice paddies ankle-deep in dung and stagnant water. The Burmese had come through before King Mongkut had thrown them out; so had the Khmers and gangs of bandits and other trouble-makers, but the people never changed. Work the land. Trade at the market and barter for the best deal. Make babies and hope for boys. Pray to Buddha and honour the *bonzes*. Constant. Now we're here and even when they hear the planes fly over, they seldom look up. It just isn't important. In time, all *farang* go away.

Review the facts. The TWIX was real. Fact one. Lion doesn't have the mission on its schedulte. Fact two. The Command post may not have known. Not a fact, but a strong suspicion.

'Blazer One.'

'Go, Lion.'

'Your tanker will be Red Anchor Six-three. Fly heading zero-zero-five, maintain twenty-four thousand.'

Click-click. 'What frequency?'

'Uh ... three-two-zero-five. Can I be of assistance?'

'No problem — just want to check in.' South changed channels, but stopped himself before transmitting.

'Lion, this is Blazer One.'

'Go ahead, Blazer.'

'A tanker just passed me — towing some Phantoms. I need his frequency.'

'Okay, Blazer. You going to make your own arrangements?'

'Negative, Lion. Say frequency.'

'Three-zero-three-point-three, Blazer.'

Click-click. South switched channels again.

'Tanker north of Khorat, this is Blazer One.'

'Orange Anchor Seven-one — go ahead, Blazer.'

261

'Evenin', Orange. How long you gonna be up in your anchor?'

'Short-time. Drop off these F-4s and head for home.'

'Rog. Who's scheduled in behind you?'

'Don't know ... have to check the schedule. Hang on for a sec.'

Click-click. South adjusted his heading back to 005.

'Blazer, this is Orange Seven-One. My nav says we're the last act in the area today. You need some help? We've got *mahk-mahk* gas.'

Fuck! 'Negative, Orange, but thanks for the offer. I'm a late add − I'll catch somebody later on.'

'Roger ... be glad to hang around, sir. No hot dates tonight.'

'Appreciate that, babes − have a good one.'

'You too, Orange Anchor.'

South switched back to Lion's frequency. 'Lion, Blazer One is back up.'

'Roger, Blazer. We're moving all our business into White Anchor. The weather's starting to drift north. Fly heading zero-two-zero.'

'Roger, zero-two-zero. How far's my tanker?'

'One hundred miles at twelve o'clock. He is Red Anchor Six-six on three-two-zero-point-zero, copy?'

Click-click. 'Red Six-six, Blazer One radio check.'

'Five-square, Blazer. What kind of a load can we give you and which way are you headed?'

'Fill my tanks and drag me northeast as far as you can.'

'Blazer, this is Lion. Fly zero-two-five, sir. Range eighty miles.'

Click-click. 'Red Anchor, say your altitude.'

'Twenty thousand.'

'Rog. Lion, Blazer One is descending to one-niner, steady on heading zero-two-five.'

'Thank you, sir. Range sixty-eight miles. Red Anchor turn to heading two-zero-five.'

'Turning, Lion, Red Anchor.'

South scanned his instrument panel. Everything seemed

to be working smoothly. What the hell was this thing all about?

'Range fifty miles. Blazer, your tanker is at twelve o'clock.'

Click-click. What if Wainright was flipping out? Than-Lohn was more restricted than a nun's shower room. He could be taking a big gamble, but the TWIX looked real. The fucking TWIX! If the damned piece of paper hadn't been there, he'd turn around, but it *was* there. Still, it smelled like a setup. If the TWIX was a fake, the CP wouldn't have one — that would account for it, but Elise couldn't talk to them ... it really hadn't been verified either way. No choice but to keep going.

He had to admire Wainright. The bastard was smart. Here I am hauling ass for Than-Lohn and he's in the clear, sitting in his office. If I take out the target, he's going to ride me again. *Me.* If I botch it, it's my fault. South? Have no idea what he was doing up there. This was a perfect war for Wainright because the flow of information was screwed up all the time. No way for reporters or even for the brass to dope out a lot of things. With a remote base and heavy combat load, it's very easy to cover your tracks. This time he'd done his homework; no choice but to keep going. What if the TWIX is real? What if the President has ordered this mission? Could abort — that would be a way out, but the aircraft was sweet. Be hard to back that up and what would the rest of them think once they heard that? Hell, it could be for real; it was just crazy enough to come from Washington. Maybe he's jockeying for position against the Russians in the Middle East. Christ, who could tell? Out here, we don't know a damn thing about what's going on. They tell you only what you need to know.

'Twenty miles,' said the voice of the GCI controller.

Click-click. South trimmed the aircraft, reduced his airspeed below supersonic and flipped the Vertical Altitude Indicator to cruise mode. He scanned the duct plugs; they were full aft and set for refueling.

'Range fifteen miles. Tanker at eleven o'clock now.'

Click-click. South scanned the sky ahead of him.

'Red Anchor Six-six, port turn to heading zero-two-five. Range nine miles.' The grey tanker flashed in the bright sun and South spotted it turning above and in front of him.

'Lion, Blazer One has visual contact. Red Anchor, you got F-4s pulling away from you?'

Click-click. 'The boomer has you in sight, Blazer One.'

'Rog.'

'Range four miles.'

Click-click. 'Okay, Lion, thanks for your help.'

'Lion clear.'

'Red Anchor, can you extend your track over the river? I got a long ways to go.'

'Can do, sir. Take you as far as you want.'

'Beautiful. You guys carrying guns these days?'

'Negative ... but we hide real good.'

Click-click.

'Blazer One, this is your boomer. How read?'

'Good, boomer. Five by five.'

'You're cleared in, sir.'

Click-click. This would be a whole lot better if the damn mission was scrubbed at the last minute. Maybe there would be bad weather. You couldn't hit in a thunderstorm. He trembled. No choice. Have to keep going. At least he was alone; that had to be in his favour.

The tanker was dead ahead. South pulled back slightly on the stick and increased his power to climb into position. A hundred yards behind the fat, slightly swaying tail he ran through his pre-contact checklist. Reposition fuel valves to load in the main tank. Pull back the air refueling handle and watch for the green A/R Ready light to come on. Blink; the system was set.

Watching rows of air refueling lights on either side of the tanker's belly, South moved closer. The boom operator's face was clearly visible, staring at him through the small window under the boom − not thirty feet away. Fighting the edges of the tanker's slipstream, South stabilized his nose just under the boom. The nozzle waved over him and darted toward the receptacle in the nose, striking home with a resounding 'thunk'. The indicator showed that fuel was flowing from tanker to fighter; he was filling up. Just like ducking into a gas station, he told himself – at six hundred miles per hour.

'Boom has a contact; fuel flowing.'

'Roger, boomer. Good stick.'

'You ought to see me with a lady.'

Click-click. South concentrated on holding his position as his weight increased. Adjust the trim. Pressure on the stick. Add a touch of power. Trim it again. Scan the instruments. How much on board now? More power, more trim. Back off a little, don't jam the boom, dummy. Back ... that's it. Can't let this man think you're a rookie. There ... everything perfect.

He glanced at the terrain. It was flat, a lush green savannah interspersed with brown blotches. To the north, small hills were already being swallowed by a purple evening haze. To the east, he could see the twisting brown Mekong and beyond Laos – starting flat and rising quickly into steep limestone ridges cut by dirty streams and white-water rivers, covered with thick forests and webs of tangled undergrowth.

From the sky, the scenery appeared to be nothing more foreboding than a soft green quilt left rumpled on a bed in the morning. Occupational blindness. Speed and distance blinded you. Supersonic override ... and JP-4 fog. It prevented you from seeing what really lurked below. Here you were high and quiet, snug, and warm like a kid in his backyard fort. Removed from the stench and decay of thick red mulch. Sight your target, get the crosshair on it, squeeze it off. Boom! It disappears. When it was over, what had you really done? Mostly ... add a mark to Wainright's board.

Like the hospital. How had that happened? Was this going to be a blundering repeat ... a crescendo of burning, crushed flesh? It would be good to walk through the wards and look each one in the eye. Man, I'm goin' back up there and I'm comin' back to roast you in that bed. Gonna turn you into a mystery meat again, asshole. What do you think of that, turkey? That's the way it should be done – not faster than a speeding bullet. Not just a split-second decision and the easy finger pressure on a switch or button. You should have to stand there and tell them, and be there to feel the debris and bloody flaps of skin raining from the fireball ... and their muffled screams of hate and fear. That's the way to fight; not like this ... too easy to forget you're one of them.

'Crossing The Fence, Blazer.'

Click-click. 'Blazer will drop off in a few minutes.'

'Rog – say when.'

South called for a disconnect and dropped back and to the side of the tanker. He'd top off again just before going off on his own. How could all that happened during this tour come down to a single mission? This was supposed to be the front end of the final ten. Milk runs. Put in your time, drop a few bombs on the monkeys in Laos and go home. Away from the war ... from the shits ... from dead men ... and bad hours, snakes, drunks and loneliness ... and from fly-drawing lifers, suck-asses and cowards. This was supposed to be the pay-back – a reward for a job well done. Instead it was Than-Lohn. Yesterday, Kep. Maybe they'll give a week off, maybe not. Then back at it again. What surprises could remain? Red China? Strafe the MiGs on Hainan Island? No choice, he told himself. No way to avoid it, now. You told the bastard you'd do the job and keep your mouth shut. Now you've got to do it.

'About five more minutes, Blazer?'

'Rog,' he said quietly. 'Movin' in again.' Now he had the feel of the bird; smooth and solid, like an extension of his body. He slid back under the boom, stabilized and watched the boomer guide the nozzle home again. Fuel flow started and stopped almost as fast. The accumulator showed about three hundred more pounds on board before beginning to stutter.

'You're venting, sir.' South strained to see his wing tips, turning and also staring into his rearview mirrors. A blue

266

vapour was pouring from them, leaving a rainbow contrail behind him. The tanks were overflowing.

'That about does it, Red Anchor Six-six. I'm dropping off to your right. Thanks for the gas. You got a position for me?'

'Rog, Blazer.' South put the PPI computer into Standby. He jotted down the coordinates, updated the navigation computer and turned it on again. As he slid back he pushed the receptacle door handle forward to close the cover in his nose. Transponder to Standby. GCI wouldn't be tracking him so easily now − but neither would the Russians in Than-Lohn. One-man-band from here on, he told himself.

He climbed quickly to twenty-two thousand and set his airspeed to conserve fuel. The sun was low behind him; its light would be almost gone by the time he reached the target. He'd be caught in twilight, neither light nor dark. Limbo.

'Six-six. Tell Lion I'm off and running.'

'Wilco, Blazer One. Good hunting, sir.'

'Thanks.' The mountains were passing beneath him. Good hunting: Who was the quarry?

Saigon Surprise

Wainright sat quietly, enveloped in a kind of serenity he'd seldom known. No more dealing and hustling; it was done. The dice were airborne. By now he figured that the various NVA defence installations ought to be painting South on their screens, wondering why a single ship was screaming in from the west. Loners usually came in from the gulf, low and fast, burners lit: get in, get done, get out. Than-Lonh. This was a big gamble, maybe even crazy: Horowitz had that much right. Everything was on the line. He had not made the decision lightly. Maybe everything would be straightened out in a few days, but the film was important and no amount of Horowitz's blubbering could alter that fact. It was gone. It concerned him that the decision might have been one of panic. Maybe he wanted the star too much. That was the truth! He'd never wanted anything so bad. Nothing. Better to not want so much he told himself; that way your spirit doesn't get crushed when it doesn't come.

Horowitz came in without knocking and flopped down at the table with his wing commander, his chest heaving violently. 'Ran,' he gasped in way of explanation.

'Lose your vehicle?' Wainright asked calmly.

'Left it in another lot. Didn't want to chase after it,' he puffed.

'Calm down,' Wainright told the other man.

'Am,' the man gasped again. 'Am calm. He was reported off tanker ... figure he's ten ... minutes from ... release ... no more than that ... no more. The tanker is ... is monitoring ... strike frequency.'

Wainright stiffened. 'What strike frequency? There isn't one − remember? I didn't assign one. I didn't want one! *That* was the idea.'

'Relax,' the vice-commander snapped angrily. 'The paperwork calls for a frequency so I wrote one in.'

'*You* assigned one? You ... who are *you*? Jesus!' Wainright shouted angrily, groping for words. 'They can tie us to it now ... what if he says something?'

'He's not going to say anything − nobody would hear if he did. I filled in a square − to make it look right. There are no copies; he's got everything with him. There's nothing here but the one copy of the TWIX,' Horowitz said. 'Besides ... I'm just following orders.'

'That's right and what are *you* gambling? Where's your ante, your risk? You're already a two-time loser.'

'Same risk as you,' Horowitz said triumphantly. 'The exact same risk.'

The entrance of Elise Mantel interrupted them. 'Colonel?

268

General Evans is on the line,' she said coldly. 'He wants to speak to you personally. I tried to buzz, but you didn't answer.'

Evans. Why was he calling now? The wing commander and Horowitz exchanged nervous glances as Wainright picked up the phone, pausing for a deep breath before speaking.

'General? Yes, I'll hold. This is Colonel Wainright.' The wing commander brushed his hair back as he waited. Five minutes had passed since Horowitz arrived; South should be diving toward the target right now.

'Sir? Yes, sir. Very fine. Right, sir. Things are going pretty well. What? Yes. We, uh, saw the error. You know our film went down in that One-thirty at Ubon today. Thunderstorm, they tell me. Bad place along that river.' Wainright smiled weakly and rubbed his temple. 'I know it's a paper foul-up. I didn't figure it was important enough to bother you about. Right, sir. Too many other things to worry about, general.' Wainright cupped the phone and whispered at Horowitz: 'He has our report — says he always reviews ours *personally*. It's all straightened out. Get to a phone and see if you can stop South. Go!' he screamed.

Horowitz didn't move. He was staring at the wall clock. 'Too damn late,' he said matter-of-factly. 'We're too late.'

'It's not too late,' Wainright said desperately. 'It's not too late. Get going.' Horowitz shrugged, picked up his hat and walked out slowly, shaking his head, a slight smile forming on his lips.

'What's that, general? It is. It's the best command over here. A lot like the old days — they're a different breed but they still fight like alley cats. South? Very well, sir. He got two more yesterday — eight now.' Oh my God! What's he leading to? Why is he puffing around on the other end? 'Bangkok, sir? I can be there. The board?' No! 'Yes, sir. I understand.' His heart raced. Don't say it, you bastard; not now; not at this minute. Christ! 'Thank you, sir. I appreciate hearing it from you.' He leaned his head on his fist and pushed hard. Of all the rotten fucking luck! He'd made it:

brigadier. What to do? Tell him. Tell him everything and hope he'll understand? No. Shut up and ride it out. Be cool. 'Yes, sir. I'll pass that along, and thank you again. I just don't know what to say. Tuesday. Right – I'll be there. Elise? Why yes, I think she'd like that. Not all fun and games for a woman up here.' He dropped the phone onto the hook and leaned back in his seat, shivering. His legs were shaking. General Jergen Wainright. A cocktail party in his honour and for Brown III. They'd *both* made it. At last, he was into the club.

The phone jarred him again. It was Horowitz. No target report, but DeSoto was reporting heavy MiG activity in the Hanoi area ... and what could be a pursuit. Wainright slumped in his chair. With this run of luck, South would probably shoot down every last one of them.

Trapped. Think what you're going to do. No, don't think. Forget it. Pour a drink and wait it out. You don't even know if he got to the target. Slow down and relax, general. He savoured the word. Wait and see. Pour a nice long drink and sit back.

He opened the top right drawer of the desk and pulled out a small box. He opened the package and touched the two silver, shining stars. All his life, he had anticipated this moment. He'd planned it, worked toward it, developed thousands of scenes of how it would happen. Now all he could do was sit and stare at the bits of metal and wonder if this was the beginning or the end.

Cat's Eyes on Yankee Station

The destroyer Dayton, code name DeSoto Radar, rolled and creaked in light swells far north in the Gulf of Tonkin. To men accustomed to batterings by thirty-foot waves and howling winds, current sea conditions amounted to a near calm. They were comfortable. Not bad duty.

Steaming north of Yankee Station, the Dayton's ancient innards were packed with the most sophisticated radar and communications equipment in the world. In the confines of his own wardroom the ship's skipper liked to brag that compared to his ship, SAC's airborne Looking Glass command centres were Tinkertoys.

The work was routine and boring, but if you were on a headset in the Comm Center, there was always plenty of action to listen in on. Commonly referred to as spooks by the ship's regular company, the electronic intelligence specialists on the Dayton called themselves the 'Voyeurs' because they eavesdropped and watched the action swarming over them.

Petty Officer Rik Yalkowsky lit another cigarette, noting that his habit had grown to nearly three packs a watch — nearly twice what it had been when they steamed out of Subic Bay six months before. His watch was only beginning, his world bathed in red and yellow lights. As he had done hundreds of times before, Yalkowsky began his watch by checking out his 'ears'. Assured that the equipment was in good working condition, he had settled back to gaze at 'Bobo' Brazil's radar scope at the adjacent station.

A brother from Elizabeth, New Jersey, Bobo sported a brillo-thick goatee and a sneer which he reserved for any non-voyeurs he encountered. The Navy, his brothers insisted, was racist. Maybe so, he countered, but not Intelligence. It wasn't part of the Navy. In the Intelligence branch, every man was a professional and nobody gave a shit what colour he was. Didn't mean shit. 'Can you do the job? Thas all, man. Thas all they ask. Thas where nuts git cut, baby.' Bobo had enlisted at seventeen to escape the juvenile authorities. There was no doubt in his mind that if he'd missed enlisting he'd have ended up doing 'hard time'. Now, for the first time in his life, he was part of the elite and nobody, black or white, was going to steal it from him.

Yalkowsky studied Brazil's scope. It was massive — a

271

deep green, the colour of slime pumped from cesspools. The yellow sweep rotated clockwise around the circular scope, igniting small clusters of yellow whenever it contacted anything solid.

'What's happenin', Bo?'

Brazil shook his head. 'Smooth, Rik. Maybe have a quiet shift. Ain't nothin' spose'd to be in there till next shift. Track a few MiGs for the boys in Air Force blue tonight. Got one blip west of Hanoi − other'n that, it be *most* cool, man.'

Yalkowsky saw the blip disappear. 'Gone.'

'Uh huh. Gettin' down low. Maybe a MiG − maybe not. Could be unscheduled picture-taker, only they ain't one on the schedule,' Brazil said tapping a thick pile of thermofax messages.

Yalkowsky was startled by sudden movement from Brazil, who lurched forward in his seat. 'Hey Rik, check this out, man.' The scope showed four blips near Hanoi. One by itself followed by three others. The black seaman scratched a red X on his scope in grease pencil to mark the single return. In seconds it was obvious that they were witnessing some kind of chase. The single ship was constantly changing altitudes, headings and speeds.

'Flyin' practice for the gooks?'

'No way, man. They are after that dude − mus' be ona ours. Recce most likely. Put chu'er ears on, Rik.'

Yalkowsky, who always wore his headset slightly behind his ears when he was off frequency, slipped the earphones into place and checked his equipment. 'Open scan,' he told Brazil. His equipment was set up to monitor an entire spectrum of UHF frequencies, including Guard on 243.0. 'If the man gets the urge to talk, we're on the line,' he told his partner.

'Judgin' by the heat they're puttin' on him, the mother-fucker ought to be yapping pretty quick,' Brazil said, as several more aircraft appeared on the screen from the south and north of Hanoi. 'They got the whole North Vietnamese Air Force flyin' tonight.' The two watched the drama in silence.

Two blips that crossed in front of the single return disappeared and the single ship made a sharp turn to avoid other contacts. 'Whew,' Brazil whispered. 'That solo's got teeth. Chalk two for the good guys ... hey Rik ... you ever hear of recce planes with weapons?'

Yalkowsky shook his head and offered his cigarettes to Brazil who pushed them away. 'What the hell's goin' on up there, Rik? Never hearda no Lone Ranger strikes in that area.'

Mayday — Mayday — Mayday. Blazer One on Guard.

Yalkowsky set 243.0 into the frequency selector on his transmitter. *Blazer One, this is DeSoto. Can we be of help?*

Rog, DeSoto. Relay message to Blazer Control. Blazer One has dropped three tons of scrap iron in the Red River. Inform Wainright dirty laundry now his own problem. Repeat. Inform Wain—

The radio was dead. Yalkowsky manipulated his radio controls, trying to screen out static as he leaned over to watch Brazil's scope. He could not pick up the signal again. The aircraft radio had been replaced by the steady whine of the scanner and the diesels that powered the destroyer.

'You write it down, Rik?'

Yalkowsky nodded. 'Yeah. I got it, but it don't make no fucking sense, man. What's Blazer Control?'

Brazil flipped quickly through his thermofaxes. 'Takhli. Must've been an F-105. What the hell's ona them doin' up there alone?'

'How the hell should I know? What's Wainright? Never heard that one before. Think that's some sort of spook operation?'

Brazil shrugged. 'Shit, man. They ain't tellin' us ev'thing that's goin' on. Better relay the message and log it in. Least we can do for the man now that he's bought it,' Brazil said as a dozen yellow blips moved back toward Hanoi.

Red River Beach Party

As South ejected free of his aircraft, he found himself in the outer edge of a black cloud; intense heat sucked all the air from his lungs and he was certain that he was dead. When his next thought came to him, he was lying face down on a beach of orange and ochre pebbles. Three dead and rotting silver minnows were lapping at the beach near his feet, their eyes staring blankly into the sky. The water line was no more than an arm's length away. Instinctively he snapped open the harness releases and broke the shroud lines away from him. He pulled the silk into him, gathered it into a tight bale and stood up, but immediately fell forward onto his face, splitting his upper lip, pushing his front teeth in and hitting his nose. The whole thing simmered for a brief moment, then blood began to pump from the wounds.

What the hell? he thought calmly. He checked his right leg. The flightsuit was gone from mid-thigh down. Burned away. Between his knee and his ankle a large sliver of bone was protruding through the flesh, peeking up at him. When he tensed the leg there was no pain, but the movement of the muscles made the bone move. He tried it a couple of times, feeling curiously detached from the situation. The leg was covered in blood which seemed to make the bone even whiter. He felt the nausea rising, felt the light-headedness coming on. Goddamn Wainright, he told himself, trying to remain conscious. Goddamn Wainright!

From the middle of the muddy Red River a launch was speeding toward shore. He had no doubt that it was headed for him. There were a couple of figures on the foredeck with weapons pointed ahead. Behind him on the beach there were voices and shouts. Putting his weight on one arm he tried to look over his shoulder, but the support collapsed in a mushroom of intense pain; he saw only a glimpse of a crowd of people rushing forward.

His visitors from land and sea arrived at almost the same moment and he could tell before any words were spoken that a sort of contest was under way. The two men on the bow were dressed in khakis and wore dark green pith helmets. The pair pointed their AK-47s at him and barked at him in Vietnamese. The crowd, all civilians, men and women, old and young, formed a circle around him brandishing sickles and hoes and a wide assortment of other implements. One of the women began to shriek and poke him with her finger. She spat on him and soon all of them were spitting and kicking at him. He rolled as best he could into a ball trying to protect himself but there were too many of them to calculate where the next blow would come from.

The crew from the boat leaped to the beach and angrily pushed the others away. South caught the attention of one of the uniformed men while the other one kept the others at bay. 'Ya know what really pisses me off, babes?' he said weakly in English. 'Here we got the makings of a hell of a beach party . . . and now I won't be able to do the limbo.'

From in front of South a small boy suddenly broke out of the ranks and rushed from the group with his shovel held high. The pilot knew the blow was coming but could not move to avoid it. All he could do was tell himself he was glad the kid didn't have an axe.

Aftermath

The teletype behind Ogden chattered and spit out a short message. He tore it off and read it twice. Blazer 1? Who the hell was Blazer 1? He called for a messenger, folded the paper neatly and put it into a priority envelope preprinted

275

to read 'Wing Commander's Eyes Only.' The guys had no idea how many screwball messages came in over the teletype for the Old Man.

The messenger met Horowitz at the commander's door and they entered together. 'Message for you, sir.' Wainright returned the man's salute and opened the sealed envelope. A smile crept across his face. He sat behind his desk and leaned back, suddenly clapping his hands together.

'This is it. We've done it, Albert. It's all right, everything's fine now.'

Horowitz took the message and read it. He felt his legs weaken.

RADAR INDICATIONS THAT BLAZER 1, YOUR COMMAND, DOWN IN NVA TERRITORY. BULLSEYE AREA. 0108 ZULU. SEVERAL MIGS IN PURSUIT. BELIEVE BLAZER 1 ENGAGED SUPERIOR ENEMY FORCE, DOWNED TWO BEFORE LOSS OF RADAR CONTACT. PILOT REQUESTED RELAY OF FOLLOWING MESSAGE TO BLAZER CONTROL.

The vice-commander read the rest of the message and shook his head, unbelieving. South had not dropped his bombs on target. He had turned away. The message was signed: DESOTO, USN.

'Shall we launch a rescue operation?'

Wainright turned serious. 'Yes,' he said quietly. 'Go right ahead, Albert. Send the entire force up there to search for him.' Horowitz nodded and left at a trot.

All the pieces had fallen into place. South had been sent in a desperate attempt to clean up a special target – he could select the specific site later. His prerogative as commander would be unquestioned. It was over. South was out of the way. Than-Lohn was intact and he was free and clear.

Wainright walked to the Scoreboard, erased the eight next to South's name and wrote in a neat '12'. Double ace. He was the only commander in the war with a single ace, much less twice that and it was likely to stay that way if the grapevine was right. The President had opened the doors during the past three months in order to force some direction

276

in the war, and it hadn't worked. Now he'd stand the force down and they'd go back to bombing in the lower route packages. Maybe even a moratorium would be proclaimed – nothing above 20 degrees north.

The wing commander fumbled with the silver stars. The new brass sparkled brightly as he admired himself in the mirror. It was odd how things worked out. Instinct told him the first time he saw South's record that the man would be a stepping stone, an excellent conduit for publicity. Of course, it hadn't gone precisely as planned, but the result was the same.

Life was like that, he reminded himself. Things never work out quite the way you think they will – but they turn out pretty well if you plan ahead. He had his star and South was gone. What more could you ask for? Now I can make an even bigger hero out of South; it is the least I can do. I owe him that much. The man had been one hell of a combat flyer and nobody could take that away from him. No ... things never turn out like you expect them to. That's the reason for systems – to cut errors, reduce Murphy's Law and human error. You can't eliminate mistakes, but you can isolate them and keep their effects within tolerance. Even with systems, you have to take risks, have to gamble, otherwise you become a reactionary. Do your homework and strike when the time is right. That's the ticket – the route to the stars.

General officer at forty-two. The second star will come quickly. I'm young and this is no dust-covered gift to a tired warrior. This is a reward, a sign of more to come. Lieutenant general is within reach and with the right breaks ...

Wainright smiled. Anything is possible, he told himself. Be satisfied with your first star. It's enough ... for now. After all, your record will speak for itself.

Comrade Up North

To those who were there and part of it, and this included the Americans, the Thai civilians who worked there, a contingent of Australian commandos and a French journalist making a documentary film, it was one of those moments that touched the soul.

Following the preliminary report from DeSoto Radar, Wainright — through the auspices of Colonel Horowitz — set into motion the administrative machinery that ultimately produced the official report governing Byron South's nine-tieth and final mission. Given the cloudy circumstances. Wainright (he reminded himself that his hunches about such things were seldom off the mark) and all who saw the report were quite certain that South was dead. Nevertheless the report ultimately resulted in a classification of the pilot's status as missing in action, or MIA. It was a technicality and for Wainright the significance in South's removal was that the pilot was out of his hair permanently. Those who fell in North Vietnam did not come back, no matter how the semantic hairs were spilt by some two-bit paper-pushers.

In many ways the community of men that comprised the Taxi Dancers of the 39th Tactical Fighter Wing was no different than hundreds of small towns back in The World. When something happened to one of the community's leading citizens it was the kind of thing that made the rounds quickly even to the furthermost reaches of the camp. So it was that the word of Byron South's death was disseminated to the Taxi Dancers, not officially through their wing commander, but unofficially in hushed calls, over fences and in chance meetings during duty. The word travelled fast.

Not long after the message arrived from the Navy, pilots

and other members of the wing, NCOs, officers and low-ranking airmen alike, began to arrive at the Takhli officer's club. This procession wound in from many directions and while the traffic was never heavy, it was steady. The men came alone, or in pairs. A few came in small groups. The men entered, found seats and sat quietly. When the chairs ran out, they stood or sat on other items of furniture. They did not order drinks and they did not talk to each other. They were waiting.

The Thais, accustomed to a kind of light-hearted air among the Americans, were stunned by the solemnity of the assembling men. The fact is that the Thais were much impressed by the quietness of the gathering. It had been their observation that Americans were culturally immature, lacking the adult discipline and perspective that would allow for quiet and serious contemplation of the greater mysteries of life. And death. If this were true, then the American society must be shallow like a thin layer of topsoil waiting to be washed away by the first stiff rain to come along. On this night, however, the Thais saw something new: compassion, resoluteness, depth of character, reverence. It was an impressive display that changed forever how this particular small group of Thais viewed their nation's guests. Until this moment the Americans represented only a fortunate economic windfall, a gift from Buddha. On this night they saw the childishness for what it had been all along − a veneer; underneath these Westerners was a depth and intensity of frightening proportions. With their technological know-how the Americans were already a force to contend with, but knowing that they also possessed moral depth made them even more impressive. It was a sobering experience.

No one was sure how many people were there that night. Estimates range from five hundred to more than a thousand. Whatever the actual count, the club was full. Outside, the rain, which began falling around sundown, continued to come down steadily, its drops beating a steady tattoo on the tin roof of the facility. There was no thunder, no lightning;

just a steady cadence. Inside it was oppressively hot. The air conditioning failed under the humidity of the weather and the crush of humanity. But there were no complaints.

Captains Danny Buggs and Mike Romero were among the first to arrive. They went directly to the stag bar and took up positions near the bar. Tommie, the barkeeper, recognized they were in no mood for idle banter and retreated to a stool in the shadows where he drew up his legs like a fetus in the womb and leaned back with growing anxiety over the tension. He didn't care to be noticed.

Around eleven o'clock Buggs pointed a finger at the boy. 'Tom. Set up a shot for each man.' Buggs did not look around to get and estimate of the gathering's size; he could feel it.

'Not enough *shotgrasses*,' the boy said nervously after a quick scan of the crowd.

'Then use water glasses, paper cups, whatever.' Buggs carefully placed five crisp one-hundred-dollar bills side by side on the bar. He had been saving them for his own hundred-mission celebration, but this seemed a more fitting use. 'If you need more booze send over to the NCO club. I want every man with a drink. Understand?'

'*Chi*,' Tommie answered promptly. He disappeared into the back of the club and soon young waitresses were moving through the throng with trays of drinks in a bizarre assortment of containers.

It was just before midnight when Vincent Katsu finally arrived. The men inside the club backed against each other to make a path for him as he strode solemnly into the stag bar. As he passed through the ranks, the hundreds of men came to their feet in anticipation.

The Chief was an impressive sight. He wore a loincloth fashioned from some kind of tanned hide, and moccasins that rose to his ankles. His short hair shone and a small collection of dark feathers was attached to the back of a leather headband. Rain still dripped from him. His face was painted black from the cheekbones down, vermilion above. His shoulders, back and pectorals also were painted

280

black and a single thin scarlet stripe led down the rippling muscles of his belly from his throat. Around his neck he wore a bearclaw necklace. When the Chief reached the bar, Buggs handed him a shotglass and beckoned for him to stand beside them. There were tears in Romero's eyes.

Buggs turned to face the men and the limp striped flag at the rear of the room. He held his glass aloft and the multitude did the same.

'Gentlemen,' he said with a steady voice. 'To our comrade up north.' The assemblage repeated the words, then each man drained his glass, carefully set down the empty and departed into the blackness and the warm rain.

Part III: Epilogue

May 29, 1973

Operation Lazarus

Byron South limped slowly up the rickety metal steps. He was careful to keep most of his weight on the good leg because the left one still throbbed when he tried to use it for anything more than a fleshy prop. He clutched the railing tightly as the primitive ramp swayed in the late afternoon winds sweeping in across the North Vietnamese flood plain from the Gulf of Tonkin. The wind was brisk and cool; it made his skin tingle. He was not used to being out in the open. Or in the light.

At the top of the stairs South paused and deliberately lifted his bad leg over the metal runner at the bottom of the hatch. There was nobody behind him so he felt no compulsion to move quickly. Once inside, he shuffled down the aisle and took the first empty seat he came to. He tensed as he lowered himself and winced when the dead leg got caught under the seat in front of him. It took several seconds to extract it and he knew that the activity, as much as he tried to be subtle about it, could draw their wrath. With the leg free, he kept his head bowed and waited for someone to come to roust him for once again displaying disrespectful behaviour. When nothing happened, he let himself relax a little. For the moment he was not being rebuked as an incorrigible war criminal.

The seat was soft and thick, its fabric and texture unfamiliar. It was something new and it made his skin hot and irritated his lower back and arms. For as long as he could remember he had been forced to sit on cold concrete floors and he had gotten accustomed to them. Now the soft cushions made his back begin to ache and he considered getting up to find a more comfortable sitting place on the floor, even if it meant a beating. But none of the others were moving and he knew he dared not. He kept still and riveted his eyes on the rubbery grey floor covering under the new black sandals that pinched his toes.

Litter cases were loaded last and attached to wall racks aft. Occasionally one of the stretcher cases would moan, but for the most part they kept their pain to themselves. It was the only way.

Throughout the loading process South had moved without speaking. It was a familiar shuffle, the ancient sound of darkness mixed with wisps of mildew and vomit and the guttural grunts and sing-song of the ape-faced guards. South learned to keep his head bowed in respect, as they taught him to do, and to shut his eyes and listen. They took his sight, not by blinding him, but by not allowing him to look and punishing him immediately and violently when he violated the rules. It was not allowed. You couldn't see when your chin was on your chest all the time, so like the blind, you learned to compensate with your other senses. Hearing was best. You depended on your ears for warning, for information, even for entertainment. When there was no other way your ears could serve as eyes, as your nerve centre, and over six years South's hearing was as keen as his sight had been in the old life.

The others in the aircraft were like ghosts, well-ordered phantoms sighing in their seats. They had seated themselves with no thought for choice, no preference for seating partners, no quibbling over who gets the window, who gets the aisle.

When the plane was loaded, an airman in a faded grey flightsuit, its seat burnished by thousands of hours in a seat over the Pacific, passed quietly down the aisle counting heads. Tally complete, he stood amidship and coughed several times for their attention.

'Call out when I read your name,' he said nervously. Then he went through the list which had been provided by the North Vietnamese. He read the names smoothly, without hesitation, without error. South's name was not called.

The man pored over his list once again, his brows arched in great V's that gave his face the appearance of a bird of prey. 'I missed somebody,' the man said. 'Who is it?'

South heard, but kept silent. If they wanted him, the bastards could figure it out for themselves. It was their fucking problem. Never speak up. He'd made that mistake many times before and he had scar tissue and fingers that jutted out at strange angles to show for his effort. If they wanted him, they could find him. They always had.

The sergeant coughed again. 'Gentlemen,' he said softly. 'I got sixty-seven people in this aircraft and only sixty-six on my manifest. Now . . . whose name did I miss?'

South felt guilty. If he held out too long somebody else might get hurt. That was the way. They were all criminals so what did it matter who you punished? Beatings were indiscriminate, dished out at random. South decided to not let them control the game. He raised his hand meekly. Here we go again, he told himself as the enlisted man approached him.

'What's your name, sir?'

'South, Byron. Captain.' South said. He also gave his serial number. It was an old record, a familiar beginning. Sessions always started with name, rank and serial number. Then they went for more and they *always* got what they wanted. When it came to extracting information the North Vietnamese were crude, but very effective. And they always took their time. The best you could hope for was to pass out. That was the goal. Make them work to get the same information they'd gotten before. Get them so pissed off they beat your brains out and send you into the comforting arms of unconsciousness. Going off the air didn't stop them from abusing your body, but it ruined their game plan, at least temporarily. South prepared himself for the onslaught.

The man touched the pilot's arm. South felt the alarm surge through him but he did not flinch. He held tight, refusing to show the slightest acknowledgement of the touch. Even if the kicking and punching began he would keep his face passive throughout.

'Uh ... Cap'n South. What's your social security number, sir?'

'Social security?' South stuttered, fumbling the phrase as if it were from an unknown language.

'Yes, sir. What is it?'

South shook his head, trying to clear his mind. What the hell *was* that number? He'd known it once. Why did they want that? This was a new approach and he put himself on guard. Maybe they'd take another number. He had lots of them. Hell, he'd made them up when it was necessary. When they wanted numbers, you gave them numbers and swore on your mother's honour they were accurate. They didn't really want the numbers; they just wanted you to get into the habit of providing information. Like Pavlov. Ring the bell. Give them their fucking numbers.

'No sweat, sir,' the sergeant said as he jotted down South's name and serial number. 'We'll get it from you later.' You bet your ass you will, but you'll have to work for it, South told himself. Be cool. Let them do what they want. You're Raggedy Andy − their flesh-and-blood punching bag. They can throw you all over the room and wrap you up in the ropes but you keep your mouth shut and don't say a word. *Nada.* Fuck 'em and the horse they rode in on.

No blow came. No kick. No slap. No screaming. The man left with a gentle pat on South's shoulder. 'Glad to have you aboard, captain.' The man walked forward and stopped. 'Gentlemen, can I have your attention?' Fucking eh, South thought. You've always got it. What choice do we have?

'Might as well,' somebody said.

'Can't dance,' came another response.

South cringed. Assholes! Don't smart off. Don't give them a reason to get worked up or they'll come down on all of us. He'd learned his lesson. Shoot off your mouth to make you feel good and somebody else gets his head staved in. Effective crowd control.

The man in the flightsuit smiled. 'We'll be taking off in a few minutes, so everybody just relax while we get this monster cranked up. For those of you who are unfamiliar with this bird, it's a C-141 Starlifter.'

Taking off? Cranked up? South could feel the tension in the group, but he didn't dare look up to see how the rest were taking the information. Taking off. What did this mean? Another staged event for propaganda? The words were almost magic, words he hadn't thought about in years. Once they had meant something, but not now. They were just words. Not important. Think about something else, he told himself. Fight false hope. There is no hope. You got what you got and that's all there is. The future is one second from now. No longer. Escape. Yes, think about escape. Code of Conduct. The first duty of every prisoner of war. Escape to fight again. This time put the bombs where they belong − right on top of the filthy little bastards. Roast them all. Turn them to liquid jelly, all of them − men, women, children. Animals. Grinning, drooling hairless apes. Get the schools first. Napalm would be best. Or Willy Pete. Watch them run to jump in the water. Watch their eyes bug out from their flat, ugly heads. Pour lighter fluid on them. Mock them as their lungs collapse and their testicles melt and their black tongues pop out of their mouths like dead frogs. All of them should die the hard death. Maximum agony. Escape. Duty. Escape and come back. Pray for escape and a mountain of rockets and bombs and ammo for the cannons. But don't hope.

You are blind, he told himself. You are deaf. You are mute. Make them believe you are a vegetable. Get them off guard. Watch them from the hiding place in your broken carcass. Stay in there where you can be alone and they can't intrude. Hide in your mind and watch them. Do as Wainright had done. Wait for the right moment. Wainright? Strange to hear that name. Who said it? Where did it come from? An intruder! Inside my mind? No . . . don't say it again. Don't think it. Remember it, but keep it on the shelf for later. Not now. Ancient history, fool. Go elsewhere, anywhere, but not with that name.

Quiet now. They don't know you're here, you know. It's a small cove ... and very dark. Cardinal Farley is over the hill beyond the broken slate walls. Old Jake Rupert is out there too − or his ghost − out there on the Fishing Ground Road. Moving up the trail away from the Polio River, through a tunnel, a narrow corridor of sumac, bright orange, blazing in the sunlight. Careful now, South! Chingachgook afoot. Freeze! See it coming. *There* it is. Watch the grass tips. *See it?* Steady with the gig, boy. Ahab is hissing. Steady lad. Patience. Aim it, aim it. Pick a spot and hit it solid. Be deliberate, you won't get two chances. Aye, laddie. That's the spirit. Drive off your back leg. *Now!* A hit, boy. Square. See the bastard squirm under the point? Now, now, black snake. Don't carry on so. This is the way it is. You shouldn't have been playing along the road. You know the price; you can't cry, you didn't know. You were told. All your kind were told. Now you have to learn the lesson, just like I did. Pain is necessary. Please understand: I take no pleasure from this. It's my duty to teach you humility, to follow the rules, is it not? Ah, you choose not to speak ... that's your decision, of course. But it doesn't change what I have to do. Answer a few questions and maybe I'll be lenient. Where are the other snakes? Tell me. You won't? Please reconsider. I'm not violent by nature. The truth is that I already know. We all do. But you must demonstrate a cooperative spirit. The others − those serpents in khaki with rotting yellow teeth and fish breath − they want you. Please let me help you. Please only the *facts*. Not your facts, *my* facts. *Here I write the history books.* Enough. It's time. I gave you an opportunity. What's this moisture on my back? Still safe in hiding? What is it? Easy now, Barney. Only sweat. Good. It might have been blood again. Escape. Kill. Make a list. Nob-Nose. Death Breath. Clubber. Grin-and-Kick. The Grunter. Canadian Club. Bossman. Remember me, gentlemen. Remember me. I'm

290

going now. But I will be back.

A new sound. Listen. Concentrate, South. No. Not new. Old sound. Familiar . . . yet . . . very old. New York Central barreling toward Poughkeepsie. No . . . not right. Where is the goddamn river? The Fence! The river is The Fence. Yes. Depend on The Fence. Yes, yes. No − dammit! Keep it straight. River, yes. True. Fact One. But not the Mekong. No. It's the other one. The Hudson of Henrik. Now you're cooking, babes. You're on the river bank at sundown. And there is the whine and roar behind where they are running up the jet engines. Damn! *God* damn! Trains have diesels, not jets. Listen to the sound. Analyse. It begins low, a high whine, gains pitch and grows to pure vibration, shattering. Not on the river. Closer. The river is a dream − the past. Get out of hiding now. It may be too late. *Get out of hiding, South! Clear your head, son. This is no time to be hiding; it's time to seek. Blink your eyes, boy. Clear your mind. Concentrate, South . . . you're a pussy!*

Everything runs together. Don't fade. Hang in there. Press on. This time you've got to stay alert. This is your chance, South. There won't be any more, so use this one right. They've never done this before. Watch and wait. A split second. A dropped guard, go for the throat. Pop out his eyeballs and make him eat them. Cut open his belly and choke him with his own intestines. Cook his children and make him drink what's left. Figure out a plan, South. This is it. *Gotta go. Gotta go. Gotta go.*

The engines of the C-141 started in quick succession. The aircraft shuddered and vibrated.

Under your feet. Feel it? A deck. The deck of a ship. No! Not the ferry boat to Kingston − an aircraft. *Good God.* It's a flight deck. What are they up to this time? Several engines to count. One. Two. Three. Four. Listen to the bastards scream. A thump. Hold tight. Armrests. Parking brakes? *Yes.* Moving slowly forward, straining. Taxiing? *Oh . . .*

South swayed in his seat as the Starlifter lurched from its parking place. He listened to the scream of the inboard engines as the unseen pilot deftly jockeyed throttles, brakes and nosewheel steering to maneuvre the craft toward the pock-marked runway. The solid rubber tyres thump-thumped as they made their way.

South felt drowsy. So much activity and vibration. It soothed. Caution, his mind whispered. Don't be fooled. What are they doing? This is an aircraft. Fact. We are taxiing. Fact. We are going to take off. Fact. No, only speculation. An elaborate game to lift you, then drop you hard. Don't believe them. Don't anticipate *anything*. Play every moment for itself. Don't look ahead. *There is no future.*

'Please check your seatbelts,' a voice said with a tone of suggestion rather than the power of authority. It seemed to come from the walls. Always voices came from walls. In the Rhinecliff station. In the cell. Walls could speak.

A thin hand with pearl-coloured fingernails touched his lap and tugged gently on the lap belt, then disappeared as mysteriously as it had appeared. An apparition? No. Fact. Real flesh and blood. Real. Nails. Long and polished. Pale gems mounted on tanned flesh. Not like his own. Not irregular. Not broken and mangled and caked with six years of filth. They order you to wash, but there is no soap. How can you do what they want? Dirt's in the pores, part of the pigment now. Ashamed, he slipped his hands under his legs.

Cautiously he glanced down the aisle. Buttocks! A woman? His heart raced. Hyperventilating, he told himself. Slow it down. Inhale. Hold it. Let it out s-l-o-w-l-y. That's it. A woman! Round-eye. Inhale. Hold. Exhale. Don't look back. Inhale. Forget it. Hold it. You'll get another chance. Exhale. The bastards! Patience. Fool them again. You are sleeping. Inhale. Hey everybody! Look at him sleeping there. A round-eye Capitalist female touched him and he's sleeping. It must be true. He's broken. No sense in bothering with that poor dumb bastard anymore. Yes, master. Exhale. No, master. Not I, master. Certainly not, master. Fuck you, master. Inhale. Something touched his arm.

292

Fact. Hold. A faint voice whispered from the adjacent seat. Exhale.

'Did you see that?'

'Shut up,' South whispered harshly.

They were moving faster now and his ears popped. Cabin pressure. Pain! Right ear blocked. *What have they done to my ears now!* Not that. He lowered his head, pinched his nostrils together and blew the ear clear. Valsalva, his subconscious mind told him. Yes, valsalva, he answered. Strange to do it after so long.

Voice from the walls again. 'Evenin', gents. This here's your aircraft commander speaking. Our next stop is the Filly-Peens. We're gonna try to give you fellers a real smooth ride. If you get to feelin' uncomfortable, you tell somebody. Hear?'

Philippines? Islands. Fact.

'Christ,' somebody muttered hoarsely.

'Thank God,' said another, louder.

'Can it,' a third voice ordered. 'If they hear you, we're all gonna catch it.'

'Fuck 'em,' came the reply. 'We're going home!'

'Our Father who art in Heaven,' several voices began to pray.

South felt the power build in the engines before he heard it. It increased quickly and he felt himself being forced back against the soft cushion. He went with it, not fighting, enjoying the speed, the howling of the wind along the skin of the fuselage, faster, bumping loudly on pitted concrete, building speed, faster, nose wheel off, main gear struts thumping as they lifted, the sinking feeling between flight and ground effect and then they were airborne, the nose up at a steep angle of attack and they were climbing free of the earth, up, up, the sound drowning him like a windstorm in a forest of dry leaves, banking right, Mr. G pushing on the top of his head, savouring it, drinking in the force like a refugee from the desert gulping his first clear water, embracing all of it like a lover who had been away too long.

As the plane began to level, the passengers remained quiet. They stayed in their seats and looked at each other, trying to comprehend the enormity of the moment. Then it began. A lap belt was undone and clattered against a set. Then another, then all of them, up in the aisles, on the seats, stumbling around, the aircraft in another steep climb knocking them off balance. They were cheering, crying, laughing, pounding each other's backs, shaking hands, tears streaming down their cheeks in small rivers. Some had been in North Vietnamese prisons for ten years and in all that time they had learned to guard their emotions, to mask their feelings. Now they cast off the restraints like drunks fallen off the wagon and went wild.

'We're out! My God, we're really out!'

'Yes!'

'I can't believe it. I can't believe it.'

It was tumultuous. They were all over the cargo hold, all trying to talk at once. They pounded the litter cases with affection and the wounded and hurt forgot their pain for the moment and joined in, one of them almost toppling to the floor in celebration. At first the nurses and orderlies tried to calm them, tried to get them to sit, but it was a plague, a wonderful plague and all were infected and they were kissing them, hugging them, touching them, weeping and smiling. None of them had ever felt such powerful and compelling emotions. Hope had been answered with action.

The man next to South nearly fell in his lap as he cheered, but South could manage only a small smile. He was tired and wanted sleep. Inside him, a wall crumbled. He understood now. It was over. The nightmare had ended.

Thirty minutes later the celebration was still going full bore. The loadmaster made his way carefully through the maze of bodies to South's seat. He touched the officer's shoulder gently, not wanting to startle him.

'Captain South?'

The pilot looked up. The man was smiling; there were tears in the corners of his eyes. Fact.

'Like to visit the cockpit, sir?'

South recoiled.

'Don't have to if you don't feel up to it, sir.' South stared at the man, carefully examining him. Not North Vietnamese. American. Not a gook. He hesitated, then nodded and the sergeant's strong arms were under him, helping him up, clearing a path through the celebrants, holding a grey door open for him.

Cold air blasted his face and took his breath away. It was freezing. It had been a long time since he had felt artificially chilled air and it made him tremble. Ahead of him a man was standing behind the copilot's seat on the right side, motioning for him to slide into it. Shielding his bad leg, South let the crew help him, and he slid back into his world, among the gauges and switches and a window to the sky.

To his right there was water and a shoreline and it was moving away from them, becoming fainter in the evening mists that always shrouded the coastal plain. How many times had he roared in over the coast feeling all powerful and invincible? But no more. Now there were only whitecaps to stare at and he found himself estimating the surface wind at five to ten knots. The instinctive response pleased him. It was still there, tucked away for safekeeping, waiting to be called back into the light. Rusty to be sure. But it was there, held miraculously in trust for future use.

He scanned the coast for landmarks, but found nothing familiar. How many years had it been? A lot surely had changed. He was glad to see the coast vanishing. It was falling behind them now. Over. A bad memory to block out until it was time to come back and finish the job. To go back.

South turned to the instruments and gasped. Hanging from the control column was a battered blue batting helmet with a white Old English 'D' above the bill. He touched it and traced its outline, running his hand over the cool plastic.

'Put it on, babes — 'bout time you dragged your sad-sack ass out of retirement.' The drawl was familiar. South stared, unbelieving.

'Buggs?' he whispered.

Flashing his toothiest Georgia grin, the pilot grabbed South's hand and pumped it violently. 'Damn irritating to be workin' while you been off playing hookey an' me left to make excuses. Shit, you dint even answer my letters.' They sobbed as they embraced. It was Buggs who finally tore away and poked at his copilot, carefully avoiding South's face, afraid that he would go to pieces in front of his crew and his friend.

'Where are your manners, co?' Buggs snapped. 'Can't you see the captain here needs him a nice cold brew?'

'Yessir,' the lieutenant chirped nervously as he pawed through the navigator's black leather satchel. It had been lined with plastic and filled with crushed ice. Beer cans gleamed invitingly in the red cockpit light. The young officer snapped a tab on the top of a can and passed it to South.

Buggs coughed loudly. 'Got an awful scratchy throat, co. Think you can find me something back there to wet it down? Medicinal purposes.' The copilot grinned as he fished for another beer in the bag.

'You're on duty, A.C.,' the younger man reminded his aircraft commander as he passed the can forward.

'Wrong, my boy. Cap'n Autopilot's got this hog. I'm just along for the ride for a while.' He tapped the control column. 'I'm on break.'

South did not speak. He felt the alcohol in the beer immediately and it made his head swim. Buggs. His former wingman hadn't changed a bit. He looked exactly the same as he had the last time he'd seen him ... he couldn't remember exactly how long ago it had been. 'Buggs?' he ventured again.

'Roger that, babes.'

South muttered the name several times, almost inaudibly. He placed the batting helmet on his head and pushed it down. He was nearly bald so it was too big and settled down against the top of his ear. Far ahead a massive thunderhead was beginning to come apart, its anvil signalling its end. In a few hours the sky would be clear and the process which built the gaint clouds would begin anew, starting on the surface of the sea itself. Eventually everything grew to size and died and was replaced by something else.

South studied his friend Buggs. His flesh still looked like rawhide and he still sported a heavily waxed handlebar — its peculiar shade of red making it look unnatural, like it had been glued under his nose. Buggsy. He'd thought a lot about him, and Romero. But only in the early months. He'd learned there was no time for others, no purpose in remembering. He tapped his helmet. 'How long you had this?'

'Since the night you went down. Six years.'

'Mike?'

Buggs shook his head. 'Bought it.'

Their eyes met.

'Am I going home, Buggs? Am I *really* going home?'

'You're going home, Barn. C-H-I-Dooey.' Buggs' voice cracked as he spoke. For six years it had been 'if' for South, not 'when'. Buggs knew his friend was in shock. All the POWs were going to be in shock; all the special airlift crews had been thoroughly briefed at Clark Field to let the POWs lead the conversation. Don't ask questions, the experts warned. Don't force anything, they cautioned. They've been through a hell of a lot. 'Damn straight, old buddy. Damn straight. Old Buggs is takin' you home. We are gonna are-tee-bewe to the you-ass-of-eh. Next stop: The World.'

South stared dumbly at his friend with a distant smile and propped his good foot on the bar across the instrument panel. 'Buggs,' South said. 'Need paper. Can you send message for me?' His voice was tired, deep and raspy like an old man's.

'Can do.' The pilot ripped a piece of paper off a small note pad and handed it across along with a ballpoint pen.

South worked carefully and slowly. When he was done, he folded the paper and gave it back to his friend. 'Do me a favour, Buggs. Send that for me.'

'No problem, babes.' He flicked the paper backward to his navigator who caught it, opened it and stared back. 'Send it,' Buggs said with a cool voice.

There was warm air pouring against South. Sleep was closing in, hitting him in ever deepening waves, taking him under.

Buggs handed his beer back to the copilot and turned his attention back to his instruments. Their indicated air speed was bleeding off a bit. He touched up the throttles and rechecked his heading. The temperature outside had dropped slightly since their departure from Hanoi. 'Coffee,' he said over his shoulder as he dug in his leg pocket for his sunglasses. He cocked his headset so that the ear nearest to South was uncovered — just in case. But his friend was sleeping now, deep sleep, and the beginnings of a snore, a heavy thick rasp that Buggs had once hated, was beginning to manifest itself with fury. As the aircraft slid on, the snoring grew louder and deeper and Buggs' eyes clouded.

The pilot felt the warm air embrace him and let himself relax under its influence. He hadn't felt so good in years. He triggered the mike button on the stick. It was too bad that Romero was gone. He would have appreciated this.

South's snoring had reached a thundering crescendo. Buggs chuckled out loud. '*That*, gentlemen, is music to this old fighter pilot's ears.'

Click-click.

Project Boomerang

It was dark in the room. Only the low floor lights were illuminated. The screen at the front of the room was filled with the images of a global map. General Evans, the USAF Chief of Staff, was engaged in a long, technical explanation about a new alert mechanism being installed in Minutemen missile silos. The alert mechanisms would provide independent satellite-directed backup to the normal communications apparatus through which missile crews could capture go-codes and other critical signals from an airborne Looking Glass Command Post. The signals were sent off the earth into a high and wide parabola; at zenith the signals turned back and dropped back into the intended receiving stations.

Major General Jergen Wainright felt no interest in listening to the description; Evans was reading from a detailed memorandum he had prepared. It had been his project. He had code-named it Project Boomerang. Instead of making notes, he was doodling — long strings of free-hand stars. What held his interest was a comment made by Evans just prior to their entering the meeting room.

'It's been a long road since the Big War,' Evans said as they walked down the long sterile hallway, their heel taps echoing ahead of them.

'Lots of memories; lost of scars,' Wainright said.

'I'm going to retire,' Evans said suddenly. It had been in the wind for months, but the general was not much on letting people in on his thinking. As Air Force Chief of Staff he had become a political animal and he played the game close and tight. The unexpected revelation caught Wainright off guard. 'As such, they're going to have to replace me. I've already talked to the President. He wanted my recommendation. You. Some will push for Brown, but I told the President that you're the man; you're better suited to the executive duties this job requires.'

'I don't know what to say,' Wainright said in a voice that was almost a frightened squawk. 'You have plans?'

'Been offered a job at William and Mary. Teaching military history. Always wanted to do that. Leaning toward that right now.'

'Hmm,' Wainright said, still not sure what to say to his superior.

'Don't say anything about any of this,' the general said

299

just before they reached the meeting room. 'Let General Brown do all the talking; sooner or later he'll choke on his own foot. These kinds of things aren't decided easily or lightly. What you need to do is keep a quiet, professional profile. The wrong statement. A poorly thought out opinion. An emotional shortfall. The least little hint of a bad odour will sink you. Trust me. I've taken a lot of care to put the whole thing into motion. All you've got to do is keep a low profile and stay out of Brown's way until it becomes official. Understand?'

Wainright nodded and followed him into the room.

Now he wondered what was going on behind the scenes. The idea of a fourth star triggered his adrenaline and made him dizzy. He'd had a little bad luck at the start. But from then on it had been a strong breeze that blew him along. Nothing had been able to stand in his way. He wondered what the others in the room, especially Brown III, would think if they knew what was coming. The thought made him quiver with anticipation. He decide that when the moment arrived, he would personally acquaint Brown III with the facts. The real facts of life. He began rehearsing the scene in his mind.

As Evans called for a back-lighted slide projector to be turned off, a young lieutenant colonel in 1505s came quietly into the room and dropped an envelope in front of Wainright's place. For a moment the general ignored the message, his mind wrapped up in an imaginary diatribe against his long-time foe. The message was not likely to be important. A lot was going on, but it was all routine. There was a problem with a missile test at Vandenberg the day before; they'd been forced to destroy the vehicle out over the Pacific range. A chopper had strayed off course near the Korean DMZ earlier in the week and drawn a short burst of ground fire; the North Koreans were raising hell in the United Nations and State was crying about the need for better controls for border flights. The *San Antonio News* had broken a story the day before about a homosexual ring in the Basic Training Center at Lackland AFB. Evans was getting nasty notes from a Pennsylvania senator who was unhappy with a secret Air Force recommendation to purchase a new tactical pilot-directed missile guidance system from a Fench contractor, and threatening to go public with it if the Air Force didn't reconsider with an eye toward an American company — especially one in Pennsylvania. Wainright wondered if the politician had stock in such a company; it might be worth investigating. For bargaining power. The trick to success was to look ahead; always forward. And be prepared.

Having played out his dream, Wainright tapped the envelope against the table to settle its contents, then folded the other end of the envelope. When it was properly creased, he laid it along the table edge and tore it open with a quick, silent motion. He inflated the envelope with a puff of breath and extracted the message and began to read. Evans was concluding his presentation.

Wainright's flesh took on a chalky cast. He sat deathly still, flexing his shoulders, opening and closing his fists, folded the message, placed it on the table, got up and shuffled out of the room without excusing himself.

Brown III was two places away. He motioned for the man between him and Wainright's seat to pass the envelope along. The general opened it and read the message to himself:

ATTN. COL. J. WAINRIGHT: EIGHT LIVES DOWN; ONE TO GO. PLEASE REMOVE HANOI FROM RECOMMENDED R&R SELECTION LIST. IT AIN'T WHAT THE POSTERS SAY IT IS. SEE YOU SOON.

The 'COL' had been scratched out and 'GEN' penned in above it. The message was signed 'Barney'. Wainright's long-time opponent did not know what it meant but inside him there was a feeling, a solid one, that this was the break he'd been waiting for, that this was the ticket he needed. Brown III smiled, tucked the paper into an inner pocket of his tunic and returned his attention to the meeting.

'Brownie,' Evans questioned. 'What's going on?'

'No problem, general,' Brown III said. 'Think Jergen's

301

just feeling a little under the weather right now.'

Evans glanced at the door. 'Seemed okay before the meeting; hope it's nothing serious,' he said out loud as he searched through his papers for the next document and gathered his thoughts in preparation for the next agenda item.

Who knows, Brown III thought. Maybe it's terminal.

THE END